HALLELUJAH, ALABAMA!

HALLELUJAH, ALABAMA!

a novel

ROBERT ELY

MBF PRESS
Montgomery

MBF Press
105 South Court Street
Montgomery, AL 36104

Library of Congress Cataloging-in-Publication Data
ISBN-13: 978-0-9785311-3-3
ISBN-10: 0-9785311-3-2

Design by Randall Williams
Printed in the United States of America

FOR MY SISTERS, YVONNE, BARB, AND JAN.

OUR LAUGHTER HAS MADE MY LIFE RICHER (IF NOT RICHARD)

Alabama, my new found land!
Whoever despises you
despises the human race!
      — Paraphrasing Brendan Behan
        upon his arrival in America

CONTENTS

NOTE

This is a work of fiction. There is not now, nor has there ever been, either a Hellespont or a Hallelujah, Alabama. There is, of course, a Montgomery, but I have taken considerable liberties with its geography. I have also altered the interiors of many of its well-known buildings. Except for actual historical figures (such as former Alabama governors, Civil War generals, and the first U.S. President Johnson), the characters depicted herein do not bear any intentional relation to real persons, living or dead. Any similarity with such persons is purely coincidental.

It may be objected by some that it was General Wilson who commanded the occupying Union Army in Montgomery in 1865, but this objection is in error. Wilson only stayed in Montgomery approximately three days before heading for Columbus, Georgia, leaving General Smith in charge of the occupying forces.

Acknowledgments

It is elementary Alabama courtesy to thank those who have been courteous to us. For that reason and others, I would like to thank the following individuals, without whose encouragement, support, and wise counsel I would not have written this book. I owe an enormous debt to Dr. James Hollis, director of the Jung Center in Houston and the mentor of a lifetime. The more substantial, astute, and helpful psychological perspectives contained in these pages are drawn primarily from his superb teaching and many inspired books on Jungian psychoanalysis. If I have misinterpreted, the fault is entirely mine. My deepest thanks also go to Dr. Juanzetta Flowers, who gave me a beautiful place to write when I needed it the most. Mary Ann Neeley, who knows Montgomery history better than anyone, helped me enormously with historical accuracy. I am truly grateful as well to those who read all or portions of this book as I worked to finish it and offered encouragement at just the right moments. You know who you are. Dr. Margaret Stephens did a splendid job of proofreading on very short notice, and I thank her greatly. I wish to state once again my profound gratitude and admiration for my editor and publisher, Randall Williams, a great American and a great Alabamian who continues, against all odds, to leave us a priceless legacy. Finally, I would like to thank my mother and good friend, Alberta Ely, for stoically enduring the curious task of raising one who has never seen things quite as other people do.

Hallelujah, Alabama!

Upsy Baby!

Like a juggler about to engage two live chain saws and a bowling ball, Professor Richard Featherston Steick, PhD, Esq., shot his sleeves, squared his shoulders, and prepared to do business. With less confidence than a juggler, however, he squinted. He squinted until he gritted his teeth, and this made his jaws ache. The pain radiated intensely in all directions, particularly into his temples, an almost daily occurrence which he had come to recognize as a sign of stress and therefore an insult to his lofty and serene intentions.

Yet the adversary he was preparing to assail on this bright June morning in central Alabama was not the monumental stupidity and foolishness of the human race in general, as it so often was. He had, instead, deeper and more immediate concerns. His septic system had backed up, making life in his faithfully restored, elegant Italianate house on the hill at the edge of the small town of Hallelujah next to impossible. All of the local experts, as well as the consultants from Montgomery whom Steick had summoned, had agreed, with predictable negativity, that there was little he could do but hook up to the Hallelujah city sewer system. This would have been perfectly agreeable to Professor Steick except for the necessity of running secondary lines from the mains to his house, a distance of some two hundred yards. Owing to some foolish Bowie County Commission rulings, he would be required to bear all the costs of installation himself, and this he was not prepared to do. Certainly not when he had a perfectly good system in place, one that had functioned impeccably since he had purchased the charming old house twenty years earlier and lovingly restored it with the help of his former wife, Gloria.

He had concluded, on the basis of his own extensive research, that the problem lay in his septic tank's antiquated baffles. These were rectangular iron lattices, like rusty Venetian blinds, designed to regulate the outflow of effluent. So he had the tank pumped more or less dry, rented an oxyacetylene welding torch from ABC Rentals, and donned appropriate attire. He wore coveralls and boots (which he called "Wellingtons"). He covered his dark, neatly trimmed hair with a short-billed, 1950s-style driving cap turned backward. With the smoked welding goggles resting on his forehead, he resembled an aviator of the 1920s, and this delighted him. A slender, well-groomed man in his late forties, Steick always presented a dapper appearance regardless of the circumstances. "One dressed for oneself or not at all" was his motto.

He securely positioned a wooden ladder inside the ancient, cylindrical cast iron tank, tested it for stability, and cautiously descended into the pit to begin his overhaul of the annoying baffles. He held the welding torch in his right hand above his head. Though unlit, the torch caused him to smile (pain radiating into his temples) at his heroic posture. He thought of the statue of Vulcan on Red Mountain in Birmingham and the Statue of Liberty in New York. With a PhD in literature, Steick was well acquainted with myths of the underworld in various cultures throughout history, beginning with the *Epic of Gilgamesh*. In ancient Greece, of course, there were Orpheus and Euridice, Persephone, and Odysseus, to name but a few, and his thoughts of Greece reminded Steick of the absurd controversy concerning the name of his town.

Until quite recently, Hallelujah had been known as "Hellespont," a name which had struck the founding fathers of the quaint nineteenth-century Greek revival crossroads as singularly suitable. It was, after all, situated roughly between Athens, Alabama, to the north, and Troy to the south. The name possessed a mellifluous sound and abundant heroic connotations.

A few years ago, however, some of the more naive and ill-educated members of Steick's own church, Camembert Covenant, had found offense in the name "Hellespont" because it contained the word "Hell." Many of these "worsted wool rednecks," as Steick called them, figured that "pont" must be the equivalent of "point" and that their town had somehow blundered into the regrettable name of "Hell's Point," which was quite opposite the parishioners' view of their charming, tranquil, and astutely Christian municipality. This mistaken interpretation of the ancient Greek place name had hopped from church to church like fire jumping from house to house in a medieval wattle-and-daub village. From Covenant it flared to First Baptist, and from there to First Presbyterian, First Methodist, and so on to the numerous Pentecostal churches, including the leading black congregation, the Precious and Divine True Light Missionary Baptist Gospel Outlet Church, or the "Gospel Outlet," as it was known for short.

The furor over the "Hell" in "Hellespont" escalated and resulted finally in a massive town meeting at the high school gymnasium. Various business, civic, and church leaders voiced their opinions, and alternate town names were suggested. It fell to Covenant's own pastor, Dr. Thurston ("Thirsty") M. Balm, to suggest what he put forth as a "compromise" name, to wit: "Hallelujah." His appeasement argument ran that both "Hellespont" and "Hallelujah" began with an H followed by a vowel, two L's, and an e. In addition (and most interestingly, Pastor Balm argued) each name had ten letters, which ought to ease the transition for the geographers and cartographers. Indeed, Balm explained, "The name 'Hallelujah' is like a sign, a blessing from God!" The matter was put to a town referendum on the two names. Pastor Balm's logic easily prevailed, and "Hellespont" was born again as "Hallelujah!"

THUS, PROFESSOR STEICK found himself in Hallelujah, embarked on this bright day upon his own heroic, archetypal journey into certain unknown depths, and somehow it all added up. There was that Spanish mystic, St. John of the Cross, as Steick recalled, who had written about the way down also being the way up, and considering the circumstances, he found that insight mildly reassuring.

The distinguished professor of Law, Literature, and Society at Oppenheimer State University was much better prepared for such philosophical ruminations than for the task of welding which he had set for himself. He adjusted the gas valves on the torch, scratched the igniter at the port, and nothing happened. He increased the oxygen (at least he thought it was the oxygen), scratched the igniter again, and still nothing happened, even though a very audible hiss emanated from the tip of the torch. He scratched twice more with the torch hissing like an angry bobcat before he concluded it might be wise to retreat upward. One could never tell about gases. They had a way, he knew, of filling cavities and detonating unexpectedly, all to the definite disadvantage of anyone, like himself, untrained in space travel.

With increased respect for the flint and steel igniter, he gingerly ascended the ladder, dragging the torch and hoses behind him. He considered and rejected the idea of reading the welding manual and trying again, concluding that there might have been some metaphysical message contained in the failure of the torch to ignite. He recognized in himself an overly zealous do-it-yourself attitude which he always attributed to his Swiss and German pedigree, his rigidly prudent parents, and his childhood on the farm outside Cullman in north Alabama. This farce with the gas welder was no doubt another case in point. He had been trying for more than half his life to unlearn the lessons of stubborn self-reliance he had soaked up in his youth and to adopt the far more measured, graceful, and aristocratic mentality of the Black Belt in south central Alabama.

In other words he knew (intellectually, at least), that it was not his proper station in life, not the highest and best use of his talents, to be buried inside the metal vault of his septic tank, ostensibly attempting to mend it, but more likely acting out a perverse, childish wish to become a human cannon ball. Certainly he could afford to have someone do the work for him. He could, for that matter, afford the connections to the city system and never miss the money. It was simply the *idea* of paying that rankled.

He would not pay it. Why should he, when all of his neighbors had their sewer connections made at county expense? He needed to rely upon his true strengths, which were his charm, intellect, learning, experience, and good connections. He needed to lead with his strong suit, and welding was not it. Instead of attempting to repair the baffles, he would wig-wam with Hoop DeMinus, director of Solid Waste Liaisons for the Department of Public Health at the state capitol in Montgomery. He would, in short, do an end run around the irritating county regulations and get hooked up to the Hallelujah city system at no cost to himself.

In a moment, he had formed a comprehensive plan. He would return the welder to ABC Rentals and demand a refund, since it wouldn't ignite and was, therefore, clearly defective. Next, he would secure the necessary county permits and get a man with a backhoe to connect him to the Hallelujah city system. He would pay the costs himself for now and seek reimbursement from the county later. He was, after all, entitled to it. If he couldn't get the job done through the back door with DeMinus and lobbying the county commission, he would litigate. Steick was a licensed attorney in good standing with the Alabama State Bar, and he knew how to sue the county. Equity and good conscience, if not the letter of the law, were on his side, and he would prevail in the end. Meanwhile, as soon as his contractor had hooked up his lines, he could return with confidence to the graciously antiqued and peaceful amenities of his early nineteenth-century house on the hill in Hallelujah.

He packed the welding torch, hoses, and tanks into the back of his cushioned, leather-upholstered, twelve-speakered, platinum and bronze four-wheel-drive Japanese SUV that had never seen a dirt road and likely never would. He turned on the ignition and aimed for ABC Rentals on Water Street. The vehicle moved with a hushed eight-cylinder purr so soft that when he slipped some Vivaldi into the CD player, he was able to hear the highest notes in spite of an increasing hearing loss that had begun to bother him in his early forties. He noted gratefully that his squinting forehead, aching jaws, and throbbing temples had all softened like a sculpture made of relaxed elastic, and suddenly he felt more or less pain free. The beautiful Alabama sunshine, the Mediterranean luxury of the early blooming crepe myrtles, and the Oriental aspect of the kudzu-covered gullies and red clay hillsides added to his growing sense of contentment. What a lovely day it was, now that he had taken himself out of the mechanical trades and once again entered the calming realm of music, nature, his own thoughts, and fine leather upholstery!

He turned down Water Street and wheeled into the parking lot in front of ABC Rentals. He took a few moments to align his comportment suitably and select an opening that would help him sound like one of the guys. Then he squared his shoulders, got out of the vehicle, and unlatched the rear door. He removed the welding paraphernalia and wheeled the rig into the store, where he met George Abazey, the owner, behind the counter.

"Whatsa matter, Doc? You got problems with that welder?" George asked.

"George, I couldn't make this mean ol' thing work at all. There I was, down in that tank, on a hot day like this, with the tank still drippin', and I couldn't get any fire out of this thing. Must be something wrong with it. I want to turn it in and get me a refund. I've got another idea about how to fix that problem I've got out there anyway. Just might be a better way to go."

"You must not know how to work that torch, Doc. Gridley Johnson just had it out, and it worked fine. Ordinarily we don't make refunds once our tools leave the store, but for you, I'll make an exception. Here ya go."

George Abazey, like most citizens of Hallelujah and quite a few in Montgomery, liked Steick and thought highly of him in spite of certain obvious quirks that complemented Steick's "absent-minded professor" image. Most people knew Steick's publications enjoyed respect in academic circles, and he had even testified before a Senate subcommittee in Washington concerning a technical matter of constitutional law and civil procedure. Early in his career, he had drafted the Uniform Act for the Disposition of Estrays and Properties Adrift, which had eventually been adopted by all of the states except Louisiana. At the same time, Steick kept up a small but active law practice which he operated from a quaint office near the courthouse. He charged modest fees, and he had done good work for quite a few people in Hallelujah, Montgomery, and the surrounding area. He had experienced some phenomenally good luck with several major wrongful death and insurance fraud cases early in his career, and the fees had left him quite well off. Indeed, he paid but slight attention to his personal finances, and he was actually in far better shape than he knew. He definitely did not, however, want to give up approximately fifteen thousand dollars to run secondary sewer lines simply because of some silly Bowie County regulations.

There was only one minor blot upon Steick's impeccable record of scholarship, academic achievement, and public service. This had occurred back in the early 1970s, when he had worked as a graduate assistant, teaching in the English Department while he got his PhD at the university. In those days, the English composition professionals were writing lengthy textbooks in which correct grammar, spelling, and punctuation were degradingly labeled "Inklush," and those teachers who insisted that their students dwell upon such trivialities were known as "Inklushes." The whole idea, at the time, was to get freshman writing students to have emotions and express them in words. Punctuation and all that nonsense would come later, it was argued, as a matter of course, once the students had realized the great personal and social importance of their deepest experiences, thoughts, and observations, as well as their great need to communicate these matters clearly. Consequently, the "T.A.'s" (as the teaching assistants were called), as well as some of the junior tenure-track faculty, took it as their duty to "mess up the minds" of naive freshmen from Millbrook, Slapout, and Bayou LeBatre. These teachers would pull bizarre stunts like faking a shooting in the classroom. Then, smiling knowingly as they wiped the ketchup from the actor-victim, they would assign the class of stunned students to write an essay detailing what they had observed and their personal reactions, their *gut feelings*, about the situation as they recalled it unfolding.

Steick had enthusiastically ingested this academic potluck. As it turned out, he ingested it with too much vigor. One fine autumn day in Composition 101, he wrote the following assignment on the blackboard: "Write a substantial paragraph in which you describe your own asshole or the asshole of a classmate. Be sure to use a topic sentence ('My asshole is like an inside-out fountain,' for example) and lots of specific supporting details. A number of hand mirrors have been provided for your assistance. You need not proofread for errors in grammar, spelling, and punctuation." He provided plenty of mirrors to add sincerity. He devised this whole exercise "to get the students to think about questioning authority," as he later explained at length to the academic vice president.

The problem was that while a number of his students were dumb-founded, a considerable portion of the class took the assignment seriously. The results were predictable, even for the early 1970s. A young girl from Eufaula and a young man from Fort Payne (both Baptists) complained to the chairman of the English Department and then to the dean of Arts and Sciences. They were later joined by a number of other students, of all races and denominations, who brought the matter to the attention of their parents and the president of the university. Steick was allowed to explain his behavior, but in the middle of the semester he was summarily stripped of his assistantship and the meager stipend it allowed. This caused him to take a job at Hardee's to make up the financial deficit caused by losing his teaching position. It also caused him a great deal of humiliation, though not among his fellow T.A.'s, who staged a protest on his behalf. Fortunately, his father had been a fraternity brother of the university registrar and nimbly arranged to have the whole matter expunged from Steick's academic record. After a couple of headlines in the student newspaper and various newspapers around the state, the matter gently died down, and Steick had not been troubled by it any further.

Perhaps it was for this reason that Steick was generally quiet and stayed out of local and state politics almost entirely. He was semi-active in the Camembert Covenant Church and even sponsored a Little League baseball team entirely at his own expense. This made him a hero to the young players, an image that was somewhat eroded by his firm insistence that the team be called "The Hallelujah Dreadnoughts."

Abazey gave Steick his refund, and with an almost pain-free smile Steick said, "Thanks, George. I'll be back next time I've got a do-it-yourselfer on my hands. Listen. Who can you recommend has got a backhoe and would do me a good job of running some sewer secondaries up at my house? I think that's going to be my best bet after all."

Abazey recommended DeVon Snipes, a hardworking black contractor who knew how to operate a hoe, charged reasonable rates, and was as honest as the church treasurer. Steick found Snipes out at work on a job for a local homebuilder. Steick talked to Snipes briefly, and the two struck a deal for Snipes to begin work at Steick's house the next morning.

Thus, by early afternoon, things were looking up. Now all Steick had to do was convince the proper authorities to pick up the tab for his materials and labor, and he would feel as if justice had been done, as if he himself had grown into a more natural and wholesome relationship with the State of Alabama, Bowie County, the City of Hallelujah, and his own byproducts. To this end, Steick telephoned his old friend and well-known idiot, Hoop DeMinus, at Alabama Solid Waste Liaisons, slipped some Berlioz into the CD player, and aimed his leather-lined SUV toward the interstate for the effortless glide into Montgomery.

Hot Tox, Doc!

With his tactical plan well-established and his SUV on cruise control, Steick allowed his thoughts to wander. He ruminated on the pastoral beauty of the Alabama countryside, delighting in its kudzu-covered hills and mimosas in full blossom. Eventually, he fell into an amused reverie, recalling with fondness the events of a criminal case he had been appointed to handle by the Montgomery County Circuit Court early in his legal career.

Young attorney Steick's first problem was that his client, Ninety McWilliams, had been lost by the Alabama Department of Corrections. Ninety was charged with attempted murder for cutting up a guy named Freddie Timmons at a juke joint out past Carver High in west Montgomery, and it was Steick's job to defend Ninety to the best of his ability.

But first he had to find him. Ninety was supposed to be in the Montgomery County Jail, so Steick went there, got buzzed in, signed in, and scrutinized by an inmate deputy who told him that Ninety had been transferred to Kilby State Prison east of town. Steick phoned Kilby to see if they had Ninety in custody, but they said he had been transferred back to Montgomery County. After many hours of relentless detective work, the young lawyer discovered the problem and located his client, who was indeed in the Montgomery County Jail. An intake clerk had mistakenly registered Ninety's name as "Tiny Williams" in the computer system, leaving the uncommon "Mc" off the inmate's last name, and thereby causing endless confusion. The clerk's "Tiny" misnomer was highly ironic, since Ninety had been built by the same firm that put up Stonehenge.

After locating Ninety in the county jail, interviewing him, tracking down various witnesses, and reviewing his client's almost endless record of knife fighting, the diligent young attorney knew he was whipped. He liked Ninety, who bore a regal bearing, like a King of ancient Benin, as well as an enormous keloid scar on his neck from an earlier event in his long career with knives. But his client had been drunk, got into a fight with Freddie Timmons concerning the proper interpretation of the Book of Job, and turned Timmons into a human cutting board. Steick begged, pleaded, and finally cajoled both the assistant district attorney and Ninety into a deal wherein his client agreed to plead guilty to first-degree assault. Although Ninety continued to maintain that he was only acting in self-defense, he was grateful to Richard for all his hard work and dutifully walked off to do another couple of years at the state prison.

But shortly, Richard left his amusing memories behind. In what seemed like only a moment of driving, the older and wiser attorney found himself parking his spotless SUV on a street in downtown Montgomery. He got out of his vehicle and prepared himself for the task at hand.

THE OFFICE OF HOOP DEMINUS, director of Solid Waste Liaisons for the Alabama Department of Public Health, was on the twelfth floor of the RSA tower, the most commodious and elegant building ever to grace the Montgomery skyline. A softly lighted, mirrored elevator, trimmed with spotless chrome, brass, and dark-veined pink Italian marble, gently eased Steick upward and quietly opened its doors allowing him entry into the realm of the truly health-conscious. He stepped onto the cushioned burgundy carpet of the empty hall and craned his neck in several directions before his eyes fell upon a small, tasteful sign directing him to Solid Waste Liaisons. As he opened the massive mahogany door and entered, he was warmly greeted by a stunning and immaculately dressed black receptionist, Melinda Foyle, who smiled graciously and said, "Please have a seat, Dr. Steick. Mr. DeMinus is expecting you and will be with you in just a moment."

Richard tried to thank Melinda but was constantly interrupted by the telephone. Every ten seconds she was required to repeat into her small microphone, "Solid Waste. May I help you?" She did this with such a lovely rising inflection, such sincerity, competence, and sophistication, that Steick wanted to embrace her and cry, "Yes! Yes, you can help me in many ways! But please begin by teaching me how to speak like you!"

Several minutes passed with Melinda gently warbling "Solid Waste" as if it were a term of endearment, and this gave Steick an opportunity to admire the pastoral landscape from a huge window facing northward over the Alabama River into Autauga and Elmore counties. The sun was bright on the river, and the green fields were hazy where Montgomery faded into the fringes of rural Alabama. Some 360 million years ago, near the end of the age of the dinosaurs, a massive meteorite had slammed into the earth near the present site of Wetumpka, northeast of Montgomery. It had been one of the greatest explosions in geological history, and Steick thought he could just make out the remnants of the astrobleme at Bald Knob, but he wasn't sure.

Then Melinda purred, "You may go in now, Dr. Steick."

Once again, Steick aligned his comportment. He selected "Good Ol' Boys" (Axis 1) and "Righteous Indignation" (Axis 2) and squared his shoulders. He was about to open the door when DeMinus beat him to it, extending a huge, friendly white paw and clapping Steick on the back with the other paw so vigorously that Steick was temporarily winded.

Steick had spent a lifetime explaining to friend and foe alike that his last name was German and properly rhymed with "bike." His efforts had, of course, gone unheeded and, quite naturally, what stuck was "stick," an eventuality which his parents had not foreseen when they had dubbed him "Richard." Endless puns had tormented him from grade school onward, and DeMinus immediately seized the opportunity to make a linguistic circus of Steick's parents' gaffe.

"Well, if it ain't ol' Dick Stick," he guffawed. "Doc Dick Stick, no less! Sticky Dick! Sticky Doc Dick! Or is that 'Sticky Dick Doc?' Hew-wheee! How ya doin', partner, you ol' stick in the mud? Long time no see! How's your mama and 'em up in Cullman? Come on in here and let's talk. Haven't seen you in a long time. What you been up to, anyway?"

Steick and DeMinus had been at the university together as undergraduates. Steick noticed a game of solitaire in progress on the computer screen occupying the credenza behind the elegant, massive, and greatly littered mahogany desk bearing Hoop's brass nameplate on a walnut and marble base. Steick caught his breath and replied, "They're just fine, Hoop. Looks like you're doin' pretty well yourself up here in this marble palace."

"Solid Waste has been good to me, Doc."

DeMinus was a professional Alabama bureaucrat who had worked for every Governor since George Wallace. It was a family tradition. His father, Big Hoop, had been a pal of Big Jim Folsom when Folsom was Governor and had served as Big Jim's liaison with the power companies and the TVA. So it was natural that Little Hoop should become the state's director of Emergency Planning when Lieutenant Governor "Little Jim" Folsom became Governor after Governor Guy Hunt was convicted of felony embezzlement of campaign funds and forced to leave office. But party politics meant absolutely nothing to DeMinus or his prospects in life. "Democrat" and "Republican" were but different names for the same gentle and pleasant breeze that blew behind DeMinus as he glided along I-85 in his black Infiniti on his way to his house at Lake Martin for the weekend.

Kicking and receiving were not relevant to his life. Little Hoop always sat squarely on the fifty-yard line and feasted gloriously with his cousins at the victory banquet. When the Democrats had dominated Alabama politics, he was a Democrat. When the Republicans took over, he was a Republican. A lifetime Baptist, he would be a Buddhist come November if the Buddhist party won at the polls. He had two older brothers, Maury and Meaux DeMinus, who were presidents of Alabama junior colleges. His third brother, Dickie, ran a profitable custodial business that served the buildings of the capitol complex on Goat Hill.

Little Hoop continued on the matter of exactly how Solid Waste had been good to him. He looked squarely at Steick. "Over in Emergency Planning, you know, I had all these problems with the press claiming I didn't have any qualifications, which was bullshit. Why, I been in emergencies all my life and never got hurt yet! Ha, ha. Then that pole barn that was supposed to go for supplies during those tornadoes, it shows up somehow on my farm south of town and they want to indict me for that! They tried to do the same thing when I was in State Parks and gave them space to store a few of those old picnic tables out by my lake. Then there was that thing with calls from my cell phone when I was fishin' up in Canada. I tell you! These press around here are paranoid! No good deed goes unpunished when you're a poor, underpaid, lifetime servant of the people. It's all politics, is what it is, and it's a shame and a disgrace. It ain't no wonder we can't get more good, qualified people to go into public service. Why, they even wanted to send me to Kilby prison when I borrowed that little bit of money from Forestry. They all knew I was goin' to put that money back, with interest. I'll tell you what that was, Doc. It was more politics, just plain old politics. Why, if I hadn't got that pardon from Governor . . . Governor . . . I forget which one—anyway, the Governor, I might be sittin' out there at Kilby today stampin' out car tags instead of servin' the people of Alabama like I do best. Meantime, lots of folks are drivin' around on welfare with no license and no insurance. It don't make no sense.

"But Solid Waste, Doc. Solid Waste has been good. Like now, I'm securin' that permit for a fill down in Coffee County for my brother, Dickie, and nobody can criticize, because everybody knows Dickie DeMinus has been here in Montgomery forever, cleanin' all the capitol buildings every day. And so they can't claim he hasn't got any experience in solid waste now, can they?"

The friendly devil's advocate, Steick offered tentatively, "Well, isn't that just a little bit different, Hoop? I mean cleaning office buildings isn't quite the same as running a landfill, is it?"

"I don't see any big difference, Doc, and I don't think your average Alabama voter would either. What this state needs is vision and leadership in all departments, and I do mean *all.* I've got great plans for that Coffee County fill. I need somebody I can count on to see it through, somebody I can trust, and that's why I need Dickie. Maybe I could get him to take that 'Intro to Disaster' course the Red Cross offers. We'll see. Anyway, listen, Doc, and this is definitely for your ears only, okay? But listen to this. We're going to go toxic with that baby. All these politicians tryin' to get reelected, whinin' on '60 Minutes' about how we don't want Alabama to become the toxic waste pay toilet of America, shoot. That's nonsense. That's just political. The Wiregrass, it needs somethin' to boost it into the twenty-first century. This whole state does. What have they got down there now but peanut farms? What have we got in this state but chickens, discount outlets, some apparel, and a coupla' little car plants? Maybe a few bass lakes and golf courses. But tox is big, Doc! Tox is the future! These clean-state people, environmentalists, politicians, Auburn eggheads—what do they want Alabama to be, the Garden State? New Jersey's already got that title locked up. You think it smells good in New Jersey? You think they don't have any tox in New Jersey? Give me a break.

"I've seen the future, Doc, and it's hot tox, and it's now. Why, it's more like today now than it's ever been before! If we don't get into position, we'll get left behind as usual. In the future—which is already here in my opinion—you'll see these states killing each other to get the tox business. Used to be they'd sue each other to keep it outside their borders. Now they can't get enough of it. And why? Because of good ol' American free enterprise that's put profit into it where it belongs, that's why. You pay at the tail end of everything you buy, just like you pay at the front end. So what's new? I mean, what's gonna' happen is gonna' happen, regardless of what happens, and I'm here to make sure it does happen! I've already been up to New York and Seattle (keep this under your hat) talking to some of the really big tox boys, and we can do business with them, no doubt about it, soon as we get the computers hooked up. I don't mean just your average dioxins, PCBs, that kind of thing. I'm talking hot waste! The real thing! Irreducibles from nerve gas! Maybe some pluto! I'm talking a quarter million dollars per metric yard for permanent storage, plus an annual maintenance fee! I'm talking forget peanuts and chickens and cotton lint! I've got what it takes, Doc! I've got the people in the legislature who got the vision! We can get it through Oversight, I'm sure of it. No election comin' up right now. Not an issue. The EPA, I don't know, might have some problems there, but where there's a will . . . well, look out when Little Hoop gets determined about something that's good for the State of Alabama!

"You know what they've got at Los Alamos at the Trinity site? A monument. Well, that's what I want down in Coffee County, a monument to the people of this state who had the good sense to recognize the future when they woke up and saw they were slap in the middle of it! Forget that stupid boll weevil monument down in Enterprise! That's ancient history! We're into *real* growth now!

DeMinus took a breath, paused, and asked, "So what brings you down here into the slums?"

Suddenly there was a muffled rattle, the sound of metal and boards banging against glass, and an angry black man dropped into view in the huge plate glass window over the thick burgundy leather pad that cradled the neck of DeMinus as he lounged in his executive swivel chair.

Steick experienced a moment of "*deja vu* all over again." It was Ninety McWilliams! One moment there was nothing to see but Montgomery and the endless, beautiful green landscape of south Alabama, and the next moment, Ninety had appeared, dropping into view with a violent jerk and bouncing unsteadily on a window washer's rig that clattered, though not offensively, against the glass.

The plate was thick enough to dampen even fairly sharp blows. Pigeons, mistakenly attempting to fly through, would hit the glass, break their necks, and drop to the sidewalk below, like sacks of lead shot, without disturbing the peace of anyone inside. Similarly, Ninety now pounded forcefully on the glass without particularly disturbing DeMinus, who craned his neck casually upward, around, and backward to face the black man.

"What's that you say, Ralph? Speak louder. I can't hear you."

It was clear that Ninety was already shouting at the top of his lungs. The veins and cords were popping out on his neck, and he was pouring sweat everywhere into his white coveralls.

DeMinus swiveled back to Steick and said, "That's Ralph. Washes windows for us."

In his white uniform, Ninety might have been a certified member of a window-washing crew except for the six-digit number stenciled in black ink on his left breast pocket which identified him as a duly enrolled member of the Alabama prison community.

"That's no Ralph, Hoop!" Steick exclaimed. "That's Ninety McWilliams! I represented him a few years ago for attempted murder! He's a nice fella, but he just can't keep himself from cutting folks up."

"No, no, no, Doc. That's Ralph Sumpin' or 'Nother," DeMinus said with a knowing grin, adding, "You know how they all look alike. Heh, heh. Especially in those white suits they're always wearin'. Heh, heh. You're just confused; it's natural."

Steick knew the man dangling outside the huge window was Ninety McWilliams, and as an educated and decent man, he winced at Hoop's racial slurs. Still, he considered the source and allowed the matter to pass like a pigeon bouncing off the window. He would not even attempt to persuade DeMinus that "Ralph" was really Ninety, who, at this point, seemed to recognize Steick as someone vaguely connected with his own past. Ninety gave Steick a confused smile and a double nod of his head, and Steick nodded back, giving up all intention of enlightening DeMinus about basic matters of his window washer's identity and the fundamentals of human dignity. The cause was hopeless, and Steick had other fish to fry.

"Got him on work release," DeMinus said. "Does good work when he wants to . . . Now what's that you say, Ralph?" Since the clatter had died down, conversation was almost possible.

DeMinus eased his tall, ruddy, graying, but still athletic and rather elegant self out of his swivel chair and padded stocking-footed to the window where Ninety was standing, uncertainly perched upon his scaffolding and shouting a stream of hurried, unintelligible syllables. DeMinus leaned close to the glass, looked at Steick, and held his finger to his lips, indicating silence. He looked back at Ninety and said, "Try it again now, partner."

Through a combination of listening carefully and reading Ninety's lips, Steick could just make out what he was saying. Clearly, the man was desperate.

"Mr. Hoop! Mr. Hoop! I can't take this heat no more! I'm going to fall out if I stays out here another five minutes! It's a hunnerd degrees out here! You could fry a egg on this glass!"

DeMinus quickly improvised a code of charades. He held up his right index finger, indicating one. Then he crossed it in the middle with his left index finger in an attempt to show one-half. He held his Rolex up to the window and traced a semi-circle on the face, beginning at 12:00 and ending at 6:00. He did this several times. Then he slid his index finger under his neck in a slicing gesture that apparently referred to quitting. Finally, he pointed toward the floor and then repeated the whole routine. Steick gathered that DeMinus intended for Ninety to work another half hour before quitting and returning to ground level. Evidently Ninety caught Little Hoop's meaning, for he turned his head upward, appeared to shout, tugged on one rope, hauled on another, and vanished skyward as quickly as he had appeared, leaving only a vapor trail of perspiration behind him.

"Ralph's a good fella," DeMinus said, turning back to Steick.

"What's he in for this time?"

"I don't know. Robbery, murder, something like that. He was over in Phenix City trying to sell some jewelry in somebody's house, only they weren't home. Turns out the jewelry wasn't his to sell, either. Then the folks come home, and Ralph gets out his knife. It ends up he goes down for two to twenty. Class B. Copped some kind of a plea; I don't know. Great window washer! Comes from New York or someplace and always complaining about the heat. Truth is, he likes it! Can't wait to get out there in the morning! We've got the cleanest windows in the RSA tower, thanks to Ralph! I've got him up at Transportation doing their windows, too. Never know when we might need to make a little night shipment, require some kind of stupid permit, you know. They'll be grateful for the windows, and we'll be grateful for the permit . . . Anyway, like I was saying, what brings you round to see me, Doc? Big shot lawyer and professor and all that?"

Steick allowed Axis 2, "Righteous Indignation," to kick in at full bore.

"Well, Hoop, I've got this problem with the Bowie County Commission about my right to proper solid waste management. That is, over my right to be connected by the county to the Hallelujah city sewer system, and I thought you might be able to help me out or at least point me in the right direction. See, I've got this worn-out old septic tank still in place from like a hundred years ago up there, but frankly, I'm tired of fooling with it, and I want to get myself modernized and connected to the city system like everybody around me. It seems to me that's what's in the best interest of the groundwater and also in the best interest of the county and the state. But that's where the problem comes in. County says, 'Okay. Fine. You can hook up if you want to.' But here's the thing. I've got to pay to run the secondaries, and we're talking about maybe two hundred yards or more up there, plus materials, and it adds up fast. We're talking fifteen thousand dollars, minimum. They've got this county reg that says I have to be inside the city limits or zoned for possible an-nexation or zoned R-11 or I-9 or RI-15, or else I have to be engaged in a state-floated manufacturing business in an industrial enhancement zone or be engaged in nonprofit wildlife management or maybe one of several other things. And I don't fit any of them. My property sits just outside the city limits by a few yards, maybe twenty, and so, for a little technicality, I'm screwed. I mean, when the Hallelujah Junior Council wants to have their annual Sacred Houses Pilgrimage, whose house do you think is first on their list? Mine, of course. I even furnish the refresh-ments—white wine, cheese straws, all that. Make my own canapes—a regular Martha Stewart. And I'm glad to do it, too. The money goes for a lot of good causes they work on. I mean, it's like my Little League team, the Hallelujah Dreadnaughts. You know about them. Can't win a game, but I pay for it all myself. Good young kids. Keeps 'em out of trouble, out of juvie. All I do for the city. Meanwhile, some—you know—drags a broken-backed 1979 Blue Moon double-wide off an abandoned trash heap and up some sorry kudzu hill just inside the city limits and gets himself hooked up immediately to the city lines once he gets a simple permit which costs him maybe a few dollars at most. It just doesn't seem right, does it?"

DeMinus swiveled, jumped, and held both arms skyward like a referee signaling a successful field goal. "Say no more, Doc! I know exactly what you mean, and you can cross that little ol' problem right off your list! Let's just say several members of the Bowie County Commission owe me a few favors. And that young guy in Liaisons, whatever his name is, hell, I got that job for him! Heh, heh. Time for me to call in my cards for my old pal, Sticky Dick! Hee, hee. I'd suggest that you just go on and get the work done that needs done, and I'll see to it that the county or the state or somebody cuts a check direct to the contractor. Best interest of the groundwater and the people, after all. I got wide discretion there. 'Equity of the statute,' the lawyers call it, or something like that. Anyway, not to worry. Shoot, Doc, I'll take care of it right now!"

DeMinus gingerly solved Steick's entire problem without opening a drawer, retrieving a file, or even dialing the telephone. He simply touched a button, and Melinda purred, "Yes, sir?"

"Melinda, darlin', get me that little fella in Liaisons up in Bowie County, would you please? What's his name, by the way?"

"That would be Mr. Hank Dawson, sir."

The speakerphone went silent for a few seconds, allowing Hoop a brief interlude to demonstrate his skill as a pencil juggler, impassively snapping an unsharpened number two into the air like a baton and deftly snatching it back again, at desk level, barely moving a muscle.

Melinda came back gently, "I have Mr. Dawson on the line, Mr. DeMinus. Would you like me to put him through?"

"Yes, please, darlin'," Little Hoop replied.

There was a slight click and DeMinus smiled, winked at Steick, and jovially roared at his telephone, "Hank! Hank Dawson! That you, you ol' son-of-a-gun? This is Hoop DeMinus at Liaisons in Montgomery! How's things up in Bowie County? I ain't talked to you in seems like forever! Your good-lookin' wife and them fine little ones all okay?"

Dawson replied that he, his wife and little ones, and everything in Bowie County were just fine and that he was greatly enjoying another excellent season of Atlanta Braves baseball. "How 'bout them Braves?" he asked.

"Wonderful, wonderful, just wonderful, hope to get over there in a couple of weeks and watch 'em clean the Cubs' grits!"

Hoop then dropped half an octave into a more serious and business-like tone. "Listen, Hank," he confided. "I've got an old pal of yours and mine up here, Richard Steick, a fine, upstanding citizen of Hallelujah; does a lot for the community—lawyer, professor, baseball team, and all that. You know who I mean, don't you? Well, Dicky's got him a little problem with county regs and him gettin' hooked up to the city system, if you know what I mean. He's just outside the city limits by about two feet, and I'd like to help him out in any way we can. Get the commission to ease off a little, if you know what I mean, so he can hook up to city without havin' to pick up the tab himself, you know? Only fair, after all. You got any ideas?"

There was a brief pause while Dawson pondered the situation. Then he came back with a full dissertation about the plat map, errors in certain old surveys, virtual annexation, proper maintenance of the aquifer, the best interest of the county, and half a dozen other matters—all interest-ingly interconnected—that would, when taken together, allow Steick an exception, Dawson was certain, after he talked to one or two key members of the county commission, filed a few papers, and so on.

"Well, can you put this on the front burner, Hank? Dicky's got a mess right now and needs expedited, okay?"

Dawson confirmed that he would get onto the matter immediately and that he was positive there would be absolutely no problem if Steick simply went ahead, got the work done, and sent the contractor's bill to him at Liaisons in Hallelujah. No problem at all.

Steick liked the sound of what he heard and smiled to himself. De-Minus said a few words of farewell and best wishes to his old pal, Hank, and once again pushed the button on his speakerphone, ending the conversation. He swiveled in his chair toward Steick, locked his hands behind his head, leaned back, and smiled, saying "There ya go, partner. Mission accomplished. You know who your friends are now, don't ya?"

The two reminisced for a few minutes before Steick rose to leave. As Hoop walked him to the door, he chatted breezily, "Look, Doc. I might need a little help with statutory interp on this Coffee County thing, ya know? You wouldn't mind lookin' it over for me if I've got a problem, would you? Maybe talk to some guys in the Legislative Reference Service, Oversight, Fill Committee, that sort of thing? It's a good project. Deserves all our support. Make a better Alabama, believe me. I can count on you, can't I?"

Steick replied that he would be happy to do whatever he could, within the bounds of the law, to further the project. Concurrently, he posted a mental note to himself concerning how much he detested the whole idea of Hoop's hot tox landfill, how so many things were truly outside the bounds of the law for an ethical attorney in good standing like himself, and how he would do anything in his power to sabotage Hoop's toxic waste dream for Coffee County.

"Good. Come see me," DeMinus replied as Steick shook hands, backed out of the office, and gently closed the heavy mahogany door behind him.

HE WAVED GOOD-BYE TO MELINDA, took the luxurious elevator back to street level, hopped lightly into his leather-lined SUV, popped Wagner's *Die Meistersinger* into the CD player, and cruised triumphantly back to Hallelujah. When he arrived at his lovely house on the hill—which was now only technically outside the city limits—Steick immediately phoned DeVon Snipes to confirm that work should begin absolutely as early as possible the next morning.

The contractor happily agreed. He did a splendid job, and the work was completed in less than two days. Steick was connected to the city. The bothersome old septic tank was filled and the land above it sodded with zoysia grass. Steick phoned Hank Dawson to thank him for all his help and hard work, and Dawson said he was glad to oblige, that he had already made the necessary arrangements, and that DeVon Snipes should simply send his invoice straight to Dawson at Liaisons. Steick hung up the telephone and, full of his own accomplishments, flushed the commode several times with contentment and dignity.

Triple Threat

In recent months, Steick had become obsessed by his Cold War memories and had developed the notion that he might exorcise them through a process of total immersion. Years earlier, when his daughters were young and he was still married to Gloria, he had converted an old stable behind his house into a charming English-style pub, liberally garnished with coats-of-arms, martingales, engravings of cathedrals and ancient ruins, pictures of the Queen, Toby jugs, and the Union Jack flying proudly above the roof. His Cold War exorcism consisted of transforming this lovingly created nest of British coziness into a museum of 1950s memorabilia, a miniature Atomic Cafe which he called "Mushroom Memories." He hoisted down the British flag and replaced it with a small, dummy radar antenna he fashioned from a discarded TV dish antenna and an old oscillating fan. On the door he placed a sign he had purchased from a junk shop. The sight of it never failed to make him shudder. It was a rectangular piece of galvanized tin painted radioactive yellow against a dull black surface. Three inverted triangles, in the same scary, sulfur yellow, met at a point in the middle of a black circle about fifteen inches in diameter with a small inscription stating, "Maximum Occupancy 185 Persons," and beneath that was the large, bold, business-like announcement, "Fallout Shelter," in gleaming, evil yellow on weathered black.

Inside the former "pub" was a veritable midden of freakish 1950s trash. There was a large chrome and white Emerson table radio with the two Conelrad alert indicators intact and one of them always tuned in. Steick had framed pictures of Khrushchev pounding his shoe on the U.N. table, of Richard Nixon proudly unscrolling the roll of Alger Hiss microfilm, of

Pacific atolls at the moment of their incineration, of shock waves coursing through the desert landscapes of New Mexico and Nevada, of Kennedy pointing out the missiles in Cuba, of Appleton, Wisconsin's, own Senator Joseph McCarthy, balding, sweating, pressing hungrily toward the microphone, interrogating. There were "Duck and Cover" schoolroom posters side-by-side with posters of Marilyn Monroe in *The Seven-Year Itch*. On one wall hung an old gas mask and a protective rubber suit next to a framed blueprint for a do-it-yourself backyard bomb shelter. There were framed quotations from Khrushchev ("We will bury you!") and the Book of Revelation, photos of Willie Mays, Joe DiMaggio, and Mickey Mantle, movie stills of James Dean and Brando, and excellently detailed models of a 1957 Indian motorcycle and a customized 1957 Chevy named "Pillow Talk." Steick had installed a large-screen TV (retrofitted with dials, knobs, and a Formica-like cabinet) and VCR which, with the flick of a switch, showed a constant stream of nuclear detonations, craters the size of small cities sinking into the Nevada desert at zero hour, and his personal favorite, a hydrogen detonation in the Pacific with the old battleships bobbing about like carved toy boats in the foreground. Only occasionally did the continuous-play video tape switch to an old Billy Graham crusade or a Pepsodent commercial.

Pride of place in "Mushroom Memories" was reserved. It was not given to the grandfatherly Ike, the sober and sinister J. Edgar Hoover, the jolly and helpful General Groves, or the sad humanitarian, Robert Oppenheimer, in his slouchy, scholarly desert hat and gaunt, Upanishad-haunted countenance. Rather, there hung above the fireplace the portrait of the paunchy and rather slobbish physicist, Edward Teller, who, when his own calculations showed that the Trinity blast might set the Earth's atmosphere permanently ablaze, concluded, "Oh, what the hell. Let's just shoot it off anyway," and went on to lead the free world and then the rest of it from mere fission into the wonderfully destructive new universe of hydrogen fusion without hesitating, flinching, or blinking an eye. Was this "grace under pressure" or what? Who could possibly deserve top honors more than Teller?

All of the pewter trenchers and ale tankards in the former "pub" were now replaced by Melmac dinner plates with starburst patterns, and the glass barware had little Sputniks circling about the rims. Steick had obtained several ancient cans of genuine fallout shelter food and a huge but empty shelter water can, which he filled with beer for keggers, and these items adorned the bar shelves and various corners of his bizarre retreat. There was a Kit-Kat clock on the wall and an old Westclox alarm clock, both stopped permanently at one minute until midnight. On a shelf in the corner were several well-worn copies of the influential *None Dare Call It Treason* together with the collected works of Whittaker Chambers and an enormous, garish collection of John Birch Society literature and right-wing religious tracts. Each of them confidently projected the precise year of the forthcoming Soviet takeover of America, which seemed to recede indefinitely but always managed to remain about five years following the year in which the particular tract had been published.

It was at once a mildly macabre, sinister, but faintly encouraging scene of nameless nostalgic menace and a source of rather wan amusement to his friends when he asked them in for drinks of lime Kool-Aid and vodka served over bomb-shaped ice cubes in the Sputnik-rimmed cocktail glasses. And, though most refused with a chuckle, some of his guests gleefully accepted his invitation to kick off their street shoes and don the old white bucks and saddle shoes which he provided at the door.

INCREASINGLY, HOWEVER, STEICK preferred his own company to that of his friends who, it seemed to him, treated his "Mushroom Memories" enterprise altogether too blithely. They merely regarded it as one more of Richard's quaint fascinations and an occasion for the silly 1950s theme parties he threw from time to time (with worn-out sock-hop music played on worn-out 45s on a worn-out Motorola record player followed by endless screenings of *On the Beach* and *Dr. Strangelove*.)

Thus, Steick took to long nights of quiet, solitary reflection in the former "pub," sipping his lime Kool-Aid and vodka while the huge TV screen silently played and replayed endless atmospheric and subterranean detonations in wonderful living black and white.

He pondered first the dimensions and then the meaning and formative effect, for him, of a fundamentalist, Cold War-childhood on a farm outside Cullman, Alabama. He knew that, growing up, he had lived minute-by-minute for many years with a constant, aching fear in his hairless chest of imminent annihilation: the Triple Threat of communist troops in Cullman, all-out nuclear warfare, and the Second Coming of Our Lord and Savior, Jesus Christ. Although these three events could, and most likely would, happen simultaneously, their timing, sequence, causes, and effects would matter very little. In each case, the young Steick knew that the outcome for him would be swift, remorseless, and automatic. In each case, he could, as they liked to say, kiss his sweet ass good-bye.

According to what he read in the church tracts and what he was taught from the pulpit, the newsreels, and Bible school, or in listening to the offhand remarks of his teachers at school and the lessons at church camp, according to the fear in his parents' throats when they discussed the evening news, indeed, according to the air he breathed, Phase One would consist of sneering, jack-booted, machine-gun-toting, bayonet-armed Soviet troops battering down the door of the white frame fundamentalist church on a random Sunday morning, raping the women, and executing the children (of whom he was one) before their mothers' eyes. The Soviets would demand that everyone immediately renounce Jesus and become an instant atheist. Those who refused (like his own mother, surely) would find their children tortured more gruesomely than those who complied. Then, all the strong but gentle, clean, hard-working, crew-cut, Christian, Nash Rambler-driving fathers would be chained together and marched off to Siberia where they would be hitched naked, like sled dogs, to wagonloads of salt which they would drag barefoot through the snow for a few yards before being shot or dropping dead of exposure and starvation.

It never occurred to young Steick to ask where the Soviet troops might come from so suddenly and without warning since, quite clearly, they might be your neighbors from Double Springs, Fort Payne, or even right next door in Cullman. Nor did he wonder how the men would be herded from the church sanctuary to the frozen arctic tundra, since the Soviets were devious and clearly had their ways. In any event (and this always seemed to be the greatest tragedy of all to his parents), the farm and everything on it would immediately become the property of the new Soviet American State! Good-bye Soil Bank checks! Good-bye crop subsidies and parity! Good-bye USDA-funded soil conservation terraces and ponds and everything that allowed the few remaining American farmers to single-handedly feed the entire world with no thanks from anyone!

Phase Two would begin when our sober, exalted, righteous, and democratically elected officials in Washington learned of these terrible events in Cullman and throughout America. Of course the U.S. was definitely not a first-strike nation. But our leaders would *have no choice* but to begin dropping, lobbing, launching, and otherwise delivering, through every conceivable means available in our massive tripartite defense apparatus, thousands of multi-warheaded, multi-megatonned packages of retaliation into Moscow, Leningrad, Gdansk, Baku, and (why not China too, while we're at it?) Peking. Better dead than red. And so the Soviets and the Chinese would *have no choice* but to lob everything they had back at us, and there you are, vaporized. Or worse, dying of radiation sickness in a depopulated desert. Or perhaps worst of all, being one of the aimless few surviving briefly, intact but doomed by a huge cloud of strontium-90 rolling over the planet, becoming general, and finally bringing slow but certain radioactive death to your own pleasant little island neighborhood. Then there would be nothing. The breeze slapping a window shade against a radio microphone in San Francisco. Nothing.

But if, through some miracle, there was still *something*, if Phase One and Phase Two of *The End* had managed to miss you, there was always Phase Three, the Second Coming, which would bring you to the same conclusion, but with even more spectacular pageantry.

The script for Phase Three, the Apocalypse, was found in the Book of Revelation, a text the young Steick knew only by secondhand accounts. The gory details were recited weekly in church and Sunday school, and the exact timing and sequence of the horrible events were a source of endless fascination for his mother and aunt, who diligently debated the fine points while snapping beans at the kitchen table. "Do you think the souls already in Heaven will be able to watch?" one would ask. "Of course not!" the other would reply. "Everything in Heaven is perfect! Why would God let them watch?"

Richard was terrified even to look at the title page of the Revelation, though sometimes he would give it a quick glance and quickly slam the Bible shut, just to test his nerve. Merely the sight of the closed, limp, leather-bound, gilded black book on the coffee table sent waves of nauseating fear coursing through his skinny young frame, filling his mind with visions of seven-headed monsters, lightning, fire, brimstone, tidal waves, and whole mountain ranges rolling across the continent, leveling cities, grinding all unrepentant human life into grease, and crashing into the sea. The weeping, screaming, wailing, and gnashing of teeth would be clearly heard above the sound of thunder, blowing trumpets, and rolling mountains. What protection was your little farmhouse outside Cullman, Alabama, against the Second Coming? None at all! After it had flattened New York, Washington, and Atlanta, even Birmingham would be a mere speck on the westward path of divine retribution toward New Orleans, Denver, and ultimately, *Los Angeles,* the Sodom of all Sodoms, the Gomorrah of all Gomorrahs, the Whore of Babylon with lots of freeways!

The first signal of the really big end would be a trumpet blast sounded by one of the Archangels. Richard thought this was probably the Archangel Michael, although it might be Gabriel. Young Steick was never quite certain, since the naming of Archangels was largely a Roman Catholic matter—remote, esoteric, and vaguely illicit. The bell of the trumpet, he knew, would be at least as big as the harvest moon, and consequently, Richard was forever frightened of odd or remote sounds. Was that merely a passing train in Cullman, tooting a statutory warning to auto traffic, or was it the Archangel Whomever, blowing Jehovah's great horn to announce the end of time? Did that clap of thunder possess an unfamiliar, ominous undertone? If so, what should young Steick do? Duck and cover? Dig a fast fallout shelter? Get on his knees and beg forgiveness in a hurry? Swallow his fear and read the Book of Revelation? What?

The visual effects of the Second Coming would be equally stunning and would (he later realized) diminish the horrors of Bosch's great painting, *The Last Judgment,* to something like Disney's *Snow White.* Neither animation nor computer graphics were required for Richard to get the picture. A mere flannelgraph and two or three posters supplied by his local church did the job wonderfully well! First, there would be the trumpet fanfare. Then, the true master of ceremonies, Our Lord and Savior, Jesus Christ, would appear in the clouds over New York harbor. He would be approximately the size of France and would step down to earth on a light-slanted sunbeam. He would look like a nice Gentile with long hair, a semi-sorrowful smile, and uplifted hands ("the better to weigh and judge you with, my son"). Airplanes and dirigibles would buzz around Him like gnats. The toyland village of Manhattan would constitute, at most, a deific footprint. The sky would blaze in vivid psychedelic color!

"*Hallelujah!*" the old and truly saved would cry.

But not young Richard, even though he got saved each summer at church camp in north Georgia. He was never sure it quite "took hold" for him, never sure he was quite "saved enough," and he had an instinct for backsliding that was irrepressible. Consequently, any oddly colored cloud, any particularly enormous thunderhead, any slanting sunbeam, or even an icy ring around the moon was a sure sign to young Steick that the Big Conclusion was imminent, and he was in deep trouble. Judgment was at hand! So he would pray fervently, but he always assumed his prayers were too little, too late. At least, that was what they told him in church, and he believed them. Once the Judgment began, it was *Too Late* for anyone outside the fold.

Later in life, Steick learned that some Protestants referred to this horrible chain of events as "The Rapture." How odd a name, he thought, for what had been taught to him as a living nightmare. It turned out that these lucky people had missed all the sound, fire, and fury to be found in a fundamentalist Sunday school. They had absorbed a far more bland version of the Second Coming in which all the believers simply vanished. Poof! In adulthood (even after Steick and his educated, enlightened, and secular friends had cast off their "religious superstitions") the Rapture people told Steick they were forever frightened of empty office buildings and empty public spaces. Such scenarios always gave them a shiver, telling them they must have been "the one left behind."

He still believed, as an adult, that the Rapture folks were the lucky ones. Oh, to have been born a Methodist!

Thus did the now graying, distinguished professor find himself alone in Mushroom Memories on a Saturday night, a copy of Jung's *Memories, Dreams, Reflections* in one hand and an iced, lime Kool-Aid and vodka cocktail in the other. He would, he knew, figure this thing out yet. He had learned early and well how to be mindful, vigilant, and observant. Although he no longer lived in daily fear of the Triple Threat, he had learned how to duck, and he had learned how to cover his ass.

Contempt, Anyone?

One bright Tuesday morning in November, Steick showed up in the Bowie County Circuit Court wearing his hunting clothes. He was there to represent a client at a probation hearing, and his attire didn't exactly square with Judge Smiley's notion of proper decorum for an attorney. She fined him three hundred dollars for contempt and told him never to come into her courtroom dressed like that again. Richard was in full camo, and the judge was really pissed.

Circuit judges have wide discretion for controlling conduct in their courtrooms, which is perfectly logical, but Steick was not sure Judge Smiley hadn't violated due process or the First Amendment by fining him *that* much just for what he was wearing. Lawyers have rights, too, after all. Nevertheless, he didn't want any hassle, so he peeled three hundred-dollar bills out of his shirt pocket and counted them out to the clerk, duly noting his payment for the record. The judge almost fined him again for being so cavalier, but she couldn't seem to phrase how he had done anything wrong the second time. She just glowered like her forehead was a piece of steel, hot from the forge.

Steick knew Judge Smiley was extremely enamored of her newly elected status as a circuit judge. It is customary for all the lawyers, clients, witnesses, and onlookers to rise when a judge enters the courtroom. This is true whether the bailiff cries "All rise" or not. It is equally typical for the judge to quickly pat his or her hands downward, as if smoothing a stack of just-finished ironing, thereby indicating, "No big deal. Please sit down." Judge Smiley, on the other hand, always kept the whole courtroom standing while she drank a full ten-ounce plastic tumbler of water. Then she would swish and fiddle with her black judicial robes and finally settle her ample corpus into her throne, thereby indicating it was permissible for everyone else to sit down also. After about fifteen minutes of additional ceremony, which always included many mysterious asides to the court reporter, Judge Smiley would joggle her papers, peer out over the top of her rimless spectacles, and call the first case.

Attorney Steick would have felt less injured by the contempt citation that morning if he had actually been out hunting, which he had not. He had never killed an animal in his life and not been sick afterwards. That made him a wimp among Bowie County and Montgomery County lawyers, but he couldn't have cared less if it made him a monkey. That morning, he was just tramping around out in the woods south of Hallelujah to see what he could see, and he didn't have time to change into a coat and tie before the stupid probation hearing.

His client, a twenty-year-old black male, got his probation revoked. One could hardly expect otherwise, considering he'd missed six months of meetings with his supervisor and then got himself arrested for possession. What was the judge supposed to do? Pat him on the back? What was Steick supposed to do? Make an argument?

The deputy cuffed Steick's client and led him into a holding cell while Steick said, "Adios, partner" and picked up his briefcase and stocking cap.

He did not consider his actions a mark of disrespect for the courts or that he was stupid or crazy. In fact, he believed the courts represented society's most important bulwark against anarchy and chaos. He had received the highest score in Alabama on the bar exam when he took it almost twenty-five years previously, and he had not suffered the slightest ethical reprimand while representing thousands of clients since. His record with the Professional Responsibility Office was spotless, which was not common for a lawyer with Steick's experience. In addition, he shared a number of interesting hobbies with certifiably sane people like Hallelujah Mayor Dard Hooper. In short, Steick wasn't worried.

And yet he had the vague sense that his day of judgment was coming, since the episode with Judge Smiley was merely symptomatic of the many substantial changes occurring within Steick's psyche. His brothers and sisters at the bar began to notice these changes about two years earlier, when he began to listen to Vivaldi on his iPod while trying cases. His slight hearing loss was sometimes evident, and he joked indirectly about his "hearing aid." The judges didn't say anything, and Steick won his cases anyway. But there were snickers, asides, a lot of blushing, and little heart-to-heart suggestions from old friends who gently placed one hand on his shoulder. Perhaps if Steick had suffered some traumatic loss, such as the death of a loved one, his recent conduct would be more understandable and excusable. But there was no great bereavement, no significant life-altering experience, nothing like that at all. True, there was his divorce from Gloria some years before. And he *did* have an auto accident where a lady with no insurance or driver's license ran a red light and he walloped the side of her car. But the docs said he came out of that with only a bad concussion, and again, he wasn't worried.

It was just that he began to see the whole courtroom ritual for what he thought it most truly was: a fear-based pageant which was not only a bulwark against anarchy but also a theatrical event staged primarily for the amusement of the main players, namely, the lawyers and the judges.

So, Steick would make certain little comments. One day at a pre-trial, he told his old pal, Josh Wiggins, that Josh's $1,000 Brooks Brothers suit looked like it had chalk stripes in it. Josh just looked at Steick quizzically and said, "That's how it's supposed to look." Steick wasn't wearing his camos that day. He had on a $2,000 Gucci Italian silk that outclassed Josh's mere worsted by more than two to one. But Steick's feet were hurting, and so he wore his Nikes. His footwear, Steick knew, made Josh Wiggins look down his nose and wonder about his old friend and fellow lawyer. In this business, Steick reasoned, you learn to read other people's thoughts, whether you want to or not, and Richard could tell that Josh was thinking, "This guy's losing it." Steick also knew that Josh's sentiments were becoming more and more general around Hallelujah and that he, the upstanding citizen, was an increasing focus for gossip at Dard & Elle's Cafe, the lunch-time restaurant of choice for most Bowie County attorneys, court reporters, and public officials during the work week.

Whatever Wiggins and Steick's friends, colleagues, and clients were thinking was fine with him. The way he had it figured, after much reading and many solitary nights of contemplation in Mushroom Memories, was that he was not put on this Earth to perfect a way of life already attempted, refined, and screwed up by millions. On the contrary, he was put here to screw up his own way of life or, in other words, to screw up his own life in his own way. It seemed to him that most people, like Josh Wiggins, were so desperately attempting to avoid the living nightmare of almost being themselves that the result was either comic or pathetic, depending upon one's mood.

Opp U.

Oppenheimer State University in Hallelujah was a peculiar institution. Its unique split personality derived from thirty years of seemingly intractable federal court litigation directed toward ending *de facto* racial segregation in Alabama higher education. Opp U., as it was affectionately known, offered Richard Steick, PhD, Esq., a perfect academic venue for teaching his specialty of Law, Literature, and Society.

The institution was founded in the early 1870s by a German Missionary, one Klaus Oppenheim, for the purpose of educating recently emancipated slaves and their descendants. Over the next century, it was grudgingly and meagerly funded by the white legislature but slowly and steadily grew from an initial student population of five to approximately five thousand black students when integration arrived in the late 1960s. Its administration and faculty did the best they could with the little they had to work with, and the school had established an excellent reputation as a teachers' training institution serving black public schools throughout Alabama and the nation. It went through various name changes, from the Oppenheim Freedmen's School to the Oppenheim Colored Normal School, the Oppenheim Negroes' College, the Oppenheim State Teacher's College for Negroes, and finally, Oppenheim State College.

The black intellectual leadership at Oppenheim played an important role during the 1955 bus boycott in Montgomery and the ensuing Civil Rights Movement. By a curious if predictable twist of fate, however, integration betrayed the school cruelly. When the desegregation of higher education eventually succeeded throughout the nation, including Alabama, the best and brightest black students rapidly betook themselves to the University of Alabama, Auburn University, Vanderbilt, and prestigious

Ivy League colleges and universities formerly closed to black Americans. In addition, many of these previously segregated institutions began to offer scholarship incentives to minority applicants. Thus, there was little cause for well-qualified African Americans to enroll at Oppenheim, which still could not afford chalk, let alone scholarships.

And so the former black teachers' college suffered a serious identity crisis in the early 1970s. Deprived of its student base, it didn't know what to do with itself. It tried becoming an open-admissions, all-things-to-everyone college which welcomed every high school graduate, regardless of race, creed, color, I.Q., mental infirmity, inability to read, haircut, or unfortunate lack of a high school diploma. Students who had lost their diplomas were routinely admitted, even when their high schools had inadvertently misplaced their records of attendance and graduation as well. All were welcomed at the table of knowledge.

The formerly distinguished teacher's college quickly collapsed into an adolescent day care center and theme park substantially populated by brain-damaged Vietnam War vets drawing their VA benefits and smoking reefer. Meanwhile, Alabama's white colleges and universities flourished, as always, and multiplied significantly during the first and second Wallace administrations. In Hallelujah, a brand new, spiffy white university was spawned by the legislature overnight in the white district across town from Oppenheim State. It was justifiably said by many that in Alabama, "the more it changes, the more it stays the same." More than fifteen years after *Brown v. Board of Education,* Hallelujah had two separate but exceedingly unequal universities on opposite sides of the small city. There was the old, decrepit Oppenheim State in the black part of town for black students, and the sparkling new Montgomery University Hallelujah (MUH) in the white part of town for white students.

Segregation was thus perpetuated contrary to the law of the land, and the black leadership at Oppenheim knew it had a winning hand in the federal courts. They sued and sued and sued to absorb the new white campus, and the white establishment fought back with enormous funding and appeal after appeal after appeal.

The black and white taxpayers of the state paid the legal fees—for both sides—which, after nearly twenty years of litigation, topped $200 million. Most residents of central Alabama were tired of the whole mess, and so was the federal judiciary. An out-of-state judge was called in to mediate and bring closure to the endless lawsuit, no matter what.

The black and white constituencies remained intransigent until the judge recommended a remedy and imposed a deadline upon the parties. In the event that Oppenheim State and MUH did not accept the judge's proposed solution or enter a workable consent decree before the deadline, both institutions would be closed indefinitely until they did. Since the two sides could not work together to fashion an alternative, they agreed to accept the judge's plan.

Unfortunately, the out-of-state judge's highest and best calling to the bench was to serve as a warning to others. He ended the controversy between the warring Hallelujah institutions effectively, but the results were often comical. Pursuant to the court's final order, Oppenheim State College and Montgomery University Hallelujah were permanently merged into one institution, with its name to be determined by the parties. The university's new school colors were, of course, black and white. Its motto and mission, as directed by the court, were to be "Equality In All Things."

The court further decreed that "equality" meant one-for-one equality. Thus, the newly hybridized institution would have two of everything. There would be a black president and a white president. Similarly, there would be black and white co-tenants of all offices above directorships. There was a black academic vice president and a white one, a black head librarian and a white one, and so on. The faculty, staff, and student body were ordered to be kept constantly at a one-to-one ratio. For each black faculty member hired or fired, a white faculty member would have to be hired or fired also. For each white student admitted, a black student would be admitted as well. If a white student dropped out, no new black students could be accepted until the former white student was replaced. Any deviation from the decree would result in contempt citations with enormous fines and possible jail time for the individuals responsible. Thus, when the commingled institution created an African American

Studies degree program, it was quick to institute a Caucasian Studies program simultaneously.

The university thus created was an administrative debacle of monumental proportions. The black and white co-presidents held their equal ineptitude up to the light as if inspecting its seams. Every decision, however small, from ordering paper clips to the university logo, made the sinking of the Bismarck look like a friendly child's game.

The divisiveness naturally began with naming the new institution. Black alumni, students, and power brokers insisted that the name remain "Oppenheim State University," while the white opposition adamantly demanded "Montgomery University Hallelujah." A predictable stalemate, and precursor of many bitter disputes to come, rapidly ensued.

A solution to the university's naming problem was eventually suggested by an unlikely source, Hallelujah Mayor Dard Hooper. Mayor Hooper was a good friend of nearby Montgomery Mayor Mallard McGuire, and both were pals of General William Tecumseh Warpage, commander of Maxwell Air Force Base in Montgomery. The air base had an enormous impact upon the economy of both Montgomery and Hallelujah as well as a large portion of central Alabama. Both Mayor Hooper of Hallelujah and Mayor McGuire of Montgomery found it wise and politically beneficial to maintain a close relationship between the air base and their respective cities. This political necessity and mutual courtesy called for a regular exchange of views as well as an inordinate amount of grinning, cocktail chatter, and back-slapping between the two mayors and General Warpage.

The friendship of the three extended to a semi-regular, rotating poker game hosted by one of them or by one of the three or four other regional power players in their group. It was at one of these informal but influential gatherings that the newly merged and perpetually equal institution of higher education in Hallelujah was christened.

General Warpage had just bluffed on a pair of eights and successfully raked in a modest pot of four hundred dollars for the final hand of the evening. The single-malt Scotch had been passed once again, and the men had lit up embargoed Cuban cigars graciously provided by the General via U.S. Air Force transit from Guantánamo Bay. It was a serene and relaxing time for all. The General, by far the largest of the men and also the best storyteller, was reminiscing about some of the more enjoyable events in his history of service to the Air Force. He had experienced many things that most never had or would, and he was delighted to share his recollections. On this pleasant evening, he was recalling with dreamy-eyed awe the grandeur and beauty of atomic detonations, which he had witnessed on many occasions during the Cold War testing period.

"You fellas know what an atom bomb sounds like?" he asked.

The gentlemen responded, with considerable interest, that they could only imagine.

"An atom bomb sounds like peace and freedom. That's what it sounds like. I can remember lots of 'em out there in the Nevada desert in the 1950s. Ka-Boom!!! There she goes! And I always said to myself, 'Listen close, Bill. That's the sound of peace and freedom that's bustin' your eardrums right now.' Then the shock wave went over our trenches like a tornado, and in a little bit the C.O. would give the all-clear, and we could stick our heads up and look at that beautiful mushroom cloud, all red, white, and blue, like the tallest thunderhead you've ever seen. Them big ol' yucca tree plants would be a-poppin' and a-burnin' like Fourth of July sparklers, I tell ya. Sometimes the heat would tear 'em right out of the ground and make 'em shoot up in the air like a rocket. And one time I saw the face of Jesus in one of them clouds. I swear I did. I ain't no Catholic, or I would have seen the face of the Virgin Mary. I'm just an ordinary good Christian, like everybody else. But that was the face of Jesus in that mushroom cloud, just as sure as I'm sittin' here.

"That Bobby Oppenheimer was one great sumbitch of an American, wasn't he? Look at what he gave our country. We've always got to remember the immortal words of Patrick Henry: 'Give me death, or kill me!' Seems to me like Oppenheimer's never got the respect he deserves in the history books or from the nation as a whole. A forgotten hero, that's what he is, ol' Oppenheimer."

Hallelujah Mayor Hooper paused a moment, scratched his head, and asked the General, "Say, Bill. Who's this Oppenheimer fella you're talkin' about? Seems like I've heard of him, but I can't rightly remember just what he did."

"There ya go! That's exactly what I mean, partner. An educated man like you, and the Mayor of Hallelujah, no less, ought to know the name of Robert Oppenheimer, Dard. Go on. Don't tell me you've never heard of the Manhattan Project? Or tell me. What was it? Do you know at all?"

Mayor Hooper asked, slightly hesitantly, "Wasn't that the code name for the operation that built the first atomic bomb out in New Mexico, so we could go on ahead and win World War II?"

"Why SURE it was!" the General pronounced loudly, and both he and Mayor Hooper burst into satisfied grins. "Now Dard, same song, second verse. Who headed up the Manhattan Project and gave the world the atomic bomb?"

"I'm going to say it was a guy named Robert Oppenheimer," the Mayor replied, pleased that he had put one and one together.

"You're right again, Dard ol' boy! You just won the bonus prize. That Oppenheimer was a genius and a great American. I don't care what he did or said or what they all said about him later. He ought to have a monument in Washington or something."

The Hallelujah Mayor paused, grinned slightly, and gave the General a sideways, conspiratorial grin.

"How about a state university in Hallelujah, Alabama, bein' named after him?" he asked.

"Well, now. That would be just wonderful. I've been readin' in the paper all this nonsense about these Hallelujah colleges bein' merged and how the black folks and the white folks can't even come up with a name for it yet. You want to name it after Dr. Robert Oppenheimer, Dard?"

"Let me put it this way, General. If you yourself would get behind the publicity, I would gladly put the pressure on the leadership of both sides to give the university that name. Seems like a reasonable compromise to me. After all, the black folks want to keep it named 'Oppenheim,' and all they'd have to do is add an 'er' to that. The white people, on the other hand, aren't all that crazy about 'Montgomery University Hallelujah' anyway. They'd like the place to have some distinction, you know. With all due respect to Montgomery, Mal, they'd like to see the school in their town have a unique identity apart from our great capital city, if you know what I mean. No offense, of course. And I think the white people would all admire Oppenheimer, just like you do, General, once they got around to remembering him, and they'd probably be proud to have their city's university named after him. Whadda ya think, Mal? General?"

The General happily responded. "I think you've got yourself one wonderful idea there, Dard. Fact is, there's a connection between Hallelujah and ol' Oppy, you know. See, during the Manhattan Project, General Groves, the military commander, was in and out of Maxwell like a hummingbird, and I know for sure he brought Oppy to Montgomery with him on more than one occasion. Why, I've got no doubt at all that they drove around, saw a little of this beautiful Alabama countryside, and probably drove slap through Hallelujah just to have a look at it on some nice Sunday afternoon. I'll bet you most anything that both of those campuses sit on some of the very rocks that Robert Oppenheimer might have looked at. It's only fitting and proper that this fine new educational institution should be named after him."

"And what's even better, Dard," Montgomery Mayor McGuire interjected, "is that I'll bet you could sell it to both sides and put this silly bickering behind you so y'all could get on to bickering about the next silly thing. Or better yet, so you yourself could be the hero bringing peace to both parties. You've got an election coming up in about a year, don't forget. I don't know about your opposition, or even if you have any, but this could be a good opportunity to get the voters on your side with something quick, easy, and sensible to boot."

"Fellas," Hallelujah Mayor Hooper responded, "I think this has been a particularly fine evening of poker and an especially productive one intellectually. First, I'm going to take this 'Oppenheimer University' idea to the city council and get a resolution supporting it. Then, I'm going to put it in front of the university presidents and ask them to take it to their boards. And I'll do everything I can to get them to adopt it. Man, think of the great football team names we could get! 'The Oppenheimer Bombs.' Well, maybe not that. Could give the wrong idea.

The Oppenheimer Atoms, or something. Might go Double-A. Build up Hallelujah's economy. Who knows? Have us a little Oppenheimer museum or something. General, I thank you!"

And with that blessing upon his well-decorated shoulders, General Warpage said, "Let us pray." He delivered a stirring benediction, and the game broke up.

It took some time for Mayor Hooper to persuade the university's two constituencies to accept the new name he had proposed. The controversy was a small reminder of the debates stirred up earlier when the former town of "Hellespont" decided to rename itself "Hallelujah." But in the end, Mayor Hooper's persuasive power prevailed, and "Oppenheimer State University" was officially selected as the permanent name of the single, unified, and unalterably equal institution of higher learning situated in his small city.

There were certain problems, of course. The colloquially preferred "Opp U." held on in conversation, both inside and outside of Alabama. And thus, postal deliveries for the institution were often mistakenly directed to the town of Opp, Alabama, many miles southward.

But that was a small price to pay for ending the divisive community controversy. And, in addition, it gave the university an absolutely unbeatable advertising slogan: "Oppenheimer State. Where Opportunity Doesn't Just Knock. It Blows You Away!"

ON NOTICE

One day an event occurred that shook Steick to his foundations. It was early in the spring semester, and he had just conducted his morning seminar at Oppenheimer State. The text was Franz Kafka's novel, *The Trial.* The students were bright and alert, and Steick had been pleasantly surprised by their preparation and the liveliness of the discussion. As he silently navigated the creamy leather and burled-wood cabin of his SUV toward his law office on Peach Street, he smiled as he recalled one young black man's particularly cogent observation. The young fellow had shot up his hand and bubbled, "So what this dude Kafka says is that the universe itself don't offer no fundamental due process. Shit, man. That ain't nothin' new! Black folks been knowin' that for four hunnerd years!"

The learned professor pulled into the tiny but immaculately paved parking lot behind the restored nineteenth-century dogtrot house that served as his office. The dogtrot was a perfect arrangement, since Steick required peaceful isolation in order to fully concentrate upon cases, pleadings, offers and counteroffers, and legal research. His secretary, Betty, was the peerless and irreproachable mistress of one-half of the quaint old house, the half that also contained the conference room where Steick took endless, boring depositions. The other half was his own cozy suite, book-lined, homey, and a dash elegant. With eighteen feet of roofed but open porch space (where the dogs used to trot) between himself and Betty's noisy domain of ringing telephones, fax machines, copiers, case files, and all the impedimenta of a law practice, Steick felt sufficiently removed in his own suite to do his real job, which was to read, think, and write cogently and diligently as he prepared his cases.

He did not suffer interruptions in his half of the office. Instead, whenever he arrived, he would check in with Betty, collecting a stack of papers to sign, his telephone messages, and "tickler" reminders of forthcoming deadlines on his docket. He was devoutly religious about maintaining his calendar. Each deposition, trial date, discovery cut-off, or other important event was routinely written onto Betty's calendar by Betty and also onto his own calendar by the lawyer himself. Steick's malpractice carrier required this double-entry system, but he took it two steps further. Both he and Betty maintained computer calendars with timed, audible alarms. Thus, every deadline was recorded in quadruplicate, twice on paper and twice on computers, thereby rendering any stupid errors such as missed appointments or missed deadlines virtually impossible. Or so Richard thought, until this particularly fine and bright February morning in Hallelujah.

He opened the door to Betty's office with a cheery "Hey, Betty," as usual, and walked behind her chair to collect his papers and messages. "How's everything this mornin'? You doin' okay?" he graciously inquired, as he flipped through the meticulously prepared stack of pleadings and correspondence.

"Everything is just fine, Mr. Steick," Betty replied, wisely rhyming her employer's surname with "bike," as he preferred. She possessed an uncanny ability to read his mind and to know precisely what to do in almost any situation. She fully understood the enormous importance he placed upon meticulous attention to detail. All of these qualities made her, in Steick's judgment, a priceless professional, and he compensated her well with bonuses, liberal paid vacations, time off when she wanted it, and wide latitude to run her side of the operation in her own way.

"Good, good, good," he said, tucking his papers and turning to go out the door and into his suite.

He had just grasped the doorknob when Betty said, "Oh, yes, Mr. Steick. Mr. Jones phoned again asking if you had filed his worker's compensation case. I told him everything was fine and not to worry."

Steick's right hand froze to the doorknob while his left hand dropped his neat sheaf of papers. A nuclear hot flash traveled from the crown of his head to the tips of his toes in an instant, like a shock wave coursing across the Nevada desert after a test detonation. Enormous perspiration immediately flooded the same path. He was paralyzed, but he shook so hard that the glass rattled in the door frame.

"What's the matter, Mr. Steick?" Betty cried. "Are you okay?"

He was choking to death. He could not form words. He wanted to butt his head through the glass, fall onto the shards, and decapitate himself, but he couldn't move. His eyes were bulging. His face was bloodless.

Betty rushed around her desk and lay her hand upon his shoulder in a gentle, matronly way. She shook him but got no response. She shook harder and harder until the eloquent lawyer finally turned, faced her, and said, "Mufff." Betty waited and then shook again, whereupon Steick came out with, "Pishlloglll . . . hhhhai!" With a little more stern shaking, he eventually uttered, "I blew-hoo it, Betty! I forgot t-t-to f-file that J-Jones lawsuit, and the statue, st, statute of limitations ran three d-days ago! I, I'll be sued to the m-mooon! Kaput! Finito! No washing, no rinsing, no wiping dry! No excuse! N-Nothing to d-do! I . . . I . . . I w-want y-you to c-cancel all my appointments for the rest of the day, and no telephone calls either!"

The stunned attorney regained his equilibrium sufficiently to navigate the eighteen feet to his suite, leaving a trail of trodden white papers and pink message slips in his wake. Trembling, he went to the sideboard, grasped a Waterford double old-fashioned glass, filled it nearly to the top with Jack Daniels, and drained it, spilling the lovely amber liquid all over himself, the furniture, his papers, his books, and the floor. He poured another short one and sat down in his burgundy leather wing-backed recliner, where he leaned back and waited vacantly for the few moments until the whiskey began to fulfill its anesthetic function.

And, in only five minutes, he felt numb, dazed, but much improved! Things weren't really so bad after all! True, missing a statute of limitations is the stupidest mistake a lawyer can make, but it is also one of the most frequent. And anyone—even he, Professor Richard Featherston Steick, PhD, Esq.—was entitled to make a mistake!

There was also the backstop of his malpractice insurance. He had paid his carrier thousands upon thousands of dollars in premiums over the years with nary a boo-boo! Now he would simply have to put the insurance company, Malanon, Inc., on notice of his error in missing the statute, and they would handle the entire matter. He would be required to pay his $5,000 deductible, but after that, the ball was in the risk insurer's hands. His premiums would go up, of course, but he would merely increase his hourly rate to compensate for the added expense.

He languidly lifted the receiver and dialed his agent, Frank Ferret in Montgomery, and lazily told him the bad news. Frank asked a few questions and instructed his wayward customer to immediately put all the sorry facts into a certified letter and mail it to him at his agency. He assured the stunned attorney that everything would be fine. Steick was fully covered, and the excellent lawyers at Barratry, Champerty, and Tennis in Birmingham would take care of everything once Jones had filed his inevitable suit for malpractice.

Steick thanked Ferret, replaced the receiver, and leaned back for a few moments of reflection before dozing off. This was his first really big mistake since marrying Gloria! Not a bad record, but not his style at all! Missing the statute was a wake-up siren! His friends were indeed correct about him, and all the gossip at Dard & Elle's Cafe was right on point!

He needed help. So he would get help. Simple enough.

He slept fitfully for three hours, dreaming of Jones shaking his finger in Richard's face and hollering, *"Yura gonna goada hail!"* He awoke with a monumental headache which, in justice, should have been reserved for Edward Teller, Gloria, Judge Smiley, and his childhood Sunday school teachers.

Yes, he thought. I will get help.

THE NEW COVENANT

The following afternoon, Professor Steick set out to find the help he needed. Perhaps it would come as a word or two of advice from a friend, colleague, or counselor. Possibly it would be a mood pill. He wasn't sure. He had never given much thought to such matters, having dedicated his life to what he considered The Larger Issues: Law, Literature, Society, and a well-nourished bank account. Once he arrived at the university as an undergraduate, he had cast off his fundamentalist Protestant superstitions and consigned "spiritual issues" to their proper lieutenants: religion majors, Californians, shrinks, and shrinklets. (True "shrinks" were MDs who could prescribe medications, while "shrinklets" were mere clinical psychologists who had nothing in their arsenals but psychobabble and "reflective feedback.")

On the other hand, he had not thrown out the baby with the bath water. After many years of shunning religious observance altogether, he had cautiously joined Camembert Covenant Church in Hallelujah, and he was glad he did. Sometimes, he even attended services. The church was mainstream, liberal in the best sense, rational, and compassionate—quite the opposite of the fundamentalist chapel in Cullman where, as a child, he had learned to fear the Lord Jesus more than the devil himself. Covenant was full of good-hearted, well-educated, and affable Alabamians who loved the world and most things about it, who did not pry into others' affairs, and who, in a quiet and loving way, did good deeds in abundance without regard for earthly reward. The church was even slightly integrated! To his amazement, Steick actually enjoyed giving money to the church, occasionally serving on various committees, ushering now and then, and attending Sunday worship when he felt like it. He had seen evidence of effective pastoral counseling, and he thought that his minister, Dr. Thurston ("Thirsty") M. Balm, might help him get back on the right track spiritually and emotionally.

With hope in his heart, Steick tooled his platinum SUV down the oak-lined, appropriately named Church Street and wheeled into the impeccably paved parking lot of Camembert Covenant. The edifice was a classic example of pristine American church architecture, composed of red brick, white trim, Greek revival columns, and an immensely tall white steeple. Before gingerly hopping onto the tarmac, the religiously reformed lawyer and professor aligned himself appropriately for the situation. Axis one: loyal parishioner. Axis two: slight problem with memory and a vague sense of unease.

He mounted the six white concrete steps and entered the narthex, which smelled of warm milk and comfortable baby aromas emanating from the thriving day care center located beneath the sanctuary. He turned left, walked past the church secretary's office, and down the long hallway to Pastor Balm's study. The door was open, and Thirsty faced him from behind the littered pastoral desk where he had propped his feet next to a glazed ceramic sign that announced "Shalom" in flaming Hebrew script. With all due courtesy, Steick knocked on the already opened door, stuck in his head, and smiled.

Pastor Balm greeted Steick somewhat tentatively, scanning him as if searching for a name tag. "Well! Hello there . . . friend!" Balm exclaimed, adding, "Seems like I haven't seen you in quite a long while . . . Have I?"

"Richard Steick," the guest replied. "I wonder if we might have a word."

"Oh yes, yes, yess, Dick! Of course! Sit down. Sit down!"

The pastor's slightly confused demeanor betrayed that he had mislaid his highly secret Visual Information Pattern Encoded Refractive Spectacles, or VIPERS, as they were known by the select few who knew about them. No one in Hallelujah, not even Thirsty's lovely wife, Cookie, had a clue about his ultra high-tech eyewear. They were his deepest secret, and they assisted him enormously in his vigilant effort to endear himself to his congregation and the Hallelujah community at large.

Thirsty knew, even before he entered seminary, that he had a number of minor disabilities which he would have to surmount in some manner if he were to become a successful pastor. As a younger man, he had applied himself diligently to the task and achieved a mixed measure of success.

For one thing, he suffered frequent onslaughts of the slight speech impediment known as "spoonerism," a name derived from an English cleric, the Reverend Spooner, who perfected the disability to the degree that it was mysteriously transformed into a high art. The Reverend Balm nearly surpassed Spooner himself, particularly when Balm got involved with the consonants G, J, and L, which are often used in the Christian liturgy. During his theological education, he went to a speech therapist on the side and, with considerable practice, obtained a fair mastery over his own ever-twisted tongue. Nevertheless, the problem persisted to the degree that, at least once each Sunday morning, he came out with a real blooper. Often this would occur during the peroration of his sermon, in which he would announce, in magnificent, stentorian tones, "All jory, gloy, thanksgiving, and honor be unto the Gourd our Lod! Amen."

Thirsty had been a tank commander before entering seminary, and Steick often wondered how he had managed. It must have been terribly confusing to his crew, and not especially helpful in the desert, when he came out with something like, "Joe gleft tiny degrees on my mark! Jurn!"

The pastor's most embarrassing gaffe occurred at the conclusion of a packed, candlelit evening wedding when he ceremoniously announced that the lovely young bride and her handsome groom were "now jawfully loined together." Understandably, Balm's side income from weddings dropped considerably as a consequence. Nevertheless, his parishioners and friends in Hallelujah generally overlooked his impediment and adored him for his many other fine qualities, which included his outstanding warmth and an uncanny ability to recall names, dates, and events, a knack which he owed entirely to his highly secret VIPERS.

Pastor Balm learned of this technological marvel and obtained his own personal pair of VIPERS through his well-connected sources in the tank corps. The new spectacles were so secret that few of the top brass at the Pentagon even knew of their existence. They were, however, extremely popular among politicians at both the national and state levels, more and more of whom were sporting the electronic eyewear and rising ever higher in the opinion polls as a result.

Essentially, VIPERS were a sort of Teleprompter, with a large computer memory contained in a CPU which was about the size of a pack of cigarettes and fit neatly into a jacket or shirt pocket. A nearly invisible electric and fiber optic wire passed from the CPU through Thirsty's shirt collar and into the tip of the earpiece of a more or less ordinary pair of eyeglasses. The frames were slightly thick and black like the ones Michael Caine wore in *The Ipcress File,* but they flattered the pastor's whitish hair and ruddy face and gave him an appropriate, scholarly appearance. They were secretly available, to a very select few, with or without prescription vision adjustment. Thirsty was considerably myopic, and so his new frames came as no surprise to anyone, including Mrs. Balm, when he obtained them.

Through a simple connection to his PC, Thirsty could download entire sermons from the Internet and store them in his glasses. The lenses were slightly refractive, though not obscuring to ordinary vision, and the entire text of his sermons scrolled, perfectly paced, before his eyes as he gazed emphatically and empathetically into the faces of his congregation on Sunday mornings. With the slight touch of a button in his pocket, he also had the entire text of the NIV Bible at his disposal. Everyone marveled at his wit and recall. Apart from his speech impediment and an occasional reference to "Saint Paul's Letter to the Philippines," his delivery was exceedingly sharp and *without using a script or even any notes!*

Another distinct advantage of Balm's VIPERS was their remarkable pattern-recognition feature. By using a special scanner, which he passed over the pages of Covenant's photo membership directory, the pastor could store all the faces of his congregation, together with their names, addresses, telephone numbers, dates of birth, and spouses' and childrens' names, in the VIPERS's computer memory. Then, whenever he peered at a parishioner, the sophisticated optics of his spectacles would, instantly, match the pattern of the person's face with the stored data and give him a heads-up display of the member's name and vital statistics. He could even input the contents of his last conversation by way of a diary link with his PC.

What a boon his VIPERS were to a pastor with a large congregation like Thirsty! There was never an awkward moment when he greeted his members at the close of services. Indeed, he astonished them with an abundance of recall which clearly betokened a huge, caring heart coupled with an outstanding mind and an enormous knowledge of the scriptures. "Well hello, Mrs. Smith," he would say, "I believe we last talked at about 2:17 P.M. on Thursday, August 18. That was a year ago, of course. How is your son, Michael, doing at Tuscaloosa? I know you were worried about him. And your Pekingese, Bluie, had an abscess on his toe, as I recall. Is he okay? Oh, by the way, happy birthday two weeks from Tuesday! And take a look at Job 29, verses two through eight, as you turn sixty!"

But, to his great dismay, the Reverend Balm had somehow misplaced the refractive spectacles portion of his VIPERS unit earlier on the day when Steick came to call. They were undoubtedly located somewhere within the vast clutter of the pastor's study, but nearsighted as he was, he was badly handicapped in attempting to find them. He was staring at the open door, trying to retrace his steps, when Steick had intruded. He knew the lawyer was okay, and even somewhat prominent, but that was all he could recall.

Balm panicked. He felt cold all over. His right eye began to twitch uncontrollably.

He arose from his comfortable office chair, opened the closet for his coat, and said, "Uhhh . . . Mr. aah . . . Mr. aah . . . Dick . . . aah, I'll bet you're here for some important matter of church business . . . aah . . . some committee . . . aah . . . possibly a pishional urshoe . . . why, say, I uh . . . I have to attend a funeral now—part of our Paradise Assistance Ministry, you know—and I'm, and I'm, uh, going to have to turn you over to our Spiritual Lifestyles Coordinator, Larry Needle. You're acquainted with *him*, I'm sure! Wonderful fellow! Always ready to help! Sorry I have to run like this, but ah, great, aah, really great to see you again! Thanks for choosing Covenant as your prayer source! See you Sunday, maybe. Bye, bye. I'll send Larry in."

Pulling on his coat, Balm brushed past Steick and out the door, yelling *soto voce,* "Needle! Needle! Get in there and talk to that man, Mr. aah . . . Dick. I think he needs some help. I'm on my way to Paradise Assistance. Go on!"

Looking out the pastor's window and into the paved parking lot, Steick watched as the pastor climbed into his forest green and chrome SUV. Balm switched on the V-8, quickly cranked backward out of his "Reserved for the Reverend" slot, threw the vehicle into drive, scratched his tires, lurched, and plowed headlong into Mr. and Mrs. Ovaltine, a gray-haired couple in an antique four-door Dodge sedan. They were bringing canned goods for the church's Good Samaritan food closet and a chocolate cake for the pastor and his family. Steick noted with relief that no one had been hurt. But the cake had splattered itself all over the inside windshield of the light blue sedan. Balm was out of his SUV, dancing a jig of apology, and running his hands over his body as if they were mice, still hunting for his spectacles.

Before Steick could offer to help the pastor and his aged parishioners, Larry Needle entered the room, entirely unfazed by Steick's right index finger, which pointed out the window toward the accident. Steick and Needle vaguely recognized each other, but neither knew why. In contrast to Pastor Balm, Needle was a verbal geyser. "Hey!" he said. "Good to meet you! Mr. Dick, isn't it? I don't know why, but you sure do look familiar. What's your first name?"

Steick gave his first and last names correctly, careful as always to rhyme the latter with "bike."

"You weren't ever a lawyer, by any chance, were you, Mr. Steick?" Needle inquired.

Steick replied that he was indeed and gave Needle a brief biographical sketch.

"Aah! So that's where I know you from!" The pastoral associate began to elaborate at length. "Until recently, I was a lawyer, too! So let me tell you about myself. I was in my early fifties when I gave up law practice to become Spiritual Lifestyles Coordinator for Camembert Covenant in Montgomery, and just two months ago I came up here to help Pastor Balm in Hallelujah. When I quit the law, I had all my ex-wives and my only son fully paid off with plenty of money to spare. I had an MDiv from Harvard, thanks to a Rottweiler Foundation Theological Fellowship, and my master's degree qualified me for the job in Montgomery."

"Well, that's wonderful," Steick responded.

"My theological education naturally occurred before I 'saw the light' and transferred to Harvard Law. Ha, ha! I made law review and graduated in the top 10 percent of my class. I could have gone straight from commencement to Wall Street for an enormous salary, but I missed the fragrance of tea olive in October, and I wanted to come home. So I joined the largest bond firm in Montgomery and made a heap of money before I was forty. It wasn't Texas money, but it was enough. I had tax-advantaged accounts in Grand Cayman, Liechtenstein, and Switzerland, with all of them so papered over with close corporations and limited partnerships that the best divorce lawyers in Alabama couldn't get at my real assets."

"Thinking all the time," Steick said.

"At fifty, I found myself alcoholic, gastritic, and slightly demented, symptoms I find ever more common among lawyers these days," Needle continued. "You know, according to the latest studies, the average working life of an American attorney, male or female, has plummeted to about fourteen years. Most legal dropouts attempt to recycle themselves into productive and less stressful careers, which is why I took the job at Covenant. I could have traveled around Europe, skiing and getting laid until I got too old, but that seemed aimless and irresponsible."

Steick cleared his throat and squirmed.

Needle continued, "Montgomery is a good place to warm your hands in front of the fire, so to speak, and I wanted to give something back to the community that had given me a great start, three gorgeous wives, and tremendous opportunities for financial growth. It didn't hurt, either, that I had been quarterback at Montgomery Academy and still enjoyed a certain local fame, in spite of my age."

Steick was growing exceedingly bored and restless, but he managed to reply, "Yeah, you quarterbacks are always famous."

Mistakenly taking Steick's comment as encouragement, Needle grew more animated. "Covenant in Montgomery had a rapidly growing congregation of six thousand, thanks largely to its extremely successful cybermission. The web site really took off when the church added a new program called Pew 5.1. With the touch of a button on their home computers, our folks could experience a reverential, fan-generated breeze gently bathing them in the fragrance of old Bibles, hymnals, kneeling cushions, candles, and chrysanthemums. It's wonderful what technology can do! Why, some Sundays we'd have fewer than a hundred people who actually showed up physically at the church, but we'd get as many as eight thousand hits on the web! That tells you people are looking for something more than the same ol', same ol' liturgy!

"The enormous growth of the cyberchurch called for a new outreach to individual members, and consequently, the Council of Deacons created the position of Spiritual Lifestyles Coordinator, a job of increasing importance at churches all over the country. Covenant's budget was fat and happy, with members all making their pledges by payroll deduction or automatic bank draft, and the Lifestyles position was immediately sanctioned by the Bishop and the Synod. We kept the director of Christian Education, the lay pastors, the Minister of Music, Minister of Racial Forgiveness, and all the old what-nots, but everyone agreed that one-on-one spiritual design was the wave of the future and was bound to boost the congregation even further."

"Mr. Needle," Steick interrupted. "I, uh . . ." But he didn't get to complete his sentence before Needle plowed onward.

"It was an ideal job, and I was the ideal person for it. I had the background, the qualifications, and the connections. In addition, I had been a member of Covenant for twenty years and was a regular patron in the Lazarus chat room. Pastor Ed Johnson practically begged me to take the Lifestyles position! The salary wasn't great, but my annual dues to the Montgomery Country Club and the Capital City Club came as fringe benefits, and I wasn't in it for the money anyway. So I took the job and immediately started preparing a monthly report for the relationships marketing division of the Worship Ministry."

Steick rose and said, "I have to go now, Mr. Needle."

"Oh sit down," Needle said as he lit a small, expensive cigar. "You need to hear this. It's good stuff."

Beginning to boil, Richard reluctantly took his seat once again.

"I like to keep busy, and in a typical week, I'd have approximately sixty spiritual seekers in my office for facilitation. I would listen thoughtfully, take abundant notes, and send them off with a print-out of my suggested spiritual design. The job gave me immediate access to the deepest thoughts and longings of dozens of lovely widows and divorcees, not to mention the occasional arts maiden who woke up one day to find herself drifting helplessly into middle age. Heh heh!

"For women, I typically recommended heavy doses of scripture (the Psalms, usually) in combination with Taoist meditation, warm baths, aroma therapy, and Kegel exercises. The men were a tougher problem, however, and often I had to put them on a strict diet consisting entirely of whole wheat bread, soups, and steamed vegetables, with no liquor, golf, TV, pornography, or expensive cigars.

"I suspect, as a matter of fact, that is what I'm going to recommend for you. Such a process quickly weeds out the true seekers from those simply looking to network in new venues. The scriptural readings for the men are usually from the wisdom books—Job, Proverbs, and especially Ecclesiastes—with a bit of Zazen or Sufism added for rigor. Everyone gets fundamental lessons in attention to breathing, progressive relaxation, and basic meditation. Following my initial assessment and design, I meet with my seekers about once each month to check their progress and fine-tune the program."

Steick managed to say, "Very exciting, Mr. Needle, but I have an appointment very shortly."

As if he were deaf, Needle droned on. "The spiritual design concept was a great success for our relationships marketing division in Montgomery, and I'm proud of the work I did there as coordinator. I enjoyed a nice profile in the community and was often asked to speak at sports banquets, civic club meetings, and as a catastrophe commentator on local television.

"But I've been wanting to slow down a little bit, so just a couple of months ago I took the job here in Hallelujah. I'm a good start-up guy and glad for the opportunity. I want to bring all that progress we made in Montgomery up here to a smaller environment. Folks here need it and deserve it just as much, after all."

Steick's composure was disintegrating, and he was turning red, but Needle was oblivious.

"We also conducted excellent virtual missions in Honduras, Chile, Sierra Leone, Taiwan, and Thailand. One time I had an ex-Roman Catholic priest on line from Bangkok. In no time at all, I was able to design an individual spiritual lifestyle for him that harmonized his ingrained professional taste for dogma with his newly acquired desire to follow the Eightfold Path of Buddhism.

"And talk about high-tech sharing! Remember that earthquake in Turkey a few years ago? About thirty thousand dead and a quarter million homeless, as I recall. Anyway, we were able to download whole bushels of formulas and diagrams for making waterproof tents out of bed sheets and what-not, and that's what kept those poor people from freezing to death that winter! I mean, there's really no end to what you can do with computers, once you stop and think about it, you know."

Steick got out of his chair and had turned toward the door before Needle pulled him down by his shoulder and jumped into his story once again.

"Anyway, some members of the Board of Deacons got concerned one time that maybe we were going overboard with the virtual church at the expense of actual physical attendance on Sunday mornings. Most members thought that was nonsense, but we jazzed up the liturgy a little bit anyway, just to keep everybody happy. Interestingly, we experienced a real increase in physical attendance at Holy Communion after we made a few changes. We celebrated the sacrament on designated church holidays as well as the Sundays preceding the Fourth of July and the Auburn-Alabama game. We found that a little piece of cheese offered with the bread and the wine doubled or even tripled our attendance! (We usually served Brie or Havarti.) We also decided that Communion would be a good time to pass the Peace. This created a brief spiritual-social interlude in the worship service. Everyone enjoyed catching up on the news while sipping the wine and enjoying the bread and cheese. New friends were introduced, and old friends made plans to meet for brunch at L'Iguana or Cavalieri's. It was great! And of course we also made take-out Communion available as well. Now if I can just get it goin' on here."

Steick stood up sharply.

"So I'm at it hammer and tongs, seven days a week. What can I do for you, by the way?"

"Well," the lawyer replied, backing forcefully toward the door. "Not all that much, really, I don't suppose. I just wanted to stop in and say hello to Pastor Balm and also to meet you, as a matter of fact. I've been hearing about all the good work you're doing. You have a nice day, and I'll see you again soon, I hope. Probably see you Sunday, I suppose," he added, finally making his escape.

"I doubt it," Needle replied. "I usually just log on. But I'll look forward to seeing you again in person, too. Take care now, and stay away from all those gorgeous court reporters, if that's okay, partner!"

The pastoral surrogate followed Steick down the hallway, joking and laughing about the gorgeous court reporters.

Steick rapidly took the stairs down to the parking lot and walked in the direction of his SUV. A wrecker had arrived to tow the Ovaltines' disabled Dodge. Matters were well in hand, although Balm continued to search for his spectacles, now looking and feeling for them beneath his own vehicle. Fortunately, the distance between Steick and the accident site was sufficient, and proper manners did not require the lawyer to get involved. In fact, he reasoned, his professional ethics probably prohibited it.

So he entered his leather sanctuary, locked the doors, popped some soothing Albinoni into the CD player, reclined his seat to a forty-five-degree angle, and contemplated his next move.

Heigh-Ho Psychiatry!

Professor Steick eased his SUV out of the Covenant parking lot and onto Church Street. He had enjoyed abundant good health for most of his life, another fact he attributed to the sturdy German gene pool that had chucked him into the green and golden world of the farm near Cullman. All of his people, on both sides, lived into their nineties and died quietly in their sleep. He had never broken a bone or required a single suture. He always took reasonable precautions about his health. Most of the time, he avoided excessive drinking and fatty foods, and he had never smoked. He had been physically active, in one way or another, throughout his life. Mainly, he enjoyed solitary exercise such as swimming, jogging, walking, and weight lifting. He had played team sports as a younger man and had learned to enjoy one-on-one competition, like tennis, fencing, and racquetball, while an undergraduate at the university. Aside from the usual childhood diseases, he had not often been sick. He had gone to a doc-in-the-box here and there for what the medical marketeers dubbed "minor emergencies," but he did not have "a regular general practitioner" in Hallelujah.

In fact, there were not many from which to choose. There was Potts, who was old and senile and had twice sawed off the wrong leg when he had been a general surgeon. Potts was obviously out of the question. Then there was Denise Darling, who was young, recently divorced, childless, and whose bright smile and attractive figure matched her name perfectly. Steick had been wanting to ask her out, and thus, she was not an option. That left Dr. Lance Mangrove, who was about Steick's own age and who seemed well-liked by his patients and esteemed by the community at large.

Steick had reviewed huge stacks of Mangrove's medical records in preparing personal injury cases for trial. The lawyer had found the doctor's charts a bit scant, sloppy, and non-committal, but one had to consider that they were, after all, just medical records. Steick had taken brief depositions from Mangrove a few times and had found the doctor pleasant and genial once he had been paid his $750 deposition fee up front. On one occasion, after a deposition, the doctor had given Steick samples of a muscle relaxer for tension headaches radiating from his jaws. The attorney had received good relief from the medication, and thus he settled on Mangrove to diagnose and treat his current, vague complaints. He expected Mangrove would give him some kind of mood pill that would fix him right up.

Steick pulled the Hallelujah phone book from its compartment beneath his seat, steered into a Piggly-Wiggly parking lot, shut off the engine, engaged his cell phone, and punched in Mangrove's number.

"Dr. Mangrove's office. May I help you?" the receptionist warbled, betraying only the slightest hint of frustration at having to answer four telephone lines simultaneously.

Steick asked to make an appointment and was encouraged to find he could come in immediately if he chose. He happily told Miss Warbling Frustration that he would be at Mangrove's office in fifteen minutes. He turned the key in the ignition, and the eight cylinders of the SUV immediately hit in perfect harmony with the Albinoni.

Pleased with his clear-headed and unashamed willingness to admit he had a medical problem, Steick navigated confidently toward his new G.P.'s office, where he looked forward to all the blessings of "relation-ship medicine."

MEANWHILE, AT THE HALLELUJAH CLINIC, it was clear to his nurses that Dr. Mangrove had been hitting the samples again. No doubt it was Quaalude, his favorite. He was so high that the wheels of the black and chrome lab stool, on which he sat, floated six inches above the beige, vinyl-tiled floor of examination room number one. He grinned shame-lessly and serenely, as if he had just been handed The True Meaning of

Life by the Creator Himself. He glided about effortlessly, humming a Woodstock tune and picking up the tools of his trade one-by-one to inspect their glowing loveliness.

All stainless steel had turned into perfectly aged, fine silver. A nasal speculum glistened like a young acolyte's candle igniter at Covenant Church. A kidney-shaped emesis basin radiated all the sanctity of the chalice at Holy Communion. An ordinary scalpel gave off the beauty of a jeweled Arabian scimitar. Mangrove's examination table, which was black, projected pure sacredness, like the black stone of the Kaba in Mecca, and Mangrove contemplated kissing it. Even the sinuous lines of his stethoscope, coiled on the counter, exuded a sacred and erotic aura.

In short, for Dr. Lance Mangrove, on this lovely morning in Hallelujah, Alabama, everything was beautiful, and nothing hurt. He had just divorced his fifth wife, Mimi, and had settled upon her a new house and a new Mercedes, exactly as he had done for the four young and beautiful wives who had preceded her. His marriage to Mimi had lasted about as long as his annual continuing medical education seminar in Acapulco. "But so what?" Mangrove ruminated as he admired a glowing hemostat. "The law is the law, and the lawyers are in charge of everything in the long run anyway," he told himself. So why worry? The wives all get a new house and a new Mercedes. "It's easier for the judges that way," the lawyers explained. And, divorced once again, Mangrove was free to go happily about his business as usual.

He had suffered only one close scrape with MASA, the Medical Association of the State of Alabama, or his "master" as he disdainfully deemed the eminent organization. This unfortunate event had occurred when Mangrove had slightly over-examined a lovely young Hallelujah High School cheerleader before stunt practice. She had come up pregnant as a consequence and had ratted on the doctor to her parents. They went to the Board of Medical Examiners, which was fully prepared to pull Mangrove's ticket, or at least send him to Mississippi. But the good country doc made several well-placed charitable and political contributions, passed out a few discreet sacks of samples to the right people, hosted a glorious reception for MASA officials before the Auburn-Alabama game, and suddenly the ill-considered charges against him were magnanimously dismissed.

It turned out that the young cheerleader had been quite friendly with the Hallelujah High quarterback, Jed Mims. And why should anyone take her word against that of Mangrove, a licensed physician in good standing? Clearly she had made up the whole episode. Yes, Mangrove gave her a new Dodge Neon and a plot of vacant land he owned near Lake Martin in exchange for her hold-harmless release, but that was pure goodwill—another mark of his generosity and good citizenship—qualities which had long endeared the doctor to several thousand well-insured patients in Hallelujah. In short, as his lawyers would say, Mangrove "took a walk" from MASA.

Dr. Mangrove was much beloved by his patients because he had always taken quite literally the treatment philosophy inculcated by his professors at the prestigious School of Medicine at the University of Alabama, Birmingham, where had obtained his MD. In a nutshell, this philosophy consisted first of informed consent and, second, patient choice. Thus, from the time he began his medical practice, Mangrove always gave his patients one of two professional options. Whether the patient was suffering from an abscess, pneumonia, or suicidal depression, the doctor would listen kindly to the patient's complaints, check the necessary vital signs, and then announce helpfully, "This is one of those things that will either get better, or get worse, or stay the same." Then, as the circumstances warranted, he would ask, "What do you want? A prescription or something else?" If the patient wanted a prescription, Mangrove would simply ask, "What kind and how much?" and write the patient's preferred medicinal dosage. If the patient was puzzled, or did not wish a prescription, the doctor would ask, "So what do you want to do about this?" Depending upon the patient's response, Mangrove would recommend an appropriate specialist (often a close friend) who was better qualified than he (a mere small-town GP, after all) to treat the patient's disorder.

Dr. Mangrove was also highly popular with the drug reps who canvassed his territory. Often there were so many of these detail men and women in the waiting room that there were no seats left for his patients.

Instead of allowing the commercial travelers to take him golfing, which was normal protocol, Mangrove generously reversed the procedure and hosted the reps at the Hallelujah Country Club. He also invited them to delicious barbeques at his house on Lake Martin and sent them lovely hams and baskets of fruit at Christmas.

The reps loved Dr. Mangrove. Consequently, he always possessed enough samples of every conceivable drug to medicate an entire third-world nation for a year. These he kept neatly alphabetized, from Amoxil to Zoloft, in a huge, locked, climate-controlled room which he visited quite frequently. Every medicine on earth was readily available in the doctor's garage-sized pharmacopeia. Even highly regulated substances, so carefully controlled that they were counted out personally by the Commissioner of the Food and Drug Administration, were available to Dr. Mangrove in abundance. There were bushels of routine anxiolytics like Xanax, Valium, and Halcion, not to mention boxes overflowing with the most potent pain-killing opiates such as Lortab 12, Percodan, and Demerol. Mangrove had a far better selection of medications than the Hallelujah Pharmacy, and he was never reluctant to share his samples with friends, legislators, government officials, bankers, stockbrokers, and others who were possibly, or at least arguably, in distress.

WHEN PROFESSOR STEICK ARRIVED at Dr. Mangrove's office, he found the parking lot full, and so he parked on the street. Nevertheless, he remained optimistic. Indeed, he remained optimistic even after he discovered the waiting room full of aging adults in various stages of decrepitude, many of whom were accompanied by toddlers with runny noses. He was, after all, Professor Richard Steick, an attorney in good standing. He had been told he could "come right in," and he believed he could count upon the benefits of professional courtesy. In other words, he fully expected to go straight to the head of the line once he had completed his paperwork, preempting even the half-dozen pharmaceutical reps with their swanky clothes, run-down heels, and huge black leather sample cases.

Steick remained optimistic as he filled out an endless questionnaire detailing every medical event he could recall since his birth and then

signing a release, privacy acknowledgment, assignment of insurance
benefits, promissory note, and waiver of every conceivable Constitutional
right, all of which were conditions precedent to Mangrove's agreement
to treat the patient.

The distinguished lawyer and professor was far less optimistic when,
two hours later, he found himself sitting in the same waiting room, with
most of the same runny noses, and still reading the coverless fragments
of a three-year-old *Sports Illustrated* he had secretly snatched from the
hands of a whey-faced four-year-old who was chewing it like a puppy.
The cretin immediately began to wail, causing Steick very quickly to
retreat a safe distance before anyone over the age of six might emerge
from waiting room torpor long enough to observe that the mean old
lawyer had just yanked away a poor little baby's plaything.

One hour later, Steick's blood pressure had reached a staggering 280
over 136 as he sat, unshirted, on the tissue-covered examining table
awaiting the "be right with you" personal appearance of the good Dr.
Mangrove. Endless minutes later, there was a hopeful clank and then a
rustling of papers outside the door, and Steick drew his first full breath
in two hours.

In the hall, Dr. Mangrove glanced over Steick's new patient chart.
Vitals were fine. BP a little high. Complains of moodiness, irritability,
memory difficulties, blah, blah, blah. Okay, we'll check him out.

Wearing a huge, ruddy grin, the happy doctor opened the door and
recognized Steick immediately. Serene as he was, Mangrove nevertheless
sensed a slight limbic warning as he viewed the half-naked Steick loung-
ing casually (to all outward appearance) on the examination table. The
doctor had Steick pegged as some kind of goofy lawyer guy who didn't
know what he wanted to be when he grew up. Neither fish nor fowl.
Clearly a reptile, since he was a lawyer. Taught some kind of classes and
wrote things. Must think he's a shaman. Highly negative was the fact
that Steick was not known as a golfer. "Best take this one a little careful,"
Mangrove thought. "Bastard probably works for the DEA."

Steick stood up and shook hands with the friendly, grinning physician. "Well!" Mangrove exclaimed. "If it isn't our eminent attorney and

professor! You're lookin' good, fella! Lean, well-developed, lively affect, good vitals. Whatcha think is wrong with you, anyway?"

"Well, Doc," Steick replied, "I don't feel quite like myself lately. Been getting a little lax in my office procedures. I don't always show proper decorum in court, and people are starting to talk. I don't really care about them talkin', but a couple days ago I booted a statute of limitations, and that's going to cost me some money. Also, I get these tension headaches that seem to start in my jaws. I wonder if maybe I don't need a mood pill or something."

"How's your sex life?"

"Not worth a damn, really. I'm not motivated."

"Well, that's your problem then!" Mangrove chuckled. "You need it two or three times a day or you're goin' to get headaches and feel aimless! Only natural! Mother Nature talkin' atcha, partner! If it was up to me," Mangrove grinned, "the two of us would go shopping in my pharmaceutical cupboard until we found a combination that worked for you. Probably start you out on Xanax, say twenty milligrams four times per day, and Prozac eighty milligrams per day, and then wean you off the Xanax once the Prozac kicked in. That's basically all a shrink would do. I'd just do it faster and cheaper! But anyway, I can't do it. Damn feds and lawyers and legislature and insurance companies got it all rigged so an honest GP like me can't even practice medicine anymore, let alone make a living." He laughed.

"Gosh, Doc," Steick interrupted, "Isn't that an awful lot of Xanax? I mean, can't that stuff be dangerous?"

Mangrove laughed louder. "Xanax? Dangerous? Hell, Xanax ain't dangerous! Anything's dangerous! A horse is dangerous if you ride him too much! But just try telling that to the Washington bureaucrats. They don't get it. I guess they gotta' have something to do, since they can't do anything useful. If the damn' bureaucrats would just leave me alone, I could help more people before breakfast than they could do in a year of regulatin', regulatin', regulatin'! Ha, ha, ha!"

The doctor paused to stretch, like a cat in the sun, and then continued merrily, "But it's like I was sayin'. These days I can't hardly treat anybody anymore. If you've got a problem at all (which I seriously doubt, by the way), then I've got to refer you to a shrink. No question about it. Can't even give you a little dex to pep you up. Aspirin's 'bout all I can prescribe these days. So, what I'm sayin' is, I want you to see Dr. Max Kayahs at Heigh-Ho Psychiatry for an evaluation and possible treatment. They're in Montgomery, but Kayahs comes up here twice a week for clinic. He's as good as any. Not going to plug you into the wall or anything. He'll listen to your story and write you a script. He'll also play your case as long as HealthCon will let him, if that's what you want.

"You know HealthCon, that big insurance outfit in Birmingham? Used to be Continental Health? 'Continuously Concerned About Your Health' and all that nonsense? They write 80 percent of the health policies in Alabama, and yours is one of them. Doctors Heigh and Ho are their preferred providers for the mental stuff. You want psychiatry, you've got to see one of Heigh-Ho's boys and girls! No choice in the matter! HealthCon won't pay otherwise. So I say 'See Kayahs.' That way your insurance will pay and you won't have to drive to Montgomery. Talk to Lovie out front, and she'll set up an appointment for you if you like.

"It's all about patient choice, of course," Mangrove continued, a bit more languidly, "So you do whatever you want. If I were you, I'd probably skip Kayahs and take a three-week vacation at one of those singles resorts in Jamaica. You'd have a good time, and it's probably cheaper than Heigh-Ho in the long run. Fix you up fine, I bet. So. You get on outta here and make up your mind! I got sick people to care for. Y'all lawyers—I swear! You been representin' those malingerin' worker's comp folks for way too long! That's your real problem! It's rubbed off on ya! Ha, ha, ha!"

Mangrove opened the door to leave and called back over his shoulder, "Talk to Lovie or whatever, and check back in a year if you don't get any better."

Closing the door on Steick, the doctor extracted a tiny tape recorder from his pocket and dictated his treatment notes as he glided toward his next appointment. "Healthy middle-aged white male," he chuckled into the machine. "Alert but unresponsive and forgetful. Occasional constant headaches. Says he's not getting any. Thinks he's mental and probably is. Suspect he wants to be somebody else. Referred to Dr. Kayahs." Click.

Back in the examination room, Steick's blood pressure escalated another twenty points. To call Mangrove's work-up "blithe and brainless" would be like calling the Rock of Gibraltar "a little stone in the water." To hell with Mangrove, and to hell with Lovie! Steick would decide for himself whether to see Dr. Kayahs, see someone else, or forget about the whole business. Jamaica was sounding better and better. All he wanted at the moment, however, was to be out of this building immediately! He jammed his arms into his shirt (which he misbuttoned), stuffed his tie into a pants pocket, yanked his trousers onto both legs at once, stuck his feet into his untied shoes, and stormed out of the Hallelujah Clinic, accidentally forgetting his socks and intentionally failing to pay. He would get a year or two of monthly billing statements and nasty collection letters which he would simply throw away unopened. That was his entire opinion of Dr. Mangrove's services. And forget any more depositions with Mangrove! Steick would get his clients to pay an expert in Montgomery instead. It might cost more that way, but it would be worth it, at least to Steick.

INSIDE HIS SUV, THE LAWYER found himself half dressed with his jaws aching and his plans more confused than ever. He switched on the engine, pointed all the air conditioning ports toward his face, and slipped a Gregorian chant CD into the sound system. Nevertheless, he continued to steam as he retreated toward his only reliable safe haven at the moment, Mushroom Memories.

Arriving at his fully modernized and well-drained house on the hill, Steick parked his vehicle in a nicely furnished, commodious garage, complete with ceiling fan, a room he affectionately called "the car's boudoir." He locked the door and walked the short distance required to reach his reassuring Cold War museum-bar. He entered, leaving the lights off, and immediately clicked the dial for the big-screen TV. He watched several silent H-Bomb detonations as he prepared a cobalt Fiestaware pitcher full of iced lime Kool-Aid and vodka.

Two dozen detonations and half a pitcher later, the frazzled lawyer began to feel more relaxed. The throbbing in his jaws and temples had subsided considerably. Thus encouraged, he took out a pen and a legal pad to list his options and wrote:

1. Remain status quo.
2. Jamaica.
3. See another GDGP in Montgomery.
4. Look for a shrink in the Yellow Pages.
5. Phone Kayahs for an appointment.

He turned on Pat Boone's "Love Letters in the Sand," which he always found relaxing. He played it five times while knocking back half the remaining vodka cocktail. Then, he returned to his list and made well-considered notes after each numbered entry:

1. Status quo—not prudent.
2. Jamaica—disease, etc.
3. GP—pointless.
4. Yellow Pages—rolling dice.
5. Kayahs—Costs me nothing. Can't be as useless as Mangrove.

It was approaching four in the afternoon, with the blue Alabama sky at its airiest outside the window, when Steick made his final decision and asked himself, "What time do psychiatrists close up shop to drink and play golf?"

He suspected four would be about right. Even psychiatrists have the alleged after-hours paperwork, fictitious "rounds" at the hospital, and the occasional deposition to attend. So Steick opened the phone book, located Kayahs's number under "Psychiatrists," and found there were two: one for Montgomery and one for the satellite office in Steick's own town.

It was five minutes until four o'clock. Before he could hesitate and change his mind, Steick grasped his red "hot line" telephone and dialed the local number.

One ring. Two rings. Three (probably too late), and then four. In the middle of the fifth ring, however, a happy young female voice chirped, "Heigh-Ho Psychiatry, Hallelujah! How may I help you?"

And Steick found himself momentarily stunned. Somehow the shock of telling a woman—and clearly a younger woman, judging by the sound of her voice—that he, the learned professor and esteemed attorney, might have a mild psychiatric problem, right here in Hallelujah, left him speechless.

It seemed several seconds passed before Steick's resolution returned. But when it did, he sounded fully confident. "I'd like to make an appointment with Dr. Kayahs," he said.

"Okay," the chirpy voice answered. "What is your name, please?"

"Dr. Richard Steick," he replied.

The receptionist sounded as if Steick had said "President Franklin Roosevelt" when she replied, "Oh. Yesss! Professor Steick! The attorney and scholar. How will you pay, Dr. Steick?"

"I have HealthCon."

"Great! When would you like to come in?"

"Well," Steick continued calmly, "as soon as possible, of course, but it's not an emergency or anything. I just want a little mental health checkup."

"Fine. How about Tuesday a week, the twenty-fourth at two o'clock? Dr. Kayahs has had a cancellation."

"Fine with me."

"Have you seen the doctor before?" the young lady asked.

"No," Steick said casually, "this is my first time."

"That's just perfect," the young chirper said brightly. "Since it's your first visit, Dr. Kayahs will want to see you for an hour, and he has the whole two o'clock hour free on the twenty-fourth. So come on in. I'll send you an intake questionnaire to fill out, and you can return it to us by mail. Okay?"

"Sure," Steick replied, and then attempted a joke. "By the way—you mean fifty minutes, don't you? Doesn't a psychiatrist's hour usually last fifty minutes?"

"Well," the bright voice answered cheerfully, "it might if you're lucky. They're usually about forty-five minutes, actually. That beats the lawyers, though. Reckon y'all have thirty-five minute hours, don't you? It seemed that way when I got my divorce a couple years ago. Anyway, you come in on the twenty-fourth, okay?"

"Sure. See you then. And you should have hired me for your divorce, by the way. My hours always last at least forty minutes, no matter what."

She chuckled. "All right, Dr. Steick. I'll see you on the twenty-fourth, and I'll see you the next time I get a divorce, okay?"

"Fine. See you then. Bye now."

He felt better after bantering with the young girl, and he let out a five-kiloton sigh of relief as he replaced the red "hot line" receiver into its cradle.

DON'T BE A DILDO

Several days passed without incident. Professor Steick taught his seminars in the morning, and attorney Steick drafted pleadings, replied to correspondence, and saw occasional clients in the afternoon. His classes were enjoyable, and he learned of no further professional blunders he had committed. At 6:00 in the evening he would prepare a modest meal, order out, or nuke a TV dinner in the microwave. Then he would repair contentedly to Mushroom Memories, where he would listen to a few oldies and slowly sip two lime Kool-Aid cocktails as he read Heidegger's *Being and Time* or Pound's *History of the Common Law.* He retired at 11:00 P.M. sharp, slept fairly well, and awoke at 7:00 A.M. feeling a little poleaxed as usual, although this generally passed after a shower and several cups of coffee. He was prepared for the day's events. Having made the decision to explore psychotherapy, he put the matter to rest and gave little thought to his forthcoming appointment with Dr. Kayahs. The womb of time would deliver what it would deliver, and that was that.

Then, one week before he was to see the doctor, Steick received what at first seemed an odd piece of mail. The return address on the crisp, white, almost lawyer-quality business envelope stated only "HHPH," followed by the street, city, and zip code. Richard contemplated it in mild confusion until he opened the envelope and saw the clinic's letterhead. Oh. "Heigh-Ho Psychiatry, Hallelujah." Confidentiality and all that.

The cover letter began, "Dear Prof. Steick: Welcome to our practice! We have reserved, exclusively for you, an appointment with Dr. Max Kayahs at 2:00 P.M. on Tuesday, June 24th!" It was signed by Melissa Brandywine, clinical assistant, and Steick wondered if she were the same young lady he had spoken to on the telephone when he had made his appointment. The gleeful tone of confident welcome in her letter caused him to wonder if the psychiatrist possibly ran a time-share scheme or sweepstakes gimmick on the side. As Steick read further, Miss Brandywine reminded him of the doctor's hourly rate and the patient's insurance and payment responsibilities. Finally, he was asked to fill out an intake questionnaire, which was enclosed, and to return it by mail as soon as possible before his meeting with the doctor.

Steick had reviewed a good many similar documents in the past, often when he was preparing Social Security disability cases. He understood the doctor's need for a thorough medical history and appreciated the efficiency provided by a checklist of standard psychological assessment questions. He did not at all mind filling out the form, and he was pleased to note that the doctor appeared thorough, at least on paper. The new patient was asked how long he had suffered his present "distress," whether he drank and how much, what medications he was taking, whether he used street drugs, exercised, smoked, had previous psychiatric treatment, and so on. The attached checklist covered several dozen mental states or emotions and asked him to indicate the extent to which he experienced them. The columns offered a range of five degrees. He was asked, for example, to check whether he experienced feelings of hostility "Not at All," "A Little Bit," "Somewhat," "A Lot," or "I Can't Stand It." Was he scared or frightened? Did he feel people were laughing at him? Did he feel hopeless? Did he think he was receiving secret messages from the radio, television, electrical wires, or aliens? Was he afraid of elevators? Afraid of a heart attack? Of going mad?

Steick briskly and honestly completed the questionnaire and then reviewed his work. He was pleased to note that most of his responses were in the "Not at All" or "A Little Bit" categories. He, like the doctor, looked good on paper.

There was a final page containing several open-ended questions which seemed a little unusual. The patient was asked to answer these as quickly and truthfully as possible and not to ponder or reflect. Although he had not seen anything quite like these questions before, Steick gladly complied to the best of his ability.

The first question asked, "What are the three things you think about most often? (Please list in order of frequency.)"

Without hesitation or embarrassment, Richard rapidly wrote, "Sex, God, and evacuation."

The second question inquired, "Of all the places you have visited, which has seemed the most strange to you?"

The patient quickly responded, "Wal-Mart."

The next question: "Where would you most like to spend tomorrow?"

Steick's answer: "In Istanbul."

And finally, "What, if anything, is wrong or unusual in the following situation. A doctor checks a patient out of the hospital and writes 'Alive but without permission' on the patient's discharge summary."

To which Steick replied, "Nothing."

He glanced back over his answers, dwelling momentarily on the last and wondering if the question were some sort of joke. If so, he felt he had no choice but to play along. At least his response was quick and unrehearsed, exactly as requested.

THE NEXT SEVEN DAYS OF BEAUTIFUL, high Alabama summer passed quickly. On the day of his appointment with Dr. Kayahs, Steick left the office early to get a chili dog and a malt at the Dairy Queen. This was not his typical diet, but the glorious Mediterranean climate made him feel young and almost carefree. If Kayahs turned out to be a jerk like Dr. Mangrove, Richard determined, he would simply forget the whole matter, go about his business as usual, and try not to make any more stupid mistakes in his law practice or otherwise.

And yet, as he drove toward his psychiatrist's office, the attorney and professor began to feel uneasy. He had never been to a psychiatrist before and had never thought he needed one. So what was he doing now? He had survived graduate school, law school, marriage to Gloria, two daughters, and the usual bumps and bruises experienced by practicing lawyers. He had made important contributions toward his two professions as well as his church, his community, his state, and even his nation, and he was generally well respected for it. He was approaching fifty years of age, and no doubt he had every right to feel and act a bit quirky now and then. After all, just look at everyone around him: corrupt state officials like Hoop DeMinus, unctuous parsons like Thirsty M. Balm, that ass Mangrove who pretended to be a doctor, the well-nourished and pompous Judge Smiley, and his fellow attorneys like Josh Wiggins. Even Hallelujah Mayor Dard Hooper! What were they all but a bunch of greedy materialists and bumptious morons? And that was only at the local level! Think about Congress, the Supreme Court, and the President of the United States! Impostors all! Look at the environment, the schools, the homicide rate, domestic violence, international terrorism! Just look at the world in which we live, for God's sake, and try to make sense of anything! It is no longer possible!

"Whoa," Steick said to himself. He recognized the familiar signs of rising blood pressure, perspiration, and a headache beginning to radiate from his jaws. "Getting a little bit steamed up here, aren't we?" he asked himself, as he attempted to divine the true locus of his present situation and align his emotional axis accordingly. He was, he reminded himself, surrounded by expensive burled wood and leather, riding smoothly along the nicely paved streets of the charming and well-kept village of Hallelujah. He should not react so intensely to enormous matters outside his control. He should savor the remnants of malt from the Dairy Queen. He should pop some Gregorian chant or cool blues into the CD player and try to relax. He reasoned that a little psychiatric checkup couldn't hurt after all, and having come this far, he might as well go through with it.

He settled on Nina Simone for his traveling music, fine-tuned his twelve-way, electrically adjustable seat, and eased his back deeper into his leather lumbar support. He glanced at himself in the mirror and admired his tasteful choice of Louis Vuitton sunglasses. Taking the short-est route, he wound through the byways and back streets of Hallelujah, occasionally humming along with Nina and reading the shop signs and billboards out of habit.

The professor was a connoisseur of advertising signs, reveling in the endless ingenuity and drolleries that the phrasemakers (who were apparently paid for this activity) frequently generated. As he drove, he noted with minor interest the usual collection of political nostrums, unsolicited advice, insurance bromides, and billboards where various churches peddled their radio stations and web sites.

But crossing Spring Street, his drive suddenly turned into an epiphany, a mountaintop experience, a virtual cornucopia of ludicrous messages, and Steick laughed aloud. There was a rusty, light-bulbed, wheel-away sign in front of an auto detailing shop that flashed, "Earn $300.00 Per Week Selling Flashing Signs And Bibles." Down the street, the Pentecostal church warned, "Still Religion, Like Water, Freezes Quickest." Not to be outdone in the religious advertising war, the Gospel Outlet noted, "Wal-Mart Is Not The Only Saving Place." A bit further, the Traveler's Rest Wayside Primitive Baptist Chapel, surrounded up to its walls on three sides by a cemetery, urged drivers to "Come On In And Rest A Spell." And finally, at the rapidly growing Tubbs Memorial, this message: "Kids! Get A Free Jesus Jump Rope Just For Attending Sunday School!"

It was a fine output, Steick thought, for such a short drive in a small city. Apparently some clever soul had been burning the midnight oil. "And so we shall all be converted to the One True Religion," Steick concluded, "if only we can tear ourselves away from our e-mail, lite beer, and TV sets for an hour each Sunday morning and do our share to pay the preacher." His thoughts had gravitated back to the absurd Pastor Balm and his cohort Needle. Thus, with a phrase and a wave (and not for the first time in his life), Steick cast "institutional religion" into the dustbin of meaningless history.

He located the HHPH Clinic in the middle of a small, one-story red brick strip development on the rapidly growing eastern edge of town. The "complex" of six suites lined up facing the highway was as close as Hallelujah came to having a physicians' zone. The new patient wondered momentarily if he wanted his SUV to be seen parked in front of Dr. Kayahs's office, but he decided not to be shy about appearances and wheeled into the parking slot nearest the door. A local orthodontist had located on one side of the psychiatry clinic, and a podiatrist on the other. Steick dethroned himself from his SUV and rather jauntily approached the beige door to the doctor's office. He glanced at the sign: "HHPH—Max Kayahs, MD. General Psychiatry. Tuesdays and Thursdays, 9:00 A.M.–4:00 P.M." He grasped the smooth aluminum door handle and let himself into the office.

The waiting area looked rather like a small living room. Steick noted fair-quality institutional furniture with some roccoco curlicues, good lamps, and copies of *People* and *The Wall Street Journal* on the coffee table. There were no other patients waiting, and the sliding glass door to the receptionist's office and file room was open. A lady who appeared to be in her late thirties was clasping a handful of manila folders and settling herself into a chair behind a retracted sliding glass panel. Richard had ample time to assess her complexion, figure, and general demeanor as she seated herself. She was casually but tastefully dressed in a blue summer dress which was happily low-cut and tapered nicely at the waist. "Bosomy and she knows it," Steick thought to himself. "34-C or possible -D. Knows how to dress, too. Flawless, fair skin: soft, unwrinkled. High quality, understated jewelry and no wedding ring. Pretty ash blonde hair, obviously dyed. Good Alabama country girl with class. Wonder if this is Miss Brandywine? Time to look sharp and not crazy, whoever she is," he concluded.

The lady cast him a pleasant, assured smile as she asked, "You must be Professor Steick, right?"

"Yes, I am," he responded, noticing her good teeth and casting his own best smile and copulative gaze deeply into the black pupils of her sky-blue eyes and, he plotted, directly down her optic nerve, past her cerebral cortex, and straight into her brain stem. He could flash his own baby blues like the headlights on a new Infiniti and focus with a laser-sharp intensity when he wanted to, and he suddenly found that he wanted to. Besides, he reasoned, he needed the practice. Suddenly, he was magnetic. In his mind, he starred in a cast of thousands.

"Are you Miss Brandywine?"

"Yes. That's me," she replied, continuing to smile brightly. "You're right on time. Just have a seat, Professor Steick, and Dr. Kayahs will be with you in a moment."

He was delighted to note she had rhymed his name with "bike" and not "stick." He casually slipped his right forefingers under the flap and into his jacket pocket, exactly as he had admired President Kennedy doing so often on television when Steick was a young boy. It was a mannerism the middle-aged lawyer had cultivated to perfection for more than thirty years, and he never missed a chance to check his delivery of the gesture against the miles of newsreel footage that survived the assassination of the suave and charming JFK.

He decided a bit of Kennedy's speech pauses and inflections also might be appropriate to the moment. "Just call me Richard. But don't we—uh—have a little paperwork to do?" he asked cheerfully. "I always thought doctors were curious about insurance and things like that."

"Well, of course the doctor likes to be paid, Profess—well, Richard—but I thiiiiink we've got all that insurance information on your intake. Let me look anyway, just to be sure, okay? I'll grab your chart, and—let's see here. Yes! There it is. You've got HealthCon, so everything is covered. But—wait a minute—I don't see your airline card number here. So if you would, uh, Richard, just give me your airline card, and I'll enter the number here so you'll be sure to get your frequent flier miles."

"My what?" Steick asked, momentarily stunned out of his flirtatious mood and into a genuine perplexity.

"Your airline card. So you can get your miles."

"My miles?"

"Well, I guess maybe you don't know about the program. See, HealthCon gives you 250 frequent flier miles for your visit today and each time you visit a CCCP. Isn't that great? Here. This brochure will explain everything for you."

She handed Steick a colorful, glossy tri-fold featuring a masked but obviously smiling physician holding an elderly patient's hand as she lay in a hospital bed with a 747 jumbo jet zooming overhead. The main caption read, "Live Better! Get Well Faster! And Fly Farther With HealthCon's CCCP Physicians!"

A smaller caption at the bottom of the brochure proudly announced, "And now, if you should die on the operating table, all or a portion of

your miles, plus five thousand free Condolence Miles, are fully transfer-
able to your estate!"

Steick removed his hand from his pocket and ran his fingertips from
his right temple to just behind his ear, smoothing his hair. This was
another well-practiced Kennedy mannerism, but he was on autopilot
now and hadn't planned the gesture. He was plainly puzzled as he said,
"Uh—Miss Brandywine, I uh—"

"Oh shoot," she interrupted, "call me Melissa."

"Oh. Okay. Thank you. I uh—I will. But I'm a little confused. What,
uh—what's a CCCP?"

"That's a 'Constantly Concerned Care Provider,' silly. You must not
get sick very much, or you'd know all about this already!"

"No, I guess I don't get sick very much, and I'm—uh—I'm not sick
now, either. I just want to see if the doctor can help me organize my
time and focus on my cases a little bit better. You know, I like your wrist
watch, by the way. Maybe that's what I need to get better organized—a
new watch. But I still don't quite understand about CCCPs and frequent
flier miles. Maybe you can—uh—fill me in, Melissa."

"Well, since it's just between you and me," she replied with a furtive
glance, "I personally think it's kind of weird. I mean, offering people
rewards for going to the doctor. But that's the HealthCon policy. If you
go to one of the doctors on their list of CCCPs, and if you're compliant—or just 'follow doctor's orders' like we used to say—you get 250
frequent flier miles for each visit, kind of like using a credit card or a
phone company. See?"

"Yes," Steick said, again smiling and gazing. "Yes, I guess I do. It seems
a little strange to me too, but if that's the way they want it. By the way.
What happens if I go to a doctor who's not a CCCP?"

"Well, Richard, I'll bet you can guess the answer to that one."

"Come to think of it," Richard grinned, "I'll bet I can. But I want
you to tell me anyway, Melissa."

"Welllll—of course you know HealthCon will only pay 5 percent of
a non-CCCP doctor's reasonable and customary charges, right?"

"Okay."

"And you know you also have to fill out a complicated claim form to recover that much, right?"

"Naturally," the lawyer replied, nodding slightly.

"Sooo," Melissa continued. "What do you think?"

Steick snapped his fingers, raised his right digit, grinned broadly, gave a brief neck twist and announced happily, "I've got it! NO frequent flier miles!"

"That's right, Richard! You win the prize! No miles! Now, do you want to try for what's behind door number two?"

"Why not? I can tell I'm on a roll today. Go ahead and ask me the bonus question."

"Okay! Sure you're ready? Now, what happens if Richard is a bad boy and doesn't follow Dr. Kayahs's orders? You have three seconds to answer, so take your time."

"This is getting too easy, Melissa," Steick smiled. "The answer once again is, 'No miles!'"

"You are correct, Richard! *No miles!* You are indeed a clever fellow! It's no wonder you're a famous professor! Now for the really tough part. What happens when you get better?"

Being a lawyer, Steick had already considered that possibility but couldn't conceive an answer. So he had to admit defeat. "I give up. That's too tough for me. Tell me what happens when a patient gets better."

"Why, bonus miles, of course. HealthCon's goal is to treat and dismiss each patient within a minimum prescribed number of visits. For true paranoid schizophrenia, for example, you should get back to normal on eight visits per year. For true manic-depression, you get six. For ordinary, garden-variety depression, anxiety, or obsessive-compulsive disorder, four should do the trick. I'm not sure, but I'd guess that with someone as healthy as you are, with just some minor focus problems, HealthCon will want the doctor to fix you up in two visits."

"So, what happens if I don't come back in after today?"

"That's where the bonus miles kick in," Melissa smiled and jabbed his arm, which he had leaned upon the Formica countertop. "For each visit fewer than the HealthCon goal allotment, you get five hundred free bonus miles! So, Richard, if you don't come back and see me—I mean the doctor—after today, well, five hundred miles are added to your account. And of course you can always click onto our web site for unlimited virtual visits at absolutely no charge at all!"

"Hmmm," Steick reflected. "I think I just might want to come back after today anyway, even if I am, like you said, pretty healthy. But clarify something for me, if you will. Suppose I were really sick, like I thought the FBI or the CIA had planted a transmitter in one of the crowns on my teeth and were tracking me by satellite and I couldn't leave my house or something like that. Would that get me eight visits per year, or what?"

"Sounds right to me, Richard. Plus unlimited virtual visits on our web site. Now, here's the hard part. Let's test your math. What happens if you only saw the doctor four times in one year with that diagnosis? Take your time now."

Steick touched his forehead. "Let's see, eight minus four is four, and four times five hundred is two thousand. Sooo—I'd get two thousand free bonus miles, right?"

"That's right, Richard! Aren't you sharp! Three in a row! I'm just going to have to tell Dr. Kayahs that I don't think you need to see him at all!"

As if on cue, the door on Steick's right opened inward, and a tall, athletic, boyish figure entered the waiting area. He was in his forties, casual, natty, and tweedy in dress and appearance—all Brooks Brothers and Ralph Lauren from the top of his longish, slightly graying hair to the soles of his laid-back loafers.

"Hey, man," he grinned, rather shyly. "You Dr. Steick?"

Steick grinned back, and inwardly, he was elated. Not only had Kayahs pronounced his name correctly, but he had also given the professor the courtesy and respect he deserved by acknowledging Steick's own hard-earned terminal degree.

"I'm Max Kayahs," the doctor said, extending his hand in a frank, manly gesture of welcome.

"Glad to meet you, doctor. I'm Richard Steick," the new patient replied.

"Good. You all done with the paperwork?"

"Yeah, I was just chatting with Melissa here about the frequent flier program, a—uh–a unique concept."

"Yeah, I guess it is," Kayahs chuckled. "Well, come on back to my office, and we'll get started."

The doctor held the door for the professor, and the two walked side-by-side down a short hallway toward the psychiatrist's office. "You doin' okay today?" Kayahs asked.

"Yeah. I think I'm pretty good, Doc. Just havin' a little trouble with concentration. Lots of clients. You know how it goes."

"I sure do," the doctor sighed, and again held the door open for Steick to enter the consultation office. Like the waiting area, it had the homey feel of a living room. A few books on the shelf, some bibelots, nice art work, a computer monitor on the desk, and the mandatory box of Kleenex on a side table.

"Sit down, sit down. Make yourself comfortable," the doctor said. "You want some coffee or a Coke or something?"

"No, Doc, I'm fine," Steick replied, seating himself in a nicely uphol-stered armchair as Dr. Kayahs unhinged his lanky frame into a matching chair in front of his desk a few feet away from his patient.

"Well. Okay then," the doctor said. "I've reviewed your intake ques-tionnaire already, but I always want people to tell me about it anyway. So—you were fine until what happened?"

Steick had never thought about it that way. He had always thought he was fine, or at least he thought he had thought he was fine. But suddenly he found himself curious about what he had really thought all those years. As he contemplated the doctor's question, one memory tumbled back onto another like a line of dominoes. Had he ever been "fine?"

Steick winced. He wiggled. He rose to his feet and rubbed his right hand across his forehead, along his temple, and onto the back of his neck, where he began to massage. "I'm sorry, Doc. Give me a minute, okay?"

"Sure. Take all the time you need. No rush. It isn't a question you get every day."

Steick walked a couple of steps to the window, pulled down a mini-blind with his index finger, and peered out into the parking lot, remember-ing. He did not feel embarrassed or rushed. Dr. Kayahs was a calming presence. Steick turned, noting that the doctor sat with good posture and his feet flat on the floor the way the orthopedic doctors recommended. Kayahs looked—bemused by life. The patient felt instant, absolute confidence in his doctor. He knew he could not say anything the shrink had not heard dozens of times before or anything that would shock his affable demeanor. Somehow, Kayahs had got beyond all that. He looked like a laughing, Episcopalian Buddha, except he was slender.

Steick continued to take his time. The lawyer in him was analyzing. The professor was recollecting. Back and back and back, he recalled, he had—perjured himself. He could not really remember being fine, although he could easily recall a lifetime of pretending to be fine.

He sat down, heaved a tremendous sigh, scratched his head vigorously, lifted his face to the doctor, and peered into his pupils. It was a non-sexual version of his gaze at Melissa a few minutes earlier. But there was an important difference this time. Steick knew he really wasn't looking at Kayahs at all. He was looking at himself.

Steick held his gaze, scratched again, looked back at the doctor, and said, "Doc, I was fine until I was two."

"Really? So what happened then?"

"I started to get nightmares."

"What kind?"

"Well, Doc, they're hard to describe. They were hellish. Lots of fire. Labyrinthine, like a maze or something. Monsters chasing me. That sort of thing. I couldn't get out, and I was scared to death. I'd wake up screaming and crying."

"That's a long way back to remember. You recall anything else going on about that time?"

Steick sat motionless, chin braced upon his palm, and stared vacantly. Finally he said, "Well, all I can think of is that's about the time my mama got me down to pray me."

"Pray you?"

"Yeah. That's what I call it. I guess she thought it was time I should learn how to pray. I hated it down there on my knees. It was spooky."

"So what did y'all pray about?"

"The usual, I suppose. 'Now I lay me down to sleep.' When we came to the part about 'If I should die before I wake,' I asked Mama what 'die' meant. I'd never heard it before."

"What did she tell you it meant?" Kayahs asked, curious, concerned, but still mildly bemused.

"I remember that real well, Doc. She said, 'It means you never wake up.'"

"Yeah, that happens a lot."

"So you've heard that one before, then?"

The doctor nodded, "Yeah. Lots of times. So what's going on now? Divorced, I see. That cause you any problems?"

"Not really. It was all used up."

"Hmm," the doctor hummed. "Your symptoms still pretty much like you wrote on that intake I sent you?"

"Yeah. I was as honest as I could be about all that. No point otherwise, is there? So, doctor, what's your differential diagnosis?"

"Academic attitude disorder," Kayahs replied, "secondary to being stunned by dildo."

Steick shot out of his chair like a piece of toast from a cartoon toaster, muttering, "Yes. Thank you, doctor. I think I'll be going now."

He had his hand on the doorknob before Kayahs could exclaim, "Wait! Wait! It's not what you think."

Steick turned, lowered his head, and stared like a bull about to charge, keeping a firm grip on the knob.

Dr. Kayahs smiled shyly and said, "I forgot you're not an MD. You asked me a question in doctor jargon, and I answered in doctor jargon. It's kind of a joke with us. Sit down. Sit down. You're normal."

Steick shook his head from side to side and held his ground. "So what's this stupid joke about a dildo, anyway?"

Kayahs grinned again, shamefaced, and responded, "I'm really sorry about that. I make that diagnosis about thirty times a week, in my head, anyway, and it just slipped out this time. It stands for 'Death In Life

Disorder.' Most people have it these days, including me. Sit down. It's okay. You're not crazy, and neither am I. Your mind works fast, you're high-functioning, stressed-out, and your mental health is generally as sound as a Maytag. I thought you might have read about 'dildo' some-place. I really didn't intend to shock you like that."

Steick relaxed his grip on the knob and slowly, tentatively, baby-stepped his way back toward his chair. "Dr. Kayahs, neither 'Death In Life Dis-order' nor 'dildo,' as you call it, sound at all like any medical diagnosis I have ever read about anywhere, and I read a lot of y'all's sloppy records in my disability practice, not to mention a fair bit of medical literature. So what the hell are you talking about, anyway?"

"I don't blame you for being a little pissed, but try to get over it while I explain," the doctor said calmly, and began to elaborate. "See, we talk to a lot of patients. We've got this reference book called the *Diagnostic and Statistical Manual.* You might have heard of it."

"Sure. I refer to it all the time in my disability practice."

"Well, I'm not surprised, since it's written mainly for lawyers and insurance companies. It's filled with standards and diagnoses and numeri-cal codes. It's basically like putting mail into a slot. I write one number, and it means you've got obsessive-compulsive disorder, or 'OCD' as it's sometimes known. I write another number, and it means you've got attention deficit disorder, or 'ADD,' as it's called, and so on. You know all about this, right?"

"I thought I did, until now. I've sure never seen 'dildo' in it."

"Like I said, 'dildo' is a little joke among shrinks and sometimes other MDs. Actually, a lot of non-shrink MDs don't get it either. Of course you won't find 'Death in Life Disorder' in the *Manual.* But 'dildo' is useful shorthand for us. The thing is, people aren't like pieces of mail. So you can't just stick them into slots according to some book or grid. It's not scientific, and often it's not even helpful. On the other hand, we've got to use the diagnostic abbreviations for insurance, legal, and administrative purposes, and everybody uses verbal shortcuts."

Kayahs continued, "You've got to understand also that all mental illness is multifactorial. That is, it results from a wide range of factors from genetics and brain chemistry to how your father reacted when you got a different haircut. About 20 percent of these disorders are little understood and basically intractable. We just try to keep the people alive and functioning. Another 20 percent, approximately, are helped greatly by some combination of medication, cognitive therapy, behavior modification, reflective feedback, depth analysis—whatever. A lot of things work, but you have to find the right combination in order to help, and it isn't easy."

The doctor paused, grinned, and looked straight at his patient, saying, "That leaves about 60 percent of us, more or less, who suffer in various ways from 'Death In Life Disorder,' or 'dildo.' It's kind of like a tree. One branch might be anxiety disorder, another OCD, another depression, another dependent personality disorder, and so on. But when you talk to thousands of patients, you begin to see a clear pattern of self-sabotage emerging among that 60 percent or so. That self-sabotage is like the trunk of the tree, and we call it 'dildo.'"

"So why don't you call it 'tree trunk disorder' then?"

"'Death In Life Disorder' is a lot more descriptive, because that's more or less the way lots of us go about living. Most people love what they fear, which is death, and fear what they love, which is life. Hence, 'Death in Life,' a paradox that makes us uneasy at best, and antisocial or suicidal at worst. It's a lot like what Thoreau meant when he wrote, 'Most people live lives of quiet desperation.' I think everybody these days suffers from it in one form or another. I mean, look at history. All our meaningful connection with the Creator, the Almighty, the Great Mystery, or whatever you want to call God, was essentially wiped out by the scientific revolution, right? Also, today, the half-life of knowledge is about eight minutes, down from thirty years just one hundred years ago. So the pace of change itself unhinges the mind's natural quest for stability and order. There are no significant rituals or rites of passage. All gone. Nobody really connects with anything or anybody else deeply or for very long. Fifty-percent divorce rate and climbing. Kids and parents in different states and haven't seen each other in decades. Twenty-five percent of the population of Montgomery changes every three years. Did you know that? And in those remote parts of the globe that continue to maintain vestiges of traditional culture, the multinationals are busy selling 'information,' which translates into 'profit.' You can sell 'information,' but where's the money in a 'Wisdom Superhighway?' There isn't any. It's a wired world, and consequently, we're all wired people. Kids don't learn anything from their parents anymore because their parents don't know anything except how to navigate the Internet. Most people are like strangers, lost even to themselves. We've become mere tourists in our own lives. We blunder from one materialistic, narcissistic obsession to another, without any real sense of action, purpose, and meaning. We're 'distracted from distraction by distraction,' as the poet, Eliot, put it. Life is like a stale vanilla milkshake. Or it's like you said about your former marriage. It's 'all used up.' Meanwhile, the church, the government, the schools, the universities, the professions—everybody—runs around putting wallpaper over what amount to earthquake fissures in the foundation. Get it?"

Steick pondered this at length. Yes, he got it. It was something he had read about and knew, but only in the abstract. He had always thought himself "connected," "purposeful"—in a word, just "fine." Now he saw that all of this was false. He was himself caught in the web of "law, literature, and society" that he purported to study. But it seemed less like a web than floating in a vacuum. He saw himself as a spacewalking astronaut cut loose from his tether and abandoned. Upon reflection, he realized that was precisely how he had always felt when he wasn't pretending to be "fine."

He stared straight at the doctor and said, "Sure. I get it. So what do I do now?"

"I don't have any idea. You'll have to find that out for yourself, just like I do. Don't get me wrong: I sincerely enjoy talking to you. Especially someone like you who can grasp this and not badger me for The Big Answer. But truthfully, right now I'd rather be playing the saxophone. I really enjoy that more than anything. I practice all I can, get lost in the riffs and blue notes, and dream about hitting the road for New Orleans. Except I've got this big house and mortgage, two kids, a wife,

I don't know how many cars, insurance to pay, the whole bit. So don't feel alone. I've got plenty of conflict, too," Kayahs confessed, standing, shuffling papers, and winding up the session. "I get distracted, lose case files, lose my temper, daydream about missed opportunities, ponder the years passing, the infinite—all those things. Maybe it's the friction that makes life interesting after all.

"Anyway, what I'm going to do is give you some samples of Normalol. That's in the latest generation of serotonin antagonists. Take one twenty milligram capsule in the morning, with food or not, it doesn't matter. If it makes you sleepy, take it before bedtime. If you have a chemical imbalance, this will help, and you'll probably be able to tell pretty quickly. If you don't have an imbalance, you'll just pass the Normalol out like aspirin or vitamins. Very few side effects with this medication. Takes about two weeks to reach its full effect, so I'll give you two weeks' worth of samples. If it helps, call the office and I'll phone you in an Rx. If it doesn't help, call and let me know how you're feeling.

"In either case, come back and see me in six weeks. Meanwhile, think deeply about your life. And I'll tell you this, which I truly believe with all my heart and mind: you and I and all of us have a friend inside that wants us to succeed, that never gives up on us, that gives us overwhelming clues about where we ought to be headed. But the blinders we've put on ourselves through our personal histories typically prevent us from looking at those very obvious clues. You saw some, and that's why you're here today. So you're luckier than most people. At least you're starting to notice things and listen to your friend. Call it psyche, the soul, your true self, whatever. It doesn't matter. It's all the same thing. Get serious with your friend. Meditate, write your life story, go fishing. Do anything that helps you. What is the direction of your narration now, and where is your friend leading you? Those are the big questions. Whether or not the medicine works for you, they still mean just as much. Normalol will only take you so far, and then you're back on your own, okay?"

"Sure, Doc," Steick replied, slightly bewildered. "But before I go, just one more thing. What is that 'academic attitude disorder' that you said I have secondary to dildo?"

"Oh, yeah, I forgot. That just means you see all sides of everything and don't give much of a damn which way the building falls as long as it doesn't land on you. It's normal for people who work in their heads a lot. Take me, for example. I genuinely care about my patients' health and welfare, and I'm deeply interested in the theory and practice of psychiatry. But I don't subscribe to any chunk of ideas for very long. I'm incapable of it, and I'd still rather play the saxophone. So go figure."

The doctor walked Steick to the door of the consultation room and said, "See Melissa, and tell her I want to see you again in six weeks."

"Sure, doctor," Steick replied, furrowing his brow and adding, "Uh—thanks a lot. I'll uh—I'll see you then."

Dr. Kayahs shook hands warmly, grinned, opened the door for his patient and said, "Remember now, 'Don't be a dildo,' okay? That's your motto from now on."

"I'll try not to, Doc. But do me a favor. Don't write that bullshit on my chart. Those things can be subpoenaed, you know."

"I know. I know. I never write 'dildo' on anything. We'll just refer to the *Manual* and call it 'attention deficit disorder,' if that's all right with you," the doctor said cordially.

"That's fine, Doc. See you next time," Steick said as he turned and walked down the carpeted hallway toward Miss Brandywine.

He was ruminating deeply about his own thoughts and Dr. Kayahs's comments as he wandered rather blankly and aimlessly up to the check-out counter. He smiled wanly at Melissa and sucked his cheek.

"Are you okay—uh—Richard?" she asked.

Steick shook his head from side-to-side as if to clear it, smiled like a distracted Kennedy, and said, "Yes. Yes—uh—Melissa. I'm fine. Just fine! I was just thinking about some of the things Dr. Kayahs said, that's all. He told me to give you these," he added, handing the cheerful receptionist a small sheet of paper upon which Kayahs had scribbled some scant, undecipherable notes: "Norm samp 20 x 2 wks. ret. 6."

"Well, you must be," she replied brightly. "This is what everybody gets. He wants you back in about six weeks, so when do you want to come in?"

Melissa looked at her computer scheduling screen, and Steick selected a date and time for his next appointment. "Dr. Kayahs might release you PRN after your next visit," she confided. "That's the usual routine, anyway. We've got to think about HealthCon, you know. Now, just let me get you your Normalol, okay?"

She went to a cupboard slightly above shoulder level. Steick could see the curve of her breast as she reached up, but he was still contemplative and experienced only a minor flicker of interest. She took down two yellow and blue boxes, each about the size of a pack of cigarettes, and put them into a white paper bag which she then handed to Steick. Her hand brushed his ever so slightly.

"This is great stuff if you need it," she said. "I take it myself since—since my divorce. It helps me feel more composed and less distracted. Well, anyway, I won't bore you with all that. He told you: one per day, right? And to phone back for a prescription in two weeks if you see improvement? Okay? You got that, Richard?"

"Yes. Yes, Melissa. I've got it."

"It's just that you seem a little distracted right now, but that's typical when patients see Dr. Kayahs for the first time. If you're like me, the medicine will help. And then thinking about what he told you, too, you know. He's a pretty smart guy, I think."

Steick collected himself in preparation for a cordial exit. "Yes. I think he's very bright, Melissa. He got me to think a lot in the short time I was in there. Well, hey! It was great meeting you," he said, extending his hand.

Miss Brandywine shook it firmly and smiled, saying, "It was great to meet you too, Richard."

"Good," he replied in a slow, smiling, yet puzzled retreat. "I guess I'll see you again in about six weeks, won't I?"

"Yes! I guess you will!"

Steick waved good-bye crisply as he grasped the aluminum door handle and pulled it open, glancing at Melissa for the last time that day. "Thanks! See y'all later!" he said, as he stepped into the bright Alabama summer sunlight.

Get a New Lid

Richard Steick decorously determined "not to be a dildo," as Dr. Kayahs had put it. He took his sample Normalol capsules each morning for two weeks, as prescribed, and then phoned the doctor's office for a regular prescription. He felt improved, but he wasn't sure how much or whether it was enough. He thought he was less distracted, as he had hoped. Yet he locked himself out of his SUV twice in one week. And, in the following week, he drove out of his driveway with a large stainless steel cup of coffee perched on the shiny roof of his well-groomed vehicle. Miraculously, the cup stayed where he had placed it until Steick was about to enter the roadway, when he was flagged down by the postman.

"You've got something on your roof, Professor Steick," the postman said.

"Oh. Thank you, Kenny," the absent-minded professor grinned as he exited and looked at what the postman was indicating with his finger. Steick felt like a fool, but at least he had saved his cup of coffee.

On the basis of several events such as these, he concluded that perhaps he should consult further with Dr. Kayahs. He returned to the doctor's office for his six-week appointment, and the two agreed that he should come in once a month until he felt better focused.

In a short while, the professor found himself looking forward to his monthly visits. Dr. Kayahs was extremely bright, perceptive, entertaining, and helpful, and these were all qualities Steick encountered far too rarely among his male friends and acquaintances. In addition, his monthly visits gave him an opportunity to chat with the doctor's receptionist,

Melissa, and Steick found himself showing up earlier and earlier for his appointments and chatting with her more and more, both before and after he saw the doctor.

In spite of his well-known eccentricities, Steick was generally regarded as a fashionable and desirable middle-aged bachelor by single Hallelujah women of a particular social class. He knew that his money, his reputation as a skillful attorney and scholar, his good looks, and his natural charm gave him a certain appeal. His charitable activities on behalf of the Junior Council put him into regular contact with plenty of attractive divorcees. He had readily increased his civic efforts after his own divorce from Gloria, and not without sexual dividends. The Junior Council ladies, in particular, had provided him with considerable warmth, companionship, and pleasure.

There was Vonda Vainbeaucoup, for example, the first woman Steick dated seriously after his divorce. An attorney like himself, Vonda was tall, with a good figure and raven black hair. She had done well in her two divorces from the same dentist. Thus, she only practiced law fifteen to twenty hours per week, devoting the remainder of her time to her young son and daughter (both of whom Steick despised) and running around town organizing the Council's annual rummage sale and serving on various committees. Steick soon learned that Vonda drank too much, however, and consequently, she snored all night with uncommon brutality.

These habits and the almost constant presence of her whining children caused Vonda to be superseded by Bitsy Assalotta, another Junior Council member with not much to do. In marked contrast to the glamorous Vonda, Bitsy was a delightfully freckled, auburn-haired tomboy with an energetic disposition who liked to play softball in summer and work out constantly at Gem's Gym in the winter.

Her incessant physical activity cranked up her hormones, and she enjoyed extending her vigor into her intimate life. Steick was delighted by Bitsy's enthusiasm and inventiveness, but the problem was what to say afterward. She had majored in therapeutic recreation at the university and boasted triumphantly of never having read a book in her life. Thus, despite her considerable appeal, Bitsy shortly found herself slowly eased away by a slightly exhausted and exceedingly bored Richard Steick.

Quickly recovering his strength, Steick took up next with Jennifer Relentless, who was followed by Monica Sotrendy and one or two additional attractive women, each with her unique charms and demerits. After a couple of years, the thoughtful and generally tolerant Richard felt himself changing. He found himself increasingly irritated when attempting to kiss a woman with a cell phone pressed to her face, and he dated less and less.

Melissa Brandywine was a refreshing contrast to the women Richard had been seeing. She was shorter than himself, lithe but well-built, and always neatly dressed. She had a sunny disposition and did not put on airs. Her fair complexion, stunning blue eyes, and ash blonde hair struck him as Irish. Her fey sense of humor harmonized nicely with Richard's own, and he was delighted to learn they shared many common interests.

Melissa had an undergraduate degree in English and had almost completed her master's before her career was interrupted by marriage to an architecture student. She went to work full-time for several years to support his studies before he flunked out. The man's scholastic failure was the beginning of a long slide downward. He sold insurance, went hunting, and began to drink. He told Melissa that he did not want a wife "who was smarter than he was" and forbade her from continuing her studies. He wanted a wife who would stay home with their children, in the traditional manner, when they had them. She was a politically conscious, free-thinking, emancipated woman, and she did not take her husband's attitude well at all. But she was also raised in a conservative family which was part Primitive Baptist, part Methodist, and part Presbyterian. Therefore, she took her vows to "love, honor, and obey," "for so long as you both shall live," and so on, with a seriousness which caused her to make every effort to keep her marriage alive. The couple's failed efforts to have children were a great blow to both of them, although Melissa suffered it the most. After several attempts at *in vitro* fertilization and exhausting all extraordinary remedies, all the doctors concurred that Melissa would never have children. This left the couple fifty thousand dollars poorer and more alienated than ever from one another. Her husband's response was to drink more heavily. Melissa's response was to chafe ever more painfully under the oppressive weight of the man's obsessively controlling behavior.

She was not a woman who wore her heart on her sleeve, and she attempted to accept her situation stoically. She had great admiration for Jackie Kennedy and could distantly recall the former First Lady's incredible grace under pressure when her husband was assassinated. Melissa aspired to endure her own living death with similar fortitude, but she knew she was living a lie. Mrs. Kennedy's grief was instantaneous and acute, and her exemplary behavior was a necessary matter of public decorum. Melissa's suffering, on the other hand, was a dull, chronic, routine imprisonment that left her joyless. She was not teaching a nation how to manage its grief. She was simply a bright, sensitive resident of the small city of Hallelujah, with no public obligation of composure.

She slowly realized that she was no longer herself. She had become someone completely different. There was no "hallelujah" in her heart as there once had been. The spontaneity and happiness she had experienced as a child and college student had vanished. In their place were an endless series of pointless and unrewarding days. Just as Dr. Kayahs had reminded Richard Steick of Thoreau's famous observation that "Most people live lives of quiet desperation," Melissa recalled it as well, and she knew that it applied to her.

Eventually her situation became intolerable, and she decided to seek professional help in spite of her reservations about opening up to anyone. Like Professor Steick, she summoned the courage to change.

Her first step was to make an appointment with Dr. Max Kayahs, who, she had learned, was well regarded among those in Hallelujah who were bold enough to discuss such forbidden matters as unhappiness and the meaning of their lives.

She was pleased to find Dr. Kayahs the kind, sympathetic, and bemused soul that he was. Halfway through his first consultation with Melissa, Dr. Kayahs had formed a fair assessment of her psychological health. He gave her an initial diagnosis of 300.40, dysthymia, two sample packets of Normalol, and told her to phone back in two weeks if she felt better.

She did feel better, and so she phoned back and obtained a regular prescription. At her six-week follow-up appointment, she had a clearer mind and a more objective view of her life.

Kayahs greeted her warmly, as he did all of his patients. They walked down the hallway and settled comfortably into the armchairs in the doctor's office.

"So. How are you feeling today, Melissa?" the psychiatrist asked. He quickly noted that her affect was much brighter and more alert than during her first visit.

Melissa herself felt far less apprehensive and guarded about finding herself in a psychiatrist's office. The doctor's pleasant demeanor and the helpful effects of Normalol put her much more at ease than on her first visit. She felt she could be candid with Kayahs and that he would not judge her.

"Well, doctor, I'm feeling a lot better, thank you. I'm not as sad as I was, and I feel like I can see more—angles of things—than before. It's kind of like I was a horse wearing blinders, plowing the same field over and over, and now someone has taken off the blinders, and I can see a whole different world out there with more possibilities. Does that make any sense?"

"That is a textbook description of what people typically say when Normalol has been effective for them. So what do you see in that whole different world that you weren't seeing before?"

"I'll just give you a minor example. You see, we have a number of oriental carpets with fringes at our house. I'm a neat and tidy person, which is fine I suppose, but those fringes used to just drive me nuts! They were messed up all the time. It seemed like I spent about half my time at home straightening them out. I used to try flipping them carefully to shake them all straight, but I found it was much easier to use a coarse hair brush. So I was always running to grab the hair brush when I noticed that the fringes were out of whack. My husband said it was me who was out of whack, but he's drunk most of the time when he's home now, like I told you last time. Anyway, a couple of days after I started taking Normalol, I noticed that the fringes didn't bother me as much. They're part of the carpet, after all. So now I just touch them up once a day and let it go at that. It gives me more time to do the things I enjoy, like reading. Before, whenever I got settled in with a book, I'd usually have to jump up and check the fringes on all the carpets, even if I'd just straightened them. Now, I don't even think about it, and I can concentrate on my reading a lot better."

"That's great, Melissa, and also typical. You're less obsessive and compulsive now, and that's a sign of improvement. When people are sad, they often try to compensate, or make up for it, by controlling things in their physical environment. We're all a little superstitious, you see. If something is wrong deep inside us, we think we can somehow control it if we can just control our physical environment. So we'll spend endless time straightening up pictures, books, our closets, or the carpet fringes, like you did. This is also one of the reasons we have so many workaholics in our society. People believe that if they can work enough, perfectly enough, and achieve enough, they won't be sad anymore. So they throw themselves fiercely into their jobs, and then they don't even have the time to think about their lives any longer. It's a form of relief for them. Have you noticed anything else, besides the carpet fringes?"

Melissa gave a short, frustrated sigh. "Well, there's the parking," she said.

"What about the parking?"

"I know this sounds silly, Dr. Kayahs, but I used to have to park just a certain way in our driveway. I had to have the front wheels nice and straight and the door post exactly lined up with this beam in the carport. I called it 'east Tennessee parking' if I didn't do it just that way. Sometimes I'd have to go back and re-park if I didn't get it right the first time. But now I don't worry about that anymore. In fact, I don't even think about it. I just park the car and get out."

The doctor smiled and said, "That's the same thing as the carpet fringes, Melissa. Once again, you're responding typically and well to a medicine that you clearly needed. But a moment ago, you told me you saw 'a whole different world out there now,' and I'm curious to know what you saw in that world."

Melissa blushed visibly and looked down at her hands. She paused and almost imperceptibly tapped her toe. And yet she did not pause long.

She looked up at Kayahs, glanced away, glanced back, and then looked him in the eye and said, "I guess I see I don't have to take his stuff anymore."

Then she quickly returned her gaze to her folded hands.

"Okay," the doctor replied. "I think I know what you mean in general. You told me last time about a lot of things that were making you unhappy in your marriage. You particularly resented your husband's attempts to control your behavior. You disliked his drinking. You said that the two of you no longer had anything in common, and you hadn't had any fun with him for a long time. So when you tell me that you see 'a whole different world out there' and that you 'don't have to take his stuff anymore,' tell me what you mean in particular."

The patient glanced up at the doctor, then back at her hands, and then returned his friendly, inquiring look.

"I-I-I can't, really. Not at this point."

"That's fine," Kayahs reassured her. "You have to take these things at your own pace. You've only begun therapy, but you're already about a year ahead of most women and two years ahead of most men. Men always start out at least a year behind women, you know, because we're more likely to dull our emotions through work, drinking, sports, horsing around—general guy stuff—and we're taught we're not supposed to have emotions anyway, you know. But tell me something. Do you have any inkling about what you mean when you say you 'don't have to take his stuff anymore?' Anything at all particular out there since the blinders have come off?"

"I really don't know, doctor. All I know is that I do have several women friends in Hallelujah who have made big changes in their lives and have told me they've felt so much better since they did. One changed her career, and I can think of at least two who got a divorce and are doing fine. This is the first time I've really noticed this. I mean, before, those were just things that other people did. And what other people did had nothing to do with what I'd chosen for myself. See what I mean?"

Kayahs nodded and responded thoughtfully. "Yes. I see exactly what you mean. And you're correct, of course, that what other people did or what they do has nothing at all to do with what you've chosen for yourself. But you are free to make new and different choices, aren't you, Melissa?"

"Yes! I am, and I know I am! I think that's what I've been trying to say during this whole session, doctor!"

"The Normalol has been wonderfully effective for you, I believe," the doctor said smilingly. And then he let the conversation drop into silence.

Melissa squirmed a little and didn't know what to say.

Finally, Dr. Kayahs said, "Our time is up now, Melissa. Do you want to see me again?"

Leaning forward, she advanced one foot, braced her right elbow on her right knee, propped her chin on her right palm, looked squarely at the physician and asked, "Doctor, do you really think I should get a divorce?"

"I have no idea, Melissa. That's something you'll have to figure out for yourself. No one in the world can do that for you, and certainly not me. It's a matter we can explore in further sessions if you like, or I can just keep you on maintenance Normalol. It's entirely up to you. What are your heart and mind telling you that you should do now?"

Melissa responded with conviction. "I think I'd like to have another appointment, doctor."

"That'll work," Kayahs replied. "How about in one month? See Sheila at the appointment desk, and she'll set you up."

"Okay, Dr. Kayahs," Melissa smiled, extending her hand.

"Good. Keep taking your medicine, and tell me next time what you're seeing outside those blinders you were wearing."

THOUGH OUTWARDLY CHEERFUL AND CAREFREE, Melissa was actually a rather shy, insecure, thoughtful, and deliberative person. Once she had settled upon a tentative course of action, however, she was intrepid about following her intuitions. She saw Dr. Kayahs the next month and the month after that. At that time, they set up a regular monthly appoint-ment for her. Between their conversations, she slowly began to see more and more outside her "blinders." And during her office visits, she felt increasingly free to share what she saw.

On a number of occasions, the patient would ask her doctor outright if he thought she should get a divorce. And on each occasion, the doctor's response was the same. He told her plainly that whether she should di-vorce or not was a decision that only she could make. He asked her to attend to her dreams, and sometimes they would talk about the ones that interested her most. Kayahs always wanted to know what she thought her dreams meant, and she usually said she had no idea. Occasionally, however, when her doctor pressed her to consider various elements of particular dreams, she would have what she called "a little insight." He also urged her to ask what sort of future life she desired and counseled her against weighing what her mother, father, husband, friends, or neighbors might think of her wishes. He ended each session by encouraging her to follow her heart and find her passion.

Melissa continued to take her therapy seriously and found that learn-ing more about herself was an enjoyable experience. At one office visit, a little more than a year after her first, she told Dr. Kayahs that what she had with her husband "wasn't really a life at all, but a sort of death in life." Kayahs suppressed a smile and kept all references to "dildo" to himself.

About a week later, as she finished drawing her nightly bath, Melissa found herself staring with uncommon intensity at the pool of water in her tub. She could not take her eyes off of it, and suddenly it seemed gray, bottomless, and menacing. A moment later, she saw her marriage for what it really was: an anchor to the past and its values, chained firmly about her neck, and pulling her ever deeper into a sea of everydayness, loss, and silent self-reproach. In that moment, she knew precisely what she would do and exactly what she would ask Dr. Kayahs at her next appointment.

When her office visit arrived, she hoped her doctor would answer her question, and he did. Once they had settled comfortably into their armchairs and exchanged brief pleasantries, Melissa looked squarely at Kayahs and said, "Doctor, I know I want to ask my husband for a divorce, but I'm afraid, and I don't know what to say. Can you please tell me?"

Kayahs looked at her with more seriousness than usual and replied, "Now there's a question I can answer, Melissa. Basically, you just have to say what you just told me, but try not to be afraid. Select a quiet moment around the house, one when you're sure your husband hasn't been drinking. Ask him to sit down, and seat yourself in a chair facing him. Doing this across a table is always good. In a calm and rational voice, simply tell him that you want a divorce. Try hard not to become emotional. You're not required to apologize, make excuses, or give acceptable reasons for your decision. It's your life, after all. Definitely do not argue with him. In the event that he should become verbally combative, tell him that you want to take a time out. Tell him you're going for a drive, and then get in your car and go. You will be the best judge of when you should leave, if that is necessary. You have told me repeatedly that he is not a violent man, and the way you've described him persuades me that you're probably correct. Nevertheless, use an abundance of caution. Call a time out and leave at the moment he shows any marked signs of anger. Do not return until you've talked to him on the telephone and agreed to meet him at a neutral location, like Shoney's. If he won't talk to you on the phone or meet you in a public place, then you must see a lawyer immediately and spend a few nights at your mother's house. Your lawyer will take it from there. It's as simple as that."

They devoted the remainder of her visit to Melissa's fears and her plans for the future. The doctor assured her that it was normal to feel frightened in her a situation as well as vague and worried about what the future might hold.

As her session ended and she indicated she was about to leave, Dr. Kayahs explained, "Human beings fear change, Melissa, because it represents the unknown, and there is nothing more frightening to us than the unknown. People less brave than yourself will endure anything, however horrible, rather than risk change. As long as we remain in the known world, we feel safe. We have a certain place in society. We know our role and the moves we're supposed to make. Those moves and that fearful way of thinking become habitual, and our brain simply shuts out other alternatives. We put blinders on ourselves, you see. A brain deficiency of the chemical called serotonin makes habitual patterns of thought become ever more embedded. Normalol can restore our serotonin balance and allow us to see the world more freshly. But the rest is up to us. It becomes a matter of courage and will. I can tell from our discussion today that you have the courage to make a move that you find best. My last bit of advice is 'don't hesitate.' Having reached this point, I think you should act quickly. Good luck, and be careful."

MELISSA PONDERED HER DOCTOR'S words carefully and found herself resolute. She was determined to make her views clear to her husband at the earliest opportunity, which would likely come that night, provided he didn't stop in at a bar on his way home.

Entirely unknown to Melissa was the fact that her husband had been having numerous affairs and one-night-stands with insurance clients, other sales representatives, secretaries, and almost any woman he could pick up. Their marriage had become as boring to him as it was painful and oppressive to her. He didn't care much anymore, one way or the other. Consequently, their discussion of divorce went quite smoothly. The only real issues were the possibility of restitutional alimony and the division of property. They decided that each of them would hire a lawyer and try to work out a settlement that was fair to them both. Melissa remained in their house, and the two avoided each other as much as possible.

Melissa's attorney, Josh Wiggins, explained that domestic unhappiness was like a cancer, and lawyers and judges were the surgeons who removed it. He explained that she would probably get the home place and an equitable portion of the remaining marital estate. After about a month of dickering and phone calls between the lawyers, Melissa's husband proved remarkably compliant, and the couple met at Wiggins's office to sign the final papers. They filed a simple, uncontested divorce with the property settlement attached. The circuit judge promptly signed their decree, and they were divorced within the week. Melissa ended up with her house, a good car, considerable furniture, her personal possessions, and a reasonable sum of alimony in gross. Her husband had treated her fairly, but she had monthly payments to make and no choice but to work for the best wages she could find. Her plans to return to graduate school in English were thus put on hold indefinitely.

She discussed her situation with Dr. Kayahs at her first office visit after her divorce had become final. She expressed such a profound sense of relief and genuine joy in living that the doctor was proud to be a psychiatrist. He chalked her up mentally as a stunning professional success. He recognized a remarkable, multi-talented person in her. And, as chance would have it, the doctor's receptionist, Sheila, had just given her two-weeks' notice. Seizing the moment, Kayahs asked Melissa to come to work for him. The salary he offered was several thousand dollars more per year than what she was earning as a school librarian. She liked Kayahs, liked the office environment, and liked the idea of a career change. Thus, she gladly accepted the doctor's offer. She quickly adapted to office procedures, liked the patients, and took substantial satisfaction in her work. It had all been a good move. The many changes in her life had made it much richer and more interesting.

She was surprised, however, to discover that she experienced considerable reticence about dating. She was a beautiful and charming woman who tended to underestimate her assets. She knew that she was good-looking, appeared younger than she really was, and possessed an excellent figure. But, on balance, she considered herself "just average." She enjoyed quiet pursuits, like reading, and she was terrified of singles bars. Most of her friends were married women, and they frequently set her up with eligible bachelors of their acquaintance. Melissa enjoyed going out for dinner and a movie but was less enthusiastic about football games and days at Lake Martin. She dated quite a few men once, twice, or even three times (which was allegedly a magic number, although not with Melissa). Her interest was never greater than mild. More often than not, she found herself bored in conversation and wondered if there was something "wrong" with her. She even considered asking Dr. Kayahs if she should increase her Normalol or take some other or additional medication. For the most part, however, she was contented with her life and genuinely cheerful as she watched and waited for whatever might happen next.

THIS WAS THE MELISSA BRANDYWINE who added an extra measure of pleasure to Richard Steick's monthly visits with Dr. Kayahs. It was she for whom love's magneto began to spin ever more rapidly in his heart.

He had noticed encouraging signs from her at his first office visit when he focused his laser gaze into her large pupils. She had returned his look with similar intensity and a slight embarrassment, which Steick correctly interpreted as generally receptive. Their subsequent banter that day grew into an easy familiarity at his later office visits. He relaxed, tried to grin like JFK, and leaned upon his folded hands and forearms at the reception desk. Although they were separated by the opened, sliding glass window, Melissa turned away from her telephone and paperwork and leaned forward also. On Richard's lucky days, her decolletage was notable and enticing. Her conversation was cheerful and forthcoming, yet slightly modest. They were happy to learn that they shared interests in books, classical music and blues, museums, the theater, travel, and ballet. They touched upon the issue of divorce, which each had experienced. And Steick was decidedly pleased that Miss Brandywine was a former patient of Dr. Kayahs who had come to work for him. She had once stood where he, Richard, did, and therefore she could not reasonably find his treatment by a psychiatrist an unsavory reflection upon his personality.

On his fourth monthly visit, Steick had been delayed in court on a motions hearing and was fifteen minutes late for his appointment. When he showed up at the doctor's office, Kayahs was standing behind Melissa going over some insurance papers. The patient barely had time to flash a grin in her direction before the doctor summoned him into his consultation room.

The lawyer followed his physician down the carpeted hallway without even saying "Hello" to Miss Brandywine, who found herself feeling slightly neglected and hurt. She consoled herself that Steick was a busy man, but her insecurity lingered. She felt justified in her disappointment. She had dressed that morning with Steick's appointment in mind, choosing a simple black dress which she knew displayed her substantial assets to good advantage.

Richard was disappointed also, and he hoped he hadn't hurt Melissa's feelings. On the other hand, he was eager to get down to business with Kayahs and contemplated a longer than usual conversation with the attractive receptionist following his appointment.

The doctor and his patient shook hands and seated themselves in their customary armchairs.

"What's up, Doc?" Steick inquired.

"Oh, I don't know," Kayahs replied. "I might have to see an ortho. You know what a 'boogie board' is? I was down at the beach and jumped onto one my son had and twisted my back, and it hurts. But I'll be fine. So, how about yourself? Still feeling like the Normalol helps you?"

"Yes, I think it does, but I'm not sure how much or if it's enough. I've just come from court, which is why I was late. Sorry about that. I was on time for my motions hearing, but I was playing electronic roulette when Judge Smiley arrived at my case. I'd just won a nice chunk of play money when she called my name. I wasn't paying any attention, and I didn't notice what was going on until the third time she called and bellowed out my name like a mad bull. I got confused turning off the roulette machine and turned on the sound instead. So it played this loud, silly jackpot trumpet music for about half a minute, and everybody in court laughed except the judge, who fined me two hundred dollars for contempt. I don't mind that. I just don't want to do something worse, like really screw up a case, you know?"

"Do you like electronic roulette, Richard?"

"No. But it gives me something to do, and it's better than sitting there listening to a bunch of other lawyers mumble about cases I know nothing about."

"Well, I don't think that's much cause for worry. I've had to testify in court quite a few times, and it's about the most boring place I can imagine. So what else have you been thinking about since the last time we talked?"

In previous visits, Steick learned that Kayahs had earned both undergraduate and master's degrees in philosophy before turning to medical school, and that background had advanced the doctor considerably in the professor's hierarchy of serious persons. They had read and been influenced by many of the same thinkers. Indeed, it was Schopenhauer who had led Kayahs to his interest in the saxophone. Thus, Steick was uninhibited about expressing what really concerned him.

"Well, Doc," he said. "I've been trying hard not to be a dildo, like you recommended. We both know where you and your shrink pals are coming from, historically, with that cute abbreviation, don't we? Dildo is the outcome of rapidly advancing spiritual atrophy since the scientific revolution in the West, isn't it? Matthew Arnold's 'vast, receding sea of faith,' and all that. Right? And we know about various counter-visions of the existentialists, like Kierkegaard and Nietzsche, the phenomenologists, the Jungians, and others as well, don't we? But I still can't get a handle on it. I can't embrace any great ideology or cause, and I'm not a creative artist. I feel like a spare part in the universe, like a leftover, if you know what I mean. I've always liked what Greta Garbo once said, you know?"

"So what did she say?"

"She said 'Life would be wonderful if we could only figure out what to do with it.' In short, I don't know how to avoid being a dildo. I don't know how to live in the moment, among other things. I'm always in the past or the future. Sometimes I don't think I know how to live at all."

Kayahs pulled his typical bemused expression and said, "I know what you mean, Richard. I'm pretty much the same way myself. We've both got academic attitude disorder, seeing all sides of everything and all of them at the same time as well. It makes us tend toward emotional paralysis. About all I can do is listen and give you a few hints that might help. Want to hear one?"

"That's what I'm paying you for, isn't it, doctor?" Steick replied, looking a little bemused himself.

"Well, get a new lid."

Richard briefly rolled his eyes toward the ceiling before replying, "Oh, that's very funny, Doc. I come in here, paying you good money, and you tell me things like 'Don't be a dildo. Get a new lid.' I suppose this is some more of your shrink jargon, right? Is that what they taught you in medical school? How to play word games? Or are you just pulling my leg? I know I need a new lid, or at least an improved one, or I wouldn't be here in the first place, would I? So what the hell is 'a new lid?' if you don't mind my asking."

Kayahs seemed reflective. "I suppose you're right. We do play a lot of word games in my profession, and maybe that's half the art of it. Words are all we have to work with, in the end. So let's play it on out, okay?"

"All right. Let's play Scrabble."

The doctor looked at him and said, "Okay. We don't want to be dildos, right?"

"That's correct, doctor. We don't want to be dildos."

"And 'dildo' stands for what, professor?"

"'Dildo,' as you put it, refers to 'Death in Life Disorder.' This is a common condition y'all shrinks refer to that seems to describe the emotional architecture of a lot of people these days, including me, you said. We love what we fear, which is death, and we fear what we love, which is life. Thus, we inhabit a spiritual limbo, a 'death in life,' a 'life of quiet desperation.' It's as if we're alive but without permission. We're afraid of solitude, so loneliness is rampant, the quest for relationship—or what passes for relationship—is relentless, and fear of genuine change terrifies and rules us. We might just as well call 'dildo' plain old 'neurosis,' in my opinion. Which reminds me. Freud said that 'civilization is built upon neurosis,' you know. So, at the collective level, with most of the populace suffering from dildo, we get rampant addictions, gangs, drive-by shootings, mass murder, suicide pacts, and pathological politicians who bring us nothing but corruption, deceit, self-interest, and wars, wars, wars with no end in sight. How's that so far?"

"That, Professor Steick, was an excellent review of many of the things we've discussed together. Now, Richard, let's take our little word game to the next level. I want you to answer the following question quickly, without any reflection or analysis. Are you ready?"

"Sure. Fire away."

"What's the opposite of 'death in life?'"

"Well, 'life in death,' of course."

"Correct! And the first letter of those words spell . . . what?"

"Lid," Steick responded, smiling. But he quickly furrowed his brow. "Okay. That's very clever, Doctor Crossword Puzzle. But what's a new 'Life in Death?' What sizes do they come in, and where do I have to go to get one?"

"I'm afraid I can't answer that one for you, Richard. You'll have to figure it out for yourself, just like everybody else. And don't go analyzing it to death with your keen lawyer's mind, looking for the Big Answer, because there isn't one. You have to listen to your heart, feel your way along your journey, and forget about ever getting it just right, because you won't. Nobody ever does. The best we can do is blunder along with our difficult questions, screwing things up, and increasing our self-knowledge a little bit along the way. We don't ever really 'arrive,' you know. But we can live our journey with ever greater richness and interest if we take life's questions seriously."

Richard looked puzzled. That's what he thought he had been doing for so many years—taking life's questions seriously. He even suspected that taking them too seriously was possibly what brought him into the psychiatrist's office. Wasn't he a well-educated man, a lawyer, a well-published professor in the field of law, literature, and society? He knew he wasn't going to become a monk. So what else was he supposed to do? He didn't know, and so he inquired of his inscrutable physician.

"All right, doctor, how can I take life's questions more seriously? How can I find a new life in death?"

"Once again I have to say I don't know, Richard. Like before, about the best I can do is offer a few clues, if you're interested."

"Of course I'm interested. You know I am, or I'd just take my Normalol and stop coming back here. What kind of clues have you got this time?"

"We all have to begin by facing things. The two most common enemies of self-knowledge, and therefore the primary causes of dildo, are repression and fantasy. Take the mundane but important matter of death, for example. We're all 'beings toward death' as our friend Heidegger, the philosopher, put it. Nothing could be clearer, and we all know that it's true, but we expend tremendous amounts of psychic energy repressing the idea of death and fantasizing that it won't happen to us. Most people would rather do anything than admit their own mortality, and therefore they pursue perpetual diversion—which erases feeling—with an intensity that would be better spent in learning about their own lives and feeling their existence with authenticity and depth while they are here. We've become a society of Eliot's 'Hollow Men,' where narcissism and materialism overwhelm all sense of connection to anything eternal. Thus, fashion has become our true religion and entertainment our primary occupation.

"Such lives are bound to be a mere death in life. Almost everyone would rather practice this foolish self-deception and be a dildo than simply face things. Death is everywhere. Just look around. We're all headed that way. So the thing is to embrace nature, our natural destiny, ripen into a love of dying, and find all the authentic joy and life we can within the confines of the simple facts of our existence."

"All right," Steick replied. "I follow you. But how do we avoid self-deception and the narcissism and materialism we see everywhere? How do we avoid devoting ourselves to mere diversion, and all that, and find this great joy and 'life in death' you're talking about? It all sounds fine in the abstract, but let's get down to cases. Like mine, for example. What am I supposed to do that I'm not doing already?"

"I'm sorry, Richard, but only you can answer that question. About all I can do, once again, is possibly offer some clues."

"Okay. I'm still listening, doctor. Let's play Clue now. You're starting to sound like Sherlock Holmes."

"Nothing that gritty and exciting, I'm afraid. Just some more facts. Look. I think what we all want is a life of action, purpose, and meaning. The action is out there, no question. It's the purpose and meaning that are tough to find these days. I mean, we're a long way from the Middle Ages, aren't we? For better or for worse. Nevertheless, people haven't changed that much. What we really want is to feel connected to something eternal. And action alone doesn't cut it."

Steick nodded affirmatively. "You're certainly right about that, Doc. There's plenty of action. If all I wanted was action, I'd have stayed with Bitsy Assalotta or gone on one of those singles cruises that your colleague, that jackass Mangrove, recommended. Remember? No. I've been down that road before. So where are we supposed to find purpose and meaning? You want me to take saxophone lessons, or what?"

"It's good therapy, Richard, and I think you ought to try it or something like it. Probably do you good. But to your larger questions about purpose and meaning, try to think for a moment about the Holocaust survivors. What do we know about them? They lived with death every moment, at Dachau, Auschwitz, Belsen. They 'lay them down to sleep with death' every night, didn't they? And yet, some of them survived. What do you think those survivors have to tell us? You ever have a chance to study that or think about it?"

"Yes, I have, Doc. But I'm not sure I internalized it. Give me a quick refresher, or tell me what you have in mind."

"Three things. Three things seemed common to the survivors. One. Often they had a deep personal love, a mother, husband, wife, or child outside, and that love kept them going. Or, second, they had significant work, a sense of mission. Some of them wrote whole books and even symphonies on scraps of waste paper and smuggled them out or kept them hidden for years. Remember? And finally, for some, their suffering itself transformed them and gave them purpose and a will to live. Is this coming back to you now?"

"Okay, I can take a hint. Just let me summarize for a moment. You're telling me to get a new life, a new 'lid' as you put it. And to do that, I need to face things and get comfortable with reality. That includes death, and I suppose you also mean it includes the fact of inevitably screwing things up. A deep love for another person or a group can help. So can work, if our deeds have a satisfying sense of purpose and connection. Finally, even suffering can give our lives substance if we can find its meaning. Am I on the right track, Dr. Kayahs?"

"Yes. I think you're on the right track, Richard. You recall Dante's *Inferno,* don't you? And your etymology is pretty good, isn't it?"

"Well, I think I can give modest assent to both of those questions, doctor."

"Okay. So what was the real name of Satan at the center of Dante's Hell? Remember?"

"Sure. Satan was called 'Dis,' doctor," the patient replied.

"Okay. And the prefix 'dis' means what, professor?"

"'Dis' means separated, or cut off. As in 'dis-connected' or 'dis-aster,' which is, literally, 'to lose our stars.' Am I correct?"

"You are indeed. And I think you've chosen two very good examples to illustrate the point I'm trying to make. You're a little disconnected now. You've lost your stars. And without them, you're adrift and finding it difficult to navigate your own, interesting, unique journey to who-knows-where. And now to the bonus question. What is the Latin origin of the word 'religion?' Do you know?"

"I'm afraid I lose the bonus points, Doc. I hope this won't affect my frequent flier miles. So tell me, what is the origin of the word 'religion'? I'd like to learn."

"The word 'religion,' comes from the word *'religio,'* meaning literally, 'to bind back.' And so, partner, I think you've become a little disconnected from things that are genuinely important to you, and what your soul, or psyche, really needs, more than anything, is to be bound back into a sense of connection. Okay? That's what any true religion is all about."

"This all makes good sense to me, Doc," the patient said. "And if you'll give me just one or two more minutes, I'd like to ask you a question about where I'd like to begin this project."

"Okay. I don't have another patient for fifteen minutes, so go ahead and ask."

"Well, Dr. Kayahs, love sounds like a lot more fun to me than work or suffering, and Melissa and I have been chatting quite a bit before and after my appointments here. She's a wonderfully charming woman, you know, and I'm wondering if I might ask her out. Is she seeing anybody right now, that you know of?"

"Not as far as I know."

"You don't have any professional prohibitions against that, do you?

My asking her out, I mean. Of course I wouldn't want to do anything that would violate your ethical code or compromise her job in any way."

Dr. Kayahs looked uncommonly serious as he replied, "Well, the last time I checked, it's still a free country, and we all have a First Amendment right to freedom of association, don't we? You're the lawyer. Isn't that what the law says? It would be different, of course, if she were the doctor treating you, but that isn't the situation here. So I have no objection. But let me tell you something personal, okay, Richard? You're correct that Melissa is a 'wonderfully charming woman,' as you put it. She is also extremely intelligent, multi-talented, creative, and fairly contented with her life at the moment. Without breaking any patient confidence, I can tell you frankly that she is also rather insecure, in spite of her appearances to the contrary. She has been through a lot, and she's recovering nicely from some difficulties. In short, I don't want to see her hurt. She's not one of your Bitsy Assalottas. You understand that, don't you? You've got to treat her right, or don't treat her at all, okay? And if you don't treat her right, I'll refuse to treat you in the future. Get it? I'm not joking around. Handle her carefully and consider her best interests. Frankly, I think you might be good for her, Richard. You're a true gentleman, and y'all seem to have a lot in common. So, yes, you're free to date Melissa as far as I'm concerned, as long as you treat her like a lady, as I know you will. Is that all right with you?"

"I wouldn't have it any other way, Doc," Steick assured his physician. "There's definitely something different, deep, and vulnerable about her. I promise to treat her well, and I thank you for your advice,"

"Okay then. See you next time?"

"Next time, Doc," Richard said, as the two shook hands warmly and he turned to walk out the door.

HE FELT HIS HEART RATE INCREASE and his palms begin to sweat as he made his way down the corridor, past the reception office, and through the door to the waiting room. He turned right to face the receptionist's sliding glass window, which was open. Melissa was just concluding a phone call and swiveled to her right to look up at the handsome, well-dressed, grinning patient standing in front of her.

"Well. Hello, Richard," she said. "I didn't think you were even going to talk to me today. How have you been?"

"I've been fine, Melissa. Just fine. Thanks for asking. I'm sorry I couldn't greet you properly when I came in, but I was late, you know, and Dr. Kayahs seemed ready to get started with me."

"That's okay. I know you're a busy man. So what's the news from my boss? Are you all cured now, or do we need to make another appointment?"

"You know, Melissa, I think your boss is a pretty wise fellow for a guy so young. He has helped me a lot already, but I think I've still got some more things to learn from him. So we're going to keep up with my regular appointments for a while longer. He wants to see me again in about a month. What have you got for me at about that time?"

Melissa turned to consult her computer for the doctor's appointment calendar. She wiggled the mouse, tapped a couple of keys, and asked, "How about the same time on Tuesday, the twenty-second?"

The busy Richard had already pulled his planning calendar from his breast pocket. He consulted it briefly and said, "That would be just perfect, Melissa. Would you please hand me a pen so I can make a note?"

The attractive receptionist picked up a white plastic pen imprinted with the Normalol logo and HEIGH-HO PSYCHIATRY, HALLELUJAH. Their hands touched only slightly, but with immense voltage, as she handed the pen to the lawyer, professor, and patient.

"There!" Steick said as he completed his entry.

He quickly did a full Jack Kennedy impersonation—right forefingers lightly brushing back at his right temple, top half of his left hand inserted and withdrawn from his jacket pocket, his grin polished to its most charming—before clasping his hands and leaning forward informally to rest his forearms upon the Formica shelf. He focused his laser headlights deeply into Melissa's receptive pupils and directly into her brain stem, completely bypassing the optic nerve and all intervening cerebral matter, before saying anything. Then he happily chirped, "Now it's my turn to cross-examine. How are you, Melissa?"

"I'm very well, thank you, Dr. Steick. But not so fast. I think your cross examination is a little ahead of schedule. We're not finished with you yet. You see, I'm a little worried about you."

Steick grinned even more widely, knowing a put-on when he saw one coming.

"You are, Melissa? Now why is that?"

"I'm referring to your Health-Con sky miles account, Richard. I'm afraid the company doesn't like you one bit! According to their schedule of treatment, you should have fully recovered about three visits back. As it is, you're already in the red with your sky miles, and you're getting in deeper all the time. If this keeps up, Health-Con will have you sitting in airplanes that fly backward and land you at destinations you don't want to visit. Then you'll have to pay for air fare back to Montgomery. Whatsa matter, professor? Don't you want to get well fast? Don't you want to collect your miles so you can visit all those faraway places with the strange sounding names, all for free?"

The patient chuckled and turned up his laser gaze even brighter. "Now, Melissa, I'm sure you know the answer to that one already. As long as I feel like I'm learning something from Dr. Kayahs, I intend to keep coming here, and Health-Con can go to blazes. Besides, I might not get to see you anymore if I stopped my appointments, and that would make me sad."

"Well, I'd be sad too, Richard," Melissa responded, fine tuning her own lasers to new levels of soulfulness.

"And as for my sky miles, I accumulate those everywhere all the time and have plenty enough to take us to Paris, Istanbul, or wherever you like, and probably several times. So that doesn't worry me very much, I'm afraid."

"Ummmm," she murmured. "Sounds interesting."

Then Steick performed a psychic maneuver he always employed at critical moments such as this. He completely dropped all his inner defenses and forgot entirely about aligning his personality with the situation at hand. His normal insecurities, nervousness, and JFK mannerisms simply evaporated. In short, he allowed his deep, genuine inner joy to shine forth. He was the personification of contagious cheerfulness as he addressed the charming receptionist.

"You know, Melissa, there's something I've been wanting to tell you for a long time."

"What's that, Richard?" she inquired, while her own pulse rate popped up like a jack-in-the-box.

"Do you know that you have an absolutely adorable little philtrum?"

Melissa blushed visibly. She didn't know how to respond.

"Uh. Thank you, Richard. But don't you, uh, don't you think that's getting a little personal? I mean, we, uh, we hardly know each other—yet—do we? And, uh, what's a, uh, 'philtrum,' by the way?"

Steick was as merry as Santa Claus. "Yeah. Your philtrum. That's the tiny little vertical crease between the bottom of your nose and the top of your upper lip. Yours is just cute as a button!"

Melissa was at once relieved, flattered, and happy. "Why, thank you, Richard! What a kind thing for you to say!"

"It's true," he said, continuing, "Listen, Melissa. There's a great comedy playing at the Alabama Shakespeare Festival in Montgomery, and I'd like to ask you to go with me on Saturday night. We could have a late supper at the Capital City Club afterward. What do you say?"

Melissa beamed, blushed slightly, and said, "Why, I'd love to go with you, Richard, but there's one little thing that concerns me."

"What's that?"

"Well, I work for Dr. Kayahs, and you're his patient. I mean, I'm not sure it's allowed, you know? Wouldn't that be some kind of conflict of interest or something? You're the lawyer. You tell me."

"There's no problem. I was just discussing it with your taskmaster in there. He said it's fine, as long as you don't start slipping me samples of heavy narcotics. So! How about it?"

"Richard, I'd love to join you. Thank you for asking me."

"Great! And you're very welcome," he said, adding, "Melissa, I'm sorry, but I have to run right now. Would you please just write your home number on a piece of paper for me? I'll phone you, at your convenience, of course, possibly this evening if you like. I can get directions to your house, and we can work out the time I'll pick you up. Would that be okay?"

"Certainly," she said, and quickly wrote her number on the back of an appointment card. "Here you go. I'm sorry, but I don't have a cell phone."

"You're wise not to. They're a great nuisance. But what time would you like me to phone?"

"Why not about 8:00? Would that work?"

"That would be just fine," Steick replied. Having long abandoned the old-fashioned rule forbidding a man from extending his hand to a lady, he reached toward Melissa, and they exchanged a friendly handshake.

Richard flashed her one last grin and walked importantly toward the door. His feet had hardly hit the sidewalk before he started doing a little tap dance and humming "I'm in Love Again."

Driving back to his own office for an appointment, he reflected upon the past hour.

"Doc's right," he thought. "Connection. Binding up. Authentic love and significant work! Those are the keys! I'll take a pass on the suffering for as long as I can. But Richard Steick, PhD, Esq., is going to get a new lid!"

Ground Zero

Melissa Brandywine did not put out immediately, and that was perfectly fine with Richard Steick. He had always held to the view that a man and a woman ought to be friends before becoming lovers. She was shy, and he had no instinct or desire to become a human version of the equine Secretariat. It was their conversation and companionship that drew them together.

The couple went to the theater and a late supper on the Saturday night after Richard first asked Melissa for a date, and it was a splendid evening for both of them. They continued to chat in the witty, easy manner they had already assumed with each other at the office of Dr. Kayahs. As the night ended, Richard drove Melissa back to her home in Hallelujah. The atmosphere in his leather-padded SUV was palpably sensual as Beethoven's *Moonlight Sonata* played soulfully on the vehicle's magnificent sound system.

Experience had taught Richard to address important issues in a mature manner. "Melissa," he said, as they passed the Hallelujah city limits. "I've had a great time tonight, and I'd like to see you again. Would that be all right with you?"

"Why yes, Richard, I've had a wonderful time also, and I'd like that very much. Thank you for asking."

"So what if I phone you at about 8:00 P.M. on Tuesday, like last week, and we can discuss the details?"

"Sounds good to me," she said, as he drove into her driveway. "I'll look forward to your call!"

The agile Richard slid his gearshift into Park, pulled up the parking brake handle, and leaned to his right to kiss Melissa, all in one move.

But she had already opened her door and was hopping out before he could turn off the ignition.

"Wait, Melissa," he said. "Let me get that for you." But she had closed the vehicle and planted herself on the ground in an instant. She stood waiting for him to walk her to her door. Richard rounded the front of his SUV and, observing a certain confused reticence in Miss Brandywine, he offered her his arm, European-style.

She took it, and they walked to her door in silence. Upon reaching it, she removed her arm, grasped his hand, and gave it a tender squeeze. She looked at him forthrightly and said, "Richard, I like you very much. But I want you to know that I'm really a lot more shy and insecure than I appear. In addition, I was raised in a conservative environment, so I hope you won't take offense if I don't ask you in—tonight."

"Of course I won't, Melissa," Steick replied sympathetically. "I understand entirely. I just want you to be comfortable, okay?"

"Okay! Phone me Tuesday night." And then she offered him her cheek. He kissed it gently, and, in an experienced manner, moved his lips toward hers.

But they weren't there. She had turned toward the door and was looking back to say "good night."

Richard quickly shifted into full Kennedy mode. "Uh, Melissa," he grinned. "I'll uh, be happy to give you five hundred of my Health-Con sky miles for one more little good-night kiss. How about it?"

"Richard Steick, you know you're way too far in the red with those sky miles to ever own a single one! Besides, what kind of a girl do you think I am? But okay. One more. And only because I work for Dr. Kayahs, you know."

This time he found her lips quickly but only momentarily. They embraced and kissed briefly while Richard accepted the fact that anything further would have to wait.

THEIR COURTSHIP DEVELOPED rapidly, easily, and with ever-greater depth of understanding and feeling. One evening, Richard went to look around inside Mushroom Memories. It had occurred to him that Melissa had never visited his retreat, and he was eager to find out her reaction. He discovered his 1950s museum of banality and terror dusty, with cobwebs in the corners, and a general aroma of disuse. It dawned upon him that he had not visited it since he first began dating Melissa. Obviously his cleaning lady had noticed this fact also and took it as an opportunity to lighten her burden. To Richard, it was a significant moment of insight. "Maybe I'm getting a new lid," he thought. "Or at least the one I have is changing for the better. This place looks a little bizarre. I wonder what Melissa will think of it?"

He concluded that he would simply have to find out. He wanted Melissa to know him deeply and well, just as he wanted to know her in the same way. So he busied himself with tidying the unusual "recreation room" he had designed in hope of exorcising his fears of the Triple Threat.

On the next day, a Saturday afternoon, he took Melissa to a movie and then said there was something he wanted to show her before dinner. She had visited his tasteful Italianate house on the hill only one time before, and she had found it stunning. She was not quite prepared, however, for Richard's unique and slightly sinister annex.

"I call this place 'Mushroom Memories,' Melissa," he said, as he opened the door for her.

"Oh," she replied, as she surveyed the puzzling array of "I Like Ike" bibelots and atomic *objets d'art*. She was somewhat younger than Richard, and he suspected that perhaps she could not recall and truly connect with the significance of his collection.

"This used to be an English-style pub, but a while back, I converted it into this 1950s memorial," he explained. "Would you like a drink? The specialty of the house is lime Kool-Aid with vodka, served in these Sputnik cocktail glasses I found at a flea market. Or I've got most anything you want. Beer, Coke, Sprite, wine, mixed drinks, whatever."

"Thank you, Richard. I'll have a Coke if that's all right."

"Certainly. One Coke coming up." He fished in his pocket for a nickel, deposited it into a vintage red Coca-Cola machine, slammed the gray metal handle downward, and an ice-cold bottle of the esteemed beverage thunked into the dispenser.

"Would you like that over ice, Melissa?"

"Uh. No. I think straight out of the bottle is more in keeping with the spirit of your, uh—recreation room, Richard."

"Fine," Steick replied, popping off the cap. He prepared a house special for himself, and the couple seated themselves on a yellow Naugahyde love seat facing the giant TV screen.

"Would you like to watch the total annihilation of the Bikini atoll, Melissa? I've got some uncommonly good footage."

"The what?" she asked. Then she blushed and said, "No, Richard. I would not like to watch anything titled 'The Total Annihilation of the Bikini' at all. And I'm shocked and embarrassed that you would even ask me. Frankly, I'm a little ashamed of you, too. I suppose if you want to sit out here and watch pornography on this big TV screen, well, that's your business. But I never watch it. And you'll never get me to watch it with you, either. Period."

"Not 'at all,'—'atoll.'"

"No. Not at all. It's as simple as that."

"But I didn't mean 'at all,' Melissa. I meant *'atoll.'*"

"*No,* Richard. Not even a little bit. Why is this so hard for you to understand? I'm starting to wonder if maybe you shouldn't discuss this issue with Dr. Kayahs."

"Wait, Melissa! I'm not asking you to watch anything pornographic. I don't watch that stuff either. This is something entirely different. I think you misunderstood my meaning."

"Well, I'm sorry, then. But what is this movie called 'The Total Annihilation of the Bikini' all about anyway? I've never heard of it. It sounded like something naughty to me."

"I was referring to an atoll, A-T-O-L-L, in the Pacific Ocean called 'Bikini.' In the 1950s, the U.S. government detonated an H-Bomb on this small island, forever erasing it from the face of the earth. It was a historic moment."

"Okay. Now I get it. Please forgive me for misunderstanding and making an assumption about you. I could hardly believe it myself, actually. It just didn't seem to fit with the Richard Steick I know. Now that I think about it, though, I can see how a movie like that would fit in with your—uh—decorative theme here."

"Not a problem, Melissa, and there's nothing to forgive. It was a simple misunderstanding."

"Well, it sounds a little creepy, but kind of interesting too. I hope there weren't any people living on this Bikini atoll when the government decided to blow it up. Certainly there weren't, were there?"

"As I remember, there were maybe a couple dozen native residents who were 'relocated,' as the Defense Department put it at the time. I imagine they handed each of them five dollars and put them inside some waterproof tee-pees on top of some big canoes or something. That would be about typical, wouldn't it?"

"Well, I hope it was more than that. Yet you're right, of course. That would be about the typical government treatment of original landowners in our history. But why are you so fascinated by all of this, Richard?"

"Watch, and then I'll tell you," he said as he hit the Play button on his remote.

The entire scene lasted approximately forty-five seconds, with the shock waves surging into the vast ocean for endless miles from the small island and the phenomenal round mushroom cloud slowly unscrolling upward into the stratosphere.

Melissa was somewhat at a loss for words. Finally, she said, "That was pretty scary, and this is a, uh, a very interesting sort of place you've made here, Richard. Do you have a particular interest in 1950s history or something?"

Steick appreciated the opportunity to explain a side of himself that he had rarely revealed to anyone. He told Melissa about growing up on the farm outside Cullman in constant fear of the Triple Threat and how he spent his formative years knowing that Armageddon was definitely scheduled for any moment prior to the next school recess. He explained his therapeutic theory of total immersion. He told her how he thought constant exposure to the insipid and cataclysmic relics of the Cold War might help him exorcise the demons that continued, he believed, to haunt his adulthood in peculiar ways. For Richard, this confession of his early fears was a greater catharsis than any he had achieved with Dr. Kayahs.

Melissa listened to Richard's account with sincere interest and compassion. She felt an immense surge of sympathy and even pride in the fact that the outwardly confident lawyer and professor was able to share his innermost secrets with her. She was touched by his insecurity and wisely surmised that it was probably one of the factors that had brought him under the care of Dr. Kayahs.

"It all reminds me of a black gospel song I've heard called 'Jesus Hits Like the Atom Bomb,'" she commented.

Having listened carefully to Richard's self-revelation, Melissa described her own childhood thoughts about The Big Ending. It turned out that she was one of what Richard considered "the lucky ones" who were taught to believe in the Rapture. She explained that her own childhood beliefs had made a lasting impression upon her as well. She said that even yet, should she find herself alone in an empty mall, public arena, or even a strange house, she would often feel an involuntary frisson of fear. She instinctively assumed that the Rapture had occurred, and she was "the one left behind," adding that others she knew, who were also raised on Rapture, reported similar experiences (which Richard had heard before).

Thus, seated upon the yellow Naugahyde love seat inside Mushroom Memories, Richard and Melissa began to see much more deeply beneath the masks that each wore in public.

He had hit the "mute" button on his remote, and one atomic explosion silently followed another and then another upon the giant screen.

Melissa leaned her head on Richard's shoulder and took his hand in hers. The couple nestled in comfortable silence as vast tracts of the Nevada desert caved inward and whole fleets of battleships bobbed like toy boats surrounding immense mushroom clouds at sea.

At length, Melissa said, "Richard. I wonder if we might go inside your house now. There's something I'd like for us to do."

"Certainly, Melissa," he replied, having no idea what she had in mind, but eager to please in any event. He shut off the TV and the lava lamps and locked the little museum of horrors behind them. Melissa tenderly took his hand and led the way.

They walked the few feet into the main house which, in its elegance, was a warm and pleasant change of venue. Richard closed the door, and suddenly Melissa was kissing him passionately, then arching and turning her neck to invite his kisses there. He was not slow to oblige. Then, taking his two hands in hers, she said, "Let's go to your bedroom, Professor Steick. I'd like to see it."

Smiling broadly, Richard led Miss Brandywine to his antique four-poster bed. He tripped and fell flat on his face while getting out of his underpants, thus eliciting from Melissa an enormous burst of friendly laughter.

After a few minor, technical adjustments, the countdown concluded with a multi-megaton detonation of immense significance for both of them.

The City That Smells Right

Mrs. Thistleton-Wills IV despised her own sense of smell and emphatically disapproved of it in others. Black or white, rich or poor, old money or new—it did not matter. The sense of smell was a shame and a disgrace. She particularly disapproved of its existence in foreign nations, such as Europe, because of all the filthy things those people kept in the streets. "Just think of it!" she thought. "Camel residue! Goat carcasses!"

Known by her friends in the Hallelujah Garden Club as "Helena," Mrs. Thistleton-Wills IV could not bear to imagine such odors, or any odors at all. She had hoped to have her own sense of smell surgically disconnected, but she could not find a physician in the entire Southeast who would perform the necessary operation. They all said it would be unethical, or some such nonsense, and urged her to see a psychiatrist, an idea which Helena naturally disdained. It was perfectly normal, she considered, for any reasonable person to detest odors in general, not to mention the nasty ones in particular. *All* odors were, to her mind, inherently offensive, and she could not imagine it otherwise.

There were, of course, a small number of acceptable fragrances, such as a few of the flowers of her garden club friends and possibly the ladies' section of a fine department store. But the exceptions only proved the rule, after all. Was it really worth it, she wondered, when one had to endure everything from food and wine to fresh rainwater and wood smoke, even when one was extremely cautious?

"By no means," she answered, taking great pride in the fact that she herself owned no cologne or *eau de toilette,* however expensive. In addition to being an unpleasant reminder of the existence of *foul* odors, allegedly "fine" colognes and aerosols of any kind aggravated her allergies terribly, and Helena was pleased to note that 100 percent of her friends in the DAW ("Daughters of All-American Wars") had precisely the same reaction. She loved her mansion, her carpets, her fine ceramic cats, her city, her state, and her nation. But she could happily do without Alabama's magnolia and gardenia flowers—even its Confederate jasmine!—and she would gladly say so to anyone, including Governor Sid Scroulous.

Her favorite flower, of course, was the camellia, the official Alabama state flower, which has no fragrance at all. Choosing the camellia, she thought, was one of the few truly wise decisions in the history of the Alabama legislature, in which so many of her ancestors had served. That and the decision to secede in 1860, naturally.

Mrs. Thistleton-Wills IV had a vested interest in detesting aromas of any kind. By virtue of inheritance, she was the majority shareholder of Alchemelia Corp., the world's only manufacturer of the highly prized product internationally known as "Methyl-Smellright."

Methyl-Smellright completely eliminated any and all odors, period. It was made possible entirely by an extremely rare, amber-colored mineral, discovered and appropriately named "smellenium" by Helena's maternal grandfather, Farthing Worthy. As far as geologists knew or endeavored to discover, smellenium was found in only one place on earth.

That place was a small island in the Alabama River just north of Montgomery, and that small island had been entirely owned and passed down to his beneficiaries by Helena's grandfather.

FARTHING WORTHY WAS a bit of a white George Washington Carver in the inventions department. Born into cotton money himself, he was a progressive, scientifically minded man who wanted nothing more than to do good for the public with Alabama's natural resources. Unlike Carver—who had to work—Worthy's inheritance left him with little to do except to pursue his passions and hobbies, which included the life cycle of the catfish and geology. Although he married, in accordance with the customs and conventions of his time, he did not particularly care for women, who were forever wearing oppressive powders and ointments which Farthing loathed.

One hot summer day in 1932, while checking his catfish traps near his island, Farthing sighted a bright, rock-like amber outcrop glistening in the sun, and he decided to investigate. Using a boat oar as a spade, he dug and dug. The deposit seemed endless! The amber substance resembled iron-hard rock candy, and it was not easy for Farthing to collect a specimen. Eventually, using an ordinary rock for a hammer and part of his boat anchor for a chisel, he managed to dislodge a chunk approximately four cubic inches in size.

Farthing took the glowing amber sample back to his laboratory in Hallelujah and tried to identify it. But his geology books revealed nothing quite like what he held in his hand. It was too hard to be amber and was impervious to chemicals that would typically dissolve pine resin. It was too opaque to be amber quartzite, and it lacked that mineral's prismatic, crystalline structure. And so he took it to the experts in the geology department at the University of Alabama in Tuscaloosa.

The learned professors were equally baffled. The substance seemed to be an anomaly, unidentifiable and previously unknown. And so Farthing Worthy, amateur fish scientist and geologist, took the shiny specimen back once again to his laboratory in Hallelujah to see what useful purpose it might be made to serve.

Years later, long after Farthing's death, spectrographic analysis confirmed that smellenium was indeed a substance unknown previously or elsewhere. Radio carbon dating was of little or no use. But the appearance of the mineral, its surface texture, and all other information available suggested that it might be the detritus of a large meteorite approximately 360 million years old, which put it at about the same age as the Wetumpka astrobleme.

The best hypothesis was that some wandering star stuff from the Earth's asteroid belt had slammed into the planet up at Bald Knob, spitting debris for hundreds of miles around. One peculiar glob of goo had evidently fallen to earth and congealed in the area later inundated by the Alabama River, and Farthing's island consisted almost entirely of an above-water remnant of that pre-historic collision.

Without the benefit of such advanced scientific speculation, however,

Farthing Worthy had, in 1933, commenced to determine what useful purposes the amber substance might serve.

It was too brittle to make ball bearings and too soft to cut stone. It did not prove a hospitable medium for any organic material. It seemed, in short, a rock, like alabaster, best employed when carved into decorative items.

But Farthing continued to tinker, until one day he made a serendipitous discovery. Like Charles Goodyear bumping into the vulcanization of rubber, Farthing accidentally dropped a small chunk of what he soon dubbed "smellenium" into an uncovered one-liter beaker of an acidic compound known only to himself.

The dice-sized piece of curious amber substance bubbled, hissed, sent up an angry thirty-second geyser of steam-like vapor, and then it was gone.

But "presto-chango!" as folks were saying in the 1930s. Farthing's usually smelly lab, which housed a large number of catfish carcasses (in various states of decay) as well as a plethora of odd-smelling chemicals and old books, immediately had *no odor at all! None!* Its aromas were the only thing Farthing did not like about his laboratory. Thus, he was delighted to discover that the large room and its closets remained completely neutral to the olfactory sense for days and days afterward!

Farthing's heart leapt when he grasped the significance of his achievement. "What a blessing to the world I have discovered!" he thought. "A chemical vapor that neutralizes odors!"

He tried it on dozens of offensive smells, and it never failed. Cigar smoke was nothing to smellenium! An outhouse in high summer? Not a problem!

Farthing Worthy died suddenly in 1935 when he inadvertently inhaled potassium cyanide while performing an unusual experiment. But this was not before he had enlisted his lawyers to patent his process for producing Methyl-Smellright and to double- and triple-check his land title to the little island in the Alabama River.

Thus, Farthing Worthy discovered smellenium, created Methyl-Smellright, locked in a perpetual monopoly on the product, and then died.

Several decades later, Farthing's only son, Fairley Worthy, was rummaging through his father's derelict laboratory, cleaning things up in preparation to sell the property. He encountered a tightly locked cabinet with no key in sight. This naturally made him curious. With a gesture reminiscent of his father's, when prizing loose the first known specimen of smellenium, Fairley grabbed a nearby rock pick and made short work of the locked drawer.

He was amazed at what he discovered inside. Neatly laid out and arranged in meticulous order were a large sample of the mysterious mineral, the chemical formula for producing Methyl-Smellright, patent documents, and the carefully scrutinized deed to the small island in the Alabama River. There was also a narrative description of his father's discovery, a list of its useful purposes, and suggestions for commercial applications of the product.

Fairley Worthy was not a scientist like his father, but he knew a good thing when he saw one. He had devoted his life to preserving and expanding the vast financial empire of his family. He recognized that he lacked the technical and marketing expertise necessary to exploit Methyl-Smellright to its fullest potential. But he also knew there were plenty of corporations that would be more than happy to do so.

Fairley locked his father's crumbling laboratory, drove to his home office, and immediately began contacting his army of lawyers, investment bankers, and business community leaders.

There followed one and one-half years of intensive fact finding, marketing research, production analysis, financial and legal negotiations, and all of the heavy paperwork that goes into the formation of a new industry. At the end of this time, with banner headline announcements all over Alabama, plans emerged for a major new manufacturing business in Montgomery. It was to be called "Alchemelia Corporation," a wholly owned subsidiary of Conglomo, Inc., a multi-national chemical manufacturing concern headquartered in New York City.

Alchemelia Corp. was hailed as a great achievement for Alabama in general and the City of Montgomery in particular. Hundreds of new jobs would be created! The economic spin-offs would be tremendous!

Enhanced tax revenues would allow the state to finally do something to improve its abysmal education system.

One year later, dignitaries from throughout Alabama, as well as other states, New York City, Washington, D.C., and several foreign nations assembled at the ribbon-cutting ceremony for the new Alchemelia plant on the banks of the Alabama River near downtown Montgomery. The fanfare and the instant success of Methyl-Smellright heralded an unprecedented surge in the value of Conglomo Corp. stock. Methyl-Smellright was an immediate hit worldwide. Wherever there was an unpleasant or undesirable odor, Methyl-Smellright was there to snuff it out. Tourism promoters in the seamier sections of Tangier, Calcutta, and Rio discreetly sprayed it in the streets, improving their revenues by 20 percent in the first six months.

And, as an added bonus, Montgomery quickly became the most fragrance-free city on earth, due to the constant, unavoidable leakage of the precious gas into the ambient air of the streets and highways for miles around. To the relief of all Montgomerians, the recurrent, odious doses of noxious odor released from the Union Camp paper plant in nearby Prattville disappeared forever!

Thus did the State Capital of Alabama, which was ground zero for so much important Civil War and Civil Rights history in America, adopt a new motto, to the general approval of all: "Montgomery. The City That Smells Right. And Is!"

Tourists from throughout the United States flocked in to enjoy the pure, unscented air. Allergy sufferers claimed instant cures, and health spas popped up like mushrooms overnight. Suddenly, every city and town in America wanted to be just like Montgomery. Even Des Moines!

In short, no one wanted to smell anything at all.

Up Above My Head

Richard Steick and Melissa Brandywine were deeply in love, but they were exceedingly cautious as well. Each had endured the difficulties of divorce, and neither had any intention of repeating the experience. They found their love a growing thing, unprecedented in its intensity, and they desired above all to keep it that way. Each understood that the other had achieved a hard-won independent personality and unique individual habits. Each exercised restraint before treading into the other's private domain. Thus, they did not rush headlong into marital arrangements, as others might have done. Rather, they proceeded deliberately, one step at a time, with mutual respect and abundant conversation, companionship, and good humor.

None of their mature thoughtfulness prevented them, however, from discreetly sleeping over at least one night each week. Richard was Vesuvian in his verbal eruptions at peak moments of passion, and after the Hallelujah police once arrived at Melissa's house to see if anything was amiss, the couple determined it was best to hold their pajama parties at Richard's more-secluded dwelling.

He found that his life had improved dramatically by any standards or measures. He was a better teacher than ever, overflowing with enthusiasm and insight in his seminars. His law practice grew in volume and quality with less effort on his part. When he focused upon a case, no distractions intruded. And his friends at the courthouse also noticed the difference. No longer was he the puzzling eccentric of recent years. Rather, he was once again the acute analyst and advocate so much admired earlier in his career. He again felt himself the brilliant gladiator of his youth, strengthened now by experience. It was as if he had entered a second adulthood in which he actually knew, for the first time, what he was doing and why.

With the exception of having produced two lovely daughters, he now
viewed the fruits of his first adulthood with dismay. In spite of his many
early achievements, the first adulthood seemed a series of necessary and
inevitable blunders strung together with little connection to each other
or to anything especially enduring and significant.

ONE CLEMENT AFTERNOON, attorney Steick made an amazing discovery.
He was deeply buried in land title records in the Montgomery County
Probate Office. He had been employed by a real estate developer to
examine and assure the legal ownership of a tract of land overlooking
the Alabama River near Montgomery. The developer was on the verge
of closing a deal for the purchase of some seven hundred acres which
he planned to transform into an exclusive, gated, and well manicured
suburb with stunning vistas of the river.

The land and the developer's concept were worth a good deal of money.
But the seven hundred acres required for the project were owned by more
than forty different individuals, families, and land holding companies.
The title work was tedious and time consuming, but it paid well, and
Steick derived a certain satisfaction in perusing the microfilm as well as
the ancient and dusty bound volumes of the various records involved.

The chain of title for one important pie-shaped tract was extremely
confusing, however. The apex of the wedge encompassed a small island
in the river known as "Farthing Worthy's Island," the world's only known
source of smellenium. It seemed clear that the ownership of the island
was securely possessed by the Alchemelia Corporation.

And yet, something was wrong. In running backward through the
grantor and grantee indexes, it appeared that the island had somehow,
at some time, become detached from the remainder of the tract.

The result was a legal impossibility. As Richard clearly remembered
from law school, "Seisin can never be *in nubibus,*" meaning that the
ownership of land can never be "in the clouds," attached to no one.
Real estate cannot float up into the air. There always must be an owner
somewhere. And yet, there was a clear gap in the title to Farthing Worthy's
Island which, try as he might, the lawyer could not reconcile with all of

the available microfilm, title indexes, plat books, and surveys. If nothing else, it was an intriguing puzzle which piqued Steick's natural curiosity.

He had carefully traced backward to the bound volume of the grantor's index for the year 1865. One page, recording a sale of the island from the City of Montgomery, felt uncommonly thick. Richard put his thumb and index fingers together, ran them along the margins, and felt definite irregularities in the paper. Oddly, the back of that page was blank and of a different color and texture than its other side. When he inspected more closely, it seemed that two pages, nearly identical in size and shape, had become stuck together. In fact, they were stuck together so carefully, and aligned so well, that it appeared they might have been intentionally glued.

Richard always kept his fingernails well groomed, but he found he had enough nail on his thumb and index fingers to begin prying the pages apart. And once he had carefully begun the process, there was little difficulty, since the glue (if it was glue) was old, dry, and only slightly adhesive. In a moment, he had separated the pages without damage to either of them. The new page he discovered had not been sewn into the volume. It bore a slight sheen of some ancient adhesive upon its face, but this did not in any way interfere with its clear, unstained legibility.

The detached page was a historical document of immense value as well as a startling revelation. It was an indenture signed and sealed in ink by the Mayor of Montgomery as well as General A. J. Smith, Commander of the occupying Union army, and Andrew Johnson, President of the United States.

Steick furrowed his brow and studied the document with his greatest possible care. The folio-sized page allowed room for many recitals. At length, he concluded he had discovered the deed to end all deeds to Farthing Worthy's Island. The uncovered page was an absolutely bulletproof conveyance transferring permanent ownership of the island, its mineral rights, and all profits, uses, and benefits of ownership to a group of black firemen (and their heirs) who had heroically saved Montgomery from self-destruction at the conclusion of the Civil War. The document declared that the grant was a token of the City's appreciation to "the valiant Negro volunteer firemen" for their brave efforts in extinguishing a blaze that threatened to burn the city to the ground.

Steick vaguely recalled this event from Alabama history class in grade school and thought he had read about it since in *Alabama Heritage* magazine or some similar publication. As he remembered, in the very last days of the war, the Yankees were advancing eastward from Selma, having defeated the Confederate army and destroyed the iron works there. The citizens of Montgomery, sensing inevitable defeat and occupation, did not want valuable assets falling into the hands of the invaders. Thus, at 5:00 P.M. on April 11, 1865, they instituted a well-intended but ill-conceived strategy. They removed all the baled cotton from under the protective roofs of the huge wooden warehouses on the western edge of the city, placed it in the open air centers of the warehouses, and set it ablaze, somehow failing to consider the prevailing westerly winds. A strong wind whipped up at just the wrong moment, blowing the flames into the wooden warehouses and nearby frame structures, and the result was a near conflagration. It was as if someone had torched a medieval village, with the fire hopping rapidly from one wooden building to the next. Had it not been contained, the fire would have been awkward and embarrassing, to say the least. The city would have burnt itself to the ground, thus performing a little part-time job on behalf of the notoriously wicked Union General Sherman, who had not considered burning Montgomery worth his time.

What also made the deed Steick had found so interesting was that those who wrote it had sincerely intended it to be insurmountable by any subsequent legal maneuvering. All possible reversions and rights of reverter, as well as the Rule Against Perpetuities, the Rule in Shelley's Case, adverse possession, and sundry antique land laws, were declared to be forever null and void on the island. The effect was the same as an original patent or territorial grant from the United States. It was practically as if Farthing Worthy's Island had been made a state itself, or, at minimum, something like an Indian reservation. The document permitted the subsequent sale of the island, but only at fair market value, and only in cash in hand paid to the gallant Negro firemen or their heirs. And, as a final benefit, the island would be forever immune from tax assessment or levy of any sort by any governmental entity.

The lawyer was astounded by what he had discovered. If the document was indeed authentic, it would shake up Alchemelia Corporation, the City of Montgomery, and the entire State of Alabama more than a little. Alchemelia would lose all or a substantial portion of its tremendous profits from the island, past, present, and future. The city and state would have to cough up millions, or perhaps even billions of dollars in previously collected taxes. Even the United States government would be required to make restitution. The black beneficiaries would number many thousands and would be scattered to the four corners of the earth. The massive effort of tracking them down, and the monumental legal processes involved, staggered the imagination. It would be an enormous task, vigorously contested in the courts, but highly lucrative to the beneficiaries and the hundreds or thousands of lawyers employed on all sides.

Then Richard Steick had an epiphany. It was as if the author of Deuteronomy had personally whispered the book's famous phrase in his ear. "Justice! Justice shalt thou pursue!" Immediately, the lawyer knew that he had his next few years cut out for him. He would pursue justice valiantly! Just as the heroic black firemen had done their job a century and a half before, he would do his job now! And not only would he pursue the justice decreed by the document before him. He would also use what he alone knew, combined with his intellectual acumen, native cleverness, and network of influential friends, for the betterment of the entire State of Alabama and all its citizens!

The state was of course hip deep in a quagmire of fiscal, environmental, health, education, welfare, and public policy dilemmas. In other words, it was business as usual, and soundly covered by the universal Alabama chorus of "It's all just politics," as if politics were nothing more than the third cousin, twice removed, of the Auburn-Alabama football game. Steick had been blessed with a magnificent sonar system that kept him keenly attuned to current events around the state and in the legislature, even when he didn't have his ear pinned to the earth. Like a diviner, he knew what was moving and shaking underground, who was doing it,

and why. Recent notes in the newspaper, courthouse gossip, and matters
he heard discussed at Dard & Elle's Hellespont Cafe (which had never
changed its name), had alerted him to the fact that things were even
worse than usual for the state. For one thing, he knew that the demonic
scheme of the state idiot, Hoop DeMinus, to grant a license for a toxic
waste storage facility in Coffee County, was moving forward.

Steick immediately concocted a plan to squash that project in its
infancy by use of the ancient deed he held in his hand. Indeed, there
seemed to him no end to the good he could do for the state with the
unusual document he had uncovered. It was even conceivable that he,
Richard Steick, might achieve the impossible, not only by bringing the
races together, but also by saving Alabama from itself through other
means that would unfold in time.

Steick reflected upon his conversations with Dr. Kayahs about significant work, and he knew immediately that some invisible, synchronistic,
spiritual force had just handed him his life's calling, his authentic *vocatus,*
on a platter. Thus, in addition to his enormously deep love for Melissa, he
now had a job of immense public and historical significance to perform.
He had never felt more alive. He had never enjoyed such a resounding
sense of action, purpose, and meaning. He had never felt less like a dildo.
In short, he knew he had a great new lid, and the fit was terrific!

Eager to begin his high calling, Steick thought for a moment about
the crime of tampering with public documents and then carefully slipped
the detached, ancient deed into a file folder in his briefcase. It might not
be a public document after all. It might just be an accident, an error, or
some long deceased person's idea of a joke. Then he prepared a preliminary "To Do" list. First, he would place the incredible document in the
fireproof safe at his office. Second, he would check the old Montgomery
newspapers, and anything else he could find, for accounts of the nearly
disastrous fire, the heroic black firemen who had saved the city, and any
mention of a reward or remuneration made to them. Next would come
the minutes of the city and county council meetings from the date of
the fire until after the date on the deed. Then, he would have to locate
at least one documented heir of one of the original firemen-grantees.

Finally, he would fly to Washington, D.C., to confirm the validity of the grant in the land patents records. He would also have to employ a well-qualified handwriting expert to examine and confirm the authenticity of all the signatures.

Steick knew that the law does not permit assertion of third-party rights, and thus finding a bona fide heir was essential to using what he had discovered for the good of the state. With a documented heir, he could get into court. Without one, he could not. It was as simple as that. He also knew that the birth and death records of freedmen were a chaotic nightmare with colossal errors and omissions. Thus, he concluded that locating a legitimate, provable heir to one of the firemen named on the deed would be his most daunting and time-consuming task.

Out of curiosity, and in anticipation of the job before him, he removed the deed from his briefcase. Earlier, he had noticed a list of names of the original grantees on the document. But he had been so overwhelmed by its contents at the time that he hadn't troubled to scan the list. He had no illusions that doing so now would advance his work in the slightest, but he would have to do it sometime, and probably hundreds of times. Thus, a quick look-see was the natural thing to do.

There were some two dozen names, alphabetized. Steick spent several seconds examining each one. Midway through the list, near the top of the second column, he read: *Ninety Ton McWilliams.*

He suddenly felt like a living geyser, or a plastic ketchup dispenser squeezed violently. It was as if all the blood in his feet and legs went coursing upward into his abdomen and chest, squeezed through his neck, and blasted out the top of his head. At the same time, he felt as if he had entered an express elevator in a skyscraper. The cabin was slowing down at the ninety-first floor, but his stomach was still on the first floor. The room began to swirl about him. He loosened his tie to breathe. He paced the floor. It took him twenty minutes to stop shaking.

This was no mere coincidence, any more than discovering the deed was a coincidence. It was proof positive that the Almighty Himself had personally appointed Richard Steick, PhD, Esq., a Highly Important Man With A Mission.

WITH MALICE TOWARD NONE

Every time Alabama State Representative Ernest Grones tried to paint the snowman black, it melted. He had already destroyed three and was running out of snow and spray paint.

Grones was himself black and one of the most powerful members of the State Legislature. He was a short, handsome, cherubic man cursing gently through clenched teeth each time a snowman fell into a puddle at his feet. He was worried that the snow and the paint might damage his expensive Brooks Brothers suit.

He was tenaciously dedicated to the interests of his black constituency, and he was determined that there should be a black snowman beside the white snowman that a playful black child had lumped and rolled together on Goat Hill, the site of Alabama's stunning, white, antebellum capitol building.

On this rare occasion of a late winter snow storm in Montgomery, four inches of wonderfully moist, packable snow had accumulated, and the city had never looked lovelier. A blissful, picturesque tranquility pervaded the atmosphere. The white snow contrasted beautifully with the waxy green leaves of the magnolias, holly, evergreen shrubbery, and southern pines. Every building and office, public or private, was closed, and there were no cars on the streets. The only things moving were the dozens of ecstatic children sledding down the hill, an occasional emergency management vehicle, and Representative Grones.

On this exceptional day, Grones was out to make a statement: "Everything in Alabama must be racially balanced, equal, and neutral." His snowman would play well, he thought, on the evening news.

He was loved by many and hated by many. A source of genial amusement to most, he was admired by friend and foe alike for his unwavering dedication to the various causes of his voters and to destroying all remnants and reminders of racial segregation in Alabama.

Grones was a pit bull, a banty rooster, the gadfly of Montgomery. And he had been remarkably successful in his life's calling. The Confederate flag had come down from the capitol dome because of his intense efforts, and most Alabamians, black and white alike, murmured a sigh of relief. More recently, he had succeeded in having the First White House of the Confederacy re-named "The Pre-Reconstruction White House." His ultimate dream was to have all official state references to "the Confederate States" or "the Confederacy" replaced by "the slave states," or words to that effect. But, as a consummate politician and practical man, he knew that such a thing would never happen in his lifetime, and so he took his victories where he could. His current cause was a fervent attempt to have all slave-era manuscripts and artifacts in the state archives assembled into what he proposed naming "The Museum of Slavery."

More pressing at the moment, however, was his black snowman project, and he wondered if food coloring might work. It worked on Sno-Cones, didn't it?

At this instant of revelation, Grones's cell phone warbled, as it so often did. He sometimes regretted that he could never get any peace, even on such a placid day as this one. Grones, who was a professor of political science at Oppenheimer State as well as a legislator, thought of himself as the contemporary Adlai Stevenson of Alabama. Everyone knew him. Everyone sought his power, influence, and advice. Everyone wanted his time.

But such, he reasoned, was the price one had to pay for greatness, and so he took off his gloves, reached into his silk-lined suit pocket, fetched out his cell phone, punched the tiny "Talk" button, and answered "Grones!" as he always did.

The caller responded, "Hey, hey, hey! Ernst ol' buddy! How ya doin' partner? This is Hoop! Hoop DeMinus over at Solid Waste."

"Yeah," Grones replied, "I recognize your voice Hoopy. What you doin' today? Sleepin', I reckon, same as every other day, ain'tcha."

"Aw come on, Ern," Hoop demurred. "You know how hard I work

over there runnin' that agency. Poor, underpaid public servant is what I am, and you know it. Not some high-roller like you. Just a sorry white man. Ain't this snow somethin'? Bet they got their hands full over at Emergency Management. So what you doin' with your sad ol' hide today, anyway?"

"Look, DeMinus. I'm not like you. I can't lay up all day drinkin' Jack Daniels just 'cause of a little snow. I got important work to do all the time, so get to the point. What do you want?"

Little Hoop paused briefly before replying. "Well, ain't nobody workin' today except you and me, Ern. You know that. I got my laptop right here in my bed. Reports, budgets, long-range planning, all that kinda shit you know."

"Yeah, I know you're in the shit business. So what kinda bullshit you up to now? I ain't got all day, so get to the point."

DeMinus cleared his throat and said, "Well look, Ern, just between you and me, I got this little development concept for folks down in Coffee County, you know, that's gonna' bring in jobs and money for everybody in Alabama. Do somethin' for our education system at last, and I know how important that is to you, and I need your help in the legislature. Oversight and all that. Like to set up a meeting with you, tell you all about it. Maybe take you to lunch at the Sinai. Whaddaya say?"

"Well, Hoopy, everybody's always wantin' to take Grones to the Sinai, but the food's good, and I knew your daddy, and you seem to be all right most of the time. So when do you want to make this thing, anyway?" the statesman responded.

DeMinus sang out, "Good deal, Ern! Hey! Great! Wonderful! But look, we gotta' ride out this storm, now, don't we? What say Thursday about noon? Streets should be clear by then, power back on, everything back to normal. Weather Channel says it'll be in the mid-sixties. Thursday work for you?"

"Just a minute," Grones responded. "I've got to check my appointment calendar."

The busy legislator again reached into his silk-lined jacket pocket, this time retrieving his buttery leather appointment book. "Yeah," he said.

"Thursday at noon will work, so let me write that down."

"Faaantastic, Ern ol' buddy! Where you gonna' be so I can pick you up?"

"I'll be in my legislative office in Montgomery," Grones responded. "I got committee hearings that afternoon, so you just make sure your ass is on time. I always like a white chauffeur, but he has to do his job, and that means bein' on time. So you be there at noon, okay?"

"Gotcha, partner! That's terrific! I'll be early, man! Be good to see you again. Catch up on you and your family, you know. You take care now, Ern."

"Okay, Hoops. You come on by, and I'll see you then," Grones responded, and clicked off his cell phone.

He placed the phone and his appointment book back into his pocket, put on his gloves, and once again resolved to create a black snowman. There was the possibility of food coloring. Then, he thought, there is also a craft shop in town that sells huge balls and bales of polystyrene in various colors. Maybe he could fake it up with black polystyrene balls, if they had any. Or maybe white polystyrene would take black paint better than the snow did. He wasn't sure.

And so the distracted and preoccupied Grones decided to try both options, forgetting that all the stores in Montgomery were closed. He headed first for a craft shop on the Eastern Boulevard, engaging the four-wheel drive on his immaculate black SUV and driving carefully over the lightly dusted streets. He knew all about snow and how to handle it. But, he reasoned (as every sensible person in Montgomery does) that "You can't be too careful in snow because we're not used to it."

Grones received three calls on his cell as he glided cautiously down I-85 toward the Boulevard, accompanied only by semi-trailers. When he drove within sight of the craft shop, he readily recognized that it was closed like everything else. So he pulled into the parking lot, put the SUV in neutral, and pondered where he might find a grocery store that was open so he could buy some food coloring.

The day was growing shorter. Grones had six more calls in a row on his cell phone as he sat in the parking lot. By the time he had finished with the last of them, it was quite dark. The statesman was tired and hungry, and so he decided to delay his snowman project until the next morning.

At which time, of course, all of the snow had melted, including the white snowman, and Representative Grones's project was moot.

AND CHARITY TOWARD ALL

By 11:00 A.M. the following Thursday, the air in Montgomery had turned balmy and Mediterranean. It was shirt-sleeve weather. The Japanese magnolias had noticed the change in a hurry, blossoming overnight and adorning the city with delicate pink and white blossoms.

Representative Grones sat with his head in his hands in his legislative office. He was attempting to draft a race-neutral nomenclature bill for submission to the Alabama House in time for preliminary hearings that afternoon, and the precise wording eluded him. He felt sympathy for his students, who often told him they "knew what they wanted to say but didn't know how to say it." Grones always told them their complaint indicated they really didn't know what they wanted to say at all and that they needed to re-think their essays. Now he found himself in the same situation, as sometimes happened. All he had been able to achieve that morning was a proposed statute, which he phrased and re-phrased on a yellow legal pad, trying to be accurate:

> Hereafter, no person in Alabama shall be white, black, or other. Period.

> or:

> Hereafter, no person in the *Code of Alabama* (1975) shall be white, black, or other.

or:

Hereafter, all persons in Alabama shall be others, and all references
to such others in the *Code of Alabama* (1975) shall be deemed as others,
regardless of race, creed, color, or national origin.

He found his first and second efforts concise but lacking in clarity,
while the third was limp as a sock and longer than he wanted. He knew
he could send the matter to the Legislative Reference Service, although
that would take forever. Grones pondered his dilemma and considered
he might have better luck if he had his Opp U. teaching colleague,
Richard Steick, try to draft something appropriate. "The guy's a lawyer,
and he's sympathetic about these issues. They say he's good at this kind
of work," Grones was thinking, when he felt himself growing hungry,
and his appointment calendar came into view.

He knew he was having lunch with someone because he always had
lunch with someone. But he didn't know who it was going to be on this
beautiful day, and so he opened his leather schedule planner.

"Oh. It's that dumb peckerwood DeMinus," Grones thought, catching the entry quickly. He pondered what kind of nonsense this Hoop
fellow might have in mind, consoling himself with the fact that at least
the food would be good. DeMinus was just another agency director to
Grones, of course, and he would get no special treatment. But at least
he knew how to pick his restaurants, and that was always a good thing
to Representative Grones.

IT WAS FIVE MINUTES before noon when the receptionist announced
on the intercom that Mr. DeMinus had arrived. "Tell him I'll be right
there," Grones said as he drew on his jacket, still wondering what kind
of present his host wanted from the legislature.

He opened the heavy, brass-fitted mahogany door, stepped into the
nicely carpeted hallway, and walked toward the reception area. Settling his
jacket neatly onto his shoulders, he walked briskly past the receptionist's

desk. The blonde woman was busy summoning other members of the legislature to luncheon appointments and did not have time to stop and look up.

In contrast, Little Hoop didn't just look up. He shot up from his comfortable wing-back chair like a tall jack-in-the-box with white barn doors for teeth.

"Ernie, ol' buddy! How ya doin', man?" DeMinus almost shouted as he thrust his substantial paw halfway across the room toward the shorter Grones. Hoop thought he might try a little black hand jive, but reconsidered just in time.

"Ernest to you, DeMinus," the statesman replied, accepting the metal-crushing grip of his host. "Unless you want to call me 'Representative Grones.' Maybe that's what I ought to have you call me anyway. Teach you a little respect. Where you parked?"

DeMinus replied, "Out there on the street, partner. Where you expect me to park? In the lot? I didn't want to make you walk."

The pair moved swiftly toward the large main door of the legislative office building. Grones, slightly galled, inquired, "What do you mean 'out on the street?' You know that's all 'No Parking' out there! You white guys get away with anything you want to, don't you? I park out there and the city gives me a ticket. And me a duly elected leader of this House, too! Just proves there ain't no equal protection of the law in this state, you know."

"Aw, c'mon, Ern," DeMinus replied, slapping the representative on the back so hard that Grones almost choked. "You know this is Montgomery, son! We don't fuss about little technicalities around here, now do we? You just throw them tickets into the trash where they belong, like I do. Now c'mon. Let's go."

They had reached Little Hoop's sparkling Infiniti, and the director considered opening the passenger door for his guest but declined on the basis of manly etiquette and his instincts of male camaraderie. He tapped the rubber switch on his remote, and his Infiniti's door locks shot upward with a satisfying "thunk." Best allow Grones to let himself inside, DeMinus concluded.

Settling into the leather-lined vehicle was an act the representative accomplished with youthful grace. DeMinus threw his own long foreleg into the cockpit, pulled his left leg briskly behind it, and buckled-up with one hand while starting the engine with the other. He was pleased to note he had not received a parking ticket. That few dollars he spent each year for a vanity license tag ("Hoop-D") was more than worth the money.

DeMinus eased the vehicle onto Washington Street and grinned, "Hey Ern! Look at this! I got me a talkin' car! You want some music? Tell me what kind."

"Ain't no such thing as a talkin' car, DeMinus, and I don't want no damn music. You crazy or somethin'?"

"Sure there is, Ern! Just watch this! You want some sooooooul music? Well, here it comes!" DeMinus said, using his thumb to punch a button on his steering wheel. Then he glanced at his instrument panel and slowly but crisply uttered, "Play sooooooul track nine," whereupon Aretha Franklin shouted "R-E-S-P-E-C-T!" so loudly that the unprepared Grones almost jumped out of his seat belt.

"FIND OUT WHAT IT MEANS TO ME!" Aretha continued, while the statesman shouted, "Damn you, DeMinus! Turn that thing down! What the hell's the matter with you anyway?"

Hoop, sensing a blunder, popped the thumb button on his steering wheel once again, and Aretha went silent immediately. "Sorry Ern, ol' buddy! Just wanted you to see my talkin' car is all. Simmer down. Simmer down. We'll just ride and talk."

Grones smoothed back his neatly groomed hair and peered at the dashboard. "What kinda car is this anyway, DeMinus? I never saw no CD player like that before. I might want to get me one."

The pair chatted amiably about vehicles, the weather, the NBA, and their respective families during the ten-minute drive to the Sinai Restaurant near the south side of old Montgomery. The lunch crowd formed a substantial line trailing out of the front door of the restaurant, just as it did every day except national and state holidays. It was correctly known as one of the finest restaurants in the Southeast and a favorite of local politicians, bureaucrats, lawmakers, judges, journalists, wannabes of all sorts, the elderly, and the wealthy.

DeMinus swung gracefully across the street and into a parking lot behind the restaurant. The well-dressed duo unbuckled, hopped out of the vehicle, and made their way straight toward a nondescript back door which the genial Hoop opened with the skill of a hotel doorman, nodding his guest inside and into the distinguished eatery.

In an instant, there were greetings all around. Each of the many waiters was black and impeccably dressed in shiny black shoes, black tuxedo trousers, white shirt, black bow tie, and red bellman's jacket. They all knew both DeMinus and Grones and grinned, nodded, or waved and said "Hello." The white owner and *maitre de hôte* smiled also, clasping first the representative's hand and then the director's, and asked them where they wished to sit. The hungry public servants shook their heads side-to-side, indicating that it really didn't matter, and Grones said the first available would be fine. The owner said their place would be ready in just a couple of minutes, and in less time than that, a familiar waiter named Lewis was showing the impressive arrivals to their booth.

The decor of the Sinai was not elegant, nor was it by any means shabby. The booths were commodious, with benches and seat backs of nicely tufted black leather. The tables were also black and covered with thick beveled glass. There was window lighting but little direct lighting. Each booth had an art deco table lamp with a dimmer switch. There was a nod toward a Sinai Desert theme here and there. Plaster camels were ensconced in niches, and the ceiling had Arabesque tracery. Mainly, the atmosphere was an inspired mixture of hominess, money, power, and Alabama politics. Former Alabama Governors and political wheels peered down upon guests from framed photos that were hung above each booth. With nice irony, DeMinus and Grones sat beneath a portrait of Little Hoop's daddy, Big Hoop, political wizard for Governor Big Jim Folsom, but neither of the arrivals bothered to notice or comment. It was all in a day's work that they should be sitting where they did, as each had done so many times before.

The chatter of those in line, occasionally greeting their friends who were leaving the restaurant, created a pleasant murmur. The bartender was shaking ice and putting on a good show for the early starters. There was a larger room with tables and more murmuring through a pointed archway next to the booths. The trial lawyers and the garden club were meeting in separate, private rooms at the back.

Lewis handed each of the hungry gentlemen a menu, described the specials of the day, and asked if they would care for anything to drink. Both replied that they would like sweet tea. The waiter said he would be right back with their drinks and glided gracefully out of sight.

Grones and DeMinus studied the menu. "What are you havin', Ern?" Little Hoop asked.

"Four vegetable plate, probably," Grones responded. "Doctor said I got to watch my cholesterol. How 'bout you?"

"Reckon I'll have the mahi-mahi," the director said, adding (as everyone did) that the Sinai fish was always excellent.

The pair laid their menus aside. It was a visual cue that the joking and stroking phase of their meeting was over.

Grones forthrightly addressed the true purpose of his pleasant lunch with the agency director.

"Okay, DeMinus. What do you want, anyway? Representative Grones is listening."

"Well, Ern, I don't want nothin' except what's good for all the people of the State of Alabama. You know that. That's all I've ever wanted, same as you. Just like my poor ol' daddy lookin' down at us here. You know what I mean."

"Yeah, yeah, DeMinus, I know what you mean. Now get down to business. What do you want?"

"Well, Ern, you know Coffee County, right?"

"'Course I know Coffee County. You think I'm stupid or something? What about Coffee County?"

"The thing about Coffee County, you know Ern, is 'what have they got down there, anyway?'"

"What do you mean, 'What have they got down there?' DeMinus, you know as well as me what they got. People, land, peanuts, roads, schools. Cotton bug on a pole in Enterprise. They got lots of things down there."

DeMinus grew animated. "They ain't got a damn thing, Ern, and you know it as well as I do. No schools worth a durn. Portable classrooms everywhere. Little black and white kids can't get books. Unemployment about 15 percent. No industry. Grow some peanuts and cotton and look at that boll weevil monument like you said. Sit around and wait for Elba to get flooded again. They ain't got nothin' but empty space. But space these days can be valuable, Ern, and we can turn it into an asset for Coffee County and the people of Alabama. You and I can, if you'll help me."

"Now how we gonna do that, DeMinus? You want to sell dirt or something? You want to sell the air out of Coffee County or what?"

DeMinus leaned closer across the table.

"I mean STORAGE space, Ern ol' buddy! Storage space for hot tox! Every state in the country is going to be fightin' for it before long, and Alabama needs to be the firstest with the mostest, just like old General Forrest said. Hot tox is the future, Ern, and we need to be leading the way!"

Grones was confused. "What the hell you talkin' about 'hot tox,' DeMinus? Why don't you try speakin' English?"

"I'm talkin' about hot toxic waste, Ern. The whole United States needs space for it. I mean chemical irreducibles of nerve gas, pesticides, petro solvents, PCBs, maybe even a little plutonium. I'm not sure yet."

Grones was stunned speechless. He was paralyzed. He stared at De-Minus as if he were a robed and hooded Klansman just elected president of the NAACP.

Recovering slightly, he glanced first downward to his left and then downward to his right. He raised his eyes toward the taller DeMinus, who was grinning broadly and bobbing his knee. Grones first mumbled, "My God," followed by, "You really are one crazy cracker dumbass, aren't you, DeMinus? What in the hell has got into your mind, anyway? You mean you got some stupid notion you want to store deadly chemicals down in Coffee County? I think you might be as crazy as you seem to be. Haven't you ever heard of Emelle over in Dallas County? Aren't you supposed to be in charge of doin' something about that? Don't you know that Alabama is already the toxic waste pay toilet of America? It's a national scandal already! Now you're tellin' me you want to do more of the same, or worse, down in Coffee County? You must be jokin', man. You bring me out here to eat so you can tell some kinda stupid joke, or what?"

DeMinus just kept grinning and bobbing his knee. "Oh no, Ern. This ain't no joke, and it ain't nothin' like Emelle, either. This stuff is clean and safe! All boxed up in ten-inch-thick lead coffins. Can't leak. Can't cause nobody no problems. Just gotta have a safe storage facility, that's all. Put lots of barbed wire around it. Hire some armed guards. No civilians allowed, you know. Maybe jazz it up a little bit on down the road. Have a theme park, day care center, something for the family to enjoy. That sort of thing. And listen at this. State gets ten mil per metric yard, plus a nice annual maintenance fee! Now that's good money, Ern! And Alabama needs the money! Everybody knows that. Just think about it. Think about all we could do for our schools with that much money! Get the right facility, and we could store at least a thousand yards. That's ten billion dollars, Ern. Now THAT would be good for Alabama and good for your voters! They'd love you for it! We could have a good school on every crossroad in the state. You gotta believe in this, Ern. You just gotta!"

"I'll tell you what I believe, Mr. Solid Waste. I believe you want to poison every black person in south Alabama. That's what I believe, and that's the only way I can make any sense outta what you're tryin' to tell me here. C'mon. Let's get the check and leave before I call the looney catchers to come and get you. I ain't got time for this kinda bullshit."

At that moment Lewis, the waiter, ceremoniously appeared beside the booth and announced, "I have your orders, gentlemen," causing Grones to call a truce and allowing him and DeMinus to pull back slightly from the table before them. The waiter gracefully deposited two large, steaming platters of Sinai delicacies before the powerful public servants. Saying, "Enjoy your meals, gentlemen," Lewis took a step backward and turned away from the booth. Grones and DeMinus did not pause to look up, but gave their linen napkins a snap, placed them upon their laps, and tucked into their lunch with vigor.

The delicious Sinai cuisine had an immediate calming effect. Neither Grones nor DeMinus said anything for several long moments. At length, DeMinus swallowed, took a long drink of sweet tea, smoothed his mouth with his napkin, and leaned back in the booth.

"See what I mean, Ern?" he asked.

"I see you're one crazy peckerwood mother. That's what I see, DeMinus. How much are these waste companies payin' you to put this deal together, anyway? How much you takin' off the top? I oughta report you to the Ethics Commission, is what I oughta do. I think I will, in fact. How'd you like that, Bozo?"

"Now don't come at me that way, Ern," DeMinus replied, offended. "I ain't done a thing wrong, and I don't intend to neither. What I'm doin', I'm doin' for the good of the State of Alabama. Period. Ethics can look it over all they want to, far as I'm concerned. We're just in the plannin' stages anyway. We're not even close to any contracts, naturally. I just want your help gettin' approval from Oversight and all that crap when and if we can come up with a deal. Whadda ya say, partner?"

"Number one, I say again that you're crazy. Number two, I say you're probably not crazy. Just a crook on the make like most of y'all lifetime bureaucrats. Number three, Representative Grones don't want no part of it. It's political suicide. Now let's eat. I got serious work to do."

DeMinus could take a hint and returned in silence to his mahi-mahi. But the aromas of the Sinai, the taste of his food, the amiable chatter surrounding him, and the soft ambient light were gradually working a transcendent effect upon Representative Grones. He felt his brow unfurrow. A pleasant warmth suffused his existence as the silence continued.

Some moments passed before Grones uttered, "You just want to poison all the black folks in south Alabama. That's what you want to do, DeMinus. You got some Hitler in you or somethin'."

The agency director thought of a reply but did not take the bait. He continued to eat in silence, reassuring himself that his intentions were pure and that people like Grones would forever be on guard against a white conspiracy lurking inside any progressive idea.

"Aw Ern, c'mon," he finally said, as if injured.

Representative Grones finished his collard greens and pondered. He took a final draught of sweet tea and leaned back in the booth, eyeing DeMinus cautiously.

"How much you say this nonsense idea would bring in for the state?" he finally asked.

"Could be ten billion or more, plus annual maintenance forever. Maintenance would be indexed to costs, of course."

Grones ruminated further. "Well, we sure could use that kinda money, couldn't we? But how do you know that stuff ain't goin' to leak out some day and start killin' folks? You can't guarantee that, now can you, Hoop?"

"We've got the benefit of the best engineers and technical experts in the world, Ern. It's the same system they use in Germany and all over Europe, and you know those German engineers don't take any chances. It's just good, honest, clean money, Ern. We want to help boost Alabama into the twenty-first century, don't we? You don't have to commit to anything now. Just keep an open mind and think about it, okay? Be a while before it comes up in the legislature, no matter what happens. Michael da Vinci didn't paint Rome in a day, you know. Like to have you on board as a co-sponsor of the bill, if we get one. It's up to you, of course. Just keep an open mind for now. That's all I'm askin'."

The representative removed his napkin from his lap and tossed it onto the table in a gesture of finality. "Grones has always got an open mind. Everybody knows that. Listen, DeMinus, you ever hear about what I'm tryin' to accomplish over at State Archives?"

"No, Ern. Can't say I have. That's pretty small potatoes for a guy like you, isn't it? You're interested in jobs, fair wages for your people, equal representation in the legislature, better schools, important stuff like that. What do you care about State Archives? Buncha' dusty old papers and Hank Williams's cowboy boots is about all they got over there, isn't it? Like you told me before. You got important work to do. I can't see what you'd care about what goes on at State Archives. But you go on and tell me about it anyway."

"Well, Hoop, there's a lot of importance attached to symbols, you know. I mean, look how everybody was so happy when Grones finally got that old Confederate flag down off the capitol dome. Even most white people liked it, didn't they? Now I got me a new idea how to turn state archives into something. Make it a symbol of the New Alabama. Tourist attraction sort of thing. Bring some revenue into Montgomery. Make a lot of black folks happy, too. What I want to do is collect all the slave period stuff into one big exhibit and call it 'The Museum of Slavery.' Have a whole wing of the archives building set aside just for that. Drape the doorways in black crepe. Have interactive videos and all that high-tech stuff. Sorta like that Holocaust Museum in D.C. Sounds like a winner, doesn't it? You're white, DeMinus. What do you think? People would go for it, wouldn't they? Lots of white folks want to know about the bad old days, same as black folks do."

DeMinus patted his mouth with his napkin one more time before answering. Then he grinned enormously, settled back into his booth, shook the ice in his glass, and said, "Ern, ol' buddy, I think you're an absolute, positive genius. 'Bout time somebody made something out of that archives building! This could be the biggest thing in Montgomery since the Civil Rights Memorial, and I'm on your side, partner! You got vision. That's what you got. You got vision! And that's what we need in this state. You're brilliant, Ern, and my hat's off to you. You need any help from your old pal Hoop on this thing, and you just let me know, okay? Glad to go to bat for you in any way possible."

Representative Grones was flattered. He grinned slightly, blushed a little, and glanced quickly from side-to-side.

"Matter of fact, Hoop, there is something you could do that might give me a little boost. I expect a lot of resistance to this idea, see? Just like when I got the First White House of the Confederacy renamed the 'Pre-Reconstruction White House.' People are gonna think it's silly. White folks gonna say it's just Grones tryin' to stir something up again. So what I need, see, is lots of good-hearted, progressive academics, historians, and people like that on my side. Make it a popular movement. Now I'm thinkin' you've got a couple of brothers that are presidents of state junior colleges, ain't that right?"

"That's right, Ern," DeMinus answered, sensing the lay of the land. "I got Maury, who's president down at Bryant State, and Meaux over at Slapout State. You want me to put a bug in their ear or something?"

"Well, you know, Hoop. If it ever comes up at y'all's family get-to-gethers or something like that, or maybe if you're talkin' to them on the phone, you might just mention you heard about it and tell them what you think, kinda like you just told me, that it would be a good thing for Montgomery and the image of the state and that sort of thing, you know. Get 'em on old Grones's side at the git-go. This is gonna take a lot of good PR work if it's gonna become a reality, so any help I can get, I'll appreciate it."

"Ern, ol' buddy. Tell you what I'm gonna do," DeMinus replied generously. "I'm gonna get on the phone with those brothers of mine as soon as I get back to the office. Get them to start rallying the troops. Anything I can do to help out the people of this state, I'm gonna do it. You know that, don't you, Ern? We've got to put all this racial division and politics behind us now. When you get down to it, you and me are on the same side, aren't we? We both just want what's good for Alabama, seems to me. We got to ignore all those political hacks and newspaper writers and get on with some good, progressive policies. Count me in, Representative Grones. We're going to make this state a great place to live in, aren't we?"

"That's right, Hoop. That's what we're goin' to do."

DeMinus caught the attention of Lewis, the waiter, who brought the check. Little Hoop pulled out his American Express card and paid the bill, adding a handsome tip.

The two dedicated public servants departed discreetly by the back door, waving and nodding as they went. When they reached DeMinus's shiny Infinity, the director of Solid Waste Liaisons magnanimously popped his remote lock button and opened the passenger door for the distinguished Representative. The two rode blissfully back to the state office building, chatting about the balmy weather, their families, and basketball.

Arriving at the seat of Alabama government, Little Hoop parked in front of a "No Parking" sign, got out of his car, and walked around to open the door for his amiable lunch guest.

Grones hopped out gingerly and shook hands with DeMinus.

"Thanks for lunch, Hoop. Enjoyed it."

"Me too, Ern."

"Come see me," Grones said, and turned toward his office.

Take 15% Off!

Governor Sid Scroulous was known everywhere for having "the tightest nuts in the State of Alabama." Early in his political career, the young Scroulous had introduced a bill in the State Legislature which would have made it an act of treason for "any person or group, at any time or place, and in any manner whatsoever, to advocate any increase in the property taxes paid by the citizens of this state." At length, the bill was defeated on the grounds of free speech. But not before Scroulous had become a national embarrassment to most Alabamians and, simultaneously, a deeply supported and permanent fixture of Alabama politics.

Scroulous speedily advanced to Governor with the enormous financial backing of various "special interest groups." As always in Alabama, such groups were decried in public as "just more politics." And yet they were heartily embraced as "enlightened contributors" among the fund raisers. This was especially true if the candidate supported the Ten Commandments and opposed property taxes, as Scroulous did so loudly.

By this time, however, "special interest groups" were no longer a real issue in the state. They had so fully succeeded in turning Alabama into a second-world colony that they were scarcely needed. The colony was owned almost entirely by various Northern, Western, and multinational corporations. The state, which had once taken great pride in its glorious plantations, had finally become a plantation itself. Its out-of-state owners, masters, and overseers exploited its wealth of natural resources (particularly its timber) by keeping the state's property taxes virtually non-existent. These large landowners and their front organizations, such as the massive financial and insurance conglomerate, Alfab, adored no one in the state so much as Sid Scroulous.

Alabama was suffering, as colonies typically do, and as the state had done for decades, from massive deficits and chronic underfunding of its primary obligation to promote the health, safety, education, and welfare of its citizens. Meanwhile, Wall Street and the out-of-state owners had a good friend in the state's Governor, who was facing a reelection campaign.

And Sid had a simple and easy solution to the state's financial dilemma. He termed his philosophy of fiscal government "The Wal-Mart Approach," and proposed to simply "Take 15% Off" of everything in the state. This would balance the budget, he argued, and also provide Scroulous with a clever and effective campaign slogan. Signs proclaiming, "Vote For Sid And Take 15% Off!" appeared in massive numbers on every highway and dirt back road in the state.

Scroulous was naturally reelected by a landslide. Thus, everything in Alabama government was to be cut by 15 percent, beginning with the Governor's own salary (which he did not need anyway). Also at the front of the cuts were 15 percent of the Governor's staff, discretionary fund, and office supplies, down to the last paper clip. Under the second Scroulous administration, every state-funded entity in Alabama would be required to take precisely the same approach, no matter who they were or who they knew. Fifteen percent of all state troopers, firemen, teachers, public health physicians, judges, district attorneys, highway workers, environmental scientists, and countless others, along with their associated expense budgets, would immediately be eliminated. Period.

Sid's simple approach was highly appealing, not only to the out-of-state industry and property owners, but also to the average voter on the street or the average voter struggling to keep his small catfish farm alive and growing.

The basic reason for this was that Sid had a knack with words. Prior to his reelection, Scroulous had been interviewed and quizzed by the usual hordes of reporters, journalists, pundits, and lobbyists, as well as his opponent during a televised debate. Few, however, gained anything for their efforts, for Scroulous had a highly effective, all-purpose mantra that seemed to make sense to most people. When asked about fire protection, for example, he stated, "You can't stop a blazing house fire by throwing money at it!" Asked about flood control for towns such as the perpetually submerged Elba, Scroulous replied, "You can't stop a flood by throwing money into the water!" Similarly, when quizzed about the rising crime rate, he replied without deviating. "You can't stop crime by throwing money at the criminals!" And, of course, when queried about the state's dismal educational services and declining adult literacy rate, Sid let loose his familiar battle cry, namely, "You can't solve the problem of education in Alabama by throwing money at it!"

There were many other reasons for the Scroulous reelection landslide. For one thing, many of the state's blue-collar employees, who would be the first to lose their jobs under "The Wal-Mart Plan," could not read a newspaper, or even a calendar, and therefore they had no idea of the issues involved in the election or even the date it would be held. In addition, fully 70 percent of the state's population thought the Scroulous plan would cut their income taxes by 15 percent along with everything else. And 80 percent of all voters polled said they "just plain liked Wal-Mart."

Thus, Governor Scroulous found himself seated in his rather modest office one glorious morning in May following his second inauguration. He was attempting to implement some minor details of his fiscal policy but found he had little interest in the project and almost no energy for it. He was groggy, headachy, and dressed as if he had pulled a few random items of clothing from a clothes hamper. He had spent most of the previous night on the veranda of the Governor's Mansion with a pitcher of Grey Goose martinis and a box of his favorite cheese straws.

Then, with little sleep, he had to arise at 5:00 A.M. for his morning Bible lesson with his wife, Martha. This was a ritual she had introduced early in Sid's first term when she had caught him in bed with his gorgeous young press secretary, Helen. Only after his promptly firing Helen, much pleading for forgiveness from Sid, and buckets of tears shed by Martha, did the Governor's wife relent and promise not to go public and ruin his career. But first, Sid had to promise to join her daily, without exception, in a Biblical redemption program which she had devised.

The Bible study began with Sid correctly reciting the Bible verse which Martha had assigned him the day before. Then they played Bible Lotto for a while as a prelude to Martha's favorite portion of the "spiritual experience," as she called it. This was consulting the Gospel Tarot cards, in which she placed great faith, concerning matters of mutual concern as well as issues of public policy. Mrs. Scroulous then assigned the Governor his Bible verse for the following day, and the session concluded with the couple singing an a capella duet of the Doxology. Only then was Sid free to go about his official duties.

On this particular May morning, the Governor was scheduled to speak at a 7:00 A.M. prayer breakfast at the Capital City Club atop the AmSouth Building in Montgomery. If he didn't hurry, he would be late. He splashed some cold water onto his face, followed by hot lather and a quick shave. His shower would have to wait. He donned an incongruous conglomeration of expensive clothing he had previously dropped on the floor of his closet. His suit jacket had a U.S. flag pin on one lapel and a State of Alabama pin on the other. He summoned his driver and set off for the prayer breakfast.

He arrived just in time and greeted everyone present with a huge smile, a slap on the back, or a possible hug for the ladies. For this morning, at least, they were all the Governor's oldest and dearest friends.

Making his way to the dais, he felt a little woozy, but shortly he found himself comfortably seated and feeling a little better. A local pastor delivered a splendid invocation, with sonorous, reverential rhythms of thanksgiving and praise.

Then breakfast was served, and the Governor felt ill once again. He was nauseated, in fact, as he faced his bacon, eggs, and sausage biscuits. He could still taste his cheese straws from the night before, and the martinis had given him heartburn. He could only manage to eat his grits, which were a welcome and soothing comfort to his system.

When the time arrived for the Governor to deliver his remarks, Sid straightened his tie, smoothed his rumpled attire, and rose to the occasion. A couple of well-known Alabama jokes soon had the crowd laughing. Then Scroulous settled into his brief, well-memorized, and always well-received oration upon the importance of God and property values in our daily lives, with some interesting if peculiar observations about how the two were really the same thing.

There was applause, followed by a closing prayer, and the breakfast ended promptly at 8:00 A.M. Sid grinned and back-slapped his way back to his driver, who whisked him off to the Governor's office. Safely inside, he went to his private room, stripped off his tie, set his alarm clock, and flopped down on his favorite sofa for a brief nap before his usual 9:00 A.M. meeting with his chief aide and legal counsel, Bobby Brooks.

The alarm clock sounded all too soon, and the Governor pulled himself together. By the time his secretary buzzed to announce the arrival of Mr. Brooks, Sid was seated behind his desk, massaging his temples, and pretending to study a thick stack of papers in front of him.

Bobby Brooks entered the office and waited for the Governor to say "Mornin' Bobby" and gesture for him to be seated. He was a tall, slender, handsome, and impeccably dressed young man about thirty years old. He had graduated second in his class at Harvard Law School and could have instantly stepped into a Wall Street job that would have made him a multi-millionaire in short order. But he had a sincere desire to return to his home state and be of genuine service to all of its citizens. He had moved up rapidly and planned to become Governor himself before he was forty.

Sid continued to pretend studying his papers until Brooks was seated across the desk from him. Then Scroulous glanced up at the young man and said, "So what in the goddamn hell have we got this morning, anyway? I feel like I got a little virus or something."

"Sorry to hear that, Governor," Brooks replied, making a mental note of Sid's fairly frequent episodes of "a little virus or something."

"Let's get to work, Bobby," Scroulous replied. "What's up?"

Brooks opened his neatly prepared file folder and said, "Well, Governor, first off we've got to deal with sixty-two petitions for executive pardons and clemency. As you know, your plan to take 15 percent off of everything included executions and prison sentences, and this news made its way through the inmate grapevine like wildfire. So we've got a lot of them."

"Oh, shit. We've got a cabinet meeting this afternoon, don't we?"

"Yes sir."

"Well, we'll just have to get rid of these things in a hurry, then. Give 'em three to five minutes apiece, okay? No longer. Let me know when I've hit 15 percent of those we have and then issue a press release. Get the proper letters to the Department of Corrections and the usual regrets to the losers. That's it. So let's get rollin'. Who's first up to bat?"

"Well, sir, we've only got one plea for clemency on an execution, so that helps us speed things up. This is one Arthur Childers, age now twenty-eight, who shot and killed four innocent people in a drive-by shooting four years ago. There were three eyewitnesses. Jury only deliberated twenty minutes. He's been all the way up and down the state and federal systems, and the conviction and sentence were upheld at every level. He's scheduled for the needle next Tuesday. No signs of remorse at sentencing or since then."

"What's he got in his sympathy file?"

"The usual Amnesty International and ACLU sort of stuff. The usual letters from his mother, his girl friend, and his pastor, and that's about it."

"Many demonstrations?"

"Not many. Had a couple of candlelight vigils, but only a handful of people showed up. There'll be folks at Atmore prison on Monday night, of course."

"Press say anything?"

"The press could care less," Brooks responded.

The Governor looked Brooks in the eye, drew a deep breath, did a quick, full 360-degree swivel spin on his office chair, and stopped suddenly to face his chief aide once again.

"Put him to sleep, and may God have mercy upon his sorry soul. Petition denied. Next case, please."

"Smaller fish now, Governor, and we've got to get rid of some of them. Here's one Ninety McWilliams, doing ten years split minimum for attempted murder. Been in for four years so far and wants to walk. Warden likes him, and he's been exemplary on work release. One of those fellas who likes his knife, you know. Been cutting folks up for forty-five years now. Looks like there are usually mitigating circumstances, like possible self-defense or something. He drinks, hangs around with the wrong people, and gets into a fight about some woman or something. One time it was about the proper interpretation of the Book of Job. This time it looks like he stole some pigs' feet and Twinkies. His partner tried to take them away, so Ninety cut him up a little. He usually cops to assault or some lesser-included offense and does a year or two."

"He ever kill anybody?"

"Yeah, early on. Did a deal with the D.A. for manslaughter and spent seven years at Kilby. That was his longest term in prison. Looks like he's spent about half his adult life in there."

"Sympathy file?"

"Kind of interesting. His mama, girlfriend, and pastor all claim he's a saint, of course. But he's also got a couple of letters from some other people. Here's one from Hoop DeMinus, who's our director of Solid Waste Liaisons, you know."

"DeMinus is still around?"

"Yes, sir. You reappointed him a while back, if you recall."

"Yeah. In my fraternity, wasn't he? What's he got to say?"

"Says Ninety has always been extremely cooperative when he has worked for him on work release and probably has a better right to go free than most inmates," Brooks said, reading from the DeMinus letter in his folder.

"What about the other letter?"

"This one's from Richard Steick, a lawyer up in Hallelujah. Looks like he represented Ninety quite a while ago. Ninety wrote him a letter from Kilby, and Steick wrote back. They exchanged correspondence, but Steick didn't talk to him personally. Steick says it's possible that it was self-defense this time. Says Ninety wrote him a letter in which he promised on the Bible that he would throw away his Case knife and stay off the bottle if Steick would write a letter to help him get out early. Steick thinks Ninety is in earnest, but says he can't promise anything."

"Who's Steick? He one of ours or one of theirs?"

"A pretty straight shooter, I think, Governor. Calls 'em like he sees 'em. Smart guy but not very political. Writes some professional stuff and teaches at Oppenheimer State. Drafted the Alabama statute for the Uniform Disposition of Estrays and Properties Adrift a while back. All the states have adopted it now except for Louisiana."

"Yeah, I remember that, too. Loose cows and floatin' things. Seems funny we have to have a law for that. Don't we have any fences in this state? Don't people keep their boats tied up?"

"I can't say, Governor," Brooks replied tactfully.

Scroulous shook his head from side to side, cast his eyes upward at the ceiling, and did another quick 360-degree sit spin. Once again he stopped abruptly to face his aide.

"What say we fit Ninety up with a pair of roller skates? Okay?" the Governor grinned.

THE ELEVENTH COMMANDMENT

Richard Steick had bad intuitions about the State of Alabama, and he was right. It was in worse shape than usual. During the time in which he had worked gainfully to stop being a dildo and get a new lid, Alabama government had heard alien voices and begun to suffer tics and hallucinations.

Governor Scroulous, for example, continued his policy of taking 15 percent off of everything, including the electricity. Thus, all state offices were required to consume 15 percent less electric power than they had in the previous fiscal year. State offices were required to turn off all their lights, computers, and an infinite variety of electrical equipment during 15 percent of each work shift, effectively shutting down public services during the blackouts. Traffic signals and road lighting were cut off 15 percent during their less important hours, nevertheless causing dozens of accidents, injuries, and lawsuits against the State Highway Department. Even the State Dock Authority at Mobile was included, thereby reducing the state's essential dock revenues by 15 percent. Only battery-operated electrical equipment was exempt, which at least allowed police cars to remain on the streets and highways. But they were required to consume 15 percent less fuel than during the previous year, and many patrols were therefore curtailed or eliminated entirely.

Meanwhile, orthodox religion, which historically had made Alabama a refreshing spiritual refuge from the crass materialism of modern life, had simply quit the field. The APE-Christian Committee (officially known as the Apostolic, Pentecostal, and Evangelical Christian Co-ordinating Committee) had taken over completely. Theologically, the APE-Christians made the Sand Mountain snake-handlers look like New Age liberals. Politically, they had become the leading front organization for Alfab, a massive financial and insurance conglomerate, and the out-of-state timber, oil, and mineral industries which tenaciously kept the state a wholly owned second-world subsidiary. Commerce and theology fit like a hand in a glove, with commerce being the hand. The colonial masters poured vast sums of money into the APE Committee which, in turn, touted their masters' policies as the teachings of the Bible. It was as if the traditional Alabama election mantra had become the Eleventh Commandment: "There Shall Be No New Taxes!"

And there weren't.

Thus, the colonial masters of Alabama were growing richer by the day, and the State Legislature had become more menacing than usual. With the enormous financial backing of the state's true owners, both the House and the Senate had easily fallen into the hands of duly elected APE Christians who dominated both chambers. This made for a glorious symbiotic relationship in which APE idol worship enjoyed many triumphant victories.

Two of the committee's successes were particularly cunning. It convinced a slim majority of the state's voters to approve a constitutional amendment changing both the state motto and the state flag. Alabama's time-honored motto, "We Dare Defend Our Rights," noble and stentorian, was erased. The APE Committee first proposed to replace it with "Jesus Loves Me," but the Attorney General eventually persuaded them that this would be stricken by the atheistic federal courts. Thus, the Committee settled for "Thou Shalt Not," which had strong Judeo-Christian resonance but certainly could not be accused of advancing or preferring any particular religion.

Next came the state flag. The ancient and honorable red Cross of St. Andrew was out. In its place, the APE committee designed a Hollywood movie caricature of two stone tablets bearing the Roman numerals I through X, without text, but with the new state motto, "Thou Shalt Not," emblazoned beneath it.

And thus, by craft, innuendo, and "plain old politics," the APE Christians succeeded where like-minded but less-clever souls had always failed in the past. The famous and universally recognized Judeo-Christian icon not only flew above the dome of the state capitol, but it was also painted, chiseled, stamped, or engraved upon every facade, floor, wall, and ceiling of every school and public building in the state, not to mention all public documents. In addition, it was added voluntarily to the typical American and Christian flag duo already adorning the altars of many churches. As if gilding the lily, the legislature passed a law requiring all school children in the state to append the words "And also to the flag of Alabama" at the end of their Pledge of Allegiance each morning. Thus, mandatory violation of the first and second Biblical commandments became the new law of the land. But the scheme was obviously endorsed by the Creator Himself, since there wasn't a thing the atheistic federal courts could do about it.

These events, and many others, constituted colorful grist for the national media mill. It was a rare day when Alabama was not made to appear barefoot, pregnant, easily conned, and cheaply purchased in the national press, on the radio, and on television. This unfortunate picture of the great state that had once "Dared Defend Its Rights" was precisely the image coveted and carefully manufactured by its out-of-state owners. And image, of course, is everything. The colonial powers in New York, Atlanta, Chicago, the Silicon Valley, and elsewhere profited greatly by maintaining in Alabama the typical stereotype of a subjugated populace. The suppressed group is forever depicted as a slow, technologically backward, inferior race in dire need of the cultural uplift and wholesome tutelage supplied by the more advanced civilization which exploits the colony's cheap labor and natural resources.

Thus the state burrowed ever deeper, like an auger, into the barren field of poverty, illiteracy, high infant mortality, and fiscal chaos.

RICHARD STEICK WAS A PROUD Alabamian who loved his state, its natural beauty, its proud history, its arts and architecture, and the courtesy, generosity, goodness, and intelligence of its people. Thus, he was greatly dismayed by the feudal forces drilling it into the ground. And he was determined to use the information which he alone possessed to do as much good for the state as he possibly could.

What he had learned in the ancient county land records was too exciting to be kept entirely to himself, and he planned to allow one especially esteemed confidante, Melissa, to share his secret knowledge and high aspirations for its use. He did not, however, bring the matter up immediately.

He wanted to do further research to confirm the irrevocable conveyance of Farthing Worthy's Island declared in the unusual deed he had uncovered. He began with microfilm of *The Montgomery Advertiser* from the date of the fire on April 11, 1865, until the date on the deed. There were bold headlines and stories with impassioned praise for "our brave Negro volunteer firemen," but little else. He found the phrase, "the profound gratitude of the city," frequently used, but there was no mention of any special compensation to accompany the gratitude. In the lead story of the day after the fire, the firemen were named, and one Ninety Ton McWilliams was noted especially for his bravery.

Steick then turned to the minutes of the old city and county council meetings. A note in the city council minutes, made at a special meeting some two days after the fire, was intriguing but elliptical. It stated simply that, "A rousing debate followed concerning what remuneration or reward, if any, might constitute an appropriate token of the city's gratitude to the gallant Negro firemen who this week saved the city from destruction by fire."

The professor's further reading of abundant public documents of the period revealed nothing in addition. The entire matter was proving an intriguing historical puzzle as well as a fascinating legal one.

The lawyer knew that his next stop would be to pay a call upon his former client, Ninety McWilliams, if he hadn't yet bled to death. It was impossible to believe that Ninety, if living, was not some distant kin of the courageous fireman, Ninety Ton McWilliams, who had helped save Montgomery from burning itself down in 1865. He might even be a lineal descendant, based upon the similarity of the names. If such were the case, and if Steick could document that fact, it would be further proof that God Himself was on the lawyer's side. It was too much to hope for, and yet Richard could not prevent himself from hoping.

If the Ninety McWilliams he knew turned out to be a legitimate, provable heir of the 1865 fireman, Ninety Ton McWilliams, then Steick could rest assured that any further legal efforts on his part would be properly and, without a doubt, handsomely compensated.

He would then, of course, have to travel to the land patents office in Washington, D.C., since its records were not available on the Internet. Any grant of land signed by President Andrew Johnson would certainly be recorded there, and Steick could also use the trip as an opportunity to obtain the opinion of a discreet, out-of-state handwriting expert. He needed to verify the authenticity of the former President's signature on the document in his possession and then take the expert's deposition. All of these steps would take time, money, and effort. It would be extremely pleasant for the lawyer to know that he would be properly paid and also reimbursed for his costs as he set about righting an ancient wrong, bringing the races together, and otherwise rescuing Alabama in various ways that he might devise. Being the talk of the state and a hero to many would be nice, but it would be even nicer if he were paid to do it.

Richard had been snapping his fingers and tap dancing with joy each time he contemplated sharing his discovery with Melissa. He could no longer keep his important information entirely to himself. It was essential that some trustworthy person should know about it also and bring the matter to light in the event of his untimely death. He knew he could trust Melissa's discretion and confidentiality completely. In addition, she would be thrilled by his discovery as well as flattered by being his only confidante in such an important matter.

HE DECIDED THAT THE OCCASION of his disclosure called for a small, private celebration, and so he invited Melissa to dinner at his house on a Thursday evening. It would be an enjoyable prelude to a weekend of movies and a party they had been invited to attend.

Melissa happily allowed Richard to cook for her, and he was a fair chef when he put his mind to the job. He decided upon a French motif and prepared an interesting mixed green salad followed by quiche Lorraine, a hearty boeuf bourguignon, cornbread, and ice cream for dessert. A good bottle of Bordeaux, a well-laid dinner table, and candlelight made the ambiance superb.

Melissa was to arrive at 7:30 P.M., and at 7:25, Richard began to check his window for her car. She was punctual, as usual, and he walked out to greet her as he always did. She wore a simple, classic black velvet dress with a single strand of pearls. They kissed a leisurely "hello" and then intertwined their arms as they had grown accustomed to doing since their first date. The host then led his beautiful and stylish dinner guest into his house and to the dining room.

Ever the courtly gentleman, Steick pulled back a chair to seat his companion. Evening meals were always important events for him. He considered any meal that wasn't a celebration as merely empty calories. He found that his thinking was clearest and his conversation easiest and most sincere during a toothsome and well-presented dinner. He was feeling splendid as he poured a glass of wine for Melissa and then one for himself.

"It's French night, Melissa," he said, as he described the fare, all within easy reach on a nearby sideboard.

"That's wonderful, Richard. You seem rather fond of French things, you know."

"Do I now?" he grinned, and then asked her about her day.

Melissa enjoyed telling him about events at her job, including the scheduling foul-ups and difficult patients that are inevitable in a doctor's office and which sometimes caused her headaches. He was a good listener. In fact, he loved listening to women talk, and he had learned a little about the business over the years. He knew that women preferred men to listen attentively and not interrupt with suggestions about how to fix things. He knew that fixing things was a male fascination which he himself shared, and he sometimes had to swallow suggestions that seemed necessary and obvious. But he also knew that what Melissa desired most was his attention, and that she did not, in fact, seek or require any advice about her work from him.

When she had finished talking about her day, Richard was poised and eager to share his discovery with her and to enlist her as his backstage partner in adventure. But he savored the moment and enjoyed easing into his own main topic.

"We've got a nice green salad here, Melissa, and an assortment of dressings. Would you prefer to start with that or follow the French manner and take your salad last?"

"I didn't know the French did that, and it seems backward to this American me. Doesn't it seem backward to you?"

"Yes, it does."

"But just like you like French things, you sometimes like things backward, too, don't you?" she asked teasingly.

"Well, I won't deny that either, Melissa," he smiled. "But since we're both good Americans, why don't we begin with the salad like we usually do. That okay with you?"

"It's fine with me, Richard. Whatever you like is fine with me."

"What I'd like most right now," he said, as he dished up the mixed greens, "is to share something extremely fascinating with you and ask you for your help. Would that be all right?"

"Why certainly. I love a fascinating story, and I'll be happy to help in any way I can. So let me hear all about it."

"There's just one thing. You have to promise me that absolutely nothing I say to you tonight will ever leave this room unless I die, become disabled and unable to communicate, or I tell you to tell someone else. This is important, and I'm completely serious about it. These are very sensitive and delicate legal matters I'm about to discuss, and you must pledge yourself to absolute confidentiality, no matter what. I know I can trust your discretion entirely, or I wouldn't share this information with you. You will be my only confidante in the entire world, okay? So can you promise me that you won't tell a single soul a word about this unless I tell you to or something bad happens to me? Can you promise me that, Melissa?"

Melissa was pensive and serious. "Yes, Richard, I will sincerely make you that promise. You make this sound like a Cold War spy secret or something. Are you sure you want to tell me?"

"I'm entirely certain I want to tell you, and for good reasons, which

I'll explain. And I thank you for your promise and for being someone I can truly trust. Now, let me tell you all about it," he began.

He gave her a thorough and detailed account of his recent discovery as well as his efforts to confirm what he knew, his plans to locate Ninety, and then to travel to D.C. to confirm the authenticity of his document. They had finished the salad and the quiche and were midway through the stew before he took a breather.

"All of this is absolutely incredible, Richard! I *do* feel like I'm in a spy novel. Do you think I could possibly go to Washington with you? I wouldn't want to get in your way. But it's a beautiful city, and I haven't been anywhere in ages. It would be our first out-of-town getaway together, and it sounds like fun to me. How about it?"

"Well, in fact, I'd love to have your company, Melissa. Actually, I'd thought before about asking you, but a lot of this work is going to be tedious, and I was afraid you might be bored. But if you'd like to come along, consider yourself invited."

"Great! And don't worry at all about my being bored. I'll feel like I'm being a part of history, in a way. It sounds thrilling to me. Now, you said a few minutes ago that you had important plans for using this information for the good of the whole state, which, as everybody knows, needs as much help as it can get. Can you tell me something about that also? I can see how your discovery has many vast and important implications. But can you tell me a little bit about what you have in mind?"

Steick laid his soup spoon aside, patted his mouth with his napkin, and leaned forward conspiratorially.

"Melissa, what I've discovered in that document is leverage, and leverage of the most important sort. Financial. In America, government comes at a price, and that price can always be measured in financial terms when you really get down to the facts. This is not just everyday financial leverage. It's not typical legislative *quid pro quo,* and it's not pork barrel scraps. We're talking financial leverage of monumental proportions here, possibly enough to make major influences on policy or even save the state from an even worse financial mess. It's like Archimedes wrote. 'You can move the whole earth if you have enough leverage'."

"I'm sorry, Richard, but would you please clarify *quid pro quo*?" she asked. "I've always been a little unclear about that phrase."

"You give me this, and I'll give you that."

"So what policies do you want to influence, and how do you intend to do it?"

"We can begin with Coffee County and that horrible scheme for a hot toxic waste disposal operation there. Remember the story I told you about that corrupt moron, Hoop DeMinus? He's working overtime now to get the legislature to grant a license to the world at large to store the most poisonous chemicals known on earth down near Enterprise. That would be an environmental and policy disaster as well as a human one. The slightest technical error or miscalculation could easily lead to an Alabama version of Bhopal, India. Remember that event? Hundreds or thousands of people could be killed in an instant. It would make the Three Mile Island and Brown's Ferry nuclear near-misses look like a sit-com. I don't care how many German engineers declare the process is safe. It's like the space shuttle. It's human and therefore subject to error. We certainly don't want it in Alabama or anywhere near us. No one would want to live within miles of it! It would create a desert in the middle of the beautiful south Alabama countryside. And it would also set another bad precedent for the state, as if we didn't have enough already. We don't want to be known as the one place on earth that actually invites death and disaster for the price of a ticket, do we? So that's the first thing on my agenda—to kill that project before it goes any further. And I know exactly how to do it, too."

"So—how would you go about it, Richard?"

"It's like I said, Melissa. Once I hammer down all the nails, and I'm sure we've got an airtight case in court, we'll have tremendous financial leverage. Money means power. I've learned that the lunatic DeMinus has enlisted the support of State Representative Ernest Grones for this terrible hot tox project. In fact, it's Grones who is going to introduce the bill in the legislature. You know who Grones is, don't you?"

"I think everybody in Alabama knows who Representative Grones is, Richard."

"Then you know the enormous amount of political influence he holds which he can wield as he chooses. As chair of the Legislative Black Conference, Grones is arguably the second most important man in Alabama. After the Governor, it's a tie between Grones and Slubber D. Gloss, chair of the APE-Christian Committee. The thing is, I've known Grones pretty well for a lot of years, since he also teaches at Opp U., as you probably know. Whatever anyone thinks about the man, he is absolutely unwavering in his dedication to his constituency, and you have to admire him for that. He struts his stuff, of course, but I've always found him a fairly reasonable person. I have no idea how DeMinus roped him into supporting this awful hot tox scheme, but then DeMinus is clever, even if he's stupid.

"The bottom line is that the hot tox deal is going to go through if Grones introduces it and pushes it in the State Legislature. On the other hand, it will die in committee if he doesn't. It's as simple as that. When I know all the facts about Farthing Worthy's Island and that deed I found, I'm going to have a little private conversation with Representative Grones. I'll give him an honest free peek at the evidence. Not enough to let him do anything, of course, but enough to let him know what I can do if I want to. And if I want to, I can confiscate Alchemelia's only source of smellenium, all of the company's assets, a good share of the state's assets, and probably some fair federal government assets as well, and hand them over to the legitimate heirs of those heroic black firemen who saved the city back in 1865. Those heirs no doubt number in the thousands by now and are scattered everywhere. But I would guess that the majority of them are still located around central Alabama.

"And I can also turn Grones into a star player on my team if I choose. Make him a great hero among black folks everywhere. It could possibly send him to Washington. In any event, it would put money into the hands of a lot of black citizens, and it would be money they rightly deserve according to law. Some of them might even become rich. It's far too early to tell at this point. I could give Grones enough evidence to convince him of what I've found and guarantee him a nice portion of the credit when the matter goes public. But I would also promise him that I wouldn't make a single move further until he not only dropped his support for the dangerous DeMinus project but also killed it forever dead in the legislature. Thus, another example of *quid pro quo*, Melissa. But this one is definitely in the service of justice and in the best interest of the State of Alabama. No question about it."

"Wow! You are one brilliant man, Richard Steick! I'm honored to be the only person in on this. Thank you! I'll do anything I can to help you."

"You're helping me right now, Melissa, by listening. Not only do I love you, but I also trust you completely and admire your keen intelligence. There aren't many people in the world I could reasonably trust with this information, and you're the only one I love as well as the one I trust the most. And so it is I who should thank you."

"Oh, Richard. I do love you so much!" Melissa laughed, adding, "But you said you also have other and maybe even bigger plans. Can you tell me anything more?"

"Well, I've not worked out all the details, but I think I could actually use Farthing Worthy's Island to bring the races closer together, at least in Alabama."

"Uh, excuse me, Richard," Melissa said. Then she got up from the table, walked the short distance around to his side, bent over, and whispered into his ear, "Did I tell you about the phone call I got today?"

"Why, no, you didn't, Darlin'," he said aloud.

She whispered further, "It was the Vatican calling, asking me to be the next Pope."

Then she tickled his ribs and said, "Slide your chair back, Richard. I want to sit on your lap."

He was more than happy to oblige. The sensation of her supple, callipygian bottom was far more inviting than ice cream. When she had comfortably settled her stunning legs across his and circled her arms around his neck, first she kissed him, then tweaked him under the chin and said, "Now. Tell me how you're going to bring the races closer together in Alabama. I'm listening."

He peered deeply into her bluest of blue eyes and said, "I know you think I'm being grandiose and that I'm possibly crazy, but please don't judge me prematurely. Once again, it involves Representative Grones, as well as that allegedly great American virtue, compromise. If I'm right about the tax consequences of this matter, then a yet-undetermined number of unknown black citizens might well be able to bankrupt the state for years. Remember that the grant stipulates that no taxes will ever be assessed or levied by any government against the revenues produced by the island. That means the state could owe the heirs millions, if not billions, of dollars in taxes it has collected from the profits of the highly lucrative Alchemelia Corporation over the years. And that doesn't take into consideration accrued interest, which would also be due.

"So, what I've got in mind is to slowly disclose the facts to Grones and get him to consent to a compromise, as I mentioned. Basically, I'll ask that he push his constituents, as well as the black members of the legislature, into accepting partial settlement. The firemen's heirs can have Alchemelia, its past, present, and future profits, and anything they can squeeze out of the feds in the way of illegally collected taxes. But they will all have to join in a consent decree exempting the State of Alabama and releasing it and holding it harmless against any and all previously but illegally collected state taxes. If Grones won't agree to that, and sign off on the deal under oath and penalty of liquidated damages, then I'll just keep the lid on Pandora's box."

"Those are some awful big lawyer words and phrases you're using there, Sweetheart, but I think I get the drift. 'Liquidated damages' is new to me. What does that mean?"

"That means Grones would have to pay me a lot of money if he backed out on our deal, and he wouldn't want to do that. It's kind of a sticky little drafting problem, but I can handle it easy enough. So, if the deal goes down the way I see it, there will be several consequences. Number one. There will be a media, judicial, and state government circus of unprecedented proportions. Number two. A lot of black folks will still get a lot of money they didn't have in the past, and they will be happy. Number three. Grones is going to be an even greater hero than he has ever imagined himself, and he will be happy. Number four. The legitimate black heirs will have the state by the short hairs, as we say, in the revenue department. Even white people will be grateful if the heirs forgive the tax debt. I mean, whites will know that they damned sure wouldn't make the sacrifice themselves. Thus, the black heirs will become the saviors of the entire state, just like their forefathers, the gallant firemen, had saved the City of Montgomery nearly a century and a half ago. I want to think that white Alabama will thankfully embrace their black fellow citizens as never before. We'll have to hire a good, discreet PR firm to put the right spin on the entire matter, beginning with the media circus, but that can be managed.

"So, it's like I said. Government comes at a price in this country. If things turn out the way I see it, everybody will be happy, and the state will be a lot better off. Plus, I'll get a nice, court-approved attorney's fee.

"It seems to me, Melissa, that the overall effect will be something like it might have been if Governor Wallace, before his death, had asked Reverend Jesse Jackson to deliver the eulogy at the Governor's funeral, and Jackson had done it. You see what I mean? I think it could be a great healing thing for Alabama and possibly even the whole nation. What a splendid example of racial cooperation we will become in the public eye if this thing is handled right! Still think I'm crazy, Honey? I just might be, you know."

"To be honest, Richard, what you say sounds good and does make a lot of sense. But it seems awfully complicated, with a lot of unknown twists and turns, don't you think?"

"I agree, Melissa. I'd actually call it a long shot at this point. But I think it's worth our effort, and I think Dr. Kayahs would say so, too. We're here to be of service and to do lasting, meaningful work, you know, as well as to love each other and the Almighty. So what do you say, Darlin'? Will you hold my hand through this thing?"

"Of course I will," she smiled. "You never doubted that I would, did you?"

"No, I didn't. Now, would you like some ice cream?"

"I really don't think I care for any, Richard. I'm pretty full already."

"Okay," he said, seizing the moment for a joke which had become familiar to them. "Would you like to visit Mushroom Memories for a cup of coffee?"

"Uh, no, I really don't believe so," she smiled. "But there is another room in your house that I'd like to see again. Is that okay with you?"

"That's perfect with me, Melissa," he grinned in return, as she arose, took his hand, led the way, and further aroused the already arisen Steick.

TONS AND TONS

It was shortly after Ninety McWilliams's release from prison when attorney Richard Steick set out to locate him. The lawyer had a sense of purpose unmatched since William the Conqueror. He began on the logical assumption that Ninety was in jail somewhere, and so he made a quick phone call to the State Department of Corrections. He was pleased to discover that there was no such person incarcerated in the State of Alabama and happily assumed that his letter to Governor Scroulous might have helped to effect an early release of his former client under the Governor's "Take 15% Off" plan.

The lawyer then searched his retired cases database for Ninety's ancient phone number and home address in Montgomery. He found it quickly and cross-checked it with the current Montgomery telephone directory. There was a number for "McWilliams N and H" at 410 Oak Street, and that address coincided with Ninety's old one. The telephone number was different from the one in the lawyer's file, but that was easily understandable, and he punched in the numerals with anticipation. There was something like an electronic bird song followed by a recorded message saying that "This number has been disconnected."

Undeterred, Steick weighed whether he should drive to the Oak Street address or the Montgomery city garage, where Ninety had worked for most of his life when he wasn't in jail. The garage was closer, and the lawyer knew exactly where it was located. He knew the Oak Street area but not how to find the street itself, and so he grabbed his Montgomery data map, his handheld tape recorder, and a yellow legal pad and tucked them all neatly into his buttery brown leather briefcase. He would try the garage first, and if he had no luck there, he would track down the Oak Street address.

He left his office, ducked his head into Betty's domain, told her where he was going, and then headed for his SUV. Stepping aboard and closing the door, he felt the sense of isolation and contentment that the superbly appointed vehicle typically gave him. In addition, there lingered a faint, fragrant trace of Melissa's cologne, which warmed his heart and made him smile. He turned on the ignition, chose a selection of Chopin's *Etudes* from the electronic CD file, and pointed the comfortable traveling lounge toward Montgomery.

Driving down the interstate, he once again ruminated with affection and amusement upon his early representation of Ninety McWilliams and silently prayed that the man was still alive. The highway was full of Grand Prix drivers, but Steick remained reflective and unruffled.

He drove to the garage with ease. At one difficult intersection, a black lady kindly allowed him into the flow of traffic, as customary Montgomery courtesy typically demurred to other drivers, regardless of race, sex, or age, in congested situations. He gave her the mandatory wave of thanks and shortly found himself parked at his destination.

He got out, locked his doors, and walked inside through a vehicular entry big enough for F-16 fighter planes. The work area was cavernous and dark. A white employee, dressed in a filthy white cotton shirt and trousers, sat on an oak chair behind a badly beaten desk, paring dirt from beneath his fingernails with a pocketknife. The lawyer approached him and asked, "You know a fella by the name of Ninety McWilliams?"

"Sure. He's back there workin' on a tire or somethin'." He waved his pocketknife in the general direction of deeper into the dimly lit cavern.

"Thanks," Steick said, and walked confidently into the garage, where there was arrayed an amazing variety of garbage trucks, street sweepers, pickup trucks, bulldozers, trenching machines, automobiles, and ten-wheeled vacuums with hoses and canisters large enough to suck a catfish pond dry in thirty seconds or less. The mechanics worked alone or in teams of two or three, with their jobs illuminated by bright, hanging garage lights on recoiling pulleys. The lamps' reflectors allowed little ambient glow, and the enormous hangar thus remained gray, with flashes of light here and there from the work lamps. Steick walked around, peering into faces, looking for Ninety, and asking his whereabouts. He was directed deeper and deeper into the building until he came upon a single black man changing four tires on a police car.

In spite of the many years which had elapsed, Steick recognized Ninety's regal bearing immediately. The man continued to have excellent posture and moved about with strength, poise, and grace. The lawyer simply watched him for a few moments before approaching.

Then he walked up and said, "Hey! Is that you, Ninety?"

Ninety had no "startle reaction" whatever. He turned around to face his former advocate but found himself blinded by his own work light. He squinted for a moment, allowing his eyes to adjust to the dimness, and then recognized his visitor.

"That you, Doc?"

"Yeah, Ninety. It's me, your old lawyer. Still remember me, don'cha?"

Steick was amazed by Ninety's appearance. Although he had to be in his seventies, in the dim light, he didn't appear a day older than when Steick had seen him last, many years before. The attorney noticed and recalled the amazing keloid scar on Ninety's neck and thought maybe he had gained a few more smaller ones. But it was difficult to remember them all. Steick wanted to lead carefully into his important inquiry and was thus prepared to serve a little extra helping of the usual *parlez-vous*. In addition, he genuinely liked Ninety and was curious about his life and circumstances.

"Why sho' I remember you, Doc. You always been tryin' to help me out a lot. You wrote me letters in jail and then a letter to the Governor not long ago that help me get outta Kilby this time. I never say 'thank you,' so I say 'thank you' now."

"You're welcome, Ninety. I'm glad if my letter helped. It's better to have you out here free, doin' some useful work, than for you to be rottin' away in Kilby, seems to me . . . I've got to ask you something, Ninety, for your own good. Did you throw away your Case knife, like you promised on the Bible in your letter?"

"Yes sir, Doc. I sho' did. An' I ain't been in no trouble since, neither. Not a bit."

"How about the liquor, Ninety? You promised me you'd give that up too, remember?"

"Yes, sir, Doc. I 'member," the large man replied. "An' I ain't gonna lie to you, neither. I lay it all off except maybe wunst a week when I has me one beer or maybe two at the most, and that's all. Rest o' that stuff give me a bad headache, and I don't mess with it no more. No, sir."

"Well, I'm glad to hear that, Ninety. That'll help to keep you out of trouble too, you know. So how's your family? Last time I remember, you were livin' with your mama on Oak Street and takin' care of her because she had pretty bad sugar. Is she still okay?"

"She done passed not too long ago, Doc. Can't remember when we funeralized her, but it was a little while back."

"I'm truly sorry to hear that, Ninety. I hope she had a nice, proper funeral."

"It was okay, I s'pose. But they was a mess with her sister come down from New York. She say Mama had a lots o' money an' I done poisoned her to get it. She want to 'zoom the body and ever'thing, but the D.A. wouldn't let her. He say coroner said Mama done died o' cancer and natural causes. So my auntie go on back to New York, but she sure done made a fuss while she was here. Durn neart spoilt the funederal. All I ever done was help my mama, and I was the only one that did. Made me sad with them sayin' them things about me."

"That's terrible, Ninety. I know you helped your mama and that you'd never do anything like that." And he did know it, too. "So what are you doin' now? Livin' by yourself over on Oak Street and workin' here most of the time?"

"Miss Helen live with me now. Me and her is married, I guess you'd say. What they call 'common law,' you know. We gets along pretty good 'cept when she drink too much."

"Well, you keep your hands off her when she drinks too much, Ninety. Just run like a scalded dog. Get in your car and go, and don't come back 'til she's calmed down. I mean it. Don't you push her or even touch her. Don't argue with her, either. She makes one little phone call to the police, and you could find yourself back in prison again, and you don't want that now, do you?"

"No sir, Doc. I sho' don't. I been followin' your advice already. I stays away from her when she want to make trouble. I'm tired o' the jail house. Just wants to do my job here for the city like I always done," Ninety replied.

"That's good, Ninety. Just be sure you keep it that way, all right?"

"I sho' will, Doc. So what brings you around here anyway?"

Steick felt a slight frisson of fear as the moment of truth arrived. He placed his hands in his trouser pockets, shuffled a little closer to his former client, looked him straight in the eye, and gave his head a slight nod downward.

"Look, Ninety. There's something awfully important I want to talk to you about, okay? And I mean it's really important. It's so important that you can't say a single word to anyone about it. And I do mean anyone. Not one word and not one person. That includes Miss Helen too, you understand?"

"What 'chew mean, Doc?"

"What I mean, Ninety, is that I've found some important information that might concern you. Nobody in the world knows a thing about it except me and one other person, you understand? And that person has to know in case something happens to me. That's how important it is. And what I've learned might make you a rich man. I mean really rich. Now remember, I said MIGHT make you rich. Ain't nothin' certain yet, and this could take a long time. But if I'm right, and if everything works out like I plan, then you will certainly get some money. And probably a whole lot of it, too. You would probably be richer than most white folks in Montgomery. Maybe rich like Job, when God made his bad friends bring him all those jewels and a gold earring and kill all those cows for him and all that stuff like that, remember?"

Ninety looked serious and nodded "yes," he understood.

Steick continued. "I want you to understand, Ninety, that this ain't no bullshit or some kinda con game. You got me? If I'm right, and if this all works out like I think, it's going to help you and a lot of other black folks, too, okay? Maybe even the whole State of Alabama. So you've got to promise me that you won't mention a word of it to anybody. You get drunk and run your mouth, and we're finished. Get it? So stay away from everything, even the beer. Understand? There's a lot at stake here, and you've got to promise me, on the Bible, that you won't say a thing to anybody, or I'll just have to look for somebody else to help me. What do you say? Will you promise me, on the Bible, that you won't mention this to another soul?"

Ninety looked his counselor straight in the eye and said, "Lookee here, Doc. You always been straight with me, an' I knows it. Even when Judge Fitzgerald make me take that plea for somethin' I didn't do, you was on my side. I talk about it a lot with them jailhouse lawyers out at Kilby, an' they all tell me the same thing. That you done got me a good deal. An' you not like them other coat lawyers. You come an' visit me a lots when I was in jail, an' all the other guys in there think you one helluva lawyer, you know, an' they want you fo' they lawyer too. An' then you writed me that letter to the Governor that help me get out this time. An' didn't nobody pay you, an' you didn't have to do that neither. An' so I knows you, Doc, an' I trusts you. When you tells me somethin', I believes you, an' I believes you now. An' this be like it say in the Bible, 'Ask, an' it shall be given you.' I been sendin' my money to Reverend Mike every month for a long time, and I been prayin' like he say, an' I know the Lord answer prayer, an' I think maybe this be the time He doin' it. So yes. I promise you that on the Bible. I gots mine right over here, see. I reads it on my work breaks an' at lunch. Let me go get it."

Ninety walked to a greasy work bench and picked up something that looked like a stack of limp, black paper towels. He walked back over to Steick and asked, "What you want me to say, Doc?"

Steick said, "Let me have the Bible, Ninety." Ninety handed it over, and the lawyer held it like a court bailiff. "Put your left hand on the Bible now, and raise your right hand, okay?"

Ninety did as he was asked, and Steick asked, "Do you, Ninety Mc-Williams, hereby swear upon the Bible and before Almighty God that you will never say one word at all to anyone about the things I am about to tell you? If you do, say 'I do solemnly so swear.'"

"I do solemnly so swear."

"Good. Now go put the Bible back, and let's have us a little talk."

Ninety replaced the Bible and returned.

"You suppose you could take a little break now, Ninety? I'd like to walk out into the sunshine," the lawyer said.

"Sho. It be about break time anyway. Besides, the boss man let us take break most anytime we want to anyway."

"Wonderful," Steick replied, as he led the way to the huge hangar door opposite the one where he had entered. The two walked outside and sat down across from one another at an old picnic table under a water oak tree. They both crossed their hands and rested their forearms on the table before them.

Steick again looked Ninety straight in the eye. He felt as if his heart were going to pound a hole straight through his chest as he asked, "Ninety. You ever hear of a man a long time ago called 'Ninety Ton McWilliams?'"

"Why sho', that bees my three-times-great-granddaddy."

The lawyer could not control his joy and relief. He bounded up onto the table, spread his arms as if he had just scored the winning touchdown, and jumped up and down like a kid on a trampoline. He wanted to let out a loud "Whoopee," but he had to control himself. He didn't want to attract any more attention than he might be attracting already. He quickly made two jumps down from the table, first onto the bench and then onto the ground. He beat his feet up and down double time, as if marching in place. Then he galloped to the water oak, gently bumped his forehead onto it three times, and gave it a hug as best he could. Next he bounded back to the table and again sat down facing Ninety, who looked perplexed but who had long determined that there was no point in trying to understand white people.

Puffing only slightly, Steick asked, "When you say your 'three-times great-granddaddy,' Ninety, would that be like when we sometimes say your 'great-great-great granddaddy?'"

"Yeah. We say it that way sometimes."

"So," Steick asked again, checking himself for auditory hallucinations, "Do you mean that your great-great-great granddaddy was named 'Ninety Ton McWilliams?'"

"Yes, sir. He sho' was. He was borned a slave."

Richard hardly knew what to do. This time, he buried his face in his hands, then wiped them away, and bobbed his head three times on the table before him and let it rest there for several moments, collecting his thoughts. When he raised it again, he was extremely cautious not to ask Ninety any leading questions.

"Do you—uh—do you happen to know anything at all about Ninety Ton McWilliams?"

"Sho' I do. He was a worker for the city an' volunteer fireman an' kind of a famous man for a slave. They say he was a good fireman an' helped stop the city from a-burnin' down at the end o' the war that let the black folks get free like the Isreelites from Ejip. Folks in my family always be talkin' 'bout him. Say the city gave him some kinda money or lan' or somethin' for bein' a good fireman an' savin' Montgomery. I ain't never seen no money nor no lan', but my peoples always used to be a-talkin' about it like it was real or somethin.' I thought they all jus' crazy, you know, like when my auntie thinkin' my mama had all that money hided away an' I done kilt her for it. That kinda thing. Black folks always talkin' 'bout money an' stuff they ain't got 'cept up in they minds where they thinks."

Steick had calmed a little, but he still had twitches and stammers and sat bouncing up and down on the balls of his feet.

"Any-any-any-uh-anything else, Ninety?"

"Well, Doc, jus' my peoples always be a-talkin' about it, like I said. An' they say they always be a 'Ninety' in the family ever since Ninety Ton McWilliams, you know, an' that was where I got my name from. An then, a long time ago, some of 'em start callin' me 'Ninety Megaton' 'cause I kind of a big fella, you know. But I don't know what that 'megaton' mean unless it mean a lots o' tons. An' it ain't official or nothin' down at the coat house. Jus' what they started in a-callin' me, you know. An' they say too that all us McWilliamses been a-workin' for the city ever since Ninety Ton did a long time ago. An' I likes workin' for the city, too, you know. We's always liked workin' for the city, they says."

Steick was still trembling, although less visibly. He knew he still needed to avoid leading questions.

"Where were you born, Ninety?"

"At my mama's house."

"Do you know who was there at the house when you were born, by any chance?"

"They told me it was jus' my mama an' daddy an' some white doctor Daddy brought around."

Steick was relieved to hear the word "doctor," and continued. "Do you happen to have a birth certificate that you know of, Ninety? I mean a piece of paper that says when and where you were born, who the doctor was, and all that kind of thing? You ever see a paper like that at all?"

"Oh, yes, sir. I knows I got me one. I look at it lots o' times before. My family always funny that way fo' some reason. 'Always keep yo' birth certificate,' they say. An' they always sayin' how it might be important sometime an' be worth some money or somethin', an' they treat them birth certificate like they be hunerd dollar bills theyself you know, and tell me always to do the same thing. They used to talked about it a lot when they was a-talkin' all that business about Ninety Ton gettin' some money or lan' from the city or whatever they say it was. I never paid much attention to it. Jus' thought it was some kinda family tradition or somethin' they proud of like that, you know."

Steick was afraid to continue for fear of jinxing his winning streak, but on the other hand, he knew he had nothing to lose, and he had to ask.

"Uh, you wouldn't happen to know where to find your birth certificate, would you? We could probably look it up at Vital Statistics, but it would be even easier if you had one yourself."

"Oh yeah. It be in the box at my house with all the rest o' them."

"What do you mean, 'all the rest of them?'"

Ninety looked at Steick as if the lawyer were a little slow. "It's like I tol' you, Doc. My family always say it was important to keep them birth certificate, and so everbody always done it. I got mine. I got my daddy's. I always behave an' listen to my daddy, you know. He whupped me lots, but he was a good man an' always work an' provide for us pretty good. I wouldn't go against what he say an' what all them other daddies done tol' they sons. I keep them birth certificate in that ol' safe box they come in. I got 'em goin' all the way back to my three-times-great-granddaddy, Ninety Ton, you know."

Steick couldn't believe his ears. This was too great to possibly be true. If it were true, it was still more evidence (as if any were needed) that he had been divinely appointed a sort of modern Moses himself. He suspected that if he picked up a stick and hit a rock, water would come gushing forth.

He could wait no longer to see if Ninety's facts were true. "What time do you get off, Ninety?"

"'Bout three hours from now."

"You suppose your boss man would let you off now if I asked him and told him it was important?"

"He might. He all right."

"What's his name?"

"It Mr. Smiley Jones now."

"Does he have an office in there?" Steick asked, pointing toward the cavernous garage.

"Yeah. It up toward the front. Always nice an' cool in there in the summer and warm in the winter."

"Well. Let's go see if he'll let you off a little early today, okay?"

"Sho," Ninety said as he got up and led the way to the garage office.

By the time they arrived, Steick had become the most genial man on the face of the earth. His grin almost hurt his jaws.

They walked inside, and Ninety said, "This attorney Steick, Mr. Jones. He want to ax you somethin'."

"Oh, hi Ninety," the bearded white man said, swiveling around in his chair. He was casually dressed but clean and well-groomed. Steick noticed a lot of laugh lines around his eyes. He was fairly fat but looked otherwise fit, if weathered. Steick saw some mounted fish and a nicely pointed deer head on the walls and judged Jones an affable outdoorsman.

The lawyer stuck out his hand like he was campaigning for President. Every ounce of Kennedy charm he could muster went into his handshake and his gestures.

"I'm Richard Steick, Mr. Jones. Very pleased to meet you. It's a great job y'all do here keepin' all this equipment at work and on the road. I've always said that Montgomery has the finest city services in the world. Couldn't ask for anything better."

"Well, thank you, Mr. Steick. I appreciate the compliment. What can I do for you, anyway?"

"Well, Mr. Jones, I'm workin' on a little civil matter, and I need to talk to Ninety for a while. It'll take a couple of hours. I wouldn't want to just stand around out here using up the City's time and setting a bad example for the other workers. It's kind of urgent. I was wondering if you would please let him off early today for me. I'll be happy to pay for half a day of his wages, of course. That would only be fair, it seems to me. And I always like to be fair, you know."

"Well, this is a little unusual," the supervisor responded. "But we always let guys off for medical reasons and when they're subpoenaed or got Guard duty or other things like that, you know. I don't know why we couldn't do it now, 'specially since you're willin' to pay for his time off."

"And how much would that come to, Mr. Jones?"

"Well, let's see," Jones responded. He pulled out a file drawer, fished inside, pulled out a piece of paper, and then quickly ran some numbers on his calculator. "I reckon about eighty dollars would cover it, including taxes and benefits and all that kinda thing," he said.

"I'm more than happy to pay that, Mr. Jones," Steick said, fishing for his wallet. He found it quickly, flipped it open, and pulled out two crisp hundred-dollar bills.

"This should more than cover his time off then," the lawyer said, handing Jones one of the bills. "And this is for your trouble," he added, handing him the other one.

Jones's mouth dropped open in surprise. "Why, thank you very kindly, Mr. Steick. We're always happy to help out where the law is concerned. Just let me know if there's anything else we can do for you!"

"I sure will, Mr. Jones," the lawyer replied, adding "Y'all keep up the good work now!" as he and Ninety headed for the door.

Once outside, Steick said, "Look, Ninety. Where's your car?"

"Ain't got no car. Got me a pickup truck over there," he said, pointing toward a fairly beaten Chevy three-quarter ton.

"Okay. Fine. You take the lead, and I'll follow you over to your house on Oak Street."

A STUDY IN CONTRASTS, the two-vehicle parade set out from the garage parking lot. "Oh, my God," Steick thought as he drove. "What if Miss Helen's at home now?" It was a matter he had failed to consider.

The drive to Ninety's house took about seven minutes. As soon as Ninety had parked, Steick was out of his quickly locked SUV and at Ninety's window. "Hey, Ninety, where's Miss Helen right now?"

"She at her work. She a cleanin' lady at Lee High School. She won't be home for a coupla hours."

Steick felt himself looking more and more like Moses on the Sistine Chapel ceiling. "Good. Let's go. I want to have a look at all those birth certificates, if it's okay with you."

"Sho," Ninety replied, leading the way into his clean but sparsely furnished small house.

Once inside, they walked into what Steick surmised was the master bedroom. Ninety opened a sliding closet door and pulled down an old, black, rectangular file box from a shelf. It bore plenty of signs of wear. The lawyer could just make out the words "Nashville 1858" in tarnished gold lettering. The box would be good to keep out water and vermin, but it would never survive a house fire.

"This strong box got them birth certificate in it, Doc."

"Good. Let's have a look."

"Okay then," Ninety said, as he walked to a chest of drawers, pulled open one of them, and brought out a small iron key. He put the box onto the dresser, unlocked it, opened the lid, and said, "You go on an' take a look now. They's all there, an' that's all I got. I hope you finds what you lookin' fo'."

And sure enough, the lawyer did. In chronological order as well. It was the work of a moment as he quickly but very carefully scanned through the birth certificates and a few other miscellaneous documents, including warranty deeds, deeds of trust, and death certificates. Many of the oldest papers were brittle, and he handled them gingerly.

Within five minutes he had traced a clear, definitive, state-stamped and -sealed chain of paternity and therefore inheritance from the Ninety McWilliams by his side back to one Ninety Ton McWilliams, born 1825, sold in 1840, and officially emancipated in 1865. He found interesting variations on the name, including "Eighty Ton McWilliams," who was the first son of Ninety Ton, and a later grandson named "Ninety Truck McWilliams." His former client, Ninety, had no middle name at all.

Steick turned to him and said, "Ninety, this is exactly what I've been looking for. I think your family was right all along about these birth certificates being worth money one day. They're extremely valuable, and they would be destroyed if you had a house fire. If you don't mind, I'd like to take them back to my office and put them in my fireproof safe. I'll be happy to write out a receipt for them if you want me to. Would that be okay with you?"

"That's all right, Doc. I don't need no receipt. You knows I trust you. So what you wantin' me to be doin' now, anyway?"

"Ninety, I don't want you to do anything except your job at the city garage and keep your oath on the Bible that you made in front of me today. Nothing else. Don't say a word about this to anyone. Period. Just go about your business as usual. Don't talk to Miss Helen about it. And don't drink at all. Not even beer, okay?"

"All right then."

"You promise?"

"Yes, sir. I promise."

"Do you have a phone now?"

"It been cut off fo' a while."

"All right," the elated attorney and prophet continued. "Just do what I told you, and I'll get in touch with you when I need you. It might be a while. I've got to go to Washington, D.C., about this. I'm not going to lose you or these birth certificates, I can promise you that. Here's my card. You call me in Hallelujah if you have any questions, okay?"

"That's fine with me, Doc. I'll keep my promise, and I'll be waitin' to hear from you."

"Thank you so much, Ninety," Steick said, heading for the door with the precious box in his hands. "This is going to turn out to be a very good thing, I believe."

Then he hesitated, thought for a moment, and turned back. "But I've got to get an attorney-client contract with you first. You've been my client before. Do you want to be my client again, Ninety?"

"Sho' I do. If you say it a good thing, then I believes you."

"Okay, good. I'll stop around at the city garage and have you sign a contract tomorrow. So good-bye for now, and I'll see you tomorrow at your afternoon break time, okay?"

"That's fine, Doc. I'll see you tomorrow."

The lawyer almost ran to his SUV. His heart was still pounding very hard, and it was difficult to avoid speeding. But he slowly got a grip as he contemplated the difficulties that yet lay ahead. He changed CDs, replacing Chopin's *Etudes* with Beethoven's *Third Symphony,* "The Heroic," which he played all the way back to Hallelujah.

That night, Steick very carefully drafted an attorney-client contract for Ninety to sign the next day, which Ninety cheerfully did.

Get It While It's Hot?

Richard and Melissa were enjoying a late dinner in the warm glow of the charming and historic Old Ebbitt Grill on Fifteenth Street in Washington, D.C., just around the corner from the White House. They were celebrating the end of a wonderfully successful three-day trip to the nation's capital and had just come from a fantastic performance of Stravinsky's *Firebird* ballet at the Kennedy Center. The next morning, they would fly back to Montgomery. They had long agreed that dining late, after the theater, an opera, a symphony, or a movie, was the most elegant and leisurely way to tuck into a fine meal.

"Thank you so much for this trip, Richard," Melissa said. "I don't know when I've had so much fun. It's ages since I've been away from Alabama, and I was just itching to go somewhere different."

"The pleasure was all mine, Melissa," he responded. "You've made this trip ever so much more fun for me too, you know. I was kind of dreading it before we decided you'd come along. I anticipated just a bunch of boring research, but we've had a great time together, haven't we?"

"We certainly have. And you're a very good traveling companion. You're thoughtful of me, flexible, and courteous, even when you have work to do. My ex was always the big boss. He laid everything out in advance, had it timed down to the minute, and wouldn't eat anywhere different because he was afraid he wouldn't like the food. If I were with him now, we'd be at that chain restaurant, whatever it was, that we passed in the cab just a couple of blocks from here."

"I never eat at places like that unless I have to."

"And we got to do a lot of things I never expected, like the ballet tonight, the National Cathedral, National Portrait Gallery, and the Smithsonian. I thought you'd be so busy with work that we wouldn't be able to do anything else."

"The last thing I wanted was for you to be bored, Melissa, and so I did as much research in advance as I could. I knew what I was looking for and where to find it. We ran into some very kind and helpful people, and we had excellent luck in the bargain. My membership in the Bar of the U.S. Supreme Court helped quite a bit, didn't it?"

"It certainly opened some doors. Now, please summarize just where we stand, if you will."

"Glad to. It's more for my benefit than yours. You know how I like to think and talk about important matters over dinner. It helps me clarify things and make my mental lists.

"First, we located the duly recorded, fee-paid land patent to Farthing Worthy's Island, conveying it forever to the black firemen of Montgomery and their heirs, and it corresponds exactly to the copy I found in the Montgomery County Probate Office. Thus, it's a done deal, and it's airtight legitimate. I've looked into the matter, and the island is almost like an Indian reservation, nearly sovereign itself. All subsequent ownership is, and has been, bogus.

"Second, we obtained the opinion of a famous Presidential handwriting expert, Hans Aschliman, that the signature on our deed is in fact that of President Andrew Johnson, and we've got Aschliman's deposition as evidence. It was an unexpected bonus that Aschliman turned out to be an expert on paper adhesives as well. I wasn't too surprised to learn that the small scrapings he took from the front of our deed were in fact a form of glue commonly used in the 1860s. My intuition tells me it was an intentional act that caused our document to be stuck face down in the grantor's index, and that seems the most logical conclusion, but our expert can't verify this.

"So, there we are," he said. "With our deed, deposition, and Ninety's box of birth certificates, we can sue the daylights out of Alchemelia Corporation and its owner, Conglomo, as well as the State of Alabama, Montgomery County, the City of Montgomery, and the United States of America, to name a few, beginning tomorrow."

"But you don't plan to do that, at least not immediately, do you?" she asked.

"No, Honey, I don't. I'm going to use what we know as leverage, first of all to kill that hot toxic waste facility in Coffee County. That's my first priority. That facility would be a terrible disaster for Alabama, and I'm surprised it has gone this far. My guess is that the APE-Christian Committee has got itself behind it. But if I can massage Ernest Grones in the right way, it won't even be introduced as a bill, and if it is, it will simply die in committee."

"So—how are you going to approach Representative Grones?" she asked.

"I'm just going to have to play it by ear. I have to avoid any appearance of bribery, period. I don't want to break the law, lose my license, maybe go to jail, whatever. I'm already on thin ice for borrowing that old deed from the Probate Office. That probably constitutes tampering with governmental records, a class A misdemeanor, although nobody knows about it except you and me, and I think I have a solid defense. Besides, I can get a certified photocopy and put the original back where I got it now, which is exactly where it needs to be found when and if we go public.

"There's a thin line in Alabama law between ordinary lobbying on the one hand and bribery on the other. As we all know, that line is too often unobserved and unprosecuted while incredible deals pass quietly under the table. What I want is to get the most commitment I can out of Grones without showing more of my cards than I have to and without breaking the law. It's going to be a tricky business. He's sharp as a tack, but he's also deeply committed to his constituency as well as his own advancement. I'll have to work on those angles. Wish me luck, Melissa."

"I certainly do, Richard. I love you all the more for your dedication to this important work, you know. You're an uncommonly fine man, and I'm with you, come what may."

THE FOLLOWING AFTERNOON, the couple found themselves back in Montgomery and then in Hallelujah. It took a while to unpack, and Richard did not have any classes until the next morning. He thought Grones followed a schedule a lot like his own, with Grones's classes scheduled in the morning, followed by his political work in the afternoon. Richard hoped he might catch the legislator in his office at the university.

Steick was early for his 8:00 A.M. honors seminar (titled "Rights: What Are They?") the next day. His students surprised him with their preparation and at least vague comprehension of the reading selections he had assigned. But his mind wandered frequently to the property rights granted Montgomery's "heroic Negro volunteer firemen" in 1865, the mysterious loss of those rights to history, and his plans to finally obtain justice for the firemen's heirs.

When his seminar ended at 10:00 A.M., he walked to his office and looked up Representative Grones's number in the campus phone book. He did not expect to find Grones in his office immediately, but it was worth a try, and he could always leave a message. He punched in the numbers and listened to the phone ring four times. There was a tiny click, followed by a lady's pleasant, recorded voice saying, "Your call is being answered by Audomat . . ." followed by a louder click and the single, forceful word, "Grones."

"Professor Grones!" Steick responded, as if he had reached the Almighty Himself. "Glad I caught you! This is Richard Steick over in the Honors College! It's been a while, but I hope you remember me."

"Of course I remember you, Richard. In fact, there's something I've been wantin' to talk to you about for a while now. Two things, really. What can I do for ya?"

"Well, that's interesting, Professor Grones, because there's something I've been wantin' to talk to you about, too."

"Just call me Ernest, Richard. I hope it ain't about some damn curriculum committee or something like that. I don't have time for all that junk, you know? I've got more important committees down at the legislature that I've got to work with."

"No, it isn't, Ernest. In fact, this has to do with your work in the legislature. So, since we've both been wantin' to talk to each other, when do you s'pose you're going to have a little time for me in your busy schedule?"

"Well, I was just headin' down to my legislative office now, but I don't have any appointments until lunch time. How 'bout you? You got any classes now or anything?"

"No. I'm free for the next hour, so I called you on a long shot. Think there's a chance we might work in a little conversation before lunch?"

"Yeah, come on over. You know where my office in political science is at, don't you?"

"Sure I do. Look, can you give me about fifteen minutes first? I've got something I've got to do for honors. Won't take me but a little bit."

"That's okay. Just don't keep old Grones waitin' too long. I've got people botherin' me and wantin' my time all the time."

"I won't make you wait, Ernest. I'll be over within fifteen minutes, I promise."

MOVING SWIFTLY, STEICK PUT a "Do Not Disturb" sign on his door, then closed and locked it. He quickly removed his navy blazer, loosened his tie, and pulled it over his head. He was out of his white shirt in seconds. Reaching into his briefcase, he pulled out a small, highly sensitive, flesh-colored digital recording device which he taped to his right side. He ran the short wire and attached the self-adhesive microphone to the soft spot just under his sternum. The device was voice-activated, and he quickly tested its operation. Perfect! He dressed again, checked his appearance in a long mirror, and briefly groomed his hair. He tucked up, patted down, and looked and felt prepared. The entire operation had taken less than eight minutes, leaving him just the right amount of time to walk casually to Representative Grones's office.

When he arrived at room 209, he noticed that the class schedule and office hours posted were four years out of date. He knocked confidently, and immediately he heard Grones bark "Come on!" from within. He entered grinning and saluted the Representative, who was talking on his cell phone.

Grones looked up with a smile and said into the phone, "Okay. Thanks. Look. I've got to go now. I've got somebody here to see me. We'll talk more later." He punched the phone off, put it on his desk beside another, and rose to shake hands with his fellow professor. Still smiling, he said, "Professor Steick! Long time no see! Sit down! Sit down!"

Steick took a straight-backed chair immediately opposite Grones's seat behind his desk. The office was littered with civil rights books and stacks of manila class folders which Richard guessed contained years of unmarked student essays.

"How you been, Richard?" the Representative asked. "Stayin' busy?"

"Oh yeah. You know what it's like, having responsibilities both here and on the outside."

"I sure do. But it keeps us from gettin' bored, doesn't it?"

"It does indeed," the lawyer replied, silently reflecting that perhaps Grones was one of the lucky few not afflicted by dildo. "So how's your family, and what's up in the legislature these days?"

"Family's fine. Legislature's a mess. So what's new?"

"Well, you do good work there anyway."

"You know, Richard. You're all right for a white guy. Straight shooter. About the only white person I know to contribute to my campaigns. You black inside? I think maybe you're black inside."

"Ernest, I don't always see eye-to-eye with you, but I think you're a straight shooter, too. You generally take progressive stands in the best interest of all the people of Alabama, and you represent your constituents vigorously. That's enough to win my support, no matter what color I am or you are, outside or inside."

"Thank you, Richard. I mean that sincerely. And what you just said takes me to the first thing I've been wantin' to talk to you about."

"Fire away."

"Well, there's two things really, but I'm always so damn busy I've been puttin' 'em off. Listen. The first thing is a little drafting problem I've got, and I know you're good, maybe even famous, for your legal drafting. So I wonder if you might help me write something up for a bill I want to introduce. I could go through the Legislative Reference Service, but I'm never happy with what they write for me. All I want to do is revise the entire *Code of Alabama* so there is no mention of race in it, period. I don't want to see the words 'Negro,' 'Caucasian,' 'Asian,' 'Indian,' 'black,' 'white,' or anything like that in there at all. See what I mean? Do you think that's possible? And can you help me write it?"

"To be honest, Ernest, it's a little tough because sometimes the classifications are necessary to a compelling governmental interest, such as equal protection of the laws, if you see what I mean."

"Let me show you what I've got so far," Grones replied. He opened his enormous briefcase and rifled through an immense assortment of files. But he quickly produced his abortive efforts to date and passed them across the desk to his colleague.

The lawyer surveyed them and pronounced, "I think I get the drift, Ernest, but I don't think what you've got here is going to do the job. I'll be happy to look the matter over and give you my best efforts, but that's all I can promise. Okay?"

"That's fine, Richard. I can't ask for more than that."

"There's just one thing I'd like to ask you today, Ernest, and it's strictly on the up-and-up."

"Okay. What is it?"

"I want you to sincerely listen very carefully to what I've got to tell you in a few minutes. I just want to talk to you about a possible state project and share some information. That's all. Some of this material is highly confidential. You can't talk to anyone about it. I'm not offering you anything, and I'm not asking for anything. We're just talkin' politics. Okay?"

"That's okay with me, Professor. Grones will always listen, you know. We've got a First Amendment right to talk, don't we? And if talkin' politics wasn't allowed, there wouldn't be any reason to have Montgomery, would there? So I'm happy to listen and talk. No problem. But look, Richard. Folks is always wantin' something from Grones, you know, and they'll give most anything to get it. So just don't offer me any thing of value. Okay? I know you're smarter than that."

"Of course I am, Ernest. I'm not interested in any *quid pro quo* or violating any rules of ethical conduct. I wouldn't do that on principle. And we both have too much to lose, don't we? So what was the second thing you wanted to ask me about, anyway?"

"Richard, are you acquainted with my plans for the Alabama State Archives Building?"

"I've read a little bit about it in *The Advertiser*. I think you want to create a slavery museum or something like that, don't you?"

"Exactly!" Grones said enthusiastically. "Call it 'The Museum of Slavery.' They've got a lot of space down there at Archives, with too much of it devoted to Hank Williams's cowboy hat and boots. I want a section set aside for slavery, kinda like the Holocaust Museum in D.C. We'll have black crepe surrounding all the doorways. Work songs and spirituals playin' in the background. Make it interactive, with videos and stuff, so the kids will like it. I've got an idea for a video game called 'Underground Railroad.' Want to display the manacles, gags, whips, and all those ugly things. Maybe even have a little patch of cotton to chop. Use heat lamps and make it a hundred degrees in there. You get the picture?"

"Sure. I get it. So what's your problem, and what do you want me to do about it?"

The Representative looked dismayed and replied, "It's the same old story. All the white folks sayin' 'There goes Grones again. Only got one string on his banjo,' and all that stuff. But I'm talkin' about a sound educational project here, Richard. There's no denying that slavery is a part of this nation's history, any more than there's any denying that the Holocaust happened, is there? And you know what they say about the Holocaust, don't you? 'We must never forget.' And I think we ought to take the same approach to slavery in the United States. See what I mean? Might even bring some tourist dollars into Alabama, if I'm right. And God knows, we need the money. So what do you think of my idea, anyway?"

Steick was thoughtful. Then he said, "That famous old phrase about how 'Those who forget the mistakes of the past are condemned to repeat them' has a lot of wisdom in it, Ernest. And I agree with you that we must never forget about slavery. But I'm going to be brutally honest with you now, because you deserve my best ideas, and I won't give you anything less. I think what pisses off a lot of white people is the self-righteousness and envy, or resentment, that your proposals sometimes project. *Resentiment* in French. It kinda combines 'resentment' and 'envy.' Nietzsche used that word to describe an unhealthy state of mind that keeps people from overcoming their obstacles and getting on with real achievements.

"To come to the bottom line, I think your idea for a Museum of Slavery is a good one. I just wouldn't want to see it constructed or pitched with a lot self-righteous *resentiment*. Could backfire on you and do more harm than good. Like to see you incorporate differing scholarly views. And I think it wouldn't hurt to include information and displays about the history of poor whites in Alabama as well. See what I mean? Strive for accuracy, objectivity, and balance. Try to be dispassionate.

"Don't get me wrong. I wouldn't find it easy to be dispassionate myself if my ancestors had suffered the way yours did. I'm just telling you what I think would be the best approach to your idea. So how can I help you?"

"Frankly," Grones said, "you've helped me already by being honest. I'm never quite sure what white people are thinkin', you know, and I kinda see what you mean. Could you get behind the idea and support it if we took the path you just suggested?"

"Yes. I could, Ernest. I'd be happy to help such a museum in any way possible, provided it's done right. But what do you want from me besides my support?"

"That's the main thing I need, Richard, is your support. I want you to talk the idea up with your lawyer and professor friends, your friends at church, your family, all the people you know. Maybe write a letter to *The Advertiser* givin' old Grones your vote of confidence on the project. I'm gettin' the weary blues with these labels and stereotypes white people are always puttin' on me. If you think I got a good idea here, then get on the bandwagon, okay?"

"I promise I'll support the museum in all those ways, Ernest, and I'll write more than one letter to the editor in favor of it. In addition, I won't just write to *The Advertiser*. I'll write to papers all over the state. How's that?"

Half rising, Grones extended his hand across the desk to shake on it, and Richard grasped his hand firmly. "Thank you for knowin' a good thing when you see one, Professor Steick," Grones said, and as he regained his seat, he was smiling proudly. "Now. You said a little bit ago that there was something you wanted me to listen to, and like everybody knows, Grones will always listen. So what's on your mind?"

"First of all, Ernest, you have to promise me that nothing either of us says here today will ever go outside this room. I'm not gonna try to bribe you or influence you unduly. It's just that if this matter gets out too early, there's going to be hell to pay, and something potentially great for the State of Alabama is going to be shot to pieces. You follow me? I've been honest with you, and I want you to be honest with me. That's all I'm asking. Okay?"

"Okay, Richard. I promise that I'll keep everything we say in strict confidence. You've got my interest and full attention now, so let me hear it."

"The first thing, Ernest, is that hot tox storage facility down in Coffee County. I know who's behind it—that clown Hoop DeMinus. I don't know what he hopes to get out of it for himself, but I'm sure it's a lot of money. Now I hear that *you* are going to introduce a bill in the legislature authorizing the project, and I just can't believe that. Do you have any idea how dangerous that stuff is? I've read a whole stack of information about it, and I've brought some copies for you. This thing would be humanly and environmentally disastrous for a large portion of south Alabama. Do you realize that? Do you know that one minor technical error in delivery, storage, or surveillance could mean potential death for thousands of people, both black and white, for miles and miles around? Is that what you want? You bring that thing to Coffee County, and it'll be far worse than Love Canal. It'll be a potential Bhopal, India. Remember that one?"

"Yeah, Richard, I know a lot of that stuff, and it worries me something awful. I've got a lot of doubts about that bill and that project. It's just that it's good money, and we need money worse than ever, with the dock revenues down and every other source of income down, thanks to the Governor's 'Take 15% Off' plan. So where we going to find it, anyway?"

"I can't answer that altogether," Steick responded. "But I can tell you this. That bill has got to stay out of the legislature entirely or else die in committee, and you've got the power to see that it does. You shouldn't introduce it, Ernest, and you should stomp on it like a cockroach if anybody else introduces it. That's the first thing I want you to hear from me today."

"You must keep your ear to the ground pretty good, Professor. I didn't know it had got out that I planned to introduce that bill."

"I've got good sonar. Came that way from the factory."

"What about my voters? Their schools are bein' closed down. They can't get any decent health care. Even the courts can hardly operate. We're lettin' more criminals out all the time, so we can try and catch them again, with fewer cops, so the crooks can stay out on bail and on the streets longer, committin' more crimes, and we never get around to prosecuting them at all, because the courts' dockets are clogged like really bad arteries. So what are we supposed to do?"

"I can't give you all the answers, Ernest, but I can tell you something really important to some of your voters, if you want me to."

"And what would that be?"

"This is the most sensitive stuff of all. So listen carefully and don't talk to anybody about it. Do you sincerely promise, on your word of honor, that you won't mention it?"

"Yeah, I already promised you, on my word of honor, that I won't. So trust me, and let me hear it."

"Okay. Here are the facts. I have definite legal proof that a fair number of your voters, as well as a lot of black people elsewhere, have got a lot of money coming to them according to the laws of Alabama and the United States of America."

"I know we're all due reparations for slavery, Richard, so what's new about that?"

"I'm not talking about reparations or restitution for past events. You know that's never going to happen anyway. I'm talking about genuine, present ownership by many black citizens of some extremely valuable real estate in Alabama as well as all the profits that have come from it in the past and that will ever come from it in the future. What do you think about that?"

"I think you're even crazier than DeMinus, and he oughta' be locked up."

"I suppose I'd think the same way if I were in your shoes, Ernest, but what I'm telling you is the truth, so help me God. And right now, I'm the only person in the world who knows about it and can prove it in court. I have documents. Tangible, indisputable evidence. I'm prepared to slowly share my information with you if you're interested. You can be the point man and take all the glory. All I want is a reasonable attorney's fee for my work and the satisfaction of knowing that justice has finally been done after an extremely long delay. It's going to be a tough battle, but I've got an airtight case, I assure you."

"I still think you're crazy, Richard. I think you might be hearin' voices and need a doctor. But how much money are you talkin' about, anyway?"

"I can't say at this point, Ernest. It has to get into court or else be settled out of court, and then there has to be a massive, unprecedented accounting. Just guessing, I'd say we're talking about hundreds of millions or possibly billions of dollars."

"And this money belongs to who?"

"Black people and black people only. Mainly around here in central Alabama, but some of them scattered all over the country and elsewhere, I would imagine. You take the point position, and you could find yourself in Washington when it's all over, I'd guess."

"You can't say how much at this point," Grones repeated. "Now let me guess what comes next. I ask you what real estate and what money, and you'll say 'I can't say,' right?"

"That's right, Ernest."

"Okay. What documents and what indisputable evidence? Show me something. Like I don't know the answer already, but show me something."

"I can't do that now. In fact, it would be violating an attorney-client privilege if I did."

"So you've got a secret plan with legal proof to make a lot of black people rich, and I get all the credit, but you can't tell me anything about it, is that right, Richard?"

"That about sums it up, Ernest."

"So, how'd you learn about this deal, anyway? I suppose you can't tell me that either, can you?"

"I'll tell you this much. I learned what I know through legitimate, verified public records in the Alabama court system, and that's a fact. I can let you in on the documents and the proof after due consultation with my client and other considerations, including the future of the Coffee County hot tox project. I've got a busy schedule, you know, and so does my client. I would guess I won't even be able talk with my client until that hot tox bill is killed dead in the next legislative session."

"A lot of important people are countin' on that bill! Where we gonna get the money to run this state if it doesn't pass?"

"Let those people get behind a fair and equitable tax system then. You know as well as I do that genuine tax reform is what we really need to generate consistent revenues and boot-strap Alabama out of last place in every important measure of health, education, and welfare. If they can't do that, then let them at least adopt a state lottery like almost every other state in America. We've got a lot of wonderful people in Alabama. But, just like anywhere, we've got a lot of idolaters and hypocrites who refuse to feed the hungry and clothe the naked because it might cost them a nickel or offend their highly moral sense of smell. You know that as well as I do, Ernest. You're as much in favor of tax reform or a lottery as I am. These issues are always part of your own campaign platform. We don't need to turn Coffee County into a dangerous wasteland for our children and grandchildren just to appease the rich, the greedy, and the self-righteous, do we? End of sermon."

Representative Grones swiveled his chair and looked out his window for a long time. When he rotated back to face his colleague, he looked careworn and somber.

"Richard, I cannot and will not promise you anything at all. But just let me repeat a few of the things I said a little bit ago. First, Grones will always listen. Second, you've always been a straight shooter in my book, and I trust your honesty and integrity. Third, we're both in favor of what's in the best interest of Alabama. Fourth, I've had my doubts about that Coffee County project ever since that dumbass DeMinus started pushing it on me. Fifth, I'm going to think very carefully about everything you've said before the legislature convenes next week. Okay?"

"Okay, Representative Grones. I take your word on all you've just said, and I trust your deliberations will result in a decision that's good for the entire State of Alabama, not just for now, but for future generations as well. And having said that, Ernest, I'll say 'good-bye and good luck.' I know you're a busy man, and I've got appointments, too."

Grones escorted his fellow professor toward the office exit.

"Hope you have a good lunch, Ernest," Steick said.

"Yeah, I will," Grones responded, adding, "Come see me," as he shook hands and bid his colleague good-bye.

No Known Casualties

The most significant achievement of the next legislative session was the creation of the Alabama Filling Station Hall of Fame. Most Alabamians let out a sigh of relief when the session ended and so little damage had been done. There was the usual tinkering with funding shortages, the Uniform Trust Code, registration and filing under the Securities Act, sentencing reform, further immunity for physicians against malpractice suits, and a lot of jabber about accountability and constitutional reform. Every bill thoughtfully considered and recommended by the Alabama Law Institute sailed through without a hitch. The legislators all knew that the Institute understood the law and recommended only that which was truly necessary for basic civil government. The Senators and Representatives also knew that they personally did not know a trust from the Book of Psalms, and therefore they had to have faith in an organization that did.

On the final night of the legislative session, Governor Scroulous sat in his study with his martinis and cheese straws. He was memorizing the Bible verse that Martha had assigned for his morning redemption program. The verse was Job 42:7, which stated, among other things, that "The Lord said to Eliphaz the Temanite, 'My wrath is kindled against thee, and against thy two friends: for ye have not spoken of me the thing that is right, as my servant Job hath.'" The Governor could not, for the life of him, see how the verse had a damn thing to do with property values or anything else important. Yet he had no choice. He had to memorize it. Martha seemed determined to make him learn the entire Bible, verse by verse. But somehow she never got around to the good parts, like "Ask and it shall be given you," and really Christian things like that.

The Governor had been counting on the hot tox revenues to save his administration from further financial difficulty and embarrassment, and he was wondering who had let him down. He could not call a special session of the legislature to push the bill due to his own "Take 15% Off Plan." It took him a while, but eventually he recalled that he had assigned a subordinate to goose the well-known moron, Little Hoop DeMinus at Solid Waste Liaisons, into ramming the bill through the legislature for him.

The failure of DeMinus to do so kindled the Governor's wrath considerably. He was on his third martini when he decided that the budget at Solid Waste deserved a little more trimming. It probably hadn't reached its quota of 15 percent off of everything, and Scroulous would rectify that error the first thing the next morning by taking a little more off the top. In short, DeMinus would be gone. The Governor didn't feel bad about it because he knew his old fraternity brother would turn up quickly as assistant director of Emergency Management, the Forestry Commission, Public Health, or some equally harmless position. DeMinus might miss a mortgage payment, but the Governor wanted to teach him a lesson. And Little Hoop would probably end up with a pay raise in any event.

DeMinus himself had been puzzled and dismayed when Representative Grones had not introduced the Coffee County bill in the legislature. He had gone to a lot of trouble with oversight committees, the Alabama Department of Environmental Management, the federal EPA, and various special interest groups to insure that the bill would have its best shot at passing if it were brought up in the session. He had tried repeatedly to reach Representative Grones by telephone when the bill wasn't mentioned, but neither the Representative nor his secretary would return DeMinus's calls.

So he went to Grones's office to wait him out. When the legislator found he could not avoid DeMinus, he told him he was too busy to talk and that DeMinus would have to make an appointment like everybody else. DeMinus even spent several days in the gallery and hallways of the legislative chamber trying to get an audience with Grones, but to no avail. When DeMinus caught him, Representative Grones was always too busy to talk and told him, as usual, that he had to make an appointment. And when DeMinus talked to the Representative's secretary about making an appointment, the earliest she could work him into the schedule was six months in the future.

Meanwhile, the stealthy lobbyist Richard Steick was beside himself with joy when the session ended and the Coffee County hot tox bill had not even been mentioned. The newspapers were totally silent on the issue. Representative Grones had let the word go out discreetly that he not only opposed the bill, but also that he would kill it in committee along with any legislator who dared to introduce it.

Thus, the human and environmental future of much of south Alabama had been saved through the hard work and intelligence of one lawyer and professor from Hallelujah. And Richard Steick, PhD, Esq., found that the mantle of discreet messiah fit him quite nicely. He had achieved fantastic success in the service of the state he loved, and he had even bigger hopes for the future.

In addition, he had a great human love and understanding companion in his life, Melissa Brandywine. He knew he was no longer a dildo and that he truly had found a new lid. He was eager to celebrate his victory with Melissa and also to tell Dr. Kayahs all about it.

He considered his accomplishment sufficiently significant to merit a pleasant weekend of rest, recreation, and relaxed scheming. So he bought a copy of *The Birmingham News* for its entertainment section, reviewed the bill of fare with Melissa, and booked the Governor's Suite at the Tutwiler Hotel. They would take in the symphony, see *Cirque de Soleil* at the Civic Center, and spend a leisurely Sunday afternoon at the museum.

MELISSA WAS AGLOW at getting out of Hallelujah for the weekend. When they arrived at the Tutwiler, she was as amazed as in Washington by Richard's dexterity at managing parking attendants, doormen, bellhops, reception desk personnel, *maitres des hôtes*, and all of the wonderful people who made traveling so much easier. She considered "her man" (as she now thought of Steick) a prestidigitator at tipping. With the smoothest, barely noticeable legerdemain, he tipped, nodded, winked, and sent what seemed telepathic messages to the concierge and several others, all at the same time.

As soon as they drove beneath the hotel's porte cochere, Richard went into his sleight-of-hand routine. Attendants opened the SUV doors for each of them the moment the vehicle stopped. Then, it was as if Richard reached into his pocket without moving and, still without moving, passed an invisible tip to everyone in sight. She knew he was handing out twenty-dollar bills like trick-or-treat candy, but he did it with such poise and discretion that it would take a slow-motion video re-play to decipher what was going on. He gently slapped a shoulder here, shook a hand there, and the SUV was gone. Then he had took her arm, and they were standing at the registration desk. Bellhops were giving it the heave-ho and setting Olympic speed records in the shorter dashes. Richard smiled at the busy receptionist, waved a pen over a registration form, and the happy couple glided gently upward in the elevator, leaving a substantial team of grinning hotel personnel in their wake.

When they arrived at their suite, an attendant was there to unlock the door for them, and when they entered, their luggage was already neatly stacked on a console. How it had reached its destination before them was a mystery to Melissa. She glanced about the well-appointed suite and spotted a large bouquet of flowers, a basket of fruit, a platter of assorted cheeses and crackers, and a bottle of the finest French champagne nestled in an ice-filled silver chiller.

Such was the style of Hallelujah's lawyer-professor, especially when he was in a festive mood, and Melissa was duly impressed.

The couple had plenty of time and desire, before the symphony, to relax and enjoy the amenities, including the champagne and the luxurious four-poster king-sized bed.

Melissa had been with Richard long enough to know that a certain level of indulgence stimulated his cerebral mechanism, and she fully expected him to share his intellectual product with her when the proper moment arrived.

It arrived, typically, as they were enjoying a late supper on Saturday night after the *Cirque de Soleil*. They were dining at a splendid restaurant in an exclusive club atop Red Mountain with the lights of the beautiful city of Birmingham spread all around and beneath them.

"Had a good time so far, Melissa?"

"Absolutely splendid, Richard. And how about yourself?"

"Simply magnificent. Couldn't be better. And I couldn't possibly ask for a more beautiful, intelligent, and charming companion than yourself, so I thank you.

"Little getaways like this help me to think, too, you know. It's like there's no pressure about anything, and my mind clears, goes on auto-pilot, and I gain clarity. I suspect you already know I've been thinking about our next move with Representative Grones and Farthing Worthy's Island, don't you?"

They were seated in a black leather booth beside a huge window. There was candlelight everywhere. Somewhere a piano was playing "I'm in Love Again." She reached across the white, linen-draped table and clasped his hand. "Of course I know what you've been thinking about, Richard," she said. "We know each other so well that I feel like we could almost complete each other's sentences. I'm ready to listen whenever you feel like talking, Darling, but there's no need to rush, you know. Whenever gestation ends, I'm here to catch the baby and do whatever I can to help."

"You can read me like a neon sign, Melissa. Yes, I'd like to bounce a few ideas around with you, if you don't mind."

"You've got my full attention and all of my time, Richard, so fire away."

"Okay, here's how it goes. We've got a long haul ahead, but I think the results will be worth the effort. We can see to it that some long-overdue justice is done, as well as bring the races together in Alabama as never before."

"Go ahead and lay out the program," Melissa replied.

"I still generally favor the plan I outlined before we went to D.C. It's good news that we're dealing with the courts now and not the legislature, since the rules are clearer, and any accusations of bribery are greatly di-minished. The key player continues to be Representative Grones. If I can get him on board once again, our project will be a lot easier. He asked me to come see him after the legislative session ended, and I promised I would. I want to meet with him immediately, thank him for killing the Coffee County project, and move on to phase two. I'll unravel the evidence for him to examine as slowly and as enticingly as I can. I have to be sure he continues to trust me. And I have to be certain I can trust him. It takes cooperation between us, or the whole thing could blow up like a land mine. Possibly I've played a little fast and loose with some laws and the Lawyers' Code of Professional Conduct, but that is debatable at best, and I don't think I've done anything warranting punishment. In addition, the lid is still tightly closed on everything. Only you and I know the real score. I want to keep it that way as long as possible, and I don't want any personal headaches with the courts or the State Bar. I've never had any professional discipline in my career, you know."

"So what are you going to tell Representative Grones this time?"

"I've decided to tell him the basic facts about the ownership of the island and possibly share all or a part of our handwriting expert's deposition with him. I asked Hans Aschliman the questions I did with this purpose in mind. I think his deposition identifies the contents of the conveyance sufficiently to convince Ernest that what I'll be telling him is the truth, and I don't think he will think I would be stupid enough to fake up a deposition with no particular reason for doing so. Meanwhile, the deposition remains my personal property, and Grones has no possible lawsuit, criminal action, or subpoena power against me that I can foresee."

"You mentioned going into court yourself, Richard. When does that come in?"

"After I have a firm commitment from Grones," Richard replied. "I think this is best handled as a class-action lawsuit filed on behalf of the heirs and legatees of the original Montgomery firemen. One problem with a class action suit, however, is called 'numerosity.' You have to prove to the judge that you have a certain minimum number of injured people or claimants, 'plaintiffs,' you know, in order to be certified as a class. Once you're certified, you can advertise the lawsuit and notify the whole world that they might be entitled to recovery. It's a difficult process, since we only have one definite plaintiff right now, Ninety McWilliams. But I think it might be made easier if Representative Grones joins Ninety as a plaintiff. We can argue that his legislative office *de facto* qualifies him as, as—an attorney in fact, I suppose—for a good number of unknown but legally aggrieved citizens in his constituency. It's worth a try."

"Richard," Melissa said. "I want you to listen to me carefully for a moment. It's all well and good—it's wonderful in fact—for me to be traveling with you on our getaways, 'holding your hand,' as you put it, and serving as a sounding board for your ideas about righting an ancient wrong. But I want to do more than that. I want to play a genuine part in this effort. I don't want to just sit on the sidelines and be your cheerleader. I've done enough sideline-sitting in my life. I'm fairly educated, and I have some useful skills and abilities. I know I'm not a lawyer or a politician, but I'm sure I can be of genuine use in some capacity. I want something I can sink my teeth into. I want you to put me to work, Richard. See what I mean?"

"I see exactly what you mean, Melissa. Like with a lot of things lately, it's as if you've been reading my mind. I've been wanting to talk to you about this for quite a while, but I haven't wanted to impose upon your kindness or interfere with your work with Dr. Kayahs. Still, since you're volunteering, I have a very important job I want you to handle, if you're willing."

"So tell me about it, Richard," she said, resting her chin informally on her palm and gazing into his eyes.

"Okay, it's like this. When the truth about Farthing Worthy's Island comes out, it's going to be big news. And by 'big news,' I mean national news. Interviews, all the major networks, the newspapers, and above all, steering the whole project toward the best result we can obtain. It's going to take a major PR effort, Melissa, and I want you to be in charge of that."

"Well! I'm flattered, and I'm ready, willing, and able to take on the job!" She paused, touched her cheek lightly, and said, "But there's just one thing that worries me, Richard, and that's my job with Dr. Kayahs. What do you want me to do. Quit? I love my work, you know, and I'd hate to give it up. What you're describing sounds like a full-time responsibility for me, don't you think?"

"I think it's a major responsibility, but not necessarily a full-time one. Remember that I said I want you to be 'in charge.' I don't mean for you to do all the writing, phoning, and legwork. We're going to have an astute and discreet PR firm, as well as plenty of local 'go-fers' for that, and they'll all be working directly for you. You'll be giving the orders. So there's no problem about keeping your job with Dr. Kayahs. You'll simply run the PR folks after hours. You might have to field an occasional phone call at the doctor's office, but you can keep that to a minimum. Essentially, you'll be moonlighting for our project.

"I'm talking about a couple of hours after work during the week and maybe a few hours on weekends. We want to keep enough time free for us to continue to enjoy each other—that is paramount to me, Sweetheart. But you keep track of your time and bill me monthly. I want to pay you twice what you're earning at your present job."

"What?"

"That only seems fair to me. Above all, I trust you entirely, and that's worth a lot to me. Second, I desperately need your skills and abilities. And finally, it will be overtime for you, won't it? I think twice your usual salary is fair, if you agree. So what do you say?"

"Richard, why are you talking about paying me at all? You know I'd be happy to do what you ask entirely for free. I don't need to be paid. I want to do it for the satisfaction of the work."

"That's fine," he said. "But your time and effort are as valuable as anyone's. To me, they're both priceless in all respects, as I think you know. And in the courts, as well as in the law generally, people are entitled to be compensated for their work, especially when that work serves the cause of justice. *Quantum meruit*, we call it, meaning 'what one merits or deserves.' If all goes according to plan, we're talking about hundreds of millions of dollars here, if not more. I fully expect to be well-paid for my own work under the Equal Access to Justice Act or at the discretion of the court. I'll also be fully reimbursed for all my reasonably associated costs and fees. When we're talking about the vast sums of money that are going to be adjudicated here, a few million dollars is not excessive for the lead attorney—namely, me. Big, multi-party lawsuits are like money trees. Shake them a little, in the right way, and the money comes floating down. So don't fret about being paid for your work. You're going to earn it."

"Okay," Melissa said, "as long as you think it's fair, it's fine with me. I have to confess, however, that I'm still a little worried about juggling my responsibilities with my other job."

"What I've learned over the years, Melissa, is that the key to effectiveness is not working harder, but working smarter. I think I can teach you a few tricks about that. The first one is to delegate, and you're going to have some fine people at your disposal. So don't be afraid to use them. That's what we'll be paying them for, after all. Also, I'm going to fill in Dr. Kayahs on some of the details. I know him pretty well by now, and I think he'll be sympathetic. So, whether it's on your days in Montgomery or those in Hallelujah, you can probably take a call at work now and then, and I don't think he'll mind.

"Melissa," Richard elaborated, "you have great beauty, poise, and grace, as well as a keen mind. You're well-spoken and highly articulate. I'm sure you'll have great media 'presence,' as they call it. So, in addition to what I've already described, I'm going to ask you to head up a committee we ought to form. Call it 'The Committee for Historical Justice,' or something like that. You'll be both the chair and the spokesperson. It's going to gain us a lot of popular support to have a beautiful, articulate white woman, like yourself, speaking out on behalf of an effort ostensibly led by Representative Ernest Grones. See what I mean?"

"Sure, I get it," Melissa said. "We have to massage the public, don't we? And it's like Marshall McLuhan wrote, 'The Medium is the Massage,' isn't it? So you're asking me to be the medium, massage the public, and especially massage the white folks, right? Well, I'm proud and happy to accept your invitation to become a real part of the team!"

She extended her hand across the table, and they shook on the deal. Richard kept her hand in his, gently easing her out of the booth and leading her to the small dance floor. They danced cheek-to-cheek through soft piano renditions of "Strangers in the Night," "I Left My Heart in San Francisco," "Love is a Many-Splendored Thing," and several more classic oldies before taking the elevator down to the parking garage and returning contentedly to their suite at the Tutwiler.

How May I Serve You?

It was characteristic of Richard Steick that he invited Representative Grones to dinner at the Capital City Club in Montgomery the following week. Serious matters always called for a fine meal in an excellent restaurant with a view. It was equally characteristic of Representative Grones to accept. Richard phoned the Alabama statesman on Monday, and they agreed to meet at the Club at 6:30 P.M. on Wednesday.

They were seated at a quiet table near a window. The city lights were just beginning to brighten in the gloaming. The magnificent Alabama River reflected the orange and russet sunset grandly, a perfect photo for a state tourist brochure. The tip of Farthing Worthy's Island was just visible around the north bend of the river. The Wednesday night dinner crowd was sparse, which suited Richard perfectly. He definitely did not need the distraction of possible eavesdroppers at this vital meeting.

The Opp U. colleagues exchanged pleasantries over a cocktail, talking about the university, Grones's family, sports, the weather, and the beauty of the city and the landscape surrounding them.

Once the waitress had taken their dinner orders, Grones considered that the time had come to seize the initiative. His doing so suited the once again carefully wired Steick perfectly.

"I thought you might be giving me a call, Richard. I consider you a rare thing—a white guy who's also a man of his word. I still think maybe you're black inside. Anyway, how'd you like what happened to that Coffee County bill in the legislature?"

"Ernest, I want you to know that you did a great service for the State of Alabama by stomping that sucker flat. Sadly, I don't think you'll ever get the credit you deserve for it, but generations of Alabamians to come will have you to thank for keeping south Alabama green, productive, and a great place to live, as opposed to a lethal wasteland. You did the right thing, Ernest. I'm proud of you. And on behalf of many unknown residents, now living or yet unborn, I want to thank you."

"Well, thank you, too, Richard. I genuinely appreciate your acknowledgment. I try hard to do the right thing, you know. I really do. I try. Frankly, that hot tox project DeMinus dreamed up had bothered me from the git-go. It was dangerous. I think maybe he really wanted to kill all the black people in Coffee County. Don't know how he'd spare the white folks, though. Maybe give 'em secret gas masks or somethin'."

"Trust me, Ernest. Gas masks wouldn't do anybody any good if that stuff DeMinus wanted to store down there ever got loose. Simple skin contact with any contaminated, radioactive vapors would put a person permanently underground, regardless of color. You're damn right it was dangerous. It was too dangerous for this state, and you did the right thing."

"Well, I hope so. I don't know how in hell we're going to get out of this financial mess we're in, but I suppose we've been sayin' that for the last hundred and fifty years in Alabama, haven't we? Now what 'chew got for me, anyway? Last time we talked, you were full of crazy ideas about expensive real estate, rich black folks, and all kinda nonsense that made me think you might be even nuttier than DeMinus, which is asking a lot of anyone. You got anything to say to me this evenin', or are you really just a bullshit artist like most white folks? Come on now. Cough it up."

"Ernest, I've got a lot for you tonight. More than you could ever imagine. But let's start with the easy stuff first, okay? You wanted me to draft a bill for you, remember? Well, I've got it, and here it is." Steick passed the Representative a plain manila folder with a single typed sheet of paper inside. Grones opened it and read:

The *Code of Alabama* (1975), as previously and hereafter amended, shall be revised immediately so as to eliminate, now and hereafter, any and all references to race, color, ethnicity, national origin, religious preference, or gender. All citizens of Alabama shall be referred to as 'citizens' only, unless further designation as a member of a protected class is strictly necessary to a compelling governmental interest. The Alabama Legislative Reference Service shall oversee and assure the prompt implementation of this bill by the official publisher of the *Code of Alabama*.

Representative Grones smiled broadly, saying, "This is exactly what I wanted, professor! I'll introduce it first thing next session. Meanwhile, I want to shake your hand, brother!"

He extended his hand across the table, which reminded Richard of Melissa's gesture at dinner on the previous Saturday night. He shook hands firmly with the Representative but refrained from pulling him out of his seat to dance. He said simply, "Thank you, Ernest. Glad you like it. Happy to be of help in any way I can. It's a good bill, by the way, and you were wise to think of it. We always go around thinking that we speak language, but the fact is that language speaks us. So neutralizing the *Code* vocabulary is more than a symbolic gesture. It seems quite significant to me, and I'm proud that you asked me to help you out."

"Don't mention it, Richard. Much obliged," the legislator responded.

"And here's a little something else I think you might like, Ernest," Steick said, as he passed another plain file folder to his colleague.

Grones opened the folder and read its contents with an ever-widening smile. It was a letter-to-the-editor, a concise, reasonable, articulate, and well-argued appeal for Alabama citizens to support Grones's vision of a "Museum of Slavery" for the State Archives Building, signed by "Richard Steick, PhD, Attorney at Law."

"I've just mailed that letter to *The Montgomery Advertiser* and the editors of approximately fifty of the most important newspapers in the state, and I'm going to continue to support your idea in any way I can. I think it's a good concept if handled properly, just like I told you when we talked about it before."

Representative Grones looked at Richard and smiled broadly. "Thank you again, professor. This is just the kind of thing I need to make my dream become a reality. You gotta' be black inside, Richard. You certain you ain't got some of our royal blue blood inside you?"

"Not as far as I know, Ernest, but anything is possible, I'm sure. And besides, what does it matter? Just shows you how irrelevant race can be when men and women of good will act in the common good. I think your Museum of Slavery could serve some important educational purposes and others as well, as long as you go about it the right way. If I didn't believe that, I wouldn't have written that letter at all."

At this point, the waitress brought their gorgeous green salads.

"I'm not in any hurry, are you, Ernest?"

"Not at all."

"Ma'am, would you please go a little slow with our entrees? We're havin' a good time here, and we've got a lot to talk about, okay?" Richard said.

"Certainly, sir. I'll inform the chef immediately."

"Thank you," Richard said, and as she walked away, the two diners flapped their napkins and tucked into their first course.

"Excellent timing," Richard thought to himself.

It was several minutes before either spoke of anything but their delicious salads and the excellent quality of the food and service at the Capital City Club. Then Grones again took the lead.

"What about that real estate business you were talkin' about in my office, Richard? You—uh—you had any chance to talk to your client since the legislative session ended?"

"As a matter of fact, I have, Ernest."

"And just what, if anything, did this client have to say?"

"My client told me that I could tell you just so much right now, and then we'll have to have some action."

"What kind of action? Come on and get to the point, Richard."

Steick leaned a bit to one side and pointed toward the real estate in question, which was just disappearing in the twilight.

"See that island out there, Ernest?"

"Sure I see it. Fartin's Worthless Island. What about it? Belongs to

Alchemelia Corporation and makes a lot of white folks rich."

"No. It doesn't, Ernest. It really belongs to black folks, mainly here in central Alabama, I believe, but also in a lot of other places as well. So does the money."

Grones looked as if he'd been hit with a stun gun. His fork dropped from his hand, clattered onto his salad plate, and fell to the floor. It took him several moments to regain his speech. Then he said, "You're, you're, you're gonna' have to prove that to me, Richard."

"I will, Ernest, I promise. But look what we've got here!"

The waitress had just arrived with their respective entrees: pressed duck for Representative Grones and chateaubriand for attorney Steick.

"Here you are, gentlemen," she said. "I hope you enjoy your meals. Is there anything else I can get for either of you right now?"

"In fact," Steick replied, "we forgot to order wine. Bring us a bottle of your finest Cabernet, please. That okay with you, Ernest? Go all right with your duck, you think?"

"Yeah, sounds perfect to me."

"Fine, gentlemen," the waitress said. "I'll be right back with your wine."

She had hardly turned her back before the Representative blurted out, "What in the hell are you talkin' about, Steick? You gotta be crazy like I thought!"

"Don't go gettin' your britches in a knot, Ernest. I've brought the proof with me. Let's just have a little wine, enjoy our meal, and then I'll show you something pretty astounding, I'll admit."

The waitress wasted no time in returning with the Cabernet and two fine glasses. She poured a small swallow for each of the men to test for corkage. They swirled it, sniffed it, chewed it, swallowed it, and agreed it was superb. She then filled their glasses tidily and again said, "Enjoy yourselves, gentlemen," before she turned and left.

"All right, Richard, I'm going to enjoy my meal like she said. But you better have something pretty darn good for old Grones when we're finished, okay?"

"I do. Come on. Let's dig in before it gets cold."

"Cheers," Grones replied, raising his glass.

Both men were possessed of impeccable table manners, but both devoured their food like starving hyenas. When the waitress returned to ask about dessert, both waved her away. There was less than an inch of wine left in the bottle when Representative Grones demanded, "Okay. Let's see it. Show me your proof."

Steick knew he was taking a grave risk, but it was one he felt he had to take. "Here," he said. "Read this." And he handed Grones the original deposition of the Washington handwriting expert, Hans Aschliman.

Representative Grones took it, surveyed it, and handled it delicately. He first scanned its contents and then read carefully, word for word, with the intense concentration of a brain surgeon performing a delicate procedure.

Steick knew that Grones was sharp as a scalpel and would not miss anything in the document or fail to apprehend its general significance. He had anticipated this when he deposed Hans Aschliman, taking great care to record the contents of the conveyance as well as the authenticity of the first President Johnson's signature. He took equal care, however, to avoid disclosing where the document could be located in the Land Patents Office in Washington, D.C.

After long scrutiny, Grones said, "This is astonishing, Richard. Who else knows about this besides you and me?"

"Only my client and one trusted associate of my office. That's it. And Hans Aschliman, of course, but he's bound by a professional code of secrecy."

"Okay. So where is the original deed located?"

"I'm afraid that's a client confidence I'm forbidden to reveal at this time, Ernest. Can't get it out of me with a crow bar, a subpoena, a lawsuit, show-cause order, or any legal process. I can only divulge that information when my client consents to it."

"So what's to stop me from running up to D.C. or just gettin' me a good real estate lawyer up there to look it up, anyway?"

"Absolutely nothing whatever, Ernest," Steick responded. "It's a free country, and that conveyance is a matter of public record."

"Well, I guess I'll just have to do that then, since your client won't cooperate."

"You certainly may if you wish, but let me ask you to consider the down side of that approach first. For one thing, it would be a great waste of your time and money. I already know where the deed can be found in D.C. Second, only I know where the second original is located in the Alabama court records. Sure, you might find the first original in Washington. But if you did, and I'm only speculating now, you might still find yourself up the creek without a paddle, legally, unless you can also produce a locally recorded copy. It's a complicated matter, Ernest. Buyers of land are entitled to rely upon the accuracy of local records. The D.C. conveyance, by itself, might not get you anywhere without a locally recorded deed.

"Third. I've been working on this case for months now, and I've worked out a long-range strategy that I think will be in the best interest of all concerned, both black and white alike. In fact, it would be good for 'all the people of the state' like we keep talking about. It could even help the Alabama budget, or at least prevent us from going totally bankrupt.

"Fourth, if you agree to follow my plan, I think you will have an excellent chance of being elected to Congress after this thing is all over."

Grones's eyes widened.

"Finally," Steick continued, "there are a whole lot of other good reasons why you and I should work together on this project. We can get into more details if you want to, but I'm curious to know what you think so far."

"I think I want to hear a whole lot more details before I say anything."

Just then the waitress reappeared. "Are you sure there isn't anything else I can get for you gentlemen, or would you like me to bring you your checks now?"

"Please put this all on my account. And yes, I've changed my mind about dessert. If you would, bring me the creme brulee, a Remy-Martin Napoleon brandy, and a cup of coffee, black. How about you, Ernest? Care for dessert, brandy, whatever?"

"Yeah, I think I do, after all. We're going to be here for a while, and so we might as well enjoy it, especially since you're pickin' up the tab. So I'll have the triple-chocolate cheesecake, a brandy, and a cup of coffee also, if you please."

"You want Remy-Martin or Courvoisier, Ernest?" Steick asked helpfully.

"I'm like you, Richard, I always go for the Remy-Martin."

"Great! You get all that, ma'am?"

"I certainly did," the waitress replied. "I'll be back in just a moment with your orders."

"Thank you," Richard said, and then he turned to Grones.

"Okay, Ernest. What more can I tell you? Ask me anything, and I promise to give you my best, most honest answer. But there's one thing I want to say first. I absolutely cannot and will not promise or guarantee to you or anyone any particular result or outcome. There are only two things I can promise you. First, that I will work hard for the best interests of all my clients. And second, that I will never lie to you, okay? You should run like a scalded dog from any lawyer who promises you more than that. Nobody has a crystal ball, and certainly not me. This whole thing could blow up in our faces like a hydrogen bomb. Get it? It's just like when you go to the doctor. The doctor will tell you, 'Look. I can give you this pill, this nose spray, do this little surgery, or whatever, but I can't possibly promise that you're going to get better. You might even die on the operating table.' See what I mean?"

"Sure, I get it," Grones replied. "I been around hundreds of y'all lawyers for more years than I can remember, and I've picked up a few things along the way. I've got a better than average layman's grasp of what lawyers can and can't do, but there are a lot of technicalities that I don't understand. That's one reason I want to hear a whole lot more details before I comment."

Then the waitress returned with a silver tray carrying the desserts and brandy. She served Grones first and then Steick. "I'll be right back with your coffee," she said.

As the waitress disappeared stage rear, Grones continued. "Listen,

Richard. Here's what I want. I want to just sit here and think quietly for a few moments while she brings us our coffee. Then, when we're all set up, I want you to tell me the whole deal, from the first step to the last, leaving out nothing, just the way you see it, okay? This is very heavy stuff, and Grones always likes to listen, you know."

Two or three minutes passed as the two sat quietly, with Grones staring out the window. Then the waitress returned, smiling, and poured their coffee.

"There you are, gentlemen. I think you'll find these desserts are superb, so continue to enjoy yourselves, and let me know if you need anything else, all right?"

As she left, Representative Grones swirled and sniffed his brandy. Then he picked up his dessert fork to dig into his triple-chocolate cheesecake. Before he began, however, he said, "Okay, Richard. Give me the whole story, first step to the last. Grones always listens, and he's listenin' very carefully right now."

Richard meticulously spelled out in great detail each step of the campaign he envisioned. Essentially, it was the same plan he had unscrolled previously to Melissa. First, set up a headquarters office in Montgomery. Second, hire an astute, discreet PR firm to massage the public. Third, file a lawsuit in the Federal Court for the Middle District of Alabama, naming anyone remotely in sight as a defendant. Fourth, hold a press conference. Fifth, allow those who could legally wiggle off the hook to do so if they could. Sixth, soak the rich, ruling remainder, primarily Alchemelia Corporation and its New York owner, Conglomo, Inc. Seventh, charitably grant a full release to the financially strapped State of Alabama for its unlawfully collected taxes, thereby bringing the races together as never before in the history of the state. Eighth, send Representative Grones off to Washington, if that was what he and the voters desired.

Mr. Grones had finished his cheesecake and was on his last sips of brandy and coffee when Steick concluded his dissertation. Grones pondered, looked out the window, and pondered some more.

"Okay," he said at last, turning and leaning forward to stare the attorney squarely in the eyes. "Suppose I buy into all that you've just told me. What's to prevent you from screwing me over, just like white folks always do, and turning this whole thing to your personal advantage or the advantage of a few rich friends? For all I know, you could be working for Alchemelia right now, couldn't you?"

"That's a very fair and sensible question to ask, Ernest, and I knew you'd ask me. At the same time, I could ask you the same questions. What's to prevent you from yanking the rug out from under me and running helter-skelter with this thing any way you want to at any moment? You have a lot more rich and influential friends than I do. But let me answer your question as best I can and then offer a proposed solution, okay?"

"Certainly."

"All right. First let me ask you a few questions, if you don't mind."

"Fire away."

"Ernest, long before any of this came up, you've always trusted me in general, haven't you?"

"Yes, Richard. I must say I've long trusted you and generally regarded you as a straight shooter and a fair man."

"Thank you, Ernest. I mean it. Now, second. Have I ever lied to you or let you down in any way whatever?"

"No, Richard. Quite the contrary. You've always been straight up, honest, and fair with me, even when we've disagreed on minor matters."

"That's what I've always tried to do with everyone, Ernest. So, third. Do you think I'm a good lawyer?"

"Everybody around here knows you're a good lawyer, Richard, possibly even a great one. There's no doubt about that."

"I'm glad to hear it," Steick responded. "And I've got my A-V rating in *Martindale-Hubbell* to back me up. The 'A' means I have the highest and most preeminent legal ability, and the 'V' stands for the fact that I have professional ethics that are irreproachable and beyond question."

"I didn't know that, Richard, but it doesn't surprise me."

"In addition, Ernest, I've never had the slightest discipline imposed against me by the Alabama State Bar. Not one bit. Not even a private letter of reprimand in nearly twenty-five years of practice. That's a record almost unheard of. You can check all this out with the State Bar's Center for Professional Responsibility if you want to. They keep a permanent, complete record on every attorney in the state."

"That's very impressive, Richard."

"Thank you again. Now. You've said I'm an excellent lawyer, you trust me, and you've got good evidence to support your trust. Is that right?"

"It is."

"Okay," the lawyer replied, growing in confidence with each question. "Do you genuinely believe, or do you not believe, that what I've told you is the truth?"

"Yes, I believe it. I don't think you or anyone else, for that matter, would be stupid enough to dummy-up a fake deposition and try to con a state legislator about the ownership of that island out there. There wouldn't be any point, as far as I can tell, and you'd probably land in jail. Just wouldn't be worth it, would it?"

Steick could feel the line growing tighter on his reel and his fishing rod starting to bend. "And do you believe or not believe that I genuinely have the best interests of all the people of Alabama foremost in my mind?"

"Yes again, Richard. I honestly believe that you do," the Representative said.

"Okay. Just one or two more questions. Do you think I'm out to screw you or the black citizens of this state, Ernest?"

"No, I honestly don't, Professor," Grones responded.

"And if I were your own personal lawyer, would you trust me, Ernest?"

"I would indeed. Absolutely and completely," Grones said sincerely.

"All right then, Ernest. I'd say we'd make a good team, wouldn't you? The thing is, we need to find a way to tie each of our interests to those of the other. That way, we're engaged in a cooperative venture for mutual benefit, and there's nothing in it for either of us to break faith. Get it?"

"Sure," the statesman replied. "I see exactly what you mean. It's like basic political science stuff, you know."

"Fine, Ernest. Now, I think I've found just the right way to tie our interests together, okay? I once considered a complicated contract between us with a liquidated damages clause and lots of things that we really don't need. But now I'm onto something much simpler. Want to hear about it?"

"Of course! That's what we're here for, isn't it?" Grones said, slightly annoyed.

"In other words, are you asking me for my legal advice, Ernest?"

"Yes. I'm asking you for your legal advice," Grones replied.

"Good," Steick said. "That means I'm not soliciting. So here's my best legal advice," he continued. "I think you should sign a contract engaging me as your attorney and the attorney for all aggrieved parties whom you will represent in this matter. That will put my money, my neck, my reputation, and my whole legal career on the line, you know. I'll be strictly bound by our Code of Professional Responsibility to represent you zealously, within the bounds of the law; to keep your confidences and secrets entirely to myself; to avoid any conflict of interest whatever; and to take all lawful measures to protect and advance your best legal interests as well as those of the people you represent. How does that sound to you, Ernest?"

"It sounds good so far, Richard. I'll want to review the contract very carefully before signing it, of course, but I think we've got a deal in principle and that I want to hire you as my lawyer. So draft up the contract and let me see it as soon as possible, okay?"

"I will certainly do that."

"By the way," Grones asked. "What's your timetable? When do we really get rollin' with this thing, anyway?"

"I'd say it'll take us about two months to set up the Montgomery office, hire a good PR firm, get me some help to run my Hallelujah practice, and draft the initial complaint, motions, and necessary discovery documents."

"So that's when you're going to go public with it? In about two months?"

"No, Ernest. That's when you're going to go public with it."

LAW DOGS

As it turned out, it took the "Firemen's Justice Project," as they sometimes called themselves, a full three months to prepare to attack. Richard hired two young law dogs, fresh out of the University of Alabama School of Law, to run his Hallelujah practice for him. He called them "law dogs" because they were loyal, eager, and tenacious, as most young lawyers are. They enjoyed nothing more than non-stop yapping about the law with clients, other lawyers, and anyone who would listen. They adored showing off their new suits, starched white shirts, and impeccable ties, both in the office and the courtroom. They knew all the latest research technology inside and out, were ever eager to use it, and were positively thrilled to sign their names to pleadings, demand letters, and other documents. When not signing something official, they practiced writing indecipherable but impressive signatures on yellow legal pads with their new Monte Blanc fountain pens. They desired above all to make legal history by winning the impossible case and saving the world. Otherwise, they were happy to serve routine civil government in any way they could, as long as they were provided a fair salary and given the liberty to test their newly installed law brains to their fullest potential. And, just like faithful little dogs, they were tenacious. Once on a case, they held on like the British bulldog, until their noses slanted backward. Steick could give them a little experienced guidance here and there, pay them fairly, and still earn a nice income for himself from the practice he had built up in Hallelujah and the surrounding area. This freed him to devote all of his own efforts to the Firemen's Justice Project.

He rented a small, quiet suite on the seventh floor of the Bell Building in downtown Montgomery and had it fully wired and equipped with telephones, computers, and the finest in on-line legal research services. The team printed simple stationery and envelopes, using a post office box as their only return address. They chose an unlisted number for the telephone. There were no full-time employees. The idea was to keep the office lean, lethal, nameless, and as camouflaged as possible. It was a place for Richard to work, for Melissa to work when she could, and for them to meet with clients, like Ninety McWilliams and Representative Grones.

They also hired the small but highly respected PR firm of Blow, Blowmore, and Spinit, out of Atlanta. The firm's specialty was political opinion management, and they would send a young representative to Montgomery when needed or upon request. But most of their consultation would occur via the telephone or e-mail. The firm had designed an attractive and informative new web site which Richard was ready to activate at the touch of a button. Melissa would be responsible for its constant updates.

The Firemen's Justice Project had also established a 501(c)(3) tax-exempt, nonprofit organization called "The Historical Justice Committee," which Melissa would also head up, for those who cared to make contributions, as they all hoped many would do. The overhead was a little steep, but Richard could afford to keep things running without undue hardship, and he fully expected to be duly reimbursed and compensated for his expenses and efforts.

He had carefully researched and drafted an extensive array of documents approximately one inch thick. He was quite pleased and proud of the result, and he was ready to sign and file the papers at any time. Even the style of the case was impressive. The list of plaintiffs and defendants running down the top left side of the initial filing was seven inches deep. In addition, both Steick and Grones had, in strict confidence and with great caution, begun calling in any and all special favors owed to them by anyone of influence. Without disclosing details, they had a lot of lunches with various legislators, lawyers, lobbyists, friends, supporters, and public officials. Both made it clear that something very big was about to be announced in Montgomery, and when it was, they expected the total support of anyone who valued their influence or might ever desire their support in the future.

At last, all seemed to be in readiness. All of the local and state media, as well as the national networks, the news services, and the major news magazines had been alerted to expect a major press conference on the steps of the federal courthouse in Montgomery at 10:00 A.M. on Monday morning. This was perfect timing for the evening news and the Tuesday morning headlines. Steick felt as if it were thirty seconds until midnight, and he had his finger on The Big Button.

HE AND MELISSA HAD BOTH been extremely busy with their respective preparations, but they had always set aside plenty of time for each other. Their love had grown far greater than either had expected. No work, however significant, was sufficiently important to distract them from this fundamental fact of their lives. Thus, they frequently dined together and went to movies, symphonies, the museum, and plays at the Alabama Shakespeare Festival. Their intimate liaisons had naturally become far more frequent and intense as well.

With the inauguration of their historic Firemen's Justice Project less than twenty-four hours away, the couple had a quick pick-up supper at Richard's house on Sunday evening. Although the fare was light and far from elegant, their easy affection and shared sense of humor made it seem like haute cuisine.

"Well. Tomorrow's the big day, Melissa! How are you feeling?"

"Richard, I'm feeling just fantastic! I've got my PR ducks all lined up perfectly. And how about you? Feel like you need a little extra Normalol or anything?"

"Normalol? Not at all. I've never felt better in my life! I'm dining with a beautiful, charming, and intelligent woman whom I love very deeply, and in just a few hours, I'm going to begin the most important case in my legal career. Life is truly wonderful tonight, Melissa."

"You know, Richard, you've led us into something I've been wanting to talk about for quite a while. It doesn't have a thing to do with the Firemen's Justice Project. It has to do with us, you and me, in the long term. You've dropped a lot of hints here and there and made a lot of suggestions, and increasingly so in recent weeks. But we've never really talked seriously about our future together, or if we really have one at all. Can we do that now, or would it be bad timing?"

The lawyer looked at her, patted his mouth with his napkin, and took a long swig of sweet tea. Then he said, "Melissa, Darling, would you please come over here and sit on my lap?"

"Why certainly," she said, as she pushed back her chair and Richard scooted his at an angle to accommodate her. Then she settled herself in, wrapped her arms around his neck, and kissed him tenderly on the cheek, saying, "Now. What can I do for you, Richard?"

He peered deeply and laser-like into her stunning blue eyes. It was a gaze so focused and pure that it quickly traveled the usual channels, zoomed directly into her brain stem, and came out far beyond that into an unknown future that they both anticipated and both hoped would last forever.

"What you can do, Melissa Brandywine, is please marry me. I love you absolutely and unconditionally, more than I've ever loved any other woman in my life, and I want nothing more than to spend the remainder of my life with you. Will you please say 'yes,' my Darling?"

Melissa jokingly poked her index finger into her right cheek, cast her eyes upward, squinted in a moment of mock concentration, and then laughingly returned her gaze to his.

"Why yes, Richard. I will most certainly say 'Yes!'" she said, and the couple dove into a passionate kiss longer than a windy lawyer's closing argument.

When they had disengaged, each pulled back and smiled joyfully at the other.

"Do you really think you can stand me, Melissa? I'll always be different from other people, as I'm sure you know. I'm a little eccentric and stuck in some of my ways, to say the least, but I will do absolutely anything to make you happy and to keep you happy for as long as I live. I can promise you that for certain. Are you sure you want to marry me, warts and all?"

"Yes," she responded with conviction. "And I know I've got my own warts as well. Are you sure you truly accept me and want to marry me, with all my imperfections included?"

"I certainly haven't noticed any imperfections, and you know, Melissa, we've never had a harsh word between us. Not one. So yes. I'm absolutely, positively certain that I want to marry you, or I wouldn't have asked. I've been wanting to ask you for quite a while, you know, but I've been a little timid and afraid you might turn me down. Besides, I've wanted to get your ring ready first, but I haven't had the time to do it yet. Want to have a preview?"

"Yes! I can't wait!"

He took her hand, and they left the table, following a familiar path toward his bedroom. He led her to a large closet, which he opened. Then he flipped back the carpet to reveal an obviously heavy floor safe.

"This is where I keep my important personal papers and items not related to my clients," he said.

He twirled the combination knob skillfully, then pulled open a round, four-inch thick steel door about twelve inches in diameter. Diving in with his right hand, he retrieved what was obviously a ring box.

"Let's go over here by this lamp so you can really see it."

They went to the lamp, and Richard announced, "Here you are, Sweetheart. Open it. It's all yours, just as soon as I can get it properly mounted."

Sizzling with anticipation, Melissa held the box under the light and opened the lid. And what she saw made her gasp. It was a man's ring with a diamond solitaire about the size of a glass doorknob. She didn't think she had ever seen such a stone outside a museum.

"Like it?"

"Richard! I've never seen such a magnificent diamond in my life! Where on earth did you ever get it?"

"Authentic family heirloom, in a way. Belonged to my great-uncle, long deceased. I can hardly remember him, but he must have really liked me as a young 'un. And he didn't have much family otherwise. He was one of the last of the authentic Mississippi riverboat gamblers. The story goes that he won this on two pair, aces and deuces, just beating out another two pair—kings and eights. It's 2.31 carats. Great color, and as close as you can get to internally perfect. I'll have to get it appraised again and increase the insurance coverage before I give it to you. Just show me a picture or a drawing of how you want it mounted, and I'll have it done. Whadda' ya say, Mrs. Richard Steick?"

"I say I'm the luckiest, proudest, and happiest woman in the world," she said, as she put the ring on the side table and began to undress him.

Afterward, they talked about setting a date, and both agreed it would be best to wait until the major heat of the Firemen's Justice Project had died down and the situation was fairly under control.

A Major Detonation

T he following morning at 8:30, attorney Richard Steick filed his thick stack of papers in the clerk's office at the Federal District Court in Montgomery. The press conference began promptly at 10:00 A.M., exactly as planned. Melissa had done a fantastic job of rounding up the herd, and the steps of the courthouse were packed with reporters from all over Alabama and beyond. CNN and the three major networks had all sent reporting crews, and the TV cameras poked about everywhere like reptilian snouts, jockeying for position.

At his best, Representative Grones was a superb, articulate, Roman orator, with glorious periodic phrasing and a calm, self-assured presence. He wore his best Brooks Brothers suit, and he looked and sounded positively Presidential. He stood before a gaggle of microphones and skillfully delivered his prepared statement with warmth, radiant goodwill toward all, and scarcely a glance at his notes. Meanwhile, his lawyer stood serenely in the background.

Melissa had assembled a carefully prepared PR packet containing both condensed and expanded press releases together with the major pleadings and allegations. She included copies of 1865 *Montgomery Advertiser* stories about "our brave, volunteer Negro firemen," a copy of Hans Aschliman's deposition, and even copies of the certified original conveyance signed by the Montgomery mayor as well as by the occupying General Smith and U.S. President Andrew Johnson. She had hired a couple of high school kids to distribute the packets and had instructed them to be certain that all present should receive as many copies as they chose.

Everything was handled with the essence of professionalism. After delivering his statement, Grones called for questions, and every hand not holding a TV camera shot up at once. The Representative did his best to answer questions, carefully staying within the boundaries that he and his attorney had diligently rehearsed. Steick himself was mute, except when his client deferred to him about answering a particular question. On these occasions, the lawyer invariably stated, "We cannot comment upon that matter at this time."

Melissa, willingly released from a day's work by Dr. Kayahs, also took her turn at the microphone. She added glamour and credibility to the presentation and exuded perfect grace under pressure, just like Jackie Kennedy. She announced the creation of the Committee for Historical Justice and did not hesitate to admit that she was employed by counsel for the plaintiffs and was their public relations manager. She gave the web site address for the Committee, which she promised would be updated every twenty-four hours. She ended with an appeal for all Alabamians, regardless of race or political affiliation, to join the Committee in justly fighting to right an ancient wrong. And of course she announced that any financial contributions to the Committee would be fully tax deductible.

After Melissa had spoken, Representative Grones carefully brought the drama to a superb climax by introducing Ninety McWilliams, a direct lineal descendant of the original "Ninety Ton McWilliams" mentioned so prominently and with such great admiration in *The Montgomery Advertiser* in April of 1865. Richard had conveniently arranged for Ninety to be off work at the city garage that morning. He had, of course, been more than willing to reimburse the city for the loss of his client's time while he was away from his job. He had fitted Ninety out nicely in a new suit, shirt, tie, shoes, and stockings. He had even brought in a make-up artist from the Alabama Shakespeare Festival to make Ninety's huge keloid scar virtually invisible. And naturally, he had told his client not to say a single word to anyone about anything. Ninety's one and only response, which the two had practiced over and over again, was "I'm sorry. You'll have to talk to my lawyer about that."

The plaintiffs had nothing to hide, and the press conference continued for a full two hours. At noon, the reporters and cameramen began to drift off toward lunch, and the press conference slowly came to a halt.

Melissa strictly instructed all parties and temporary staffers that they were to give absolutely no interviews or make any statements to anyone at all. Only she, attorney Steick, and Representative Grones could speak on behalf of the Committee for Historical Justice or any member of the potential claimants' class.

THE NEWS HIT ALABAMA like a hundred kiloton H-Bomb, and it sent shock waves throughout the nation. The story was carried nationally on the evening news. One anchor lisped that "a strange historical anomaly has been discovered in Alabama," while another speculated that "a small, extremely wealthy new state just might be added as the fifty-first star on the United States flag."

The story even made the front page of Tuesday morning's *New York Times, Washington Post,* and countless other daily newspapers nationwide. The bold headlines on *The Montgomery Advertiser* were nearly four inches high, the largest since the capture of Saddam Hussein.

At 5:30 P.M. on Monday night, Richard, Melissa, and Ernest convened at Mushroom Memories to watch and tape the news on Richard's gigantic TV screen. The occasion merited two bottles of perfectly chilled Dom Perignon, served in Waterford flutes, and accompanied by splendid hors d'oeuvres catered by Cavalieri's. The host would have been glad to have invited Ninety McWilliams, but he didn't want to expose his client to alcohol.

Ernest had never visited Mushroom Memories in the past, nor had he ever seen anything like it, and he was quite amazed.

"You know, Richard," he said. "You're weird. I mean, you're just plain weird. By anybody's standards, black, white, or other, you're about the weirdest guy I've ever known. But I'm glad to know you and have you in my corner just the way you are. You might be weird, but you're smart, and your heart's in the right place. Where'd you ever find all this stupid junk, anyway?"

Meanwhile, enormous teams of lawyers were huddling together all over the nation, but most particularly at the Conglomo office in New York, the IRS in Washington, and the Governor's office in Montgomery.

All of the groups were in close electronic contact with one another. All agreed that the case against them appeared airtight and bulletproof. All agreed that something had to be done, but no one knew what to do. It was abundantly clear, however, that it was imperative for Governor Scroulous to hold a press conference immediately the following morning.

AFTERSHOCKS

The Governor knew that his press conference Tuesday morning would be a "make it or break it" point in his career. Thus, in a well-intended but ill-conceived gesture of sacrifice, he laid off his usual martinis on Monday night and concentrated upon the text of his message.

Unfortunately, jumping so suddenly onto the wagon left the Governor totally sleepless, headachy, and with slight but noticeable withdrawal tremors the following morning. His Biblical redemption session with Martha did not go well. It began promptly, as usual. But the Governor could not properly recite his Bible verse, and thus Martha assigned him to memorize two new ones for the following day.

After the First Couple completed singing the Doxology, Sid got dressed as well as he could. He wasn't very good at it, even on his best days, and he had to consult his wife on several occasions. At length, he emerged cleanly shaven, well combed, wrinkle free, properly attired, and color coordinated in a crisp, expensive, and highly impressive black suit. It was the best he had looked since his last inauguration, although he remained colorless and trembling.

Promptly at 9:30 A.M., he had his chauffeur drive him to his office at the statehouse. He made a few final preparations, checked his appearance in the mirror one more time, and then made his way to the press conference room. He was trailed by a small herd of underlings, consisting of the Attorney General, members of the Governor's cabinet, and his chief aide-de-camp, Bobby Brooks.

At 10:00 A.M. sharp, the cameras began rolling, and the Governor strode as confidently as he could to stand behind his impressive lectern. He was ready to begin. He cleared his throat and said, "Ladies and gentlemen, please let us pause for a moment of silent reflection and meditation before we begin. Even the atheistic federal courts can't stop us from doing that." Then he bowed his head. It was an unusual way to begin a press conference, but the reporters and photographers didn't know what else to do except to follow suit.

Momentarily, the Governor raised his head, smiled broadly into as many red TV camera lights as he could, and cleared his throat once again.

"Ladies and gentlemen," he repeated, shaking visibly. "I want to thank you for joining us here this morning. Today, the great State of Alabama, Montgomery County, the City of Montgomery, and one of our finest industries face the worst God—God-blessed financial crisis since the Great Depression. And what I mean by that is that the Great Depression was indeed truly blessed by God, because the folks that lived then didn't have to face what we're facing today.

"I refer, of course, to the scandalous, trumped-up, false, misleading, corrupt, and greedy lawsuit filed yesterday in the atheistic federal court by State Representative Ernest Grones and some kinda group of outside agitators. And so to the Honorable Representative Grones and those agitators, I say, 'Bring it on! Alabama is ready!' And in the words of our great new state motto, 'Thou shalt not!'

"Today, I'm calling upon every real Alabamian to rally 'round our flag and support our state. Pro-business and fiscally conservative Alabamians are real. There's no doubt about that. You can't always be sure with some other Alabamians. Not all of them are real. And I just don't know what to say about the people who filed this lawsuit. They want to ruin Alchemelia Corporation, one of our best sources of personal income and state revenues in central Alabama.

"But are they content with that alone? No! They are not! They also want to ruin the City of Montgomery, Montgomery County, and our great state itself by exacting hundreds of millions of dollars, and possibly more, that they allege we collected in illegal taxes. And we're broke already!

"Maybe we made an honest mistake. I don't know. The atheistic federal courts are going to have to apply the law to the true facts and figure that one out. And we don't know all the true facts yet.

"What these outside agitators want to do, it seems to me, is to cut us up into pieces and throw our bleeding heads onto the table to stare us in the face, as someone once said. Maybe that was Shakespeare, I don't know. But whoever said it, let me say this. That is exactly what we are going to do to these outside agitators, whenever we find out who they are!

"I also want to say to the people of this great state that I'm in a mess, and you're in a mess too if this lawsuit goes forward. Which means, actually, that no one's in a mess, if you know what I mean.

"Now. We have major problems facing us today in Alabama. We have enormous fiscal shortfalls that have resulted mainly from some corrupt state officials loading the dice and refusing to take 15 percent off of everything, as they are sworn by law to do. We have major problems with crime, education, mental health prevention, and dozens of other things I could name but won't, since y'all know what they are anyway.

"But I want every citizen to know that I'm working on funding, just like I promised in my campaign, to put the people first! And now this God—this God-blessed state has to endure this expensive and frivolous lawsuit, and it just isn't right. It isn't right, and it isn't fair to the ordinary, working, pro-business Alabamian. Democracy, the courts, the law, and all that stuff used to be good things, but somehow they've gotten into the wrong hands. Well, we're just going to have to squeeze those hands until we break 'em!

"I want to close by echoing the words of two of this nation's greatest statesmen, the former Honorable Vice President Dan Quayle and Representative Gary Ackerman of New York. And I hope I can do justice to their noble sentiments.

"My friends, no matter how rough the road may be, we can, and we will never, never surrender to what is right as long as it's wrong! Sometimes, in order to make progress and move ahead, you have to stand up and do the wrong thing in order to be right, and that's exactly what this administration intends to do, starting immediately.

"There will be no questions and answers this morning, ladies and gentlemen. So God bless you. God bless the great State of Alabama. And have a nice day!"

THERE WAS A STUNNED SILENCE as the Governor left the press room, followed by his retinue of dignitaries. A few mumbled, "Good job, Governor," and slapped Sid on the back. But most appeared dazed and disappointed as they split up and headed for their respective offices.

No one was more disappointed than the young Bobby Brooks, Sid's special counsel and his most trusted advisor. Brooks had laboriously penned a brief, politically neutral, non-committal, and appeasing statement for the Governor the day before. The Governor hadn't used a word of it except "Thank you for being with us here this morning." The rest was pure, vintage, off-the-cuff Scroulous at his most embarrassing worst. In addition, his shaking had grown more pronounced as he faced the reporters and the TV cameras. The overall appearance he gave was that of a disintegrating schizophrenic.

As Bobby walked with the Governor toward the executive suite, he noticed that Sid's knees were wobbling, and he was veering a little off the straight and direct path.

"Are you okay, Governor?"

"Just fine, Bobby. Just fine. Press conference shook me up a little, and I think I might be catchin' some kinda virus or something. Just get me to my office, and I'll be fine."

When they arrived at the door, Brooks asked, "Do you want to do our daily briefing now, sir?"

"No, Bobby. Let's just put it off until tomorrow, okay? I'm gonna catch a few winks in my private office and then get to work on all this mess. I won't be needing you any longer today. Just go to your office and figure this thing out as best you can. Or go out to the country club and play some golf if you want to. Whatever. I'll see you at the usual time tomorrow mornin', okay?"

"If you say so, Governor. You've got all my numbers, so phone me at any time, day or night, as always, all right?"

"Sure Bobby. And thanks," the Governor said as he opened the door to his suite.

"Mornin' MaryLou," he said to his faithful secretary. "Absolutely no phone calls and no visitors, okay? I've got a lot of hard work to do."

"Certainly, Governor."

Sid went into his official office and then straight into his unofficial office at the back, carefully locking the door behind him. He immediately kicked off his shoes, without unlacing them, and stripped off his coat, tie, and dress shirt, leaving them all in a heap on the floor. This left the Governor in a T-shirt, dress slacks, and stockings, as he pulled a small key from inside an oriental vase. He used the key to unlock an antique decorative cabinet. Next, he shakily retrieved from within the cabinet a coffee mug bearing the motto, "Vote for Sid and Take 15% Off!" With his other hand, he pulled out a new fifth of Maker's Mark whiskey. He had a little trouble with the unopened cap, but he soon managed to fill the coffee mug with the lovely amber American beverage, which he quickly drained.

He had taken considerably more than 15 percent off the top of the bottle before the potent elixir downshifted the gears in his brain. His tremors quietly ceased. "Things aren't really so bad after all," he mused, as he grabbed his favorite Afghan and stretched out comfortably upon his sofa.

MaryLou knew better than to inform the Governor before she took off work at 5:00 P.M. At its most violent, his constant snoring had been faintly audible, periodically, through the two, thick wooden doors, ever since he had sequestered himself before lunch.

WHAT ICEBERG?

There followed six months of unrelenting legal success for the Firemen's Justice Project, and it was six months of exuberant joy for Richard Steick, Melissa Brandywine, and Representative Ernest Grones.

The legal case was a classic instance of David versus Goliath, with Steick playing David. But instead of a simple leather sling and a few small stones, Steick held a howitzer. Virtually hundreds of lawyers for all of the defendants, from Conglomo, Inc., to the United States Government, were arrayed against the solo practitioner. What made his work such a pleasure was the extremely uncommon occurrence that all of the law and all of the facts were on his side. Always at the predictable last moment, dozens upon dozens of answers, counterclaims, motions, responses to motions, interrogatories, requests for admission, notices of depositions, and all manner of procedural documents poured into the Justice Project's small suite in the Bell Building.

Steick quickly needed full-time help at project headquarters, and he called upon Lillian Murphy, a retired Montgomery legal secretary who had worked for him early in his career. Lillian was an absolute wizard with a computer typewriter, and she was unsurpassed at transforming the attorney's taped dictations into attractive, perfectly crafted, and error-free legal documents. In addition, it was as if she were clairvoyant with regard to Richard's perfectionist whims and requirements. Each afternoon, she had an enormous number of documents and letters neatly stacked and waiting for the lawyer to review and sign, all arranged precisely in the order in which he desired to deal with them. Thus, just as fast as the defendants' hundreds of documents poured into his office, Steick was ready and able to deliver prompt, concise, and thoroughly researched rejoinders.

All the defendants were consolidated. The case was set for trial, and nearly a dozen pre-trial motions hearings were held before U.S. District Judge Clark Wilson, a Harvard graduate, a brilliant lawyer, and an exceedingly fair judge. Steick handily won each and every contested matter.

In addition, under the astute management of Melissa and the PR firm of Blow, Blowmore, and Spinit, Alabama public opinion, both black and white alike, overwhelmingly favored the Justice Project. Fully 99 percent of black citizens and an amazing 83 percent of white citizens favored a full measure of justice for the heirs and devisees of the "heroic Negro firemen" of 1865. When it came down to clear cases, almost everyone in the state agreed that "What's right's right, and what's wrong's wrong." All of the major newspapers opined that the only honorable thing for the state to do was to cede Farthing Worthy's Island to its current, lawful owners, even if that meant raising taxes!

Not only that, but the nonprofit organization, the Historical Justice Project, had garnered a fair amount of money in contributions, which made Richard most grateful, and Melissa responded to each contributor with a brief, personal letter of thanks.

Thus, at the end of six months of seeing the evidence, examining it closely, and never once failing to draw the losing card, the defendants were ready to start cutting deals. They were ready to make almost any deal to preserve the status quo or at least minimize their damages. They became ingratiating and obsequious with Richard Steick, counsel for the plaintiffs. Conglomo wanted to fly him first class to New York for several days of "negotiations," which he knew would consist of a posh suite and lunch at the Plaza, dinners at Tavern on the Green, a private limo, the best seats for the latest Broadway shows, and all the attractive young women he could possibly desire. Steick wrote Conglomo, thanked them, and declined, explaining that there was really nothing to negotiate. Farthing Worthy's Island would shortly be stripped from the ownership of Conglomo and its subsidiary, Alchemelia, and handed over to Ninety

McWilliams and a yet undetermined number of black owners. Steick explained that he had visited New York many times in the past and had always enjoyed its hospitality. But he had no desire to leave his offices at the present time.

Similarly, he was invited to the nation's capital for meetings with the Secretary of the Interior and the director of the IRS. He knew that the program would be similar to the one offered by Conglomo, except that the perks would be more discreet. He wrote polite letters, thanking the eminent bureaucrats for their kind invitations, but explaining, with all due respect, that he was unable to leave Alabama at the moment.

He took the same position at the state and local levels. He courteously refused to meet with Governor Scroulous and the Attorney General as well as the Montgomery city and county attorneys. His carefully considered position was that he would only attend such hearings and meetings as were ordered by the court.

In short, all of his adversaries were eating out of Richard's hand, which is an extremely rare and pleasant situation for any lawyer to experience. But with possible billions of dollars at stake, cornered defendants will stall, stall, stall and employ any strategy whatever to save the day or at least save some money. Consequently, it came as no surprise to Richard when all of the defendants joined in a motion for court-ordered mediation.

Mediation and other forms of alternative dispute resolution are tools of great usefulness and highly favored in modern law practice. Judges are extremely fond of them.

Thus, the defendants were both stunned and enlightened by the brief hearing Judge Wilson held on their motion to mediate, which Richard had naturally opposed. The judge listened carefully to both sides and then, looking at the half-dozen counsel for the defendants, said, "Well, I don't see how there's anything to mediate here. Either this conveyance is valid, or it isn't, and everything I've seen so far tells me that it is. I think y'all are just trying to delay the process of justice. I would remind you that each of you has a sworn duty to expedite litigation. This court has neither the time nor the patience for needless and protracted legal maneuvering. Motion to mediate is denied. Ladies and gentlemen, I recommend that you all prepare for trial on the date set. This court is now adjourned."

All of the attorneys rose and, in customary fashion, murmured, "Thank you, Your Honor," even though all of them but one, Richard Steick, had just seen their case go down like the *Titanic*. The Judge's comment that "everything he had seen so far told him that the conveyance was valid" was a death knell to the defendants.

What the judge had said even stunned Richard. He knew from the time of his initial filing that he was holding four aces. Now it appeared he had underestimated his case and in fact held the unbeatable royal flush.

Eager to share this good news with Melissa, he phoned her at the Montgomery office of Heigh-Ho Psychiatry and arranged to pick her up after work for dinner at the Sinai.

The line was short at the restaurant, and the couple quickly found themselves seated in a comfortable black leather booth being served by Richard's favorite waiter, Lewis. After the waiter had taken their orders, Richard clasped Melissa's hands in his and said, "As a practical matter, it's all over, Sweetheart, and we've won everything, hands down. The rest, including the trial, is just a bunch of bureaucratic details. So when and where do you want to get married, and where do you want to go on our honeymoon?"

Melissa was taken aback with surprise and delight, and she asked Richard to fill in the blanks for her. He was positively gleeful in telling her about Judge Wilson's comment.

Her enormous, new, tastefully mounted engagement ring glistened like Venus at full phase on a clear night.

"Back to what we were talking about a moment ago, Darling, about getting married, I mean," she said. "It really doesn't matter at all to me. I'm ready to marry you at any time, under any circumstances, you know. But I guess I'd like to keep it as simple as possible. We've both been through big weddings in the past, and I'm sure we don't want to repeat that again, do we?"

"Of course not. We can just go to the Probate Judge for a simple civil ceremony, or we can have it in a church with a pastor. However you wish. So think about it and let me know. Meanwhile, what about our honeymoon?"

"Now there's a fun idea to think about!" Melissa exclaimed. "And I've been thinking about it now and then. You've been on a number of cruises in the past, Richard, but I never have, and that's something I've always wanted to do. Think we could swing it? Maybe seven to ten days or something like that?"

"I'm certain of it, Melissa. I'll pick up a bunch of brochures at WorldTrav, and you just look them over and pick out what you want, okay? Money is no object."

"Are you sure, Richard?"

"Oh, absolutely, Melissa. I'm certain about that. Don't think twice about the money. Cruises cost a little bit, but they're good value. And nothing in the world is too good for my wife, my soul mate, and my Darling."

She reached across the table, took his hand, and gave it a squeeze. "Okay, Richard. As you like it. You know a lot more about your financial assets than I do."

"Good! Meanwhile, Honey, why don't we drop in at Dr. Fleabot's lab and get our blood tests done sometime in the next few days? You could probably do it during your lunch hour on one of your Montgomery days. That okay with you?"

"Sure, Richard. That's no problem."

"And also, please get me a certified copy of your birth certificate, and I'll stop in at Probate and pick up a marriage license for us. I think they're good for six months, or something like that, so we don't have to be in any big rush."

"I'll bring you a copy tomorrow evening at the Justice Project HQ," Melissa replied happily.

SEVERAL DAYS LATER, on a beautiful, cloudless Montgomery afternoon, Richard leaned back, hands clasped behind his head, with his feet resting atop his desk at the Justice Project HQ, and ruminated in tranquility. Never in his life had he felt himself so high, wide, and handsome. First, all of the Justice Project technicalities were out of the way, and he was about to marry the woman he loved more than any other in his life. Then, he was going to wrap up the details on the biggest case in his legal career, bring the races closer together in Alabama, and become a state legal hero and possibly a national one as well. Life was indeed wonderful on this glorious day in the Bell Building in historic downtown Montgomery, Alabama!

At length, he decided it was time to have a look at the stack of point-less pleadings and motions from the various defendants which Lillian had opened and neatly arranged for him on his desk. He knew his adversaries couldn't touch him now, but the details still required attention.

He leaned forward and began to survey the papers. The first was easily dispatched—a motion to produce documents he had already produced. The second was similarly inconsequential. The defendants' lawyers were simply trying to wear him out while running up their own legal fees.

The third document, however, definitely caught Richard's attention. It had the longest caption of any motion he had ever seen in his life. The caption read:

MOTION TO STRIKE, SET ASIDE, QUASH, VACATE,
AND HOLD AT NAUGHT ANY AND ALL PRIOR PLEADINGS,
MOTIONS, AND ORDERS IN THIS CAUSE AB INITIO,
AND TO DISMISS THIS MATTER IMMEDIATELY WITH FULL PREJUDICE

Richard carefully scrutinized the grounds for the motion in the most minute detail. Its gravamen was that he, Richard Steick, PhD, Esq., was not a licensed attorney in good standing with the Alabama State Bar Association. The *Rules of Civil Procedure* were abundantly clear that each and every pleading, motion, or other document filed in any lawsuit must be signed by at least one licensed attorney in good standing. The motion further recited, with appropriate documentation appended, that Richard Steick, counsel for the plaintiffs, had ceased to be an attorney in good standing with the Alabama State Bar some ten months previously for failure to renew his annual professional license. The attached Exhibit

A was an affidavit from the director of the Alabama State Bar, stating that Richard Steick had been removed from the roll of active attorneys some ten months previously for failure to renew his license. Exhibit B was a certified copy of the relevant pages from the official roll of licensed attorneys, with Richard's name notably absent from the place where it should have been found among the "S's."

Apparently some young law dog for Conglomo had left no stone unturned. In any event, the motion was signed by counsel for all of the defendants.

Steick read the entire document three times. If it were correct, as it seemed to be, both he and his case were utterly nuked, finished, and disgraced beyond redemption. He would become the laughingstock of the legal community and the state. He would be sued to the moon by Grones and possibly by Ninety, if not by others as well. He would be disciplined by the State Bar. The prospect made the story line of *On the Beach* look like a pleasant summer outing.

Thus, it was quite interesting to Richard that he did not immediately pick up an office chair, smash out a window, and throw himself headlong seven stories down onto the sidewalk below. Equally strange was the fact that he did not set a land-speed record making his way to the nearest liquor store, bar, restaurant, juke joint, or other establishment that sold a drink.

In fact, he was amazingly calm, and he knew precisely what he had to do. First, he phoned his friend, Stephen Smitherman, director of the Alabama State Bar, just up the street on Dexter Avenue. Smitherman confirmed that his affidavit was indeed correct and that he, Richard, had truly been stricken from the roster of active attorneys ten months previously for failure to renew his annual license. Smitherman explained that all the usual, routine warnings had gone out to Richard's office in Hallelujah, but the Bar had not received any response whatever. Nor had it received Richard's annual license fee of $250 for the present year. Smitherman continued that he was sorry, but there was absolutely nothing he could do.

Richard thanked him and immediately phoned Betty, his secretary in Hallelujah. In a calm voice, he asked her to please check the date on his framed professional license. Betty quickly did so and returned to the phone to inform him that the license was dated for the preceding year.

"I thought you always took care of that for me, Betty."

"No, Richard, I thought it was something you wanted to take care of yourself. You once said it was so important that you would tend to it personally. So I always put all the documents pertaining to your professional license into your 'In' box, assuming that you would take care of them."

"And I always just glanced at them and put them into my 'Out' box expecting you to look after them," he said.

There was no point in blame, anger, recrimination, or looking backward.

"In any event, it's one of those things that just slipped through the cracks, I guess," Richard continued. "So how are you doin', Betty?"

"I'm fine, Richard. How about yourself?"

"I'm okay," he said, and then he asked her how his two young law dogs were doing.

"They're just great! Real go-getters. And they're bringing in some very nice fees, by the way."

"That's wonderful. Betty, there are just two things I want you to do for me right now, okay? The first is to set up an absolutely iron-clad, bulletproof policy for all attorneys in that office to renew their annual professional licenses on time. Quadruple calendar the deadline, and send a memo from me to my two young associates informing them of our office procedure on this matter. And Betty, hereafter, you will bear the ultimate responsibility for strict compliance with our procedures and to be sure they are carried out each year in a timely manner, okay?"

"That's fine, Richard. It will be good to have all that clarified. Now what was the second thing you wanted me to do?"

"The second thing, Betty, is that I want you to cut five-hundred-dollar bonus checks for yourself and my two young associates this month. Is that okay with you?"

"That's more than okay, Richard! It's fantastic! You've always been generous, and that's typical of your kindness, just coming out of the blue with nice bonuses like that. Thank you so much!"

"You're more than welcome, Betty. You deserve it. So I'll say good-bye for now and see y'all later, okay?"

Next, Richard phoned Melissa to cancel their usual dinner together that evening. She sounded worried as she asked him if everything was all right.

He assured her that everything was fine, but a minor glitch had come up, and he had to do a very time-consuming on-line case search immediately. She asked how he would eat, and he told her he would just grab something at the deli on the first floor and would definitely see her the next day.

After he hung up, he got a cup of coffee, sat down at his computer, and typed in the address of the most powerful on-line legal research engine in the world. Eight hours and many cups of coffee later, he knew he had exhausted all possible resources. Not only were there no recorded Alabama or federal court cases that broke his way, there were also no recorded cases in the entire history of United States jurisprudence that gave him the slightest bit of help. If anything, the few cases he turned up hurt his position more than they helped it. By the time he was finished, he knew he was truly finished. He had searched all recorded cases, not only in the United States, but also in England, Ireland, Scotland, Canada, Australia, and all of the common law jurisdictions throughout the world for the past five hundred years.

There was not even any point in disputing the matter. Judge Wilson would have no choice but to grant the defendants' motion. Thus, the battle was lost for Richard, Melissa, Ernest, Ninety, the "heroic Negro firemen," their heirs and devisees, and the vital project of bringing the races closer together in Alabama.

Richard Steick was no quitter, but he knew when he was licked. He was exhausted, and he knew it was time to get some sleep.

AMAZING GRACE

The next morning, Richard awoke in Hallelujah feeling much improved, considering the circumstances. He showered, shaved, dressed neatly, ate a hearty breakfast, and found himself feeling even better. He could see the future, and he knew exactly what to do.

Immediately after clearing away his breakfast dishes, he put first things first. He dialed his professional liability insurance agent, Frank Ferret at Malanon in Montgomery. Somewhat embarrassed, he explained that he had made a slight error or omission by practicing law without a license for the past ten months.

In his career, Steick had handled some big-money wrongful death and insurance fraud cases, and he was grateful that he had always carried high limits of coverage on his malpractice insurance. If ever he needed it, he needed it now. As he recalled, his caps were $25 million per person and $50 million per occurrence. He figured that those amounts should keep him insulated against Representative Grones and Ninety McWilliams, and he counted it a great good fortune that those two persons were the only ones with whom he had actually executed contracts at that point.

Ferret was calm and cordial. It was all in a day's work for him. He told Steick once again to put all the facts into a certified letter addressed to him at Malanon. Then he said, "Richard. This probably has an impact on that high profile case you've been handling that's been in all the papers, doesn't it?"

"I'm sure it most certainly will."

"Quite a lot of money involved, isn't there?"

"I can't be sure, Frank, but I suppose so. Depends upon who sues me and for what. I expect only one or maybe two people actually can file against me. Say. Do me a favor and check on my limits of coverage right now, will you?"

Ferret made a few quick, audible key strokes on his computer and said, "Twenty-five and fifty mil, respectively, Richard. I'll bet you're glad you paid all those big premiums on time for all these years now, aren't you?"

"I certainly am. They were a good investment and gave me lots of peace of mind, even though I never had a single claim until the Jones matter."

Ferret cleared his throat. "Uh, Richard, please listen to me for a moment, if you will."

"Of course."

"Well, I don't want you to worry about this case, okay? Just don't make any statements to anyone, naturally. You're fully covered, and our firm of Barratry, Champerty, and Tennis in Birmingham will take care of all the details, just like before. You'll have to pay your $5,000 deductible, as usual, but otherwise, you're okay. However, this is your second claim in roughly two years, and that Jones worker's comp matter cost us quite a bit, you know."

"Yes. I'm sure it did."

"Now, you're all paid up for this year's premiums plus three years' tail-end coverage. So, like I said, don't worry. On the other hand, I think I can speak with confidence on behalf of our underwriters and tell you now that you'll no longer be renewable or otherwise insurable with us after this latest claim. Understand? If you want to continue practicing law, you ought to start looking now for some high-risk carriers, okay?"

"I understand, Frank."

"We're proud of our loyalty to our clients, but business is business, you know," Ferret said, adding, "You'll no doubt be getting all this information, plus some necessary forms to fill out, by certified mail. Meanwhile, just go on about your business, Richard. I know this is tough to take, but everything is going to work out just fine. So have a nice day, and I'll talk to you later."

Immediately after he hung up, Steick sat down at his home computer to write the certified letter Malanon required, a project which took only a few minutes. He signed and copied it, prepped it for certified mailing, and set it aside.

Steick then made a second phone call, this one to his off-shore accounts manager on Grand Cayman. Richard never thought a lot about exactly how much money he had, but he enjoyed having it, and he enjoyed knowing that he generally had more than enough for his needs. He paid only cursory attention to the various financial statements that arrived in his mail, noting that all seemed well, and filing them away. At the moment, however, he felt he would especially enjoy having as much money as he could get.

After a forty-minute conversation with Mr. Smythe in George Town, running his financial numbers on a calculator as he went along, Richard was beaming. His carefully balanced, tax-sheltered investments had done far better than he had ever imagined, with some of them returning up to 40 percent per year. He was delighted to discover that he was well set up for two or three lifetimes of quite comfortable living. And all of it was safe, perfectly legal, and fully immune from any United States levy or legal process whatever, as long as he followed the rules, which he understood quite well.

HIS NEXT CALL WAS TO DR. KAYAHS. It was Thursday, and so the doctor was in Hallelujah.

"Heigh-Ho Psychiatry, Hallelujah! How may I help you?" a happy and familiar voice asked.

"Good morning, Darling. And you've already helped me far more than you could possibly imagine."

"Richard! How are you and where are you? I've been worried! Are you okay?"

"I've never been better, Sweetheart. And how about yourself?"

"I'm fine too, Richard. But I'm a little confused about what's going on."

"Don't worry, Honey. Have you seen today's paper, by the way?"

"No, I haven't."

"Well, I'm not sure it's in there yet anyway. Don't worry about it. I'll probably stop in at your office later this afternoon and explain everything. Either that, or we'll have dinner at Dard & Elle's Cafe at the usual time after work, if that's okay with you."

"Sure. So what's up your sleeve, anyway?"

"I'll tell you all about it later, Sweetheart. By the way, have you given any more thought to when and where you want to get married?"

"A little bit. There's a retired Primitive Baptist preacher who lives just outside of town. Some of my kin folks attended his church, and he's always been kind of a friend of the family. I phoned him, and he said he'd be more than happy to perform the ceremony at his house at any time we wanted. I'd like to keep it simple, you know. Does that sound okay to you?"

"Sounds fine to me, Honey. I like the idea of a pastor officiating as opposed to a Probate Judge. What is this retired preacher's name and phone number, by the way? I might want to call him about some minor matters, like witnesses and all that sort of thing, you know."

"Well, you really don't have to worry about witnesses, Darling. He said his wife would be happy to witness the ceremony. Evidently he does quite a few of these since he's retired."

"It might require more than one witness and be well to have a second one in any event. Anyway, I'd like to talk to him."

"Sure," Melissa said, and gave him Pastor Maxwell's full name and telephone number. "So what else have you got going on today?"

"Quite a bit, actually. Does Dr. Kayahs have a patient right now?"

"No. He's back there playing his saxophone. You're lucky if you can't hear it."

"Well, count me among the blessed, then, and in more ways than one. Do you think you could get him to stop for a moment? I'd like to talk to him about something."

"Are you certain you're okay, Richard Steick? You're acting a little more weird than usual today. Why on earth do you want to talk to Dr. Kayahs at this hour of the morning?"

"It's nothing but good news, Honey, and you'll know all about it shortly, just as I promised, okay? Now, can you get him on the line for me?"

"Certainly, if that's what you want. It's a pretty slow day around here."

"Good. Put him on."

There was a brief electronic click, followed by a pause, followed by, "This is Dr. Max Kayahs. Is this Richard?"

"It sure is, Doc. I wonder if we might have a few words?"

There followed a short conversation between the doctor and his patient in which Richard explained a number of things that had been going on and asked a few questions.

Immediately afterward, he dialed Pastor Clyde Maxwell at the number Melissa had given him. The two had a short conversation, and Richard hung up with a smile.

Yes, it was going to be a busy day, he thought to himself, but it would be one that Melissa and he would always remember, in any event.

How Sweet the Sound

It was only mid-morning on yet another perfect Alabama day when Richard went into his car's boudoir, opened the garage door, and glided easily in his traveling lounge down his long driveway toward the highway. As always, the soft leather and burled wood, combined with the slight fragrance of Melissa's cologne, had a calming and uplifting effect. As he hit I-65 and headed south toward Montgomery, he chose Respighi as his traveling music, and *The Pines of Rome,* in particular, filled him with energy and anticipation.

When he reached downtown, his first stop was at the Alabama State Bar headquarters near the old capitol on Dexter Avenue. He pulled open the huge, heavy brass door of the office and was warmly greeted by a young receptionist who asked what she could do for him. He asked to see the director, his friend Steve Smitherman. The receptionist buzzed Smitherman's office and told Steick he could go right on back.

Here and there along his way, he smiled and greeted staffers of his acquaintance. When he reached Mr. Smitherman's office, the secretary told him to go on in.

"Come on in, Richard," Steve said. "Always good to see you. I've been expecting you to stop in. Care to have a seat? Want coffee, a Coke or anything?"

"Thanks a lot, Steve. It's great to see you again too! You're looking fit as ever. Your family doin' okay?"

"Fine as can be. Won't you sit down, Richard?"

"Steve, I'd love to just sit here and talk, but I've got a very full day ahead of me. I know you're expecting me to come in here and bitch about my failure to renew my license and try to shift the blame onto y'all or something stupid like that. But that's not what I have in mind."

"Well, I'm glad, because you know there's absolutely nothing that I can do about the situation. I'm just sorry it had to happen."

"Me too, Steve. But look. I'm only here about one thing."

At this point, Richard pulled out his wallet, removed his outdated membership card, and handed it to the director, saying simply, "I quit. Steve, I'm voluntarily surrendering my presently invalid license to practice law as of this moment. I know I could be reinstated after a few hearings, paying my license fee, a late fee, and I don't know what else, but I'm finished. I've never had any discipline whatever on my record, and I don't want to have any. This will save y'all the headaches of the disciplinary proceedings that I know are coming and will make life a whole lot easier for everybody, won't it?"

"Yes, it will do that. But it's not such a big deal, failing to renew your license. One of those mistakes anybody could make. It's not like you've stolen a client's funds or something. Are you sure you want to do this, Richard? You've always been an active and highly respected member of the State Bar. I'm sure any discipline against you will be minimal, considering your spotless record of achievement and your lasting contributions."

"Thanks, Steve, but my mind's made up. I'm finished as an attorney as of now, if you don't mind."

"Well, Richard. We really hate to lose you. But it looks like you're pretty determined, and who am I to stand in your way? So farewell, and best wishes, my friend!"

The pair shook hands once again, and Richard said, "Thanks a lot for all your kind words, Steve. But you're right. I'm determined, and I've got a lot of things to do today, like I said, so y'all keep up the good work, and I'll be seein' ya around, okay? Bye now," he grinned as he turned to walk out the door.

"Godspeed, wherever you're headed, Richard."

Where Richard was headed was directly to the main office of his bank downtown. After about half an hour inside, he emerged with fifteen one-thousand-dollar bills in his wallet, a couple of drafts, and a few other receipts and papers. He then walked to his office at the Firemen's Justice Project HQ in the Bell Building. He took the elevator, got off, entered his suite, and greeted Lillian cordially. Then he went to his desk for one last look at what had accumulated.

Immediately on top of his stack of incoming papers was Judge Clark Wilson's order dismissing the Firemen's lawsuit. Happily and predictably, the dismissal was without prejudice and therefore could be filed again by someone else, though certainly not by Richard Steick.

He called Lillian into his office, asked her to take a seat, and then got up, pulled out his wallet, and handed her three crisp thousand-dollar bills.

"We're closing up shop as of this moment, Lillian," he told her. "This is just a little pay for wrapping up my affairs, together with a bonus, token of my appreciation, severance pay, or whatever you want to call it."

Lillian's eyes were wide and white as Honda headlights. She didn't know what to say except, "Thank you, Richard! Thank you so much! You've always been one of the most generous men I've ever known, but this beats anything!"

The ample, gray-haired lady kissed him on the cheek.

He then sat down next to her and wrote out a list of things he wanted her to do. He dictated brief letters of apology to Ninety and Representative Grones and told her to sign them for him. He gave her a draft for the remaining amount due on the office lease and blank drafts for the telephone, power, and other utility companies. He handed her a final draft and told her exactly what to do about records retention and equipment removal and storage.

Then he asked Lillian to leave, as he wanted to make one or two private phone calls. The time was just approaching noon. At this point, he knew he could get everything done before 4:30 P.M. if he hurried.

His first call was once again to Melissa at Dr. Kayahs's office in Hallelujah. She cheerfully uttered her usual greeting, and Richard said, "Hey, Sweetheart! How are ya?"

"Richard! The question is 'how are you?' I saw the headlines but was afraid to read the papers. You're sounding awfully chipper, considering the circumstances."

"Yeah. I thought it might make today's editions. The Firemen's lawsuit has been blown sky high because of my negligence, and it's all over. Also, I've just surrendered my license at the State Bar, and I'm no longer a lawyer. Finally, Lillian is closing up shop in the Bell Building. Quite a day so far, wouldn't you say?"

"I certainly would, and I'm so sorry, Richard. All our hard work, not to mention all the money you spent—all up the chimney. Isn't there anything you can do?"

"No, there isn't, Honey, and it isn't so bad. I'm only human after all. Still love me and want to marry me?"

"Of course and of course! Anytime!"

"So what are you doin' this afternoon?"

"Why, working at this office, naturally. And what are you doing, by the way?"

"Oh, I've just got a few errands to run in Montgomery. What time is Dr. Kayahs's last appointment over this afternoon, Darling?"

"As I said before, Richard, it's a slow day. But he does have one appointment that ends at 4:00 P.M."

"What are you wearing right now, Melissa?"

"Richard! Please don't try to get kinky on the telephone with me at the office! I'm wearing a blue dress. That one you like so much."

"Great! Now, I've got a final, quick question for you. How about if we skip supper after work and go on out to Pastor Maxwell's and get married instead?"

"Richard! Are you serious, or are you just acting crazy? Did the Firemen's lawsuit disaster unhinge you? Do you need to see Dr. Kayahs? Just what's going on, anyway?"

"Melissa, I've never been more serious or more sure of what I'm doing in my life. You said 'anytime,' and the time is now, as far as I'm concerned."

"This is all coming awfully fast for me, Richard. First the Firemen's lawsuit goes up in smoke, so to speak, and now you want to get married today. Don't you want to explain just a little bit, please?"

"It's really no big deal, Melissa. And I'll tell you all about it after we're married this evening, okay?"

"If you say so, Richard. I've never trusted any man in my life before in the way I trust you."

"That's wonderful and precisely how it ought to be. I feel exactly the same way about you. I love you, Melissa. But look. I've got to run now. Got lots of things to do before we get married. I'll pick you up around 4:30, okay? And by 5:30 we'll be husband and wife. We can go to Dard & Elle's Cafe then, and I'll explain everything you want to know. Is all that okay with you?"

"It's fine with me, Richard, as long as Dr. Kayahs will let me off half an hour early."

"Don't worry about Max. I've already talked to him, and everything is fine. So I'll see you at about 4:30, and we'll go get married, okay?"

"Okay, Richard Steick, you wonderful man. But you're going to have quite a bit of explaining to do at Dard & Elle's this evening, and don't you forget it. Deal?"

"No, I won't forget it one bit, Honey. Hey! Melissa. Let's change it to the Capital City Club in Montgomery. Whadda ya say? It'll be the beginning of our honeymoon, after all, and the Club was the scene of our first date, remember?"

"Sounds fine to me, Richard. You know I always enjoy the Club."

"Great! I've got to run now. Be ready by 4:30 so we can get married at 5:00. I'm phoning Pastor Maxwell just as soon as I hang up."

"Okay! I'll see you at 4:30, and good-bye, Darling!"

"Good-bye to you too, sweet Miss Brandywine."

As soon as he hung up the phone, he rang Pastor Maxwell and asked if 5:00 P.M. would be acceptable for the ceremony. The pastor said that would be just fine.

"A little like Las Vegas," Richard thought as he hung up once again.

He was hitting on all eight cylinders now. It was shortly after noon, and he still had a lot to accomplish. He hugged Lillian good-bye, told her he would see her sometime before too long, and was soon descending the elevator.

He whipped around the corner to WorldTrav, where he burst inside, slightly befuddled and bemused. He noticed that he caught everyone's attention. He told the receptionist that he wanted to talk to the manager, if that were possible.

The receptionist rang the manager, and just like at the State Bar, Richard was ushered in immediately. He introduced himself and told the manager, Larry McCall, that he wanted to book the best possible cruise for two immediately. He said he didn't care how long it lasted. And, just as he had told Melissa when they became engaged, he told Larry up front that money was no object. "Just hurry, Larry."

Larry scratched his head and started pecking at his computer until Richard thought he would be at the travel agency all day. While he was waiting, Steick phoned Betty at his office in Hallelujah and told her to round up his two young associates and have them ready for an important conference when he returned there later that afternoon.

Larry made several telephone calls, banged away at the computer some more, phoned someone else, looked in a book, scratched out some figures, and finally said, "Okay, Mr. Steick. Come on around here and see if you like what I've got for you."

Richard stood behind Larry, who continued to sit at his desk as he explained what he had devised. The ultra-luxurious new Queen Mary had embarked from Portsmouth approximately twelve days previously for a cruise around the world. It had already docked in New York, departed, and was presently bound southward. For a surcharge, Richard and Melissa could join the cruise when it docked in Miami the coming Sunday. For an additional surcharge, they could obtain one of the two remaining staterooms. For another surcharge, they could continue on the ship until it had begun another around-the-world cruise and docked once again in Miami, thus making their own around-the-world cruise complete. And of course there was a surcharge for late booking. There were also port and dock taxes, and land packages were not included.

The bottom line looked like a galactic sum to Richard until he reassured himself with thoughts of his offshore accounts, their great return in recent years, and the fact that his actual net worth was many times greater than he had ever imagined. He counted out five one-thousand-dollar bills to Larry and put the remainder of the cost on one of his several debit cards.

It took the computer several minutes to complete printing all of the documents. But when it had, Larry presented Richard with a fine new leather attache case, discreetly embossed with the WorldTrav logo, and neatly bearing all the travel documents that he and Melissa would require, including airline tickets from Montgomery to Miami and return, cruise tickets, and a reservation for the honeymoon suite at the Four Seasons Hotel near the Miami pier for the night prior to their Sunday afternoon shipboard departure.

All of these preparations took longer than he had hoped, but Richard still had time to return to Hallelujah, complete some further necessary business, and pick up Melissa at 4:30 for their 5:00 wedding. He hopped into his SUV bearing his attractive new attache case, with all travel documents enclosed, and seven one-thousand-dollar bills (plus change) remaining in his wallet. He hit the interstate as quickly and safely as he could, and once on the road, he punched the CD button for some soothing Gregorian chants.

THE DRIVE BACK TO HALLELUJAH was smooth, and he drove directly to his dogtrot law office. His young associates ("Law dogs in the dogtrot," he thought) were curious and eager to know why they had been summoned. Richard ushered them into the conference room for a speedy but highly significant meeting.

He told them he wanted to sell them his entire practice, lock, stock, and barrel, and was willing to consider any reasonable terms that would be fair to all parties and would allow the two young men to make a decent living. He asked them to make him an offer.

The two young lawyers were stunned and scarcely knew what to say. They asked Richard if they could discuss the matter alone together for fifteen to twenty minutes, and he readily agreed. When the young men returned, they had made several phone calls, and the seller and the two buyers hammered out a basic agreement in about ten minutes. Richard would receive his just portion of any fees to date. His associates would purchase the real estate, building, fixtures, all equipment and furnishings, and everything pertaining to the practice for a sum that Richard privately estimated came to about seventy cents on the dollar. The buyers would sign a contract, a mortgage, and a seven-year promissory note. They would also write a soothing letter to all of Richard's clients, announcing his retirement from the practice of law and their new ownership of the firm.

Richard summoned the ever-efficient Betty to prepare the purchase and sale agreement and essential documents. He included a mutual cooperation clause so that non-essential documents could be completed within one year, and after one year had elapsed, they would be deemed executed. Betty had the documents prepared within half an hour, and all three parties reviewed them very carefully. Then they executed them, and Betty notarized the documents.

The two new owners retired to the conference room, feeling blessed by God, while Richard walked the eighteen feet through the open area of the dogtrot to Betty's domain.

He found her slightly weepy and all choked up. They had a brief but very fond farewell exchange. Steick reminded her that the documents included a provision for her continued employment.

Then Richard said, "I've got to run now, Betty. Here's a small token of thanks for all you've done for me over the years."

He handed her three crisp, new thousand-dollar bills, which left her speechless.

"Don't worry about it, Betty. We'll be friends forever, and I'll be seeing you from time to time, I promise." Then he hugged her and bolted out of his former law office.

Time was running short, but Richard knew that he would be on time and that all would turn out well. On his way back to his house, he stopped at the 7-11 and picked up copies of *The Montgomery Advertiser* and *The Hallelujah Gazette*, each of which carried major front-page stories concerning how the "Firemen's Lawsuit," as it had come to be known, was finished and down the sewer. Richard knew that he would be excoriated, along with the entire legal profession, no doubt, in the stories and editorials within.

He would save reading them until he got home. He knew that Melissa had by now read copies of both, and he was happy to think that this would save him a lot of time-consuming and embarrassing explanations later in the evening.

Once safely inside his house, he turned off all of the telephones that were ringing incessantly. Then he glanced briefly over several pages of the two papers. He quickly discerned that he, Richard Featherston Steick, PhD and formerly Esq., had succeeded far better than he ever could have dreamed at bringing the races closer together in Alabama. Black and white people alike agreed, unanimously, upon one thing. And that was the fact that he, Richard, who had only the best of intentions, was suddenly the most detestable, scurrilous, and incompetent jack-leg attorney ever to practice law in the State of Alabama.

He reflected that in an earlier age, he would have been tarred, feathered, and run out of town on a rail, or possibly lynched, by citizens of both races. He was indeed glad to live when he did, so that he could escape safely, advancing to the rear in luxurious first-class comfort via Delta Airlines and the Cunard Passenger Ship Company.

Fortunately, Professor Steick was between semesters at Opp U. He picked up the phone and dialed his friend and the dean of the Honors College, Dr. Clifford Graves. He hurriedly explained that he was asking for a one-year unpaid leave of absence from the university, beginning immediately. Dr. Graves, who had obviously read the papers, agreed that Richard had probably made a wise decision. Steick's sudden absence would put the dean in a rather difficult situation, but he could cover it. He would have his secretary prepare the necessary papers, and Professor Steick could drop by and sign them in the morning.

WITH MOST OF HIS WORK ACCOMPLISHED, Richard quickly showered for the second time that day, donned a conservative dark suit that he had had hand-tailored for himself in Birmingham, and completed the ensemble with a white dress shirt, a great tie Melissa had given him, gold cuff links she had also given him, and fine Italian shoes with appropriate stockings. He checked himself in the mirror and found all was well. Then he grabbed the marriage license he had secured as well as the tasteful eighteen-carat-gold wedding band he had purchased for Melissa. He quickly found himself in the car's boudoir, then backing out its door, driving down his driveway, and gliding serenely through the quaint streets of Hallelujah toward the office of Dr. Kayahs.

He arrived just shortly after 4:30 and was greeted tenderly and con-solingly by his beautiful bride-to-be.

"I assume you've read the papers by now, Melissa."

"Of course, Richard, and I can't tell you how sorry I am," she replied, struggling to hold back her tears.

"Hey! Sweetheart! Come on! There's nothing to be sad about. Like I said, I'm only human, after all. It was just one of those crazy things that happen. Look. In about half an hour we're going to be married and then set out on the time of our lives, I promise you! I can't wait to tell you all about it later. Brighten up!"

And she did, too—quite readily. And Richard thought she had never looked lovelier.

"We've got to get rolling," he said. "I told Pastor Maxwell we'd be at his house at five o'clock. Where's Max, anyway?"

"He's back in the back, fiddling with his silly saxophone. Can't you hear him?"

Kayahs was playing very lightly, and Richard could just make out a few notes here and there.

"Yes, I guess I can. Let's go get him."

"Go get him? What on earth do we need him for? He already said I could leave a little early today if I wanted."

"He's coming with us."

"Coming with us! What on earth for?"

"Extra witness. Come on. Let's get him."

The bride-and-groom-to-be walked back to the most remote part of Dr. Kayahs's office.

"Well!" he greeted them. "If it isn't the happy couple! Y'all ready to head on out?"

"Ready when you are, Doc," Richard replied.

"By the way. I understand y'all are headed for a little honeymoon. Would you like me to fix you up with enough Normalol to hold you 'til you get back?"

Richard and Melissa both looked a little nonplussed. Richard spoke first, saying, "Ya know, Doc. I started forgetting to take that stuff a while back, and now that you mention it, I never take it at all these days."

"I, uh, I had a similar experience," Melissa said. "I just kind of phased it out, I suppose. And do you know what? I don't feel like I need it at all anymore. How about you, Richard?"

"Why no. I don't think I really need Normalol any longer."

"Great!" Dr. Kayahs exclaimed. "That's precisely how that medicine is supposed to work when it works. So you're both feeling fine now?"

"Just fine," they replied in unison.

"Oh, uh, Melissa," the doctor said, "here's your final paycheck until you return. I agreed with Richard to give you up to a year off, and then you can return to your job whenever you like. That okay with you?"

"A year off! What on earth for? I think both y'all are crazy, and I'm the one who ought to be the doctor!"

"Don't worry about it now, Melissa. It's going to be a great year for both of us. I'll explain everything after we're married and having a nice dinner at the Capital City Club," Richard said.

"Well! It's just wonderful to have my life all planned out for me this way! I wonder if I might have any plans of my own for the next year?" Melissa asked, arms akimbo. "Certainly no one has asked me, now have they? And what would happen, do you suppose, if I actually had some ideas of my own about the next year of my life? I mean, it's just my life, after all, isn't it? You'd better be glad I trust you, Richard Steick, and you too, Dr. Kayahs. I'll await the details with considerable interest. And I'll also remind you that this is still a free country where even women are emancipated, and I retain the right to do whatever I please with myself next year and the year after that and the one after that, forever !"

"Of course, Melissa. I've just made some tentative plans for us, that's all. You'll have full veto power over everything I've cooked up, okay?"

"Thank you, Richard, because I wouldn't be going to marry you in a few minutes if I didn't."

"All right then. Let's hit the road! Got your sax, Doc?"

"Right here in its neat little case."

"Okay! Head 'em up, and move 'em out!" Richard grinned.

After Dr. Kayahs locked the door to the clinic, the joyful threesome hopped into Richard's SUV, with the bride and groom naturally occupying the front seats.

"Great-looking car, Richard!"

"Glad you like it, Doc. Hey! I've got a sensuous sax CD loaded in the changer. Wanna hear it?"

"Sure!"

And so Richard touched a button, and the mellow, bluesy sax played them along as Melissa directed Richard in navigating the highways and back roads to the home of Pastor Clyde Maxwell and his wife, Sarah.

THE HOUSE WAS LOVELY in the old Southern style, with an enormous gallery porch surrounding three sides. There were some weeds and brambles, but the place was generally well kept, even though the house could use several good coats of paint. As he turned into the gravel driveway, Richard noticed a sign which he didn't quite know how to interpret: SEMI-PRIVATE. PUBLIC WELCOME. He parked near the house, and they were greeted by the smiling, retired pastor and his equally pleasant wife of fifty-four years. The couple stood on the porch, amid the rocking chairs, avoiding unnecessary use of the steps. The visitors climbed the stairs, and there were introductions all around, as first Melissa, then Richard, and finally Dr. Kayahs shook hands with the elderly couple.

"Reckon y'all come on out here to get married, didn't ya?" the pastor asked. "Well, you come to the right place. Step on in. We're glad to have ya. Step on in! Step on in!"

The threesome entered a house redolent of age and congeniality. Dozens of family photos, mainly antique, adorned the walls. The furniture, still serviceable, had seen better days, although Richard spotted many fine, native Southern pieces.

The Maxwells and their guests took seats in the parlor and exchanged pleasantries about the beauty of the day and the happiness of the occasion. Clyde experienced some confusion about which of the younger gentlemen was the groom, but he finally got it straight.

"Well, let's get started," he said at last. "Mr. Steick and Miss Brandywine, I want y'all to please come on into my study here for a moment. If you would be so kind, Dr. Max, just sit where you are and keep my wife company while I have a few words with the bride and groom."

Dr. Kayahs said he would be happy to, and Melissa and Richard, followed by Pastor Maxwell, entered his book-lined study. He asked his guests to take chairs in front of his desk as he walked around and sat behind it.

"All right now," he said, clasping his freckled and withered hands before him. "I've got a duty to do a little pastoral counselin', but it ain't goin' to take very long. Y'all are plenty grown up now, and I hope you're into what I call 'the second adulthood.' You look and act like you are; I'll say that. The second adulthood is a great opportunity to learn from the mistakes we made in the first adulthood, if we just try our best and ask the good Lord to he'p us. Do y'all love each other?"

Melissa and Richard beamed at each other and at Pastor Maxwell and assured him that they did, and most sincerely.

"Good. I figured ya did, or ya wouldn't be here, and I ain't never seen a couple yet that looked to be more in love than y'all do. Now listen to me. Y'all ought to pray and read the Bible together. It doesn't hurt to go to church, either, but prayin' and readin' the Bible ought to come first. There's lots of good wisdom in the Bible, and prayin' together will keep y'all communicatin', both with each other and with the Almighty, and that's the most important thing.

"Now there ain't nothin' in the world that I can say or do that's goin' to cause y'all to take any of this advice seriously, and so I ain't goin' to dwell on it. You just have to make up your own minds and live your own lives. I'm goin' to pray that the good Lord will guide you.

"I'll just say a word or two about communicatin' with each other. Communicatin' is somethin' that y'all have got to do, or you're finished. See what I mean? You've got to do it constantly, with love in your hearts, no matter how much it hurts or how inconvenient it might be. You should set aside about an hour every day, just for that purpose, if you want to remain as happy together as you clearly are right now. Okay?

"And there's just one more thing on that topic. If y'all don't remember anything else from this session today, I want y'all to remember this. Always say what you mean and mean what you say. That's the most important thing about communication between a wife and her husband.

"Richard, I want you to recite what I just said," the pastor told him, and Richard recited without a hitch.

"And you do the same thing now, Melissa, honey," the pastor said. And Melissa likewise repeated that she should always say what she meant and mean what she said.

"All right," the pastor announced. "That's all I've got to say. You got the license, Richard?"

"Right here, pastor," Richard replied, pulling it from his breast pocket.

Pastor Maxwell glanced at the document and said it all looked fine to him. "How about rings? Are y'all exchangin' rings?"

The bride and groom each said they had their wedding bands within easy reach. Richard patted his jacket pocket, and Melissa already held hers in her hand.

"Okay." the pastor said. "Let's get ready to rock 'n roll!"

Returning to the large parlor, the bride, groom, and pastor were pleased to discover that Mrs. Maxwell and Dr. Kayahs had remedied a substantial omission in Richard's hasty preparations. They had gathered and assembled a beautiful bouquet for the bride from Mrs. Maxwell's abundant, if somewhat ill-tended, collection of old-fashioned flowers outside the house.

"All right now," Pastor Maxwell said enthusiastically, " Melissa, honey, take your nice bouquet of flowers and stand back there in that doorway on the other side of the room. Sarah and Dr. Max, y'all stand up here behind this table on either side of me."

Dr. Kayahs had already removed his shiny brass saxophone from its case, installed the mouthpiece, and was sucking on a number two reed, which he quickly screwed into place on the mouthpiece.

The pastor took his place behind the large demi-lune table opposite the doorway, with Mrs. Maxwell on his right and Dr. Kayahs, ready with his saxophone, on the pastor's left.

"Now Richard, you come on up here and stand a little off to my left and also to the left of Dr. Max. Don't want to block his music," the pastor said.

"Okay, Melissa, when Dr. Max starts to play, you just walk gracefully up toward us and stop in front of me. Then, Richard, when she gets here, you walk over from the side and take her arm in yours. Got it? Then Dr. Max will stop playing, and we'll say the vows. Everybody understand?"

Everyone understood and quickly took their respective positions.

"All right. Looks fine," the pastor said. "Now I'm going to say a prayer before all the prayer in the service, and when I'm finished with this first one, we'll get started. Everybody know what to do?"

They all indicated that they did, and thus, with everyone in position, Pastor Maxwell cleared his throat and said, "Let us pray."

All bowed as the pastor delivered a short pre-service prayer. When he said "Amen," Dr. Kayahs launched into a soulful saxophone solo of "Here Comes the Bride."

It was indeed a beautiful ceremony. Melissa walked forward royally, and Richard joined her at the table and took her arm just as Dr. Kayahs allowed the refrain to die out quietly. Pastor Maxwell employed the customary vows, and both Richard and Melissa repeated after him perfectly. At the conclusion, the pastor announced, "What God hath joined together, let no man put asunder. You may now kiss the bride."

The new husband and wife kissed lovingly as Dr. Kayahs, unable to restrain himself, broke into a real kick-ass Dixieland version of Grieg's *Triumphal March*.

Then everyone hugged everyone else. Pastor Maxwell, Dr. Kayahs, and Mrs. Maxwell kissed the bride in turn. Richard pressed a $500 bill into Pastor Maxwell's hand so smoothly that no one noticed. There were cheerful good-byes from the Maxwells as the newlyweds and Dr. Kayahs climbed into Richard's gleaming SUV and then rolled out the driveway and onto the road. In a short while, Richard and Melissa deposited Dr. Kayahs and his saxophone outside his own glorious SUV back at the clinic, thanking him profusely.

MELISSA WANTED TO FRESHEN UP and change clothes before dinner, and so they returned to Richard's house, where she now kept a substantial wardrobe, make-up, and other essentials.

A little more than an hour later, the charming couple were seated over a sumptuous meal at the Capital City Club, with romantic piano music playing in the background. As they ate and enjoyed a bottle of wine, Richard delivered a detailed account of his activities during the past two days.

"So what do we do now, Richard?" Melissa asked when he had concluded.

At this point, Richard opened his buttery leather attache case, kindly provided by WorldTrav, and began showing Melissa exactly what they were going to do now. As he did, her eyes grew wider and wider with delight.

"I wondered what that briefcase was all about."

She had never expected to have such an experience in her life as that which Richard was describing. By the end of his presentation, she was jumping up and down in her chair with glee.

"What's the total duration of the cruise, Richard?"

"Two months and we'll be back in Miami. And speaking of Miami, how fast can you pack, Sweetheart? We're due there in just about thirty-six hours."

Melissa said she could pack quite quickly when she wanted to, and she definitely wanted to now. And thus, after a delicious honeymoon supper, the happy newlyweds hustled back to Melissa's house in Hallelujah for her luggage, bathing suits, and some of her better black dresses.

From there, they traveled to Richard's house on the hill, and both began to pack in earnest.

Somewhere between his socks and his tuxedo, however, Richard had a revelation.

"Darling, a quick question. If you could do anything at all that you wanted with Mushroom Memories, what would it be? And please don't say 'burn it down.' Something in the nature of keeping it but remodeling it, redecorating it completely, making it into a space we would use and enjoy together."

Melissa pondered for several moments. "That's a little tough," she said. "I guess I'd keep it as some kind of a casual rec room. Make it an alternate dining room for us, a place to entertain the way you've done in the past."

"Fine. What kind of decorative motif would you prefer? I like a rec room to have a definite theme. Choose absolutely anything you want. It's going to be your room from now on," he said.

"Gosh, Richard. Let's see. Well, I've always liked the Turkish or Arabesque style, with lots of cushions and pillows around on the floor, like in that restaurant, The Casbah, that we both enjoyed in Atlanta. Remember?"

"Great! Easy to do. That's what it's going to be, then! Just give me a few minutes, and I'll be right back, okay?"

He grabbed a portable telephone and phoned his friend, Coco Mink, a skilled interior decorator in Hallelujah. He quickly explained what he wanted done with Mushroom Memories. He wanted it gutted and all of his memorabilia neatly boxed away and labeled. The large TV could stay. Then he wanted the room transformed into a relaxing and romantic casbah, as he and Melissa had just discussed. He vaguely sketched out his fast decorative ideas as well as he could and explained that his former secretary, Betty, still had check-writing privileges on his law office account. He gave Miss Mink a budget, told her where the key to Mushroom Memories was located, and asked her to begin immediately.

Next, he phoned Betty at her house and authorized her to write checks, up to the budget limit, to Miss Mink. He also asked Betty if she would please stop all his mail at his house and kindly supervise his cleaning lady in locking it up for a long time. For her efforts, and for occasionally looking in on Melissa's house and his own, the cleaning lady was to receive a check for one thousand dollars.

Betty took it all down and promised that she would do exactly as Richard had instructed.

THE NEXT NIGHT, Richard and Melissa were bathing together in a huge, heart-shaped Jacuzzi in the magnificent honeymoon suite of the Four Seasons Hotel in Miami. The following afternoon, they boarded the Queen Mary.

Two months later, after a joyful and luxurious honeymoon cruise, they returned to Miami, both exhilarated and more in love than ever. They very discreetly returned to Hallelujah for two days. Richard checked things out and talked personally to Betty several times to be certain that all matters were generally under control. There had been countless phone calls, she said, but she had handled them all very carefully, and the number had grown fewer each day.

Richard then gave her a private phone number for a condominium he and Melissa had decided to rent for the next ten months in New Mexico, "The Land of Enchantment." Betty was to carefully screen all calls. He told her he would only speak to his attorneys at Barratry, Champerty, and Tennis in Birmingham, and one or two other persons, whose names and numbers Betty listed. Richard hugged her, pressed two additional thousand-dollar bills into her hand, and promptly departed the premises.

Returning to his house and his new bride, he noticed workmen going at it hammer and tongs in the former Mushroom Memories. He had expected the work to be completed by this time, but these projects always took longer than expected, and so he didn't even bother to look in and check on the progress.

In a few hours, Richard and Melissa were back in the air. They landed at Albuquerque, where Richard took a ten-month lease on a new Land

Rover. They drove leisurely northward, stopping wherever they liked, at Santa Fe, Taos, and finally at their unpretentious but nicely situated and commodious condo in Angel Fire.

They spent the next ten months reading, learning to know each other ever more deeply, picnicking in the glorious landscapes surrounding them, and exploring the historic pueblos of New Mexico. In the winter, they took up snow skiing with great pleasure.

Then, after one full year of absence, the happily married couple returned to their beloved home state of Alabama. And they were not at all surprised to discover that it was still the same state that it had always been.

Melissa resumed her full-time job with Dr. Kayahs, who was extremely glad to have her back. Similarly, Richard again took up his teaching duties at Opp U., where his dean told him he had been missed.

And thus, the couple lived contentedly, if somewhat quietly together, enjoying excellent drainage and a romantic casbah at Richard's beautifully restored Italianate house on the hill in Hallelujah, Alabama.

Hallelujah, amen!

∾

Printed in the United States
69850LV00002B/5